Hayner Public Library District-Alton
W9-AGV-643

RECEIVED
JUL 2 2002
BY: MAIN

The Autobiography of
VIVIAN

The Autobiography of

VIVIAN

by Vivian Livingston

as told to Sherrie Krantz

BALLANTINE BOOKS • NEW YORK

A Ballantine Book
Published by The Ballantine Publishing Group

Published in the United States by The Ballantine Publishing Group, a division of Random House, Inc., New York, and simultaneously in Canada by Random House of Canada Limited, Toronto.

www.ballantinebooks.com

Library of Congress Control Number: 2002091994

ISBN 0-345-45354-9

Cover and interior illustrations by Hilary Nordholm
Book design by Elizabeth Schwartz

Manufactured in the United States of America

First Edition: July 2002

10 9 8 7 6 5 4 3 2 1

For my loving and very patient parents and the best brother a girl could ever wish for . . . this book is dedicated to my family.♥

prologue

You know, it's funny . . . my whole life I've never really been satisfied. I mean that in a very fairy-tale kind of way. All those happy endings: the stories I read as a kid, the films that I'd see with my friends. With hindsight I think it's fair to say that I'm the product of an extremely overzealous imagination. I was sure I'd marry Prince Charming or Brad Pitt, whoever I met first. I'd walk on the wild side—if one existed in Pennsylvania. I'd dress to the nines, award show or not, and of course make an acceptance speech and thank everybody I could remember for helping me achieve something completely fantastic.

As far as I was concerned, my life was going to be my own movie, my own novel lived on my terms with all the highs and lows I could fill it with. Too many soap operas, you say? Maybe. But I was who I was and I couldn't help it. And even with all the psychotherapy in the world my prognosis has been best phrased by my mother: "Vivian my love, you are a handful!" Yup! (That *is* a compliment, right?!)

So what I am trying to say is that if I could help it, "average" was not going to be an adjective that had anything to do with me. I was me. How could I be average? With only one life to live (uh, did you catch that?), I was going to live it to the fullest. Unfortunately though, even I couldn't argue with Mother Nature: I was average all the way through. Wasn't blessed with a knack for much. I couldn't sing, couldn't dance, and wasn't that coordinated. Not very tall, not very thin, pretty good in school—and stage fright galore. I did have an attitude but that never really got me anywhere but detention.

Let me make this real clear. I was a closet overachieving rebel without a cause. I had no idea why I always made things complicated. I was just trying to have fun. I was going for this whole "thing" that I could never really figure out. All I knew was that the rush felt good and a day without an experience, without a story, without irony, a nuance of some kind—well, that was just a waste.

So it's now, at twenty-five years old, sitting here writing my own autobiography, that the joke's on me. Clarity has taken its sweet old time knockin' on my door. It's painfully clear. I know now, the chick I am today and the woman I'll be tomorrow, would not exist at all if I hadn't been so average.

Maybe I should just end the book here. Yeah right! But I assure you, nothing in my life was as easy as writing these first words. It all could have been but I never let it. Never. And that's what did "it"—from my first memory up until this very moment. Being average lit my fire, being average let me slip in unnoticed, being average let me bloom without a threat, and being average got me laid, by the best of 'em, more times than, well, you know what I mean. (I hope they let me leave that line in here—that was a good one. Basically I just went for it a handful of times, nothing I can't add up on two hands. Relax, Mom!)

See, I figured that greatness was going to have to happen for me with the decisions I'd make, the company I'd keep. I had to be a keen mean drama queen if I was going to drive in the fast lane. (And this was before I had my license!)

I also never wore a seat belt, and wait, the best part: I was sober the whole way through. That's the power of the mind for you. That's imagination—the risks for the rewards. God it's a beautiful thing. My drive, my spirit, made me who I am today and will also make for some fine storytelling if I do say so myself. And that's when I'll touch you. When you realize that us average gals have a lot in common and when set free can live a life you can only read about.

I've been a bit wild, a bit angry, and a bit awkward, but that will all rear its head in good time. I've grown up and grown out (size 6 to size 10, thank you very much!) since then.

For the many of you who don't know who the hell I am or why on God's green earth I've been asked to put my thoughts down on paper, let me get that out of the way. If you haven't heard of *www.Vivianlives.com*, well good (sort of). I'm the chick who resides on the Net, where you can hang out with me 24/7 and experience New York City and all it has to offer to a townie sans a man, without a charge card, or the highfalutin access that the adverts might suggest.

All right then, here we go. The autobiography of me, the autobiography of you (the days of our lives . . . somebody stop me!) . . .

I was about seventeen years old, and had never been out of Pennsylvania with the exception of Vermont, oddly enough. (My family had been going there for winter and summer vacations even before I was part of the Livingston clan.) My parents had ordinary expectations for their only daughter. Marry my high school sweetheart after a college education, of course, and then, very simply, become my mother. I had two older brothers (every girl's worst nightmare once you hit puberty), a loving mother, and a dad who was a college professor with lots of admirers in the academic world. (Every girl's dream once you hit puberty.)

I did my best to follow the rules of my household (when everyone was looking) with curfews, grades, and such, and likewise did my best to stay out of the vantage points of my brothers, Simon and Joseph. I thought of it as doing everyone a favor. Why let my parents down? Why piss my brothers off? It wouldn't do me any good. I was my own undercover agent. Charlie's fourth Angel, if you will. Yeah sure, I'll be the Vivian *you* want me to be and I'll be the Vivian *I* want to be. It was that simple.

Don't get me wrong, it wasn't as if I was spending my free time in the backseats of cars, shoplifting lip gloss, or anything like that. I prefer to think of these wild and unruly days as the time when I was developing my character. Creating my personality. I was headstrong and confident, a leader most of the time. I was confrontational and loved a challenge. I was a big sister to my girlfriends and just one of the guys to most of my boy friends. I liked who I was. It worked for me.

My best friend, Sophie, and I had agreed since the third grade that we'd go to college together, marry twin brothers, and be next-door neighbors forever. So we applied to one school and one school only—Penn State. We got in and lived/dormed together (and far enough from campus that we were able to make a successful case for at least one set of wheels as of semester one!). See, neither of us had big plans. College was to be four years of memory-making and, of course, finding those twins.

With little to no direction, college was still a learning experience in ways neither of us could have imagined, and the freedom it provided, albeit several hours from home, changed our lives forever.

Today, when people ask how I managed to get where I am—be who I am—I can only point to the second semester of senior year as "my moment." You know what I mean. It's that moment in time that for you, and you only, seems like a mini-motion picture, a dream that you don't have to close your eyes in order to see in a wildly vivid way.

Unlike my brothers, who were overachievers (the obvious kind—Simon followed in my father's footsteps, three degrees under his belt and ready to take the world by storm, and Joseph, more of a financier and having just received his M.B.A., was plotting quite an ambitious play in the dot-com arena), I had no plans of furthering my education. I was going to graduate, take those quintessential photos with my family in that horrible polyester cap and gown that I'm convinced only looks good on men, pack my bags, and return right back to where I started with a framed degree for my parents to gloat over.

But my future did an about-face on the afternoon of a typical day during my senior year. My schedule rocked, with only three classes two days a week and more free time than I knew what to do with. I started getting into fitness, strength training really. One of my goals was to finally be able to do a pull-up. (You remember the physical fitness tests in high school? They would calculate the percentage of your body fat with what looked like a plastic screwdriver, make you run a mile, and then have you do those pull-ups. Well, I was never able to do one. My gym teacher, Ms. Callaghan, seemed to revel in my weakness and that really pissed me off. I made it my mission to be able to do one before I graduated. Boy, I really challenged myself in college, eh? Trying to avenge my tenth-grade gym teacher. Now that's rich.) Well, anyway, I had just finished "My Version" of working out at the gym; I stopped as usual at the convenience store for my congratulatory two chocolate éclairs, and then typically walk them off. I admit it, I also love the way my skin looks after I work out (like after a day at the beach), so I'd walk around and work it (at least in my head).

Okay, talk about a tangent—back to my story: With a nice healthy glow, undoubtedly a few chocolate crunchies in my teeth, and several magazines I picked up along the way, I stopped by my favorite coffee shop on campus (favorite only because Sophie worked there so my cappuccinos were free). I ordered my drink, found the perfect vacant table in the back corner of the place (I always like a good view, very *Godfather*), and parked it for a while. I started flipping through my 'zines, got in a good bit of people watching (one of my favorite pastimes) between scoping the pages, and then for some strange reason, my eyes met an advertisement for a songwriting contest. The winner and a friend would be treated to a first-class weekend in New York City, two nights in a fancy hotel, spending money, concert tickets, and a new guitar! Well, this advert *spoke to me*. The trip was scheduled just as spring break would spring and before any final exams, so I could go. My schedule was open and a few days out of the gym wasn't the biggest deal.

I tore the ad out straightaway and ran up to Sophie. I shouted, "We're going to New York! We're going to New York! I won a songwriting contest and we're going!!!!" She pulled the ad from my left hand, my third cappuccino from the right, read the small bit, and said, "Vivian, have you even written a song yet?"

So Sophie to say that. "Not yet, Sophie, uch! (Eye roll here, of course.) But I'm going to—this weekend—and we're going to New York!" And with that, I grabbed my things and ran back to our apartment (Yup, as seniors we had transitioned to an apartment rather than a dorm—so fancy.) and I started writing, and writing, and writing.

This songwriting thing sucked. It wasn't as easy as I had assumed. And if you're asking the question "Vivian, do you even know how to play music?" the answer is "Sort of." Simon had given me his guitar on my sixteenth birthday and although I never took lessons or had huge aspirations to play, I always liked the way it looked in my room. (I'm just being honest.) Over the years, I taught myself how to play a few strings, chords, whatever, so I figured that if I could write something good, I would strum my guitar and the rest, naturally, would be featured on *Behind the Music*.

I tortured myself for the next few days. I'd listen to music that I liked and ask myself why I liked it. I went through photo albums and my journals for inspiration and in all the frustration broke my word processor. Some evenings I'd grab a bunch of CDs and cassettes, park myself in the bathroom (They don't call it the porcelain god for nothing. Some of my best ideas come to me on the toilet), and began reading the backs of cassettes, realizing that it was all about the chorus. If I could come up with a powerful chorus, the rest would be cake. Okay, maybe cupcakes.

Whatever, I did it. Part one anyway. I ended up submitting ten songs under ten different names: Vivian Livingston, Viv Livingston, Viviana Livingston, Vivian Lives, etc. . . . I was obsessed.

College hadn't been the greatest experience for me (which I'll get into at some point when I'm in a far less better mood—remembering all of this part is incredibly fun!). I had nothing tremendous to look forward to after graduation and I had told Sophie that we were going to New York. All my eggs were in this basket, or at least that's how I saw it, and I was freaking myself out. While Sophie and some of her other friends were planning trips to Florida, I was checking my mailbox. This frightening pattern went on for weeks. My mailman even found me annoying.

Since I hate it when people drag stories out, I'll get straight to it. I won. I freakin' won!!! Mind over matter and perhaps in this case, talent as well! I ran to the coffee shop and was screaming like a lunatic, "We did it, Sophie, we did it!" She had tears in her eyes. This was big. Really, really big. (She was so happy for me, it was sweet.) It had been almost four years since I had accomplished anything that I was proud of and I saw this as a ticket to ride!

We packed like you'd expect—black tops, denim jeans, and tons of Victoria's Secret panties. (We were so tragic!) I remember I bought a small black vinyl backpack special for the trip and Sophie had a tiny, almost miniature purse made out of plastic—shiny plastic. We were mall rats to the core and had no idea what was to come! (I'm sitting here laughing as I think about it.) Either way, we thought we were hot shit and I knew this was the "me" I had been waiting for!

Did I mention that we both got tips just for the occasion? I had a guitar designed on my thumb and Sophie had a stiletto stuck on her pinky! Yeah baby!!! (So scary!)

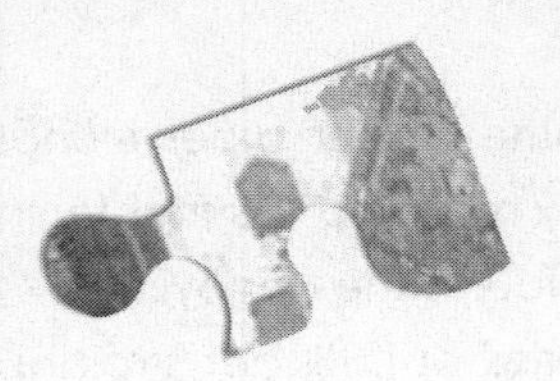

My parents, of course, had to be there for the big bon voyage. I was twenty, I think, at this point, and get this—my mom bought Sophie and me each a whistle connected to neon yellow string that she insisted we wear around our necks the entire time we were away. (For sure!) Then, even before I could ditch the necklace, there was the white super-stretch limo right on time!!! We started giggling with excitement when we saw it, gave big quick hugs to my parents, and hopped in. Plush garnet velvet trimmings, cool to the core black leather seats, rock glasses, tinted windows, and a remote control for everything. I admit it, we also opened the sunroof, stood up, and started woo-hoo-ing until I nearly lost my voice.

The poor limo driver—Les was his name, I think. I mean, we were such losers. (The worst kind, 'cause we thought we were as cool as they came!) And quite honestly, besides the concert, we had no idea what else we were going to do when we got there. Les suggested a few places, none of which were in the three thousand guidebooks we bought, so we nixed his ideas.

Entering the Big Apple and pulling up at the entrance to our hotel was another huge thrill. We felt like superstars, but much to the dismay of the tourists and such standing by, we weren't. But with Les insisting he carry our bags, closing the car doors behind us, we felt fierce! After an endless check-in, and just as the bellman left us alone in our suite, we began giggling uncontrollably. This was just too, too cool! There were two great goodie bags to dig through (part of our Grand Prize, of course) and just as I was about to order room service, Sophie hung up on the operator and was, like, "Are you kidding me, Vivian? We're going out!!!"

We opened our luggage and threw our clothes on the bed. There was no time to shower, but there was time to tease. (Big hair was in then, give me a break.) We changed (our whistles actually made for a great fashion statement—kidding!) and hit the pavement. Undoubtedly looking like two Bon Jovi groupies, we asked Les to drop us at The China Club. We waited on line for what seemed like hours and after watching about a thousand people get in ahead of us, I told Sophie to take off her jacket, work her cleavage (hell, I didn't have any!), and we sweet-talked the bouncer into letting us in.

Walking in was surreal. I didn't want to blink my eyes and risk missing a single thing (think Aerosmith à la *Armageddon* and "I don't wanna close my eyes . . .") We held hands for at least the first fifteen minutes. (To prove we weren't dreaming and afraid we'd lose each other in the crowd.) We spotted the VIP area, roped off, and knew it was so off-limits. Sophie told me to tell them I had won a songwriting contest and was here for the weekend, but after a very serious stare, she realized that wasn't exactly the best idea. So we made our way to the dance floor where everyone seemed to be welcome.

It was unbelievable! I kid you not. I danced alongside Naomi Campbell and on my way to the ladies' room bumped into Rocky!!!! Sly himself!!! I was completely freaked out—we were the same height! This was my first brush with anything celebrity-related. I had been to an autograph signing at a bookstore for Kirk Cameron in, like, the seventh grade, but he never even showed up. This was huge!!!

Toward the end of evening number one, three scary European guys offered to drive us back to the hotel but something didn't seem cool—

wait—absolutely nothing seemed cool about it, and besides which, we still hadn't hailed a cab. *That* was even an experience. We got back to the hotel and raided the minibar. I think the sun was coming up at that point. We just couldn't get to sleep—there was so much to review!!!! We had never seen so many hot guys, never been to any kind of clubs other than those filled with dartboards, pool tables, and jukeboxes. The club had a DJ, and what was that??? I was in a car pool in the fifth grade with a "D.J." but that was as far as my association went. And hello?! We boogied in the same vicinity as a supermodel! Somebody pinch me.

Not bad for day one, right?!

Sophie and I woke up the next afternoon and spent our petty cash in an instant. She decided we needed to explore the famous Greenwich Village—"the Village" to the natives. Sophie had a list of every shop she wanted to see. Every department store, every café. I should have known what I was in for. Sophie was and is a fashionista to the core, but she would never admit it. You know how awesome a first kiss is, the rush and all? Well, that's how she feels after she signs her name on a receipt!

Anyway, downtown was definitely my favorite of all the 'hoods we walked through. I loved all the different kinds of people that were crammed alongside the streets. I dug how artists and the like would set up these little lemonade-like stands where they'd display and sell their work. It was so foreign to watch everyone keep their cool while sipping caffe lattes as dogs barked at one another, motorcycle engines would rev, and a police car would go whizzing by. Were New Yorkers hard of hearing or just too self-absorbed to let the world around them interrupt their brunch?

Sophie bought tons and tons of crap. Things I knew she'd never wear but just had to have. I think it was all about carrying a lot of bags for her—

a look that she thought was pretty genius until her arms began to give out.

Inspired by some gal that passed us by, we whizzed into Astor Place, a very "Village" glorified barber shop where Sophie proceeded to chop off her long blond locks for a more New York 'do. (At $11.95 how could I argue?) She still looked like a tourist if you ask me, but she was happy. My hair? No dice. I always liked my bed head, convertibile-esqe thing and no stranger was touching my hair, especially a stylist chick named Wanda who opted to shave off hers.

From the Village we took the bus uptown to Madison Avenue where window-shopping was all I would permit. See, I had plans for Sophie and me. Vague maybe, but they were lurking, more like visions, and I knew that if I allowed her to, she'd max out her father's credit card and I'd end up a solo act. (We'll get to my "plan" in a few.)

After the most expensive soup and salad I'd ever digested, we crossed town and walked back to the hotel to get ready for the concert.

The concert that night was amazing: Sheryl Crow—I don't think I mentioned that yet. Our seats were fantastic—third row. But the two guys who sat next to us, they were a fabulous view, too. Gorgeous!!! (The needle was removed from the record once we saw them make out, which was another first in my book. Welcome to New York, right?!) Instead of clubbing it again, we hit a diner and began to plan, but not before we ordered two (fake) hot chocolates, extra whipped cream, and French fries and gravy. I couldn't get my words out fast enough. "I'm moving here, Sophie," I said.

"I know, I know, for sure," she said as she dipped her fry.

"No, Soph, I'm serious." Where my vision was more of a premonition, hers was a bit less for real. We talked for hours. My pros, her cons. At the end, my winning remark was, "Why the fuck not? Why does it have to be this huge deal?" I think I got her at that moment. If she was all into fashion, beginning in New York was not so far-fetched. It was probably the right move if she was serious about it.

"And what about you? What are you going to do?" she asked.

"I'll figure it out," I said.

The next morning, Les was at the hotel right on time and was probably surprised by our much more subdued ride home. Sophie and I had agreed over the French fries and gravy (which was pretty much sacred) that we were going to do it—move to this great city without a dime or a plan. I opened my window and fashioned myself a screwdriver sans the "screw." I let the breeze run through my hair and hopefully dry some of the sweat that was accumulating under my arms. The past was past and the future was only sixteen weeks away!

When we got back to our apartment, my brand-new Gibson guitar was at my door, and the phone was ringing off the hook. Sophie's friends were rushing over to view the goods and Omelet was the best welcome home I could have ever asked for. (Sorry if I didn't mention it earlier. There was a guy in my life—my beloved puppy, Omelet.) Joseph must have dropped him off that morning.

Things were different for me those last few months of school. I felt like I was on speed. Running around, writing more songs, strumming my new guitar, even going so far as playing gigs at a few local bars, none of which went very well. I may have had a way with words, but that's where it ended. I heard they could do a lot with synthesizers, so I held on to the notion that I'd be the brunette Stevie Nicks of the nineties once I got to New York.

Sophie's parents were a bit more modern than mine and the idea of her moving to New York to pursue a career in fashion was tolerable for them. My folks on the other hand had heard me sing and they were worried.

Nevertheless, my parents threw Sophie and me a bon voyage–type party the Sunday before we left for the big city. Because I am a nostalgia queen, my mom made a last-ditch effort to have everything and everyone I ever loved there that night. Since I wasn't a big traveler, never went anywhere without Theodore (my teddy bear), kept in very close contact with my friends from home, and only ate homemade tuna fish, I think she was hoping I would change my mind if I had an evening that had heart-strings strung all over it.

Get this: In the same room were my favorite high school English teacher, every eccentric relative on both sides, any boy who had ever felt me up since the seventh grade, chicks from my soccer team, and hors d'oeuvres that only I would appreciate. Homemade tuna fish on a bed of sliced green peppers, pigs-in-a-blanket, baked ziti (well-done of course), mint chocolate chip milk shakes, a bowl of red M&M's (I swear, I think she hand-assembled them from a box/bag you'd find at Costco), Coronas with lime, and a deadly fruit punch! I mean it was a fuckin' joke and it nearly worked! It was the best of the best when it came to anything "home," and just the mere thoughtfulness of it made me have exactly one second thought.

Looking back, they must have been so scared for me. Big bad Vivian . . . c'mon. What couldn't I handle, right? Well, evidently, in their mind, New York City was at the top of the list.

I remember my cousin Maureen, as lovable and whacked out as they come, pulling me over for a heart-to-heart. "Vivian," she said. "I just know you are going to do great things. Frank and I love you and we want you to have this. . . ." Now, see, Maureen and Frank were more like an aunt and uncle to me. Each in their fifties with no children of their own, I was their kid. And get this: Maureen is pencil-thin (a gene that skipped my makeup for sure), evidently a knockout when she was young, and quite a firecracker to boot. She was infamous for eating everything and anything that was in front of her and snatching up any and all condiments that were not glued to a table. At five foot nine, with short bleached-out blond hair and a space between her two front teeth that just screamed Madonna, I'd always thought she was the coolest. She was as real as they came. Her tiny fingers were stacked with ring after ring. As a kid, I couldn't even understand how she could sit down and write a letter. She loved vintage in a very different way than I did, but the joy of scouring flea markets was something that totally proved we were related. Frank, her hubby, was a man of very few words and had a laugh that made me think of a hyena with a sinus infection. He seemed to love Maureen as a king does his queen. He, as she, was big into vintage. He made a living out of it actually, trading and auctioning artifacts of one kind or another.

Okay, so anyway, Maureen pulled me over and insisted I accept her gift. There in her hand was one of those oversized cardboard jewelry boxes, weathered to the core. You could see bits and pieces of what was once a silver coating but had most likely disappeared after years of storage or something. The lid was kept on only by a thick rubber band, smudged with something black, and still smelling of rubber. I didn't much care what this lovely container was storing, I just died over the obvious care by which it was given to me. In any case, I opened it in front of them as Maureen was the kind that loved giving a gift more than receiving one. Once I managed to slide the rubber band off and open the box, there was this huge silver pendant that she insisted would bring me good luck while simultaneously warding off any evil that may come my way. (Noteworthy: She was telling me all this before I could even see what the tissue paper was covering.) Needless to say, I loved it. Rather, I loved them, and just as the fruit punch started to kick in and before my nostrils could flare, I saw that underneath the pendant was a plastic case of condoms, which immediately converted my tears to a giant laugh. Maureen said, "Please, if New York is anything like it was when I was there, you are definitely going to need these!" I hugged her real tight. Frank was cracking up wildly in the background and out of the corner of my eye I saw my mom, leaning against the corridor, most definitely hoping that Maureen and Frank were the accomplices she was striving for, convincing me to stay in PA.

NOT! No way. Home was what, two-and-a-half hours away??? This whole "This Is Your Life" theme party was not going to stop me from getting on the next morning's bus!

Anyway, there were others who were excited for my big adventure.

My charming ex-boyfriend was eager to visit the Big Apple and couldn't wait for me to leave. He heard the girls "were off the hook" (terrific—even more competition). My grandmother was excited. She saw my vacated room as a new shagadelic cat palace for her precious pets, and my dad, although he still won't admit it, was having visions of a converted library/cigar room. Simon sat me down, gave me fifty bucks, and told me to trust no one. Great—thanks. Joseph, on the other hand, was cool about the whole thing. We were always close and I had filled him in on the goings-on at Penn State. He was all about my fresh start and he was the one who took Sophie and me to the station the next morning.

As guests started to leave and the tuna–green pepper concoction was beginning to stink up the living room, my pal Dani came over to say good-bye. We had been next-door neighbors and friends for what seemed like forever. She was married and four months pregnant. Sophie and I had been her bridesmaids (I won't even get into the dresses . . .). Anyway, she hugged me tight and encouraged me to get out of Washington Crossing, even just for a little while. She made me promise that I'd be back for the birth of her baby, and she also made me promise to write and fill her in on what Sophie and I were up to. She was "ready to live vicariously through us." That's how she put it and that's what, looking back, made me suck it up and get on that glamorous Red & Tan bus.

Saying good-bye to my mother was the most difficult. She just had such a hard time with it. For any of you who have a strained relationship with your moms, the awkwardness of that moment will probably make the most sense to you. See, my mom and I aren't/weren't chums. She doesn't share secrets with me nor do I with her. She's the greatest as I've said, and I'm not just writing this 'cause I know that she and everyone she knows will be reading this eventually. I mean it. She put my brothers and me first, always. She made sure we had everything—from our own rooms to the best eighth-grade teachers. One hint of a cold and I was off to the pediatrician. She was at every stupid soccer game I ever played in. She picked me up from every dance, every sleepover, every lesson. And, I just have to add this: As far as nutrition went—forget about it! Her claim to fame was that she had the three of us drinking skim milk before it was even in!!!

But as I sit here and write, it's easy now to convey what we, or let me rephrase that, what *I* did not have with her. I never went to my mom with my "stuff." I was so busy not needing her, I was so busy maneuvering my way around her, that when the serious shit surfaced, we had no idea how to communicate. This sounds pathetic, but even telling her I got my period for the first time was tough. I don't even think I told her. I was twelve (of course, I couldn't get it at fourteen like the rest of my friends, or so they admitted), and instead of trying out her tampons that looked more like a deadly weapon than a feminine hygiene product, I stuffed tissues in my underpants and threw them in the toilets at school. (I developed quite a strut after several surreal months. I can imitate it for you if you want.) At some point, I don't even remember when, "pads" were mysteriously placed in my bedroom, and then things started to become clear.

Well, you'd think that being nearly twenty-one years old, with a college education, and a brand-new guitar, I would have been better at those uncomfortable moments with her, but I wasn't. I fought not to let her see that I was scared and that I wasn't sad, but I'm pretty sure she saw right through it.

Leaving Omelet was another story. Rumor had it that it would be tough enough finding a place without a white German shepherd, so as dutiful grandparents, my mom and dad offered to let him stay behind with them for the time being. I swore to him that it would be only for a few weeks and that he'd love my mom's cooking.

Picking up Sophie—with excitement so contagious—I got stoked pretty quick. Joseph stuffed our bags onto the bus and waved good-bye as we drove off into the fog. (Sunset would have sounded better I know, but it rained that day.)

The bus ride was pretty harmless . . . three-plus hours with a mini–panic attack as we headed toward and into the Lincoln Tunnel. The traffic was absurd (welcome to New York) and we sat, motionless, in that thing for the longest thirty minutes of my life. I have this confined space issue (among others). I hate tiny closets, alcove bedrooms, airplanes, old elevators, will never go for an MRI no matter what, and then there're those tunnels. It didn't make it any better when I realized that this tunnel in particular ran under the Hudson River. A very big thank-you to that overly friendly neighbor on the bus that afternoon who felt the need to explain all this to me. So that part was rough. Getting our gear (one huge backpack each) from Port Authority to Alphabet City (the eastern part of the Village for you non–New Yorkers) was another story.

See, Sophie had this cousin, third I think, who laid open his welcome mat when he heard we were making the move. He was a musician who, at the time, wasn't sharing this "great" place with a friend. The idea was that we would crash with Adam until we found a place of our own; jobs, too, of course. Adam had said it would be a breeze to transition crosstown so we gave it a whirl. With backpacks so stuffed it was hard to walk up and through the doors of a common bus, we made it to Adam's place in almost as much time as it took us to get from PA to NY. Rookies to the core.

We finally got to Adam's neighborhood and found his "palace"—both of us secretly freaking out inside and both of us too cool to admit it. We buzzed his apartment only to figure out that his buzzer wasn't working, so I just plain lost my patience and buzzed every apartment in the building until someone rang us up. (Not a great way to meet your new neighbors, I assure you.)

Four flights up, Sophie knocked on the door and there was Adam, high I'd guess, maybe on "love." We obviously had interrupted something and I remember this next part distinctly: You could see the whole place right from the door. Mini-kitchen, similar to that of a Barbie town house on the right. Bathroom, sorry shower, adjacent to the mini-fridge, and empty beer bottles lined up in this really peculiar manner. They filled the shelves where I guess books could have been, and the whole thing boyishly screamed, "Hey, I drank these all by myself!" Terrific. Where you'd assume there'd be a kitchen table of some kind was a laundry pile that you'd probably stick to if you got too close to it. The living area was a futon, with a stained (ew!) ivory cover, a desk that Adam must have taken with him from his first bedroom set (covered in incense soot, by the way), and a blue crushed velvet rocking chair. This big Martha Stewart moment was topped off with a deep red shag carpet that I'm guessing we were supposed to sleep on.

Okay. I am not a neat freak or a spoiled brat. I was grateful that he had offered Sophie and me this rent-free space to dwell in. But the novice in me was thinking, Is this how talented musicians live in New York City??? And where were his instruments, by the way? More importantly, how about the toilet? When I asked, he gave me a key and directed me down the hall. I didn't even bother making eye contact with Sophie. I knew that if I was feeling like this, she was seconds from a breakdown.

When I got back from the loo, Adam had changed his clothes, from that pile I'm assuming, and was ready to take us out for a drink. I needed one, big time, so I was more than ready to go. Sophie said she wanted to use the bathroom and freshen up, but I explained, via facial expressions, that that might not be the best idea.

The mood changed as Adam got us all riled up about our first official night as "New Yorkers." I went with it. I had to. There was no going back and no room in our budget for a room at The Four Seasons. It took a few jokes and some tickles to get Sophie in better spirits. We took the subway for the very first time across town to Don Hills, where one of Adam's friends was playing. This time there was no waiting at the door. Not 'cause Adam was "the man," but rather because there was no line. The place was pitch-black and this wanna-be Kurt Cobain was whining through his one-man show and his one single set. Adam whispered to me that this "dude" was brilliant, he was "big time." Though with no audience and not a single cocktail, it was difficult for me to believe. In any case, as a fellow "musician," I paid close attention, attempted to understand his lyrics, signed up for his mailing list, and even bought his self-produced CD. Sophie was at the bar, from what I could see, talking with Adam. I would bet it was about our accommodations and I was not about to get involved in a family matter. When his set was over, I thought it would be nice if I introduced myself to the maestro and praise his performance. But even before I could take my first step toward him, three Kate Moss look-alikes beat me to it. No wonder I didn't see them, between their combined weight and the "atmosphere" of the place, I would have needed an infrared magnifying glass. My eyes were going to have to get used to this new kind of atmosphere. Musicians and models in New York are like magnets, especially when they are struggling. (A term that Sophie inadvertently must have left out when she initially described Adam to me.)

So after a few drinks, we left Don Hills and crossed the street to some other place, the name I can't recall. Same deal, same vibe, same girls. Sophie and I grabbed a booth and conferenced. She had made a deal with Adam. Apparently, if he agreed to stay with his "friend" for a few weeks, we'd clean up his love shack, stay for a while, let him keep whatever we found for the space, and we'd be on our merry way once things shaped up for us. He went for it: free stuff and an excuse to crash with his lady friend full-time—at least until we were ready to leave and give him back his place.

Adam graciously slept on his shag that night and Sophie and I laid out our sweatshirts on the futon and settled in for the night. The sounds of the garbage trucks, police sirens, and catfights on the streets didn't really bother me. It was when I felt this odd brushy-type movement on my face—that's when I freaked. I slapped my face, demanded that Sophie turn on the light, and be my best friend and open what I had squashed in my hand. She refused, nervous to the point of tears, and Adam, our hero—not—did the honors.

"C'mon, Viv, it's just a roach. They're like flies in NYC." Chuckle chuckle. Okay. Enough. This sucked!!!!! I must have washed my graciousness off when I got ready for bed. I huffed and I puffed. I wrapped my face up in a T-shirt, took two Tylenol PMs, and passed out. When I woke up, Adam was gone and had left a forwarding number taped to his desk that I was tempted to chuck out the window.

Without jobs, a social life, or any NYC navigational skills, fumigating and redecorating Adam's space was a blessing in disguise. We started by throwing out nearly every single object in the place. Sophie had no mercy and I was relieved. I definitely didn't want to be the bad guy in this scenario. The first thing we bought were four pairs of gloves. I mean his apartment was like the most disgusting frat house you could imagine, times ten. The building's super was happy to take the futon and desk off our hands. The plush rocking chair we carried down the stairs on our own and left on the street corner. We boxed up the empty bottles and left them outside as well. When we returned from the grocery with garbage bags, bleach, nearly every cleaning product we could carry, and of course chocolate chip cookies for fuel, we noted the bottles and the chair were gone. Good show!!!!

Sophie, with her studded bandanna around her head like an outlaw of some sort, took care of "the pile" as we affectionately called it. She phoned Adam and told him that he needed to come and pick it up by day's end. "No deal," he said, unless we dropped it off at the wash and dry. Done.

We listened to the cheesiest dance music that these "new" stations offered (new city, new radio, you know?) and rocked out a bit as we cleaned the day away. Together we pulled up the carpet and we were only too happy to welcome our hardwood floors. I removed the shower curtain—I'll spare the details here—and hung up a temporary one. (My arms hurt worse than when we were schlepping the damn furniture. Wow, was it time for the gym—*any* gym.)

Finally, we each took showers and made a mad dash for someplace that didn't reek of bleach. As luck would have it, we walked right into a karaoke bar where being "too cool" probably didn't get you in. (We liked that—still do.)

We chose a song immediately and registered for our moment on the mike. Abba's "Dancing Queen"—one of our all-time favorites. Now, this whole vibe was way more "us." Girls with butts and guys with clean clothes. Light fixtures (would you believe), beers on tap, a joint where guys got rowdy, and the ladies got silly. I took a pack of matches, I remember, just so we could find our way back there some day.

After an impressive go at "Dancing Queen," a small group of boys sent us a pitcher. How sweet. Sophie naturally invited them over and "small talk" ensued!!! Six degrees of separation: My brother Joseph went to camp with one of the guys, another had gone to Don Hills once—we had a lot in common. Please, we were trying. None of these guys were from New York and all of them worked on Wall Street. Interesting, or so we thought. We listened to their war stories, which sounded all too familiar, from not knowing a soul to knowing you'd get lost every time you'd leave your apartment. The cost of things, from rent, to drinks, to takeout. Terrific. I implored them to stop (talk about a buzz kill) but they didn't. So, instead of listening to more Nueva York sob stories, I filled out another song sheet—with their names on it! Hell, I was in the mood to be serenaded and I chose the first tune that came to mind. Think *Top Gun*. Yup, ten minutes later we had half a dozen businessmen singing "You've Lost That Loving Feelin' " and I was grinning from ear to ear, fully loving it.

We closed the bar and let them walk us home. And, excuse me, but since when did a walk home equate to an invite upstairs? Our new "friends" weren't too friendly when they realized they had no shot. Sophie later fessed up that she gave "the cute one" her number. What a shocker, and I didn't recall any of them being cute. But in the end, I managed to feel like Kelly McGillis for just a few minutes. That's what I remember about the evening. Sure Val Kilmer and Tom Cruise were nowhere in sight, but remember what I said about imagination—it can be your best friend and, in this case, your saving grace during a semi-disappointing night out on the town.

We laughed as we traipsed up the stairs, thinking of the "boyz" and how off the mark they were, but the joke was on us when we walked in and realized we hadn't resolved the sleeping scenario. We had given away all the furniture and we were about to get reacquainted with the floor. Sure, the stink was gone and the Raid was sprayed, but the only cozy thing in the place to sleep with, or on for that matter, was my teddy bear and Sophie's endless collection of scarves. As IKEA didn't open till ten the next morning, out of necessity and based on exhaustion, we just passed out on the floor. How glamorous.

For the record, I never said I was cool.

Talk about "cheap chic." We had Adam's place screaming femme fatale in no time and on a very impressive budget if I do say so myself. Every neighborhood had some kind of tag or stoop sale going on, and then, of course, there were the fleas. Our one real investment was a yummy sleeper sofa but everything else was part of someone else's history with our own touch of girly flair. Sure, the deal was that Adam was going to keep whatever he wanted after the home swap, but unless he opted to play on a different sorta team for that month, Sophie and I were pretty sure we'd be able to walk away with it all! Such scammers . . .

So now we had a pad, temporary yes, but still a place that felt like home. "Apartment" was then checked off our list. Next was "jobs." All right, how hard could that really be? Neither of us were going corporate just yet. There were more restaurants and bars and stores in NYC than on any other island in the world. Surely someone could use our help.

Sophie struck gold first, landing a retail job at a shop where she ended up spending most of her salary. It was, and still is, called Atrium, located inches away from New York University. She loved it and also had a huge, huge crush on her manager. She hawked clothes to students, tourists, and the like from ten to eight every day but Monday, and made a bunch of new friends in an instant.

I, on the other hand, didn't have it that easy. I wanted something that was a bit more on the edge, with skewed hours and lots of personality. I saw myself as a "struggling musician" so I needed time to write, to be inspired, and before anything else, to learn how to play my fancy new guitar. (What a joke!) Waiting tables or bartending seemed like a good idea. After pounding the pavement I realized some new things about myself: I knew nothing about food. (What? You think I'm kidding? Go ahead. Can you tell me the difference between gnocchi and ravioli, fettuccini versus linguini?) Then there was wine. No clue about "tannins," how to open a bottle, or even pronounce anything beyond "red or white." Bartending was another disaster. Note to self: Just being able to get drunk doesn't qualify you as a bartender. Barback was more like it.

I found a barbacking job that the manager actually tried to talk me out of at this sorry-ass place called Buffalo Chips (now out of business). Chip was the owner—how creative—and he was a total sleazeball, or so the manager had said. No worries. I'd stay out of everyone's way, do whatever it was that a barback was to do, collect my cut of the night's tips, and get out of there. I was to work on Thursday, Friday, and Saturday nights and went in desperate to get the job done well, and most of all, keep it. (I had been living on Special K, oranges, and tuna fish for weeks and my skin was turning this weird shade of paste and my breath, let's just say Altoids weren't around back then.)

Night one: Everyone hated me. The bartenders were all women whose looks had faded or who were convinced they had. They each seemed scorned as hell and the sight of anyone upbeat was not only tragic but insanely irritating in their little "girl's club." And, this goes without saying, I was not invited. No hi's, hey's, or how are ya's. Just "stay out of my way, make sure there are always clean glasses, and don't even think about going to the bathroom unless one of us gives you permission." No sweat. I wanted to either cry or push one of them into the other. The nerve! Whatever, I had to make this work. Maybe this was going to be like pledging or something—see what I could endure in night one and if I stuck it out, things would be different on the second. I'd make friends with these three witches and bring them home to meet Soph.

Nope, it wasn't like that at all. I spent the night running back and forth behind a wet, sticky, narrow bar like a high-strung animal caged in a zoo, taking shit from the witches and from big pigs at the bar. People actually threw things at me to get my attention, and the more they drank the less they understood that I was the barBACK not barTENDER and could only serve them water. In what felt like an hour, nearly seven went by and at four in the morning I asked if I could pee. They laughed—no, sorry—they cackled.

I went anyway. I washed my face, scrubbed my arms and hands, and went back out there with a smile. Please, these girls thought they were going to get the best of me. Think again. As they all sat around with their thong underwear sticking out, counting their money as their cigarettes hung from their lips, I started to gather my things. "Not so fast," said one evil spinster . . . see that box over there?"

"Yeah," I said (and there were four, by the way).

"Those are the bottled beers for tomorrow."

"So?" I asked.

"So? So, you have to lay them out in the iceboxes before you leave."

I sucked it up. "Oh, okay."

I nearly broke my back carrying each box to the bar. Trick was, that the beer had to be placed by brand and stacked high. It was sort of like building a glass card house at four-thirty in the morning. By 5:15 I was nearly through. The bar had emptied out, the music was off, and it appeared that everyone was waiting for me. You'd think that in an effort to close up someone would have thought to help. Nope. It was on my last few beers that the chief bitch came over and said, "Nice work. Pretty surprising, Livingston."

(What was this—the army???) "Thanks," I said, no eye contact at all. This stacking thing required major concentration, especially for a rookie like me. And as luck would have it, just as I was nearly through, a bottle broke (I must have let go of it too soon). Hoping no one heard, I carried on desperately until that same woman started screaming at me, "You idiot! Now we've got to stay here all morning while you take out every one, clean out the case, remove the glass, and start again!"

That was it. Very much like the incredible hulk, these chicks were not going to like me when I was angry and they had gone too far. I grabbed my things, took the soda I had in my hand, and got right in her face and said, "Eat me, you witch!" I topped it off by throwing my drink in the face of the witch that pissed me off most of all and ran like hell out the door, around the corner, and literally never looked back!

Once I felt pretty safe, I started cracking up. Being tortured that night taught me a lesson. Number one, I was not cut out to be a barback, and two, I still had it in me: to follow my instincts and never let anyone monkey with my self-respect.

Now then, does anyone know of any other friendly establishments where pleasantness and decency are a job requirement?

Fuck.

After a day or two I came out of hiding. They had my address at the good old Buffalo Chips and I wouldn't have been surprised if one or two or all three of them came to pay me a visit. This was New York City. I mean, I can't be the only one who's seen *The Sopranos.*

As it turned out, a friend of a friend of Simon's girlfriend managed a jazzy little coffee shop on the corner of Bleecker and MacDougal Streets in the heart of Greenwich Village. She was pretty certain they could find a place for me there if I stopped in. (Grateful yes, but it is so like Simon to put two and two together weeks after I'd moved.) In any case, I got the job. I tried to get on their schedule as often as possible and offered to host, tend the bar (coffee/soda), and waitress. In the beginning I was given the worst shifts that were always available. Weekdays from eight A.M. to four P.M. and weekends from four P.M. till closing (usually about five A.M.). After a few weeks of being the new kid on the block, I managed to learn my way around the place, make a steady bit of cash, and, get this, even a few (eccentric) friends. Le Figaro, as it is called, was a hub for wanderers, at least in my eyes. None of us, from the kitchen to the bar to the parlor, had a thing in common, from language to background, education, and most of all, sexuality. I think out of dozens of employees I was the only heterosexual female, and I adored it. Everyone had a closet (no, not just that kind), everyone was imperfect, and whether they knew it or not, I fit right in.

When the tourists didn't tip, the manager, Miguel, would take care of it. When a rowdy bunch of guys would get "fresh" with me, Lilly would handle it. When someone would ask for my number, Natale would see to it that I was "taken." (Had my parents ever seen a glimpse of this they would have been horrified! Vivian, the undercover lesbian, would have been a Polaroid moment for sure.) Often, Sophie would drop in after she was through with work, usually with an entourage of about a half dozen. I liked them all but one: her new "boyfriend," Fernando. After hours and hours of late-night conversations that consisted mostly of me saying, "Sophie, do not date him. He's your boss," she was still completely obsessed with him. But in the end, she opted to see one of his cronies instead: Fernando. He was nice and all and a bit of a fox, if you dug guys who were big into silver jewelry and hair gel, but I had the sense that his "thing" was dating nice innocent younger women who were new to the city. He went out every night and once he woke up, would talk about his plans for the evening ahead. When I asked Sophie about what he did, ya know, for, like, a living, she would innocently say that he had a great job in the vending machine business. Okayyyyyyy.

But I was glad that she was happy. The time we spent together was always special and lots of fun and looking back, it was kinda nice that we were leading individual lives, doing our own thing. My comrades at Le Figaro were becoming my pseudo-surrogate family and surprise, surprise, my "music" was put on hold. We would all go to local bars once we got off work, listen to each other's sob stories, rock out to music at semi-historic dives, and check out each other's most recent crushes, wherever they'd be lurking. I mean working. Well, you know what I mean. Lilly and Natale, two other waitresses, were feeling like family to me already, and they definitely helped me get through momentary homesickness spells.

After a bit, I was promoted to waiting on the outside tables of the restaurant. This was where serious money could be made and where I felt that the New York City energy was abundant. My skills as a waitress were also getting pretty impressive. (I was able to juggle a bunch of tables at once and whenever things got too hectic, my charm seemed to get me through. Cha-ching!) I waited on all sorts of people, from artists to actors, tourists to teachers, athletes to musicians. I got to know my regulars and befriended a bunch of the local merchants as well. My chocolate Italian ices were always on the house at the pizza place down the street and I never paid covers at the door at any of the fine social establishments in my area. (This was where I began to understand the importance of "networking." Very clutch.)

Things were pretty amazing. Adam had officially moved in with his girlfriend so we had the place until, I don't know, until she got sick of him I guess. We did have to pay the rent now, but between the two of us it wasn't too terrible. I was making enough to save and play a bit, too. Clothes were provided by Sophie, and if we had only been the same shoe size my worries would have been over.

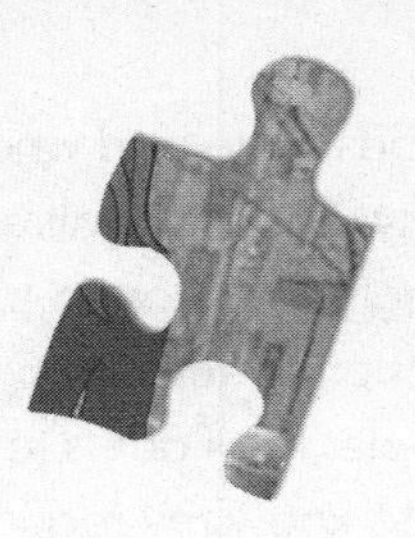

It was one night late in September when the lovely reality I had created for myself was put to the test. My section/my tables were basically two crowded rows in an L-shape outside of the place. It was virtually impossible for me to get a look at my customers ahead of time, especially on a busy night. Running in and out, placing orders, filling pitchers of water . . . any of you who are or have been waitresses can understand. Every time I looked up, or tried to catch my breath, someone needed something. Check, fork, dessert—something.

Well, I had my groove on that night. The music playing inside Le Figaro gave me just enough juice to hide my exhaustion. I saw a man with his back to me, sitting where a couple had just paid their bill, and I figured that he was my next customer. Reaching down for my pad and not paying much attention, I said hello and asked him if I could get him anything to start. He said, "Yeah, actually you can. Why don't you start by telling me why the hell you're here and what the fuck you could have been thinking not to even say good-bye?" My heart stopped.

Before I go on, I think this is probably a good time to let you in on a secret. At least something I've tried to leave back in Pennsylvania with my family ('cause they knew—eventually) and with everyone I went to school with. When I came to New York, it was only Sophie and I who knew about Mark, and actually Lilly, who I had only confessed to just a few days earlier. And that was just the way I wanted it. New York City was to be my fresh start. All baggage was indeed left behind. Or so I naively thought.

Mark was a guy I met three weeks into Penn State and the guy who I'm still trying to get over some seven years later. Not because he was just so wonderful and so amazing and because he broke my heart or something. I use the term "get over" because Mark was a creep. As close to a full-fledged monster as humanly possible. He basically ruined what should have been four fun-filled years of college and all that we're supposed to experience at that point in our lives. He robbed me blind, making off with my self-esteem, my focus, any goals, my friends, the whole nine yards. Those crucial years of my life instead became the worst years, hands down. And I let it happen.

When people think of an abusive relationship, for some reason they focus on the physical connotations, rarely the psychologial stuff. They think of women who are weak, who follow a pattern they've seen or lived through themselves. They may feel that women in "bad" relationships are drama queens, or in some strange way, like all the fights, the making up, the breaking up, the humiliation, the fear. Outsiders can't fathom why "we" stay. As if we are to blame on lots of levels and the idea of making ourselves doormats or punching bags is oddly pleasurable. Yeah sure, I decided to go to college to entrench myself in hell. As if!

But I get it. (Sort of.) Imagine possessing a frame of mind and the strength and the discipline to know, utterly and completely, that if you were in a bad situation, or even had just entered into something that just felt off in some way, that you would leave in an instant. Without hesitation or regret. How could my past and my decisions possibly make sense to someone with a true sense of self? They can't. And especially if you've been fortunate enough to never fall big time for someone whose true colors surface only after you're in la-la land. In a recent conversation with my editor, actually, she couldn't help but ask me "Why?" I mean, she knows me now, not back then. She sees someone different, so it doesn't add up. When I try to give her an honest answer, I can't really. I still don't know why I stayed so long. I still don't know what exactly I was trying to prove—to myself, to him, to my peers—no clue.

When I make time to remember what I can of those years—how it all started up, why I didn't just run for my life the minute I knew who he was and what I was in for—I come up empty-handed. I'm not too sure I'll ever really have "the" answer. I do remember what it was that piqued my interest in the beginning. That part was easy. And I'll sum it up real quick. Mark was super smart, super hot, incredibly charming, and very athletic. He was always in control, the leader of his crew. (Later, I understood that they feared him too.) He was in a frat, was always out and about, but still, big into his studies. Probably the only guy who I found attractive who did not, even once, ever make a pass at me. And this was because, I later found out, he didn't like me "that way." Not a bit. So instead, we grew to become "friends." We'd meet after class, hang out in the library, chat each other up at the local bars. But I was always the girl he'd talk to about other girls. And that drove me nuts. Maybe it was his plan all along. Basically forcing me to broach the "Hey, how about me?" topic so that he would never be at risk—who knows! But that's how it started. And I guess I was too focused on the challenge of snagging him to see who it really was that I was just about to land.

But for the sake of storytelling, let me move on, not backward. We'll get into Mark all in good time.

"Mark . . . what are you doing here?" I asked.

"Looking for you," he said with that smile of his. (He was, I admit, a striking man. Even more intelligent than he was good-looking. Six foot three and with a body that just didn't quit, dark green eyes, ivory skin, and great black hair. He played football at school, managed to graduate with something like a 3.8 GPA, and opted to continue his studies, going for his M.B.A., still at Penn State.)

Anyway, I excused myself, ran inside, and puked in the bathroom.

Natale and Lilly knocked and then pounded on the door when I had been in there for a noticeable amount of time. "I'm fine, I'm fine," I cried. I finally let them in and asked them to take his table. They said sure. "Are you okay?" they asked and I said that I was fine but I just needed one of them to wait on him. I couldn't.

I washed my face, stared in the mirror, and forced myself to get it together. "You can run but you can't hide," that's what he used to always say, and he was right, but I'd be damned if I was going to let him screw up this job for me. I waited on the rest of my tables, and did my best to pretend that he wasn't there, but I couldn't shake it. Natale said that he was "milking" his meal and asked if I wanted to have Miguel throw him out. I said no. That's what Mark would have wanted. The drama, the fighting, the scene. Not here, no way. "Tell him I said to come back at four if he wants to talk, but I'll be working till then." It was just around midnight. Just as part of me thought that he wouldn't wait the three-plus hours, the other part knew that he would. On my break I tried to phone Sophie. I wanted her to meet me at work. She was always really good at getting in his face and getting me out of a potentially bad situation, but she wasn't picking up at home and cell phones weren't as big then as they are now.

Of course, just as the clock struck four, there was Mark. I had Natale do my ketchups and cash me out and Mark and I walked for a few blocks before we started to talk. We sat on a bench in Washington Square Park. I made sure to stop in a public place. Crackheads and the homeless made for decent watchdogs. I didn't have many alternatives at four A.M. I didn't want him to know where I lived and I didn't want to see anyone I knew.

I felt so angry inside that I spoke first. "What are you doing here, Mark? Why did you have to come here? Can't you find someone else to bother? We broke up. It's over. It's all over. Please just let me be." I wanted to cry. I really did. Even as I write this now I feel as defeated as I did then at the park. Defeated because I had made a fresh start, endured what I needed to, to stay in school (no way was I not getting my diploma after four years!) and convince my parents I was "fine"—fine enough to go to New York City with Sophie and start anew. Him showing up made me feel like we were still at school. As if nothing had changed and all my efforts were for nought.

He went on and on about how sorry he was. That it was his love for me, his obsession that made him do the things he did. (See, early on in a relationship, that shit usually works. But when you hear it every two weeks for four years, you start to know better.) I told him to stop. It wasn't going to work. We were over. Gone but not forgotten; never forgotten. I would never forgive him for those years and I'd rather stand in the middle of moving traffic then ever get back in a relationship with him. I geared up for a good dose of honesty. What was he going to do really, that he hadn't done before, if I spelled it out for him and said all the things I had held inside for so so long?

I told him that I hated him. That "no, I wasn't seeing anyone else," which was what he was most interested in, of course. He asked about Omelet, which made the hair on my neck stand up

I said that if he came around me again, I'd get the police involved. I told him to go home. That we had no future together—ever. That he had disgusted me for years and that I never had the strength to leave him, but now I was stronger and this was the end. What made my blood boil was that he seemed so damn smug. Grinning, almost happy for me that I had "outgrown" him (his words) and proud of me, in his own sick way, for finally speaking up. But then he told me that I would never forget him, that I would always need him, and that I'd never amount to anything anyway. (So much for being proud of me.) "You're pathetic, Vivian. Always have been and always will be. A slut to the core and nothing that your pretty smile will ever hide." (I know this sounds harsh, but he really talked like that. No one except me would ever hear it, so what did it matter?) He spit on me and walked away. For a second I wanted to yell at him and tell him he was wrong about me. I was not the woman he saw, not the woman I showed him all those years, not the woman who stayed with him. But I just sat there. This was different, though. I was sitting there now watching my past walk away from me. Not feeling defeated or pathetic or hopeless. Rather, I sat there realizing that I was in charge of my own life, finally. I told myself that the need to show him that I was not all the things he said I was, was ludicrous. I could be the Virgin Mary and he'd still think I was shit. He was a relentless, evil, manipulative man who would always be miserable and would never change, for any woman, for anything in the world. I had worked at talking myself through these scenarios for months and this time it was finally clicking. (Yay, therapy!!!)

Seriously, 75 percent of me didn't care if I was worthy of his pedestal. His opinion of me didn't count, my opinion of me did. I sat there and felt strong. Of all of our breakups and moments, my heart knew this one was for good. Now all I had to do was work on that other 25 percent and I'd be fine.

I sat there until the sun came up, walked home, and called my folks. I asked them to bring Omelet to New York. My mom asked me if everything was okay, and I said fine (of course). I just missed my puppy.

Sophie and Fernando came in a few hours later. (Little time for a pity party, I was back at the restaurant for the morning shift.) Without even exchanging words with me she sent Fernando back out to brunch without her. She knew something wasn't right (best friend intuition is priceless!). When I told her the story she was speechless. By then, I was okay for the most part, still a little shocked but really happy about the way I handled things. More than anything, I was distracted and excited that my parents were driving down the following day with Omelet. I had already cleared it with the super and couldn't wait to see my puppy. Sophie and I had adopted him nearly six months ago, and he was, no doubt, my medicine for getting through those last tough months at school.

Sophie was never able to accept that Omelet was a he. I remember she'd pick up the most adorable feminine little collars and stuff for him. I'd get home from class and there was my confused little man with a red bow clipped in his hair or a floral cotton collar around his neck. I used to always make her take them back even though she insisted he would never know the difference. Her firstborn better be a girl . . .

Like most of the men in my life, I spotted Omelet out of the corner of my eye and just knew we were meant to be. Sophie and I were still up at Penn, having breakfast at Denny's (so glam, I know). As I anxiously awaited my breakfast of champions all for a dollar ninety-nine (does Moon Over My-Ham-EE rock or what?!) I saw an odd-looking old woman pull up in a Brady Bunch–type station wagon—only not nearly as shiny and new or with six jovial kids singing "Sha-na-na-na-na-na-na-na-na, sha-na-na-na-na-na." Her long awkward car was filled to the max—chairs, clothes, apples—I could swear I even saw a birdcage. Anyway, I watched her park the wagon, get out, and venture to the back. She opened up the trunk and there were these three adorable little puppies. Instinctively, I ran out of Denny's, left Sophie in the dust, and introduced myself to this character of a woman. She asked me if I wanted one. "One hundred bucks," she said.

"Come again?"

"All right, fifty but that's as low as I'll go," and before I could say anything I made the most delicious humbling sweet eye contact with this white fuzzy cotton ball. It felt like destiny is all I can tell you.

I told her to hang on. I ran back into Denny's, grabbed my checkbook, sucked down a strip of Sophie's bacon, and wrote the old woman a check "to cash." With no papers, no shots, no nothing, I scooped up the ball of white fuzz and brought him back inside. Sophie thought I was nuts. We had never even spoken about a dog before—unless, that is, we were talking about a guy!—and suddenly there was this yummy little thing in my lap. It just felt so right, so peaceful. I had a new—sorry, Soph—another, best friend. He slept soundly in my lap until my breakfast was served. (The waitress was nice enough to hold it in the kitchen so it wouldn't get any colder during the adoption process.) Just as I went to gobble up the first bite of my breakfast, the puppy rose on his feet, stretched as tall as he could in my lap, and ate my eggs right before my eyes. I named him Omelet in less than five seconds flat.

He was just darling. The cutest of cute. I took him to the nearest vet where I was told that I was the proud owner of a white German shepherd, approximately six weeks of age and in desperate need of a bath.

He got his shots and afterward we went to Petco, where I bought more junk than any one puppy could wish for.

I dropped Sophie off at the coffee shop and drove home with Omelet in my lap. I took him back to my apartment where Mark, who, as usual, had just let himself in, was stretched out on our sofa asleep to the sounds of a baseball game I believe. Ignoring Mark, I gave Omelet a bath. He was so tiny it took all of ten minutes and then I laid him down at the foot of the couch while I digested what had transpired over the last two hours. I put away all of Omelet's new stuff, and when I came back to check on him, I couldn't believe my eyes. (This may sound gross but I just have to put this in) Omelet had full on pooped on Mark's foot—I mean, it was everywhere—and as scared as I was of him waking up and losing it, I couldn't help but feel the camaraderie I shared with this little puppy on this, just day one, of our relationship. I carefully lifted Omelet off the couch and placed him in my room with the door shut. I was terrified of disrupting Mark and having him figure out what was on his body and how it got there. I never knew for sure what to expect with Mark and at year four of our glorious relationship, nothing really hurt anymore. I was pretty numb.

With wet warm paper towels I did the best I could to clean Mark up but he came to eventually. Fortunately, he was more embarrassed than angry. When I had finished (What, like, you thought that SOB would have gotten up and done it himself? Oh no, I was a modern-day Cinderella as far as he was concerned.), I reluctantly introduced him to Omelet and to my surprise, even a monster like Mark could be bewitched by an angel of a puppy. But then the sight of him holding Omelet began to make me nervous and anxious, so I did my best to keep them apart from then on in. I rarely left Mark alone with Omelet (who knew how he'd react if Omelet annoyed him, chewed his papers, or got in his way?). In Mark's twisted mind, that made me all the more nurturing, a loving mom, and also somehow canceled out a handful of my laundry list of horrible traits. Sick.

Back then, shall we, to Omelet and the big city. The next day, my parents arrived eventually, awkward and nervous and horrified when they saw our "palace." Omelet on the other hand almost threw out his hips he was wagging his tail so hard! (Unconditional love my friends—nothing beats it!) My parents didn't stay very long. My dad and I talked about my job, my friends, and the great graduate schools New York had to offer (as if), and my mother instinctively disappeared with Sophie. I'm guessing she got the goods on what happened the day before. My mother thought I looked terribly tired and couldn't believe my shower was in my kitchen, which was in my living room, which was in fact my bedroom, etc. Neither of them (my parents) brought up Mark, to my face anyway, which I was sort of happy about, and both reminded me of the cushy existence that awaited me back at the ranch. (No, I didn't grow up on a farm; I just like the way that reads.) Barely two hours after they had arrived, they were gone again.

So now it was the three of us: Sophie, Omelet, and me. I was psyched for myself, and relieved to have Omelet with me. I couldn't wait to bring him around to Le Figaro. I was and am a very proud mother, ya know, and they just didn't come cuter or more devoted then Omelet.

Ahhhhhh, if men were only like dogs. . . . Well, they are—oh, just forget it—you know what I mean.

After all that drama, I have to say the next few months were pretty amazing. I had virtually nothing to worry about. I loved my job, my friends, my lifestyle. I felt like I was on holiday, and more importantly, I felt like I belonged. Finally having a showdown with Mark allowed me to tear off that big "victim" patch I didn't know I was wearing.

What wasn't working, though, was my voice and my guitar playing. Sophie never had the heart to tell me, but watching Omelet hide under the sofa each time I practiced was reason enough to start rethinking my future. I might sell someone else's album working at Tower Records or something, but I was absolutely sure no one would ever be selling mine. So, unless the world went mad, I'd best start thinking of a new career—maybe music *related*?!

In time, Adam and his gal pal parted ways and he wanted his place back. Therefore Sophie and I officially had to get a place of our own. Which sucked, royally. We had no idea how lucky we were to land Adam's place when we had. Remember all that money I made/saved? Well, that went to the broker's "finder's fee," first and last month's rent, and then the freakin' security deposits!! They didn't seem to want any of

Sophie's last season's stilettos nor her "great" suede skirt, so the onus was on me this time around.

Adam felt bad for us and actually gave us the couch and a few odds and ends, but other than that we were back to square one—again! Finally, we found a very centrally located, decent-sized one bedroom apartment. My father and Joseph came down and converted it into two bedrooms. They also brought a bunch of stuff from their basement. My mother figured she ought to give Sophie and me a crack at it before she gave it all to Goodwill.

No pity here, please. Honestly, I love playing with apartments. It's like filling up a Barbie town house (I'm sort of a wanna-be interior decorator who simply lacks taste and skills). Unfortunately, the rules (Sophie's) were that unless it was for my room, I couldn't bring anything home until we both agreed on it. Fine.

As the summer slipped away and the weather started getting frosty, walking three blocks to work was pretty clutch. I rarely ventured uptown, became something of a Village rat, and paid less and less attention to what was going on around me. Not current events–wise though. I had cable, watched CNN, and always read the morning paper, but I was not "growing," as Sophie would say.

Growing to Sophie was transitioning from season to season and from one trend to the next. Growing was exploring new clubs and saving the matches from fancy restaurants. (She collects them.) Cutting or dyeing your hair, waxing your eyebrows in a different arch. Yup—that was growing. I was sanctioned from a fashion/beauty perspective. My tomboyesque qualities were dominating now that I waited tables the majority of the time and when I wasn't running or playing basketball, I was hanging out at gay bars with my friends. Getting "dolled up" wasn't too important if ya know what I mean. I cared about my looks, don't get me wrong, but when you live with "blond ambition," as I affectionately call her, having one or two of everything basic just didn't make the grade. I liked my look, thank you very much, but every now and again I'd indulge Sophie and sport something colorful and "of the moment," as she would say. I did have fun, I'll admit it, when I went out with her and with Fernando and his friends. They were cute, loved dance music, as did I, but scarily, they each knew more words to more songs than I did. Singing along isn't that macho if you ask me, but Sophie enjoyed them/him and they/he were really good to her so what could I say. (Geez, that was a mouthful.)

Looking back, I kind of went along for the ride those few months. Never really having any expectations of an evening or for a day for that matter. My funk, although disguised as "going with the flow," was still a funk and getting funkier the longer I looked at my life as a spectator sport. Really, I liked my new life. It made me forget most of my old one. But it was pretty obvious that that 25 percent was still lurking within me, and after months without even a smooch from the opposite sex, even a phone number, truth be told, it was time to start dating again. I mean even Fernando, spare me, sat me down for one of those "I'm dating your BFF and I'm concerned about you" talks.

Now that was enough to make me go out that night! Sure, it was for a cup of coffee with only Omelet as my escort, but c'mon now, it was a start. Brad Pitt gets thirsty and even *GQ*-like supermodels can go for a cup of joe. This was *somewhat* social. . . . ("Pathetic and sad, but social"—*Breakfast Club,* Judd Nelson, baby!!!)

I'm such a loser!

So I maintained my normal routine but now my eyes were wide open for the right opportunity to meet new people (okay, let's be honest, men): midnight grocery shopping, safe easy evenings at Barnes & Noble, even seeing the late-night showing of a movie all by my lonesome. I saw all of this as a genuine unforced and potentially interesting way to meet men. I actually used to (shit, still do) get dressed up to go "out" Vivian style. Sophie was busy with Fernando so on the nights that I wasn't working I needed to amuse myself. I'd sit at countless bookstores, read the ends of novels waiting for "Lance Romance" to ask if anyone was "sitting there." I'd ponder over which apples were in the best shape imagining that some "Yuppie Man," surely having just left the gym, would ask if I needed any help, and of course, during those movies I told you about, well, I'd always imagine the "Artsy Sensitive Guy" approaching me afterward realizing we laughed at the same moments and concluding that he was in love.

Pukeville, right? I know. But I'm serious, I did this shit and I thought that way. And sometimes I'd go so far as to use Omelet as an accessory. I'd look all cozy walking my beautiful white German shepherd through the parks, waiting for "Sport Man" to stop dead in his tracks, miss the quintessential football catch, and just say "Hi."

Well, you'd think with all these picturesque moments I was producing for myself that one man at the very least would whisk me away. Nope. Nada. Never. Men did not and still don't hit on me. Did my mom brand me with the word "handful"? Can men pick up on my "complicated" vibe, or do the majority of them need a brewski in their hands to get up the nerve? I think probably yes to all these questions. I say this after careful and calculated near-scientific testing five years in the making.

Look, I was holding on for this big "I knew I loved you before I met you" à la Savage Garden moment, song in the background and all, even on a train like in the video. But as I've complained, it wasn't happening. And I always took public transportation!!

Because I really did want to take another stab at a relationship and because I just didn't find Natale that attractive (sorry, sweets), I knew that I would need to step up to the plate if I was to ever meet Mr. Right or at the very least Mr. Right Now. Those magical moments that I was hoping for were going to happen all right, but I would just have to be the one with the balls.

Taking that step was a challenge for me in the beginning, seeing as how I was told that I was nothing more than a mere prostitute for all those years with Mark. (All women were sluts in his eyes except—get this—his mother. A real woman-hater he was.) Anyway, I talked myself through it and was determined that if there was a moment to be had, I'd take it.

I'd love to get into this great juicy story now about some Ed Burns look-alike that I took home on this one crazy evening, but that didn't happen—not very quickly anyway. ☺ Weeks and weeks of being on the prowl showed no results. No one captivated me. None of Fernando's friends got any more attractive or interesting, none of my brilliant and beautiful gay friends suddenly went straight, and it seemed as though only women were grocery shopping during off-peak hours.

Then, just as I was about to give up, this one night at Le Figaro there was this one gentleman (here we go) who was so attractive that I found it too difficult to tell him the specials or fill his glass with water without shaking. He was sitting with this other guy. I gave the table to Lilly—I couldn't handle it. (I should also add that he was an actor. I recognized him and I'm pretty sure he could tell.) I just couldn't keep my cool. Midway through his dinner he apparently gave a folded napkin to Miguel and asked that he give it to me. (I still have it by the way.)

When Miguel approached me and told me it was from the gentleman at table eleven, I thought he was fucking with me. When I opened it, it read: "It's too bad that you didn't wait on me this evening. I would have loved to talk to you. If you have a minute before I leave, please introduce yourself. I'm intrigued. Jimmy."

Oh my God, oh my God, oh my God . . . that's all I could think or say. What to do, what to do? I got myself together and in Mark's honor walked as calmly as I could over to his table. "Thanks for the note," I said, just as Natale ran into me with her tray. (Lovely.)

"So what's your name?"

"Uh, uh, Vivian." I'm sure that's how it sounded.

"Well, hey, Vivian," he said. "I'm Jimmy and this is my buddy Luke."

"What's up?" I said. "Nice to meet you." ENTER AWKWARD SILENCE.

"Do you think I could get your number? I'm in town for a few weeks and would love to take you to dinner."

Okay, remember how I was complaining about men who don't take the initiative? Well, that only counts when they are not actors who could melt the screen with their charm.

I told him that I was not into giving strange men my number, but if he wanted to, I would take his and maybe give him a call over the weekend.

"Well, ha, ha, ha, okay then. I get it. Sure, here it is."

My hands were surely trembling when I handed him his napkin back to jot it down but at the same time my spirit was soaring pretty high. I liked what just went down and how.

I said good-bye and carried on like it was no big thing until the two of them left. Then we all freaked out. I bet not one person in that place was served for a good ten minutes while we all completely flipped! It was a night I'll never forget, and even more so, a feeling that after just one outing seemed unlocked and unleashed for good.

I felt my own power. It had been so, so long!!!

Now what kind of gal would I be if I didn't fill you in on some of the details? I waited three days before I called him and rehearsed what I'd say with Lilly and Sophie for a good two hours before I picked up the phone. With the three of us huddled together, I called and kept the conversation brief for risk of sounding nervous or just simply losing it and cracking up. He invited me to lunch, not dinner as he was shooting now at night, blah, blah, blah. We were to meet the next day at some chichi health food restaurant—vegetarian or something.

Sophie served as my stylist that night and picked out my outfit for tomorrow's big day. Nothing like having your first date after being in an abusive relationship for four-plus years be with a gorgeous working actor. I was panicked. Small talk for me was either talking about something miniature like safety pins or keeping conversation brief. Like "Hey, what's up? Nothin'? Okay, cool, take care." What was happening here??? Life was teetering brilliantly over the edge just as I wished for and I was going mad. Sophie drove me nuts. She'd dress me up like a doll and then make me change again.

"Too 'I know who you are.' " "No, no, no. Too 'I'm trying to look like your ex-girlfriend.' " And "No, no, no. Too contemplated casual!"

"Well for Christ's sake, Sophie! Decide on something or I'm going to wear my ripped jeans and a T-shirt." (That was like the ultimate fashion sin to her and "so not funny, Vivian!")

We finally, no, *she* finally decided on a black vintage slip dress, a yummy black ballet sweater, and my favorite (and only) pair of black ankle boots. (I was in shock, too. I was permitted to wear something of my very own.) To top it off, she lent me her ruby red beaded necklace and ivory messenger bag. We agreed on my hair—half up, half down. And she taught me how to tie my sweater—the right way—around my waist, in case I got warm. And of course Jimmy and Luke were going equally as crazy over at their place! I'm so sure.

According to Soph, this getup screamed "fresh." It screamed "cool." It screamed "pretty." I told Sophie that she was hearing voices and to stop freaking me out. I needed to sleep before tomorrow would even come, right. "So enough already, please!"

I maybe got four hours of sleep that night. Of course *Steel Magnolias* and *Flashdance* had to be on cable, but having crashed so late, naturally the afternoon arrived before I knew it and I was off to a restaurant that didn't serve real food—starving, warm, and unsure of how to tie my sweater!

All right then, here we go . . . I opted to walk to the restaurant. Of course, I was running early, to say the least. In the forefront of my mind, I didn't really care much about what would or would not take place in the upcoming thirty minutes. I loved that I was moving on, I loved that I was finally back on the road of experience-making. This, I was sure, would be the stuff of storytellers regardless of what happened . . . this was the old me!!!

I strutted through the city like John Travolta in *Saturday Night Fever.* I'm sure I even heard "you can tell by the way I use my walk I'm a woman's man, no time to talk . . ." in my head. Actually I'm quite positive as I nearly got hit by a taxi, not realizing that the oncoming light had turned red and that "don't walk" sign was talking to me. Whatever, I brushed off the first of the afternoon's faux pas with an awkward delight. I was amusing myself. As I could only imagine what my expression had been prior, during, and post this near-death pre-afternoon date with a movie star moment!

I arrived before him, of course, and sat at a table for two as though it was my first time dining out publicly. Everything seemed foreign. "What's this? Oh, of course, a fork, right, right." As I pretended to read the menu, realizing that there was not a thing on it that I could ever digest with a smile (I was and am a Burger King kinda gal!), in walked Jimmy. (As leisurely and as elegantly as you'd expect.) I'm quite sure that upon his entrance, no one in that place ever expected him to shout my name, smile, and maneuver toward me. Too genius!

I stood up to greet him and quickly realized that I had worked up such a sweat while waiting that my satin slip dress was now stuck to my rear. Removing it from my bum was not really an option so I thought best to act as if it wasn't happening at all and participate in his ridiculous double pecking thing. He gave me a kiss on each cheek (the ones adjacent to my nose thank you very much) and I was thrilled to death when I got a whiff of his breath. Between you and me, it wasn't all that pleasing for a big bad Romeo, which proved to me that he was all too human whether he knew it or not!

He complained about some love scene he was filming and how he had to eat like an "herbivore" for the past two weeks. "The camera adds ten pounds to you, you know. . . ."

"Oh yes, of course," I said still staring at a menu that I had memorized by this point. I ordered a salad, having no idea at the time what tofu or any of the other stuff was. I couldn't have enjoyed this meal no matter who was sitting across from me. (And besides, you and I both know this was so not about the food!)

Once the waitress took our order and the menu out of our hands there was nothing to hide behind and nowhere to gaze but at him. Nice view for sure, but I was so not prepared. I could feel myself begin to flush just as beads of sweat began to cascade from my boobs to my belly. (What a woman!)

A little more personal background for you: I've seen almost every movie made. There's not much to do in Washington Crossing, PA, and when you're in a relationship through college with an overbearing possessive shit, renting and seeing films is almost always allowed and makes for charming solo evenings. So, basically I had the 411 on this dude. I knew his films and, in turn, all the information a tabloid could offer. I knew how old he was, I knew who had broken his heart, and vice versa, and the big trick for me was pretending as though I didn't, which I'm sure I didn't pull off.

When he asked me my age I very seriously said "thirty." Jimmy was almost double my real age so I didn't want that to be a factor. When he asked me if I had a boyfriend I said no, which was true, and when I asked him if he had a girlfriend, he smiled and said no. (He had just broken up with one of his leading ladies, according to *People* magazine—cover story—last week!) He asked me if I had seen any of his films and I said no, that I rarely made it to the cinema being that I was a very dedicated musician. SPARE ME!!!

I went to remove my ballet sweater. It was a sauna in there—at least to me—and as I carefully shifted in my seat to place it on the back of my chair, off went one of the straps of Sophie's STUPID slip dress! Moritifcation ensued. "Vivian," he said, "this is only our first date." Ha, ha. I'm not sure exactly what he saw or didn't see. Nevertheless, I just had to start laughing. What else could I do? (He also said the words "first date," so this could mean there would be a second, right???) He said that I had a great smile and an even better laugh. I told him I thought his, uh . . . forearms were awesome! (I'm shaking my head as I sit here and write this—that's what I said—*really*. I was too embarrassed to look into his eyes—big, beautiful, and blue by the way—and the only thing I could look at was his hands, wrists, and arms.)

"What?" he said. "Well you do, Jimmy. They seem strong and I love your watch. It all works." (Who was I—Sophie????) "Well thanks," he said and proceeded to raise his arm in front of him to check it out for himself, which was an opportune time for me to pick the dress out of my ass, place my napkin on my thighs, and dig in! (The waitress must have dropped off our food sometime in between all of this.)

After a bit he said, "You hate this place, don't you?"

"Yup," I confessed. I couldn't keep up this "as cool as you" charade anymore. I was getting tired.

"My dad," he said, "has this Irish pub downtown. Once this film wraps, I'll take you there."

"That would be great," I said. We went on to talk about our families, backgrounds, etc. It was a pretty nice time. I was preoccupied with my dangling slip strap and began fiddling with it until he got the check.

"You've got beautiful shoulders," he said.

I stopped fiddling immediately and replied, "Well, thanks—you already know how I feel about your forearms!" All these physical compliments were making me nervous.

He ventured to the bathroom before we left. All eyes were on him as he walked from and back to our table. Very surreal. He said that he lived just around the block and asked if I wanted to see his place. I saw my mother's face in my mind and immediately responded "Sure . . . I mean, No. No. I've got to get home. I'm meeting a few friends to jam in about an hour." (Big lie.) He asked for my number (I gave it to him. 😮) and hailed me a cab. He opened the car door, grabbed me very delicately, smooched me good-bye (on the lips, mouth closed), and shut the door. I forced myself not to turn around. I so wanted to and secretly wished that our little kiss would somehow make the gossip page of the newspapers the next day!!!

"Jimmy and His New Mystery Girl." That would be the headline of course . . .

I made the cabdriver stop about seven blocks from where we started since I didn't have enough money on me for the total cab ride home. I stopped at the first pay phone and called Sophie at work. Giggling like a schoolgirl I told her everything. She was screaming, I was screaming, it was mayhem. She begged me to stop by the store but there was no way. That ridiculous dress was coming off and I needed some time in front of a mirror. Not like a J-Lo video—stare at yourself, make sexy faces, and sing—but rather I needed to see it and believe it. Before that dress came off I wanted to see who I was and what I was feeling inside. I ran up the stairs, told Omelet to "follow me," and landed in my bathroom.

Yup, it was me. The girl with the flushed face, the slouching slip dress, and the "great smile." The girl that waited tables in New York, lived with her best friend, and just went on a date!!!

Good show me! "We did it, Omelet!"

Jimmy never called again. Buzz kill, I know, but I thought I'd tell you now instead of having you get to the next page/chapter and hope it reads like an issue of *The Enquirer.*

Going into work that evening was a huge thrill. I had a story!!! You can't even imagine what it's like to work a shift alongside drag queens, recovering addicts, dueling lovers, and the like. I was always the listener and it was delightful to be the one who held the floor for even just a few minutes. More than half my friends were beyond bummed that I didn't shag him. The others, the feminists of the group, and a few of the cooks in the kitchen who saw me as their daughter, were very supportive.

Don't get me wrong, I wasn't and never had been "prudish," but I always took great pride when it came to my bod and its suitors. For me, my body was my spirit. "He" had to be worth it or at the very least put up a good show! I admit, it's a bit of a paradox. It's not like if you lined up all the guys I've been with, you'd think they were on a Donna Karan casting call, that they'd all be insanely hot, incredibly talented, or ridiculously successful. Nope, not at all really. But they all interested me on one level or another. And I can promise you that none of them will ever say I was "easy." Even a smooch, with very few exceptions, was a sexy little labyrinth—at least in my whacked-out head. I was a huge advocate of the game, a bit of a tease, and for sure, a big flirt when someone got my attention. I'm proud to say if a guy wanted me, he needed to prove it in more ways than one. Cards, calls, flowers—lots and lots of personal attention. If I was a car, the pre-smooch drama was my fuel, and if there wasn't any gas, there was no shot we'd ever go for a drive. (Sorry, that was the first analogy I could come up with.) Very honestly, that's when I'd feel in control, when I knew I possessed that power of "when." And with Jimmy, I felt powerless on some levels. There was no chance that I'd let myself be just another diversion in his shooting schedule. Sorry. It was gratifying enough just the way it went. Fun and impactful enough that I felt it was worth mentioning in this story just as it was.

So sure, I definitely did and do respect myself, but that "power" thing, that mischievous frame of mind that I can't seem to shake, still gets in the way when seeking out or participating in a meaningful and serious relationship. I've not yet been able to allow "it" to evolve into something else just as special, whatever it is that makes people stay together happily. And this "dysfunctional fun for a while chase thing" that I loved, well, that's where the problem was with Mark. When someone asks why I'd ever be with a guy like him, it surely, on the outside, was a huge challenge—that's what I always think of and answer first. (Why did I stay for so long? Well, that is something I still haven't quite figured out.) Mark appeared on my radar first and, apparently, I had not even made a dent in his force field. And for a girl who usually "gets the guy" in the end, the challenge became so much more than just getting his attention. It got real personal real quick and touched the deepest parts of my soul, places that I wasn't even in touch with until now, so many years later.

Mark was mysterious, or so I thought. He was in a frat, played football and all, but he was different from his friends. (Yeah, right, way different.) Anyway, he seemed independent, respected, and disinterested in much of the goings-on around campus. He also was such a big guy that he made me feel like mini-me. (For any of you who are reading this and you're a "healthy" girl with curves and above five foot five, maybe you'll get what I'm trying to say.) Until Mark, I was taller than most of the other guys I dated—especially in heels. Nine times out of ten, a guy friend could easily wear my sweatpants and carry them off as though they were his own. Most guys were within twenty pounds of me and I never felt feminine in that cutesy kind of way. Being around Mark made me feel more like a woman and made him seem like a real man. And the fact that he wasn't into me, that he'd prefer to be my mate rather than my man, well, that just wasn't a good enough reality. I'd show him who I was, that I warranted his interest. That was my goal. I liked who I was—why shouldn't he? That was our beginning.

Hope that makes sense. I know it's stupid and so not what "the real thing" is all about, but I was seventeen at the time. I didn't know as much as I thought I did about love and intimacy back then.

Okay. Enough about him. Where was I? Jimmy. Yeah, he was the best thing that could have happened to me at that point. After about two weeks of checking my answering machine much like a smoker who joneses for their lunch hour to huff and puff, I realized that he wasn't going to call. And I was cool with that. I had plenty of fun in the meantime and seemed to be on a roll. I was meeting great people left and right. I had been at Le Figaro long enough that my regulars were now becoming friends and mentors. Sophie was still in love of course, but the whole "new" thing was wearing off, so she and I were seeing more and more of each other. Despite my resistance, her obsession with fashion was becoming contagious, and I began dipping into my savings a bit more than I would have preferred. We started really doing things in the city, from museums, to shows, to exhibits. Before that, NYC was just one big party, now it was slowly becoming the epicenter of all things interesting. Everything it had always been, but we just hadn't been ready to explore that side until now. In the interim, I befriended photographers, stylists, writers, artists, chefs, graduate students, more musicians, actors, and philanthropists. I'd grab a book and sit alone at a coffee shop between shifts or when Sophie was doing her thing, and by the end of the afternoon, I'd be sitting at a table squished with too many chairs, filled with friends and acquaintances all discussing this or that. I was becoming part of a community. It was wonderful.

Sophie and I made a point of filling our social calendars with any invite we could get our hands on, and being a waitress without a real goal was starting to frustrate me. My answer to the "So, what do you do, Vivian?" question was getting old. There were so many people doing so many things around me, I wanted to get involved, too. But still not a clue how.

I had become very friendly with the group of dog owners that shared the same "run" as Omelet and me. All of us were equally attached to our domesticated furry friends for different reasons, I guess. I spent my first Halloween at the run before experiencing the Halloween parade in Greenwich Village. We all dressed up our pampered pets, brought along treats just for them, and even pitched in for a gift certificate at a local doggy salon for the pup with the best costume. Omelet was the cutest ghost I'd ever seen but this pair of toy poodles dressed up as Miss Piggy and Kermit stole the show.

Seth and Alexa were the owners of the two Muppets and had become good friends after some time. They owned a skating/surfing shop just south of Houston Street and were the two most with-it forty-year-olds I had ever met. They were one of those major PDA couples. They worked very hard, always discussing the stresses of having their own business, and took holidays constantly. They made their own schedules, their own rules, and converted their favorite pastimes into their livelihood. I dug that. They had just returned from Los Angeles, where they were visiting friends and family and scoping out spaces for a possible West Coast shop, but that day they were going on and on about Nevada. They decided to spend their last evening one holiday in Las Vegas, and although they lost some cash, they had an amazing time. While Alexa loved the shows, the shopping, and the eclectic mix of people, Seth loved the slot machines. I loved listening to their description of the city and their obvious enthusiasm over Vegas. They'd been to St. Barts and Colorado in the months I had met them and never had they come back with this kind of rush.

For the rest of that day, I couldn't shake the fact that I'd never been out West and that I had been working my ass off since the day I entered that songwriting contest. Hmmmm. Could a vacation be brewing? I was deserving! I wondered what Sophie's vacation day policy was. . . .

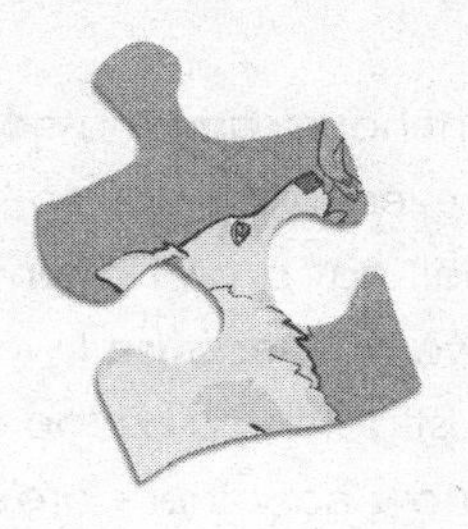

I spoke to Sophie about my brilliant idea—a vacation for the two of us, and she confessed, quite reluctantly, that she and Fernando were planning something around Thanksgiving. I felt bad for two reasons: First, that she would be concerned about my reaction, and second, that she knew me that well. I was disappointed and sort of pissed that she'd prefer to travel with him over me. I couldn't imagine a week without Sophie. Looking back, I can't even think of a time that we were apart. Sure, that might be selfish of me, possessive, and perhaps a wee bit immature, but I never said I was perfect and my friendship with Sophie was, and is, more of a sisterhood. She feels more like family to me than a friend. So it's easier for both of us to say things as they pop into our heads, treat each other as openly as sisters would, and not ever walk on glass as other friends do at the risk of offending one another. She had always been there for me in the past. We had done everything together since I could remember, and the fact that she "sprung" her romantic getaway on me was a bit of a shocker. I handled it as gracefully as I could and I think she saw that.

This also didn't help me like Fernando any more than I already didn't. He was constantly at our place and he used all our shit. We kept very different hours, and most of all, listening to your best friend have sex practically every night due to the limitations of a makeshift wall that a family member, not a professional carpenter, put up, was getting to me. And no, it wasn't because I wasn't getting any, thank you very much. Things were just getting a bit too cozy for me. Since I'm not big on confrontation (you know how there are those chicks who are amazing at verbal confrontation—their eyes never water, their nostrils never flare, their clever comebacks never waiver? Yeah, well, that ain't me, okay?), I kept my opinions about Fernando to myself up until this whole vacation thing surfaced. I met Sophie at the store the next day and told her that I felt that I was pseudo-dating her boyfriend and that I needed a little space. She accused me of feeling this way because of the whole vaca thing, but when I called her the little pet name he had for her just after "that moment" (she'd kill me if I included it in print so I apologize for being vague here), she turned burgundy and apologized. She said she wished that I had come to her earlier but was also not surprised that I hadn't until now. She said that she'd work on making things a bit more tolerable for me and also promised she'd turn up the radio from now on. ☺

Well, good then, that wasn't too horrible. She understood. Cool.

Not exactly. Fernando paid me a visit at Le Figaro that night and accused me of stirring things up. He said that I was jealous of their relationship and that, no worries, he'd stay out of my way. Great. Sophie innocently talked to him, he freaked, and now things, I just knew it, were only going to get worse at home. She ended up spending more and more time at his place and I ended up seeing less and less of my friend, which surely was not my goal in the first place, but I never told Soph about his visit.

I phoned my mom, told her what had happened and she advised me to let it go right there. Her words: I couldn't choose the boys my friends dated, I could only choose the boys I dated (and was I, by the way? No, Mom . . .). Things got sort of bad, though. I could no longer stomach Fernando at all. The mere sight of him made my skin crawl, and in his warped mind I think he felt that me not "telling on him," not letting

Sophie know about his psycho Figaro visit, meant that I was either afraid of him or that I knew he was right. I tried to shake it off. And I did, but I swear, it was like giving up chocolate or cheese or something. It was torturous!

There really wasn't anyone else but my mother whose opinion I could trust on the matter. Joseph, my brother, didn't like Fernando either for his own reasons, and it seemed like the majority of my coworkers at the restaurant loved any notion of confrontation. And as well as they knew me, as well as I *let* them know me, I was pretty sure that had I taken it any further I would have lost my best friend or just plain kicked Fernando's ass.

My mother assured me that Fernando was not a permanent fixture in Sophie's life and rather than treat him like he was there forever, dismissing him would be the best route to take. Thanks, Mom! Great advice and one of the very first times that our relationship felt real. Rather than telling me that I was overreacting, or, of course, giving me the good old defeatist "why don't you just come home," which was a constant during college, she was talking to me as an adult, as a true friend, and I relished it for hours after we hung up.

Now that I virtually had my own place, I used it as such. I had a few get-togethers, and hosted a number of poetry readings. I may have neglected to mention thus far that I began keeping a journal of sorts—more in poetry, free-writing form. My day-to-day happenings were not of interest to me at that point, not really journal-worthy anyway. Instead I preferred to take an emotion I was feeling and let it overcome me, detail how I was feeling and later go back and realize the depths of my mind—how up or how down I could be. Fascinating and a bit frightening, but interesting above all else. It would help me put things into perspective later.

Lilly was into poetry, too, so she introduced me to her circle of poetry friends. I prefered to be the charming host rather than ever read my own work aloud—a benefactor of the arts of sorts, with a tight budget—so I soon offered to hostess. There was one "poet" who captured my attention in particular, for lots of reasons. Number one, he was as handsome as any normal person could be and had this effortless vibe about him. He was from Philadelphia, so he also had a bit of home in him, and he was funny. God he was funny. Never really paying much attention to his poems, I was captivated by his performances. He was completely uninhibited. I don't know if it was out of ego and arrogance or because this was his craft. I didn't really care too much either way. I just wanted to get to know him. I asked Lilly to introduce us. You should have seen her face. "Sure, sure," she said. I panicked briefly and implored her not to be obvious about it. You didn't need to be a rocket scientist to get that Patrick did not have a problem with the ladies. I said that if tonight didn't feel right, that she could do it some other time. "Yeah, right!" she said.

I was emptying out beer bottles in my sink when a voice just behind me asked, "Do you need any help?" Thankfully I had my long hair and my smile was disguised for those few mini-seconds before I looked up and acknowledged him. (Yes, I had a feeling it was Patrick.)

"No, no—I'm nearly finished. Thanks, though." Eye contact straightaway. (After a few drinks, there weren't many shy bones in my body.)

"You know, Vivian, I have to thank you for doing this—it's so cool that you'd open up your home to us."

"Please, I love having you, I mean everyone here. Really," I said.

"So why don't you ever get up there and read out of your journal, hmm?"

"What makes you think I write?" I asked.

"I've just got this feeling. I've been watching you these past few weeks, the way you react to what you hear. I just know you're up to something." Okay, I was loving this moment. He was feeding me everything I could have wanted to hear. I wasn't thinking about sincerity, I was thinking about his mouth. Up close he had the most perfect lips and a genius smile. He had that great guy hair, too—the kind that was long enough that it looked great all muffled up and wasn't too long either so that you'd mistake him for an eighties pop star. I was smitten and conversation was not really a possibility for me at that moment.

"Of course I'm up to something," I said. "But it's really more for me than for anyone else. Would you excuse me?" I said.

"Sure, no problem," and with that I went to find Lilly. I was happy yet furious. I loved being taken off guard but hated that I felt I couldn't hold my own. This was different from the whole Jimmy thing. That was more pretend-ish for me. Patrick was a real guy, who seemed to really take an interest in me and someone who I found really attractive and I had not the foggiest idea how to handle it.

Lilly swore that she had made no mention of me to him and I took her word for it. (I was a bit relieved. At least we were playing on the same field. Our interest in each other was evidently mutual.) So with that I ran into my room. I made my bed, reapplied my deodorant, and looked in the mirror—made sure there was nothing in my teeth, or up my nose—and went back out there. Half the place had cleared out. Lilly was telling some witty story to a handful of friends on my couch and when I went back into the kitchen to grab another beer, there was Patrick playing with Omelet on my floor. (Surely, a way to a woman's heart is to make friends with her puppy.)

I did my best to ignore this major Kodak moment, grabbed a Corona, a piece of lime, and joined the others in the living room. (Let's see how interested this guy really is, I thought to myself.) Sure enough, a few moments later, he came in and sat beside me. Omelet followed him and lay at our feet. Someone cracked a joke, I don't remember who or what was said, and before I knew it, I felt Patrick sit up and raise his arm. As he went to rest his hand on my shoulder I jumped like in a scary movie or something. Then I looked at him and gave him the go-ahead. He saw that I was taken aback, but after a bit, I was really comfortable with it. It was nice to have a guy beside me. And a little while later, when he least expected it, I placed my hand on his leg—in an affectionate way—and seconds later, he put his hand on top of mine. His hand was warm and strong, and as a matter of fact, we fit together perfectly.

Ahhhh, Patrick. He was a good one. Mmmmmmmmmmmmmm. Sorry, I'll continue.

Yeah, so, I half paid attention to what was going on around me. Lilly and her friends were still winding down but I just couldn't get my mind off Patrick, nor did I want to. I felt like I was playing house and Patrick was my "Ken" or something. It was almost instinctual. We maneuvered through the rest of that evening as though we had been dating forever. We waited very patiently for "our" guests to leave. He helped me straighten up and afterward offered to take Omelet for a walk as I wanted to take a quick shower. (I was working the sweat meets cigarette stank meets alcohol fragrance and it wasn't very pretty. I don't much mind when a guy smells "weathered," for lack of a better term, but as the sexual tension was rising between the two of us, if there was going to be a first kiss, I didn't want him to think/taste/remember me as anything less than lovely!)

I confess, I shaved my legs in that shower. It wasn't exactly a "rinse off" kinda gig. I was in serious last-minute hook-up mode. I moisturized as well and tweezed a bit of my 'stache. Just being honest!

I have no idea how long I left the poor guy out there actually, and when I popped out of my bathroom to check on him, he was still fully flirting with Omelet!!! Oh, and yes, he caught me. My hair wrapped in a towel, surely red blotches above my lip, and still wearing my old Gap flannel bathrobe—SEXY!!!!

"Come here," he said.

"Negative. Look at me. Give me one."

"C'mon, just for a second." Why argue it, right? So I walked over while simultaneously removing the Disney World towel my cousin had given me some eight years prior from my hair. He stood up and just stared at me. What was probably five seconds felt like fifteen minutes, I assure you. "You're beautiful, Vivian. Do you know that? You're beautiful."

Okay—with no idea how to take a compliment well and just completely freaking out, I took one step closer to him. I don't know what I was thinking. I didn't want to say thank you 'cause I wasn't sure if he meant it. And as usual, I hated feeling vulnerable. The idea of waiting to see what, if anything, he would do next was too much pressure. Just inches away from that beautiful face, those deep brown eyes, and that GREAT mouth—okay, I'll say it—I wanted to jump his bones! There was nothing but "me" under my robe. He knew it and I knew it and the energy surrounding us was completely intense—I loved it!!!

He smiled and reached for the collar of my robe. OMG!!! His other hand was already at the back of my head grabbing my wet hair and with one sudden movement we were liplocked. I was completely out of my league. Don't get me wrong, I consider myself a high-quality kisser but the intensity . . . I couldn't remember the last time I was kissed like that. We stood there for a few small seconds and somehow made it onto my couch. He lay on top of me and well, without making this some trashy romance novel, let's just say . . . wait, ya know what? Fuck it—I'll go on. (It feels great to remember.)

He undid my robe and stood up a bit. He looked me over from head to toe in this wonderful way. The lights were out (OF COURSE) so I wasn't in that big of a panic. He took off his sweater, then his T-shirt and rested his bare chest against mine. (There's nothing better than skin on skin. Am I wrong?) He nuzzled my ears, and then kissed the back of my neck while I combed the outskirts of his body with my (trembling) hands.

His lips were meant for kissing. I couldn't help but bite on them a few times. As my body wanted to do the natural next things—from beginning to end—my brain was trying to convince me otherwise. There's really no telling what I would or would not have been able to control at that point. I was melting in his arms like a candle that's been lit for hours and my decision-making processes had definitely stepped out for a drink.

We made it to my bedroom and cuddled underneath my covers, still petting and smooching, squeezing and rubbing. After a bit, I put on some music and allowed him to take off his jeans. Poor guy—I thought my face was chafed! We fell asleep in each other's arms just as dusk turned into dawn and I remember waking up hours later with Omelet at the foot of my bed and Patrick leaning over on his side with his chin in his hand, just staring at me.

"Good morning," he said.

"Good morning," I said, while slipping my comforter over my mouth. He started cracking up, on to my bad breath prevention plan for sure, and I darted out of my bed with the bedsheets wrapped around me. I looked like a giant marshmallow, but what's a self-conscious gal supposed to do? The sunlight was vicious.

I brushed my teeth, put on an old sweatshirt and boxers, and climbed back into bed. If I had things my way, we'd still be in there to this day all cozy and new and excited, but alas, first mornings are great 'cause they're first mornings. You're strangers for all intents and purposes and as any woman snuggles in the arms of a great guy for the first time, who of us doesn't fantasize about the future while reflecting on images of the past? Patrick was my knight in shining armor that morning whether he knew it—or he liked it—or not!!!

After a repeat performance of last night's late activities, Patrick took a shower and I ran Omelet out. "Omelet honey, your mama isn't a hussy, don't worry!" I said as I grabbed a plastic bag and picked up after him. Charming!

I took another shower and left Patrick in my room to size me up by my things. I didn't like leaving him in my bedroom. What would he get about me by screening the elements that made up my bedroom? Were my books not intellectual enough? Was there dust on my windowsill? Yuck, I hope he hadn't found my photo albums!!!

"That was quick!" He laughed, seated at my desk.

"Yeah? So?" I said as I crept up behind him and planted a kiss on his neck. He grabbed me and sat me on his lap—uh-oh—same robe, same towel . . . I smooched him again but pushed myself up and grabbed a pair of panties out of my drawer. "C'mon, Patrick, I feel like a vampire, let's get out of here."

"If you say so," he said.

I put on a white T-shirt, black turtleneck, Levi's, and my Nikes. He was still in the same clothes and still looked just as fine. As I locked the door behind us he grabbed my hand before I could even think about that whole PDA scenario. We walked for a while. As hungry as I was, the thought of sitting across from him, rather than next to or on top of him, wasn't nearly as appealing as a big fluffy stack of French toast.

We ended up at some diner in the middle of nowhere but did the quintessential leave your name and stand outside hugging and kissing and giggling thing. We couldn't keep our hands off each other and I'd be lying if I said it didn't feel incredible to finally be the girl in this very scenario. I had only witnessed the weekend morning-after glow on others since I got to New York.

When they finally called our names and escorted us to our table, Patrick let me choose my side of the table first. And before I even realized it, he sat beside me, squished into this minuscule booth, rather than in the chair across from me; I tried not to smile that hugely and yes, we both got the French toast! HEAVENLY!

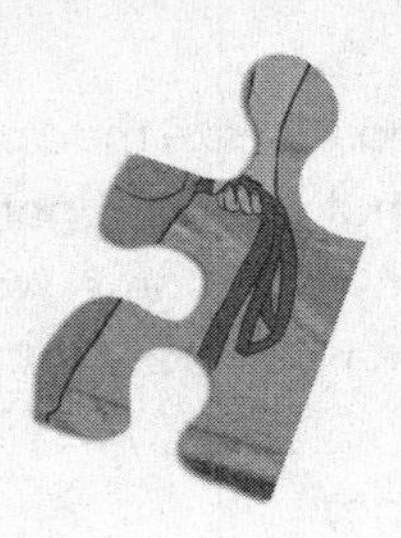

The next few weeks were incredible. Patrick was everything Mark wasn't: He encouraged me to go out with him, dress up, didn't mind me chatting with his friends, was cool with me doing my own thing—no questions asked. By that I mean: "Who were you with?" "What time did you get home?" "Why are you wearing that?" "Who are you trying to impress?" and other favorite "Mark questions." Patrick got a kick out of my friends, didn't ask me to do much for him other than to just be me—whatever that meant. Mark used to make me stay home when he'd go out. I'd have to do his laundry, clean his place, cook his meals (I still can't even cook at home without thinking about him—pathetic). Anyway, as I often say, I was like his Cinderella and Mark was like the evil stepmother, the sisters, and then some—and I put up with it no less. I rarely questioned or fought it. What was the point, really? It would only amount to huge fights with repercussions I don't care to mention.

Basically, I was on cloud nine with Patrick. Sure it was difficult not to have hesitations, question him, but I worked hard to put my best foot forward. I could only benefit, and with every scrumptious element, every sweet gesture, every tender word—the praise, the support, the affection—for every good moment, I was creating a new memory. One that I hoped would suffocate an old one. (Nice try. It doesn't work that way, I've come to learn, but it was still lovely, then.)

Patrick was cool with spending the majority of our time together at my place. He lived way out in Brooklyn and with my hours and the privacy we had at my place, it was a pretty easy decision. Sophie was still crashing most nights at Fernando's. She'd met Patrick a handful of times, gave him a tremendous thumbs-up, and everything was pretty cool.

There were three things about Patrick that I remember so fondly even to this day. First, how peaceful we were together. How being quiet was just so calming. He'd be writing, I'd be reading. I'd be napping and he'd be watching the telly. He'd tickle my arm while I listened to music, stuff like that. (I don't think I had a second of tranquillity all those years with Mark. I was always at "Defcon 5.") The second thing was that he did a mean impression of "Dr. Evil." You know, "Dr. Evil" from *Austin Powers*? I think he did him even better than Mike Myers. He'd have me in tears! He'd order in "Dr. Evil," he'd read me his poetry in "Dr. Evil," whatever. He was hilarious. He made me laugh till my stomach hurt. And last, but definitely not least, he was the worst dancer of all time. He knew it, too, but he loved clubs and house music and would dance (or whatever he'd call it) all night long. He'd boogie in my apartment with Omelet and grab me in the kitchen if the radio was on. I mean, he was so good-looking, so bright, and so talented, that if God had given him dancing feet, that just would be way too unfair. He loved to make me laugh; he enjoyed making me happy. Can a girl ask for anything more??? He was sort of an intellectual clown who sold hats by day to make his dough and wrote poetry at night to indulge his mind.

So we must have been five weeks into things and this one night, we decided to go to some after-hours party where a friend of his was a DJ. We both had had a number of drinks and we were dancing (as usual) when I caught him looking away and watched the color in his skin go from olive to ivory. He asked me to give him a minute, which I did. I found a vacated secondhand velvety chair in the corner—it looked and felt strangely familiar—and tried my best to scope him out in the crowded apartment. Bodies constantly got in my range of vision, and without a neck like a giraffe, there was no way I could have kept up with him. I hadn't seen who or what had shocked him, so I opted to mind my own business and wait it out.

After about half an hour and no Patrick, I went to find the bathroom. I had to pee and may have even been "touching cloth." I don't mean to gross you out but I had held it in since we got there and prior we had gone for Mexican . . . so I had no choice.

On my way back from the ladies' room I saw this really cute girl (with a great tan, by the way) crying as she stood beside Patrick. I didn't even know her and I felt bad for her. I walked toward them and asked him if everything was okay. (BIG MISTAKE.) This chick started flipping out. Her tears turned into something else. I could barely hear what she was saying the music was so loud. I told Patrick I was leaving and to meet me at home. We smooched quickly and I left them both behind. When I went to say good-bye to his pals, they, too, seemed odd. "Yeah, uh-huh, 'bye Viv."

What is with everyone??? I got back to my place at about four A.M. and crashed. When I woke up Patrick was nowhere to be found. There wasn't a message on my machine. Nothing. I phoned his apartment and there was no answer. I couldn't even get distressed, though. There wasn't enough time. I was already late for work. I figured I'd just see him later. My weekend night shifts always ended real late and for the past while, Patrick always met me, helped me do the sugars, refilled the ketchups, etc. He'd even double-check my numbers to make sure I cashed out right, but not on this night. He was a no-show and I began to worry.

As I walked home I could only hear Mark in my head. All the things he would say about other men, what they would really think about me, how none could be trusted, none could be honest or faithful and how none would ever really respect me. After all, to him I was this big joke—not worthy of respect—unless of course I threatened to leave him and then, quite quickly, I became his everything. And then there'd be this sick twisted make-up sex. Enough! Okay, where the hell was Patrick???

Day two. Still no word. I was too embarrassed to talk to Sophie or Lilly about it. I knew I had the worst taste in men and I didn't want to expose another failed relationship. (I mean five weeks—I can consider that a relationship right???) And besides, it was only two days! (Please say "right.") I spent most of the day at home I admit, waiting to hear from him. I even showered with the door open. But with fifteen minutes left until four P.M., Le Figaro was waiting. So I left.

Work was crazy that night. Not a moment to breathe. Fernando and Sophie came by as my shift came to a close and we hung out and laughed a bit. Sophie asked how Patrick was and I said, "Fine . . . good . . . great. Patrick's great."

"Well where is he?" Fernando questioned.

"He's out with his friends from college, yup, they came in for a visit."

"Oh, that's cool," Sophie said. "I wonder if we know any of them? Did any of his friends go to Penn?" she asked, pretty innocently.

"No, Soph, no. At least I don't think so."

They walked me home. Sophie wanted to grab some stuff for the next few days and Fernando felt the need to smoke me out of my apartment. Nearly suffocating, I took Omelet out for a quickie and there was Patrick walking toward my apartment with a bottle of wine and a dozen roses—my favorite, the hybridy pink ones with a darker version of pink on the tips. "Hey, stranger," he said.

"Hi! I was getting worried."

"Yeah, I'm real sorry. Things just got real heavy and it was hard for me to break away. Can you forgive me?" It wasn't too difficult to do. Omelet was already on his back waiting for a rubdown (he loved Patrick), and between the roses and that smile—I was toast!

I warned him that Fernando was inside (they hadn't met yet). "It's cool," he said, so we walked inside.

"Hey, Patrick!" Sophie shouted. She was so excited to introduce him to Fernando and to stay and have the four of us "bond." (Great.) Fernando gave him one of those pseudo-macho handshakes, sized him up, and told Sophie that he was tired and wanted to get back to his apartment (I started to like Fernando for a second). Sophie asked Patrick if he was having fun with his friends in town and he looked at me for some kind of explanation. I just raised my eyebrows and nodded my head, and Patrick went on to say, "Yeah, sure—great time."

"Cool. So we'll have to all go out for dinner or something this week," she said, half out the door.

"Definitely," I said. "Love you!" I shouted to her.

"You tooooooooo," I could hear as the door closed and she left.

I felt sad and scared and paranoid all at once. I didn't want to be alone with him. I mean, I wasn't alone, Omelet was there, but still . . . I was torn. Should I question him? And if I do that will he think I'm insecure? Don't I have a right to some sort of explanation? Did I even want to hear it? But would he like me more if I was one of those laid-back gals who never gave their guy a headache? Or then would he see me as some kind of doormat where he made the rules and set the stage? So many questions, all circling in my mind. Just call me Sybil. Sure I had my suspicions—I'm not naive—but I wanted this to work out so badly. Mark couldn't be right. (I was really ready to be in a relationship, eh? Not!)

So rather than deal with any of it, we opened the wine, watched *An Officer and a Gentleman* on HBO, and wound up—surprise, surprise—buck naked in bed. (Tragic.) As we rolled around I wondered who I was with—the officer or the gentleman? What did I really know about him anyway? I knew that he sure as shit didn't know me. This was all a charade. I guess that's what happens when you move real quick and fall for someone 'cause you want to.

I think my disinterest in his disappearance ended up working in my favor. He seemed to be walking on eggshells and somewhat kissing my ass that next morning. Now I was pretty sure he was hiding something.

"Why don't we ever stay at your place?" I questioned.

"You want to?" he said back.

"It's not that, but it would be nice to see your place, lie in your bed, stroll around your 'hood. That's all."

"Why all of a sudden, Vivian? Why are you asking me this now? We've been together for almost two months . . ." (Make a note: men exaggerate when they get nervous. We had three more weeks to go to make two months!)

"Patrick, you're bugging out. I just thought about it. I don't know why. I guess it's kind of unfair to you. You're always running around with your Calvin's in your bag. I just thought it would be nice of me to offer, and still I just want to be in your cave for once at least!"

He came toward me, took the coffee mug out of my hand, grabbed my waist, and kissed me. He whispered in my ear, "Whenever you want—now, tonight, tomorrow, whenever. It's really sweet of you to think about it that way. But I must confess and this may upset you . . . (Oh shit—did I really want to know/hear this?) I only have a twin bed."

ENTER HUGE RELIEF.

"Okay, let's stay here . . . and let me at least get you a roll of tokens. I insist!"

As tourist season was officially coming to an end, shifts were getting cut at Le Figaro. The weather was getting a bit brisky and as people were no longer eating outdoors, my weekly earnings began to drop, significantly. That's what sucked about waiting tables: There was really no fixed income. They were very cool about it though, and put me on as a hostess, behind the coffee bar, etc., but after a few weeks I had to make the necessary adjustments to my lifestyle. Nothing major. No more dialing "information," no more manicures, no more taxis, more cooking, less ordering, you know the deal. And unfortunately, as far as my libido was concerned, quite the contrary was happening in Patrick's world—business began picking up. So the 85 percent "see each other during the week" ratio was scaled down to about 50 percent.

Anyway, I had stopped biting my nails after college and manicures ever since had seemed like quite the ladylike luxe kind of treat—or "self-pampering" as Sophie would call it. So, because of the budget cuts, I took matters into my own hands (no pun intended) and ventured over to CVS to purchase a do-it-yourself manicure set. The results were freakish. When I was through with that cuticle cutter thing, it looked like my fingertips had been taste-tested by a bunch of tiny termites (attractive, I know). I mangled myself. Never even made it to the moisturizing phase (bummer). I've got to hand it to all you manicurists out there—you're curators as far as I'm concerned. Besides all the "coloring in the lines" there's the cutting, the filing, the buffing—who ever knew!

My point is that just as I was beginning to have my (repressed) suspicions about my "boyfriend" it looked like I was taking all the drama out on my hands. Much like any habit, I guess, for us nail-biters we can go cold turkey, but the minute we start up again, "Forget about it!!!" I made matters much worse by resorting back to the days of nail-biting. I couldn't quit it and ended up having to go for manicures every few days just to get back into the swing of things. And how about that "Nailtique," it's expensive!!! I had the best and most responsible of intentions and managed to increase my "self-pampering budget" almost 60 percent!

With lots more time on my hands (Why does that word keep popping up? Odd.) that I needed to fill and to make some extra money, I began sticking stickers everywhere I could for this local lounge just down the street from the restaurant. I got paid ten bucks an hour to "stick away!" On phone booths, streetlights, subways, coffee shops, bathrooms, seat cushions, exteriors of stores, you name it, I'd stick it! That is until I found out it was ILLEGAL, thank you very much! Two cops stopped me one afternoon while I was sticking the back of an old lady walking down the street. (KIDDING . . . KIDDING. It was the bumper of a bakery truck. Did I get ya???)

Anyway, I thought they were kidding me and I wasn't too pleased with their amusing little interruption. After I realized they weren't kidding I offered to buy them lunch at Le Figaro. That made things even worse. This "wisenheimer" spent the rest of the afternoon on a police-escorted scraping/peeling nightmare. Everywhere and anywhere I had stuck anything that day, I had to peel it away with their supervision. I wanted to kill myself. How embarrassing! In my very own neighborhood. And my fingers—you have no idea the kind of agony. . . .

It was not a good day for the hands.

I called in sick that night and soaked in a hot bath. I was furious with Sal, the owner of the lounge, for not telling me that what I was doing was illegal, and he was equally as peeved at me for my naïveté. (He was also fined I think!) It had been three days since I had seen Patrick and two since we had spoken. I sat in the tub, listened to my greatest hits (Stevie Nicks and Pat Benatar) records and as my skin began to morph into this slimy raisinlike coat, I began to feel like a giant ass. I couldn't believe that I had never once asked Patrick who the tan chick was at the party that night. Can you imagine??? Why was I so afraid of confrontation? (Well, I knew why, but why would I be afraid of confronting Patrick?)

NOW we were at about three months. What a joke. I was hiding out in my bathtub for God's sake. Real brave, Vivian. So you! Like that great scene in *Flashdance*, when Jennifer Beals sees her boss—who she's dating—with another woman at the opera and subsequently chucks a brick at his window, I wanted to be her. I wanted to do that. "Who's the goddamned blonde, Nick!!?!?!?" Or when Julia Roberts in *Mystic Pizza* catches her man from the other side of the tracks with a woman at a fancy country club dinner and she throws barrels of fish in his Porsche. Yup—I wanted to do that, too! What I liked best about both those little scenes was that on the outside without knowing anything, you'd think Jen and Jules had every right to completely lose it and confront their men, but in the end, their suspicions were wrong. No cheating. However, and this is the good part: They were able to blow off some steam, call it as they saw it, and ultimately find out that their men were true. If they could do it, why couldn't I???

So with Pat Benatar's "Love Is a Battlefield" playing in the background, I got dressed (cargo pants, Nike's, sweater, long black coat, a ski cap, and gloves—of course!), grabbed Omelet and took a cab to Brooklyn. (I know, I know—I was supposed to be watching my money, but I once got in trouble for trying to get Omelet on the subway. I'll leave that story out, okay?) I had never been to his place before, but I knew the address 'cause I sent him this totally goofy "I'm so happy I met you" card about forty-eight hours into the relationship—yeesh!—and I had the cab pull up on the corner of his street.

I don't know what I was expecting to see. I had created this big Charlie's Angels (Kelly) meets Gladiator moment. Me and Omelet waiting there at two in the morning freezing our asses off for just one small sight of foul play. I couldn't help but feel the rush of memories of catching Mark more times than I care to count in scenarios such as this. It can make you feel so low and so empty, similar to a hangover, I guess, without the great night you can vaguely remember. Did I want to catch him? Did I want to not catch him? Omelet wasn't really focusing and couldn't help me put things into any kind of perspective.

After about a half hour we walked to the pay phone and I rang my home first to see if he had called—negative. Then I called him. No answer. As I hung up I heard someone shout my name. (Was that me just talking to myself again?) Then I heard "Omelet!" We turned around and there was Patrick, just outside some old sports bar only a few windows away. "What are you doing here?" he asked

"I don't know," I said. "Love is a battlefield?"

"What?" he said.

"Nothing, nothing okay? I just didn't know where the hell you were or who she was and why . . ."

"Hold on, hold on," he said. "Let me tell the guys I'm leaving."

"Fine." I pouted. Well that was real slick, Viv!!! What happened to "Who's the goddamned tan girl, Patrick?!?!?!?"

He emerged about two seconds later and seemed incredibly happy to see me. "I was thinking about surprising you tonight, but it got real late. I wasn't sure if you'd be working and I didn't want you to think it was some booty call or something 'cause I have to be at work at eight tomorrow morning." Well that was a mouthful and I guess sort of charming. He seemed to be second-guessing himself, too. Not moving on every whim and impulse at the risk of how I'd interpret it. Didn't seem like the words of a guy who was having this lurid affair with a petite tanorexic.

As we walked back to his place he said, "So tell me, Ms. Vivian, I'm curious. What brings you here, hmmm?" He hugged/squeezed me just after he said that in a cute slash condescending way. He knew why I was there and I evidently struck a seemingly innocent chord within him; a chord I'm guessing that he was flattered by.

"Ya know what? I don't want to talk about it. Why don't you just take me up to this mysteriously swanky loft you live in."

"No way," he said. "This topic will be broached before the evening comes to a close. I assure you." Genius. I'd look like the jealous suspicious girlfriend. Perfect.

We got upstairs and into this railroad apartment, similar to that of Adam's, just a bit longer. No wonder he liked to crash with me. Who could blame him? His roommates were away and we were on our own.

"Okay. So talk to me," he insisted. "What's going on?"

After an awkward moment of silence, I said, "Okay, fuck it. I came here tonight because . . . because I don't trust you. There I said it. Are you happy?"

"No, I'm not happy. I thought things were going really well with us. I was even hoping you'd come home with me next weekend." I took a deep breath. I could feel my nostrils flaring. I could feel Mark in the room with us, just laughing at me. Being so pleased with himself that he had thoroughly and completely screwed me up.

"What?" I asked.

"Wait, why are you getting so upset?" he said. He moved closer to me and I reacted by taking two steps backward.

"Listen, maybe you're being honest with me and maybe I'm just completely off. But things have changed ever since that house party. We've seen less and less of each other, and I know about how good things are going at your job and all, but if you are fucking with me, I'll kill you. I can't take that. I need to know that you'd never lie to me. That if something was going on you'd tell me." (Here's where I started to cry.) "Who was that orange girl and why did you never come to my place that night? I have this thing—this issue, I guess. I don't know. I'm afraid to ask questions and if you want to be with me you have to be able to read my mind and answer them." WHAT!!! DID I REALLY JUST SAY THAT??? No, sorry, "fumble" through that/those words in between sniffles, snots, and skipped breaths???

Omelet was hiding in the bathroom FYI—but that's another story.

"Relax," he said. "I'm crazy about you. Don't be afraid to talk to me, question me. Vivian, please. I hate to see you this way."

"What way? Hysterical in your apartment with boogers running down my nose? (Enter sleeve.) Forget it. Listen, I think you're great. Oh! and look—there's my card—it's taped to your wall hanging on a diagonal and everything. Wow. Okay. I'm just going to go. Where's Omelet?"

He stood there in disbelief (probably) as I got Omelet, grabbed my ski cap, tore my ridiculous card from the wall, and left. It was so quiet in his building. I remember the sound of the door slamming—unintentionally. It was a heavy, old-fashioned steel door and if you'd didn't take the time to close it, the crash would travel through your bones and, needless to say, throughout the building. After a few flights of stairs I had made it to street level and this time walked to the subway entrance that was just a few feet away. Please, who was going to stop me and my dog now—three A.M. on a "school night"??? What are the odds of getting "in trouble with the law" (sounds a bit harsh I know but it's true) two times in one day?

But I was stopped. Patrick grabbed my arm just a few seconds later, out of breath and with just a T-shirt on. "Don't make me beg you. Please come home with me. She was my high school girlfriend whose fiancé just told her he wanted out. I saw her at the bar in hysterics and I spent the night at her place as she threw up, sobbed, told me the whole and I mean the WHOLE story, and I passed out on her couch. I never knew listening could be so exhausting. I was sure you'd think I was lying, so when you didn't ask, I didn't tell. I'm sorry."

"Really?" I asked.

"Really." He smiled.

(Wait, you know he was wearing pants right? I meant no jacket, no sweater, and it was no more than forty degrees outside.)

Instead of evaluating what had just transpired, we made a fort with all the blankets in his apartment and slept on his floor. (Twins beds are so not cool.) He apologized about a million times as did I. We snuggled and laughed and had a brilliant make-up session. And just as I was about to fall asleep, I heard him say, "One of these days, Vivian, you're going to have to talk to me."

I pretended I didn't hear him and he pretended he thought I hadn't.

Healthy communicative relationships . . . don't ya just love 'em?

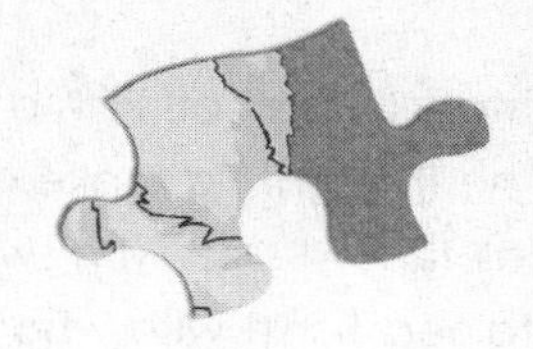

I was becoming real friendly with Zack, one of my regulars at Le Figaro, and then subsequently his wife, Laura. She was a doctor and he worked at VH1. They lived nearby, always looked as if they just came back from a J. Crew catalog shoot, and were addicted to coffee, Le Fig's amazing vanilla French toast: and my incredible service of course! Zack was fascinated with the idea that Gibson guitars was the catalyst to my living in New York. He was an avid music memorabilia collector—signed albums, guitars, photos, the works! Laura used to bitch about where they would find room for Zack's next big purchase. He assumed I was a fellow music freak as well, but as our friendship progressed he realized that that was not exactly the case. He, like many others, often asked what was next for me. What did I want to do, where did I see my career of some kind, any kind, heading? But time and time again, my answer was always the same: "I really don't know. I guess I'm just waiting for this ray of light to shine down on me from the sky and awaken some sort of epiphany within me." But at present, there was no such light, or "ray" rather. (Madonna's album was about six years away!)

One Sunday morning, he came into the restaurant with a proposition:

His assistant just ran off with a musician (surprise, surprise) and if I was interested, he thought I'd make an excellent executive assistant. "What, and leave all this?" I said with sweat dripping from my forehead, wearing a ratty stained T-shirt with who knows what all over it, and still, those awful fingertips, reeling from my homemade manicure and sticker debacle. He laughed and I sat down with him immediately and gestured toward Natale to see that my tables were all right.

Zack went on to explain what it was that he did at VH1 and what my responsibilities would be. I could barely keep my mouth closed. Get this: He was the vice president of "talent relations," whereby he would work with various record labels and managers to book guests for the station's programming and special events. "Okay," I said. "So what would I be doing?"

"Everything from answering my phones, getting my coffee (which he said I was already wonderful at—ha-ha), developing a roper with the artists and their managements, assisting me in coordinating events, scheduling meetings, etc."

"For real?!?!?!?" I shouted.

"Yes, Vivian, for real."

"Hold on a sec. Let me call my mom . . ."

I jumped up, stuck about a dozen quarters in the pay phone and got my mom on the line. As long as I had dental and the option of a "401(k)" (I had no idea what that meant) she said it sounded like a wonderful opportunity. I told her to hang on and shouted across Le Figaro to Zack. "Would I have dental? Oh, and a 601(k)?"

"Yes." He laughed.

"Yup," I told my mom.

"Then take it!" she said.

"Okay, I'll call you back!" and I hung up on her. "I'll take it," I shrieked.

"So when can you start?" he asked. I told him about a week. I knew they wouldn't have a problem filling my shifts and I was hoping they'd still let me pick up slots on the weekends. Zack gave me his card and told me to call him on Monday. I'd have to meet with Human Resources, etc.

Now this was fierce! In a week's time I'd be an executive assistant for the coolest man—heck, the only man—I knew at VH1!!! Somebody pinch me!

I immediately went to find Shirley, my manager, and gave her the 411. She was so happy for me and assured me that I was not leaving them high and dry for help. Everyone at the restaurant seemed to share in my enthusiasm and they all wanted to throw me a going-away party prior. (I thought that was very cool.)

Sophie and I met up at the apartment on Sunday night and I told her all about it. She was thrilled and felt that it would be the perfect place for me—for anyone really. And she was absolutely right. Patrick was psyched for me as well as was my entire family, who proceeded to call me over and over again for the next several days.

I spoke to Zack on Monday. He had scheduled an appointment for me that next day with HR. He gave me the address, contact name, etc. and told me to be myself (????). Who that was, I had no idea. Sophie, again stylist extraordinaire, fashioned me an outfit that "screamed music executive." (Why all of my outfits "speak" to her, to this day I have no idea.) I wore an old Rolling Stones T-shirt that Sophie cut off and up in that "distressed" look, with a fitted pinstriped blazer, red trousers, and black pointy shoes. And where did I get all this stuff? I splurged, I should tell you, and went with Soph that morning to Atrium. I needed the ultimate Fashion Emergency makeover and with her employee discount, who could resist? I was yet again talked into wearing a tiny bit of makeup: Hawaiian punchy lip gloss, waterproof black mascara, and just a bit of bronzer. And at the end of all the fussing I felt somewhat like a poser. As much as I love the Rolling Stones, until Sophie cut up the T-shirt, I most often jogged in it. The foxy red pants I was sorta digging but the fitted blazer and the "how do people actually walk in these shoes" shoes—well—that was the stretch. I will admit, however, that although I'm so not about "the clothes making the woman thing," I felt quite sassy in my new ensemble and was ready for this, the first day of my new and really first ever career!

I took a cab up to VH1's corporate office in Times Square. There was no way I could handle the steps of the subway in those shoes. They were made for getting in and out of cars only, and perhaps for big sexy photo shoots, which I, of course, was not on. When I finally got there, I couldn't believe my eyes. This was the Viacom building and where the MTV corporate headquarters were located as well. This was soooo cool! (And I did, like a dork, bring a camera, but was my own best friend and talked myself out of taking a picture with the building's security guard!)

After giving my name to the receptionist in the lobby I was told to meet Ms. So-and-so on the whatever floor. As I took a trip up the elevator I searched desperately for any kind of mirror or reflection—I wanted to give myself one last glance before the big interview. Before I knew it, the doors had opened and besides being shocked at the mere surprise of the "you're here" type bell, as I walked out of the elevator in walked Bono—yup—as in U2!

I almost puked. Literally. You know when it comes up your throat and you go through the arduous task of swallowing it? Yup—I did that. (Charming, but true!) And there was Ms. So-and-so—I'm totally spacing on her name—whom I'm sure caught my "that's so not a big deal" bogus reaction. "Oh well," I thought. "Zack said to be myself, so screw it!"

She seemed flawless in this real spooky ice-woman kinda way. Jet-black, perfectly straight hair to her shoulders. A tight black three-quarter-sleeve sweater and a very chic tight black pencil skirt with this mini-slit in the back. If I thought my shoes were pointy, hers were like arrows with heels that looked like they could kill someone if thrown with enough force. From behind, you could tell this chick worked out hardcore or that maybe she had reinvented the entire concept of support hose. Damn, I thought, she could probably kick my ass. She wore a chunky silver wrist-watch and what I'm guessing was an engagement ring—the thing was huge!!! (I rarely look gals up and down and size them up. That's more

Sophie's department, but I was wondering if that's how I was supposed to look or even if that's what I would eventually look like if I worked at VH1 for a long enough period of time. I kind of wanted to take her picture too, but again, it seemed incredibly inappropriate.)

I shook her hand—ouch—and nervously followed her back to her office. I could hear myself squishing in my own shoes. (You know that sound, right?) So I thought if I started talking she wouldn't hear my feet. "This is such a great hallway!" I said. (Good one.)

"Yes, yes it is," she replied.

Now this was getting off to a very good start. Not!

So her office was filled with signed posters from Rod Stewart, Elton John—all the big shots, really. She had the most beautiful flower arrangement on her desk, which I complimented her on by the way. "Is it your birthday?" I asked innocently.

"Oh, no," she replied. "These are a thank-you gift from one of my recruits." (God, I hope she likes Le Figaro. I could get her a gift certificate I guess???)

"Now then, Vivian," she said. "Zack has said just so many wonderful things about you."

"Really?? That's so cool of him!"

"Excuse me?" she said.

"Yeah, well, what I mean is that I'm so happy that he thought of me when the position became vacant, ya know?"

"Yes, yes . . . so moving ahead, may I have a look at your résumé?"

"Come again?"

"You do have a résumé?" I just shook my head in the no direction and smiled. "Well, maybe then, your list of references?"

"References?"

"Yes, from your previous employers."

"Well, to be honest, Zack didn't mention anything about a résumé or anything like that. We're friends—sort of I guess. He's one of my regulars—although he hates when I call him that, although his wife doesn't seem to mind . . ."

She looked horrified.

"Wait a minute—you think . . . NO WAY!!!" I laughed. "I was a waitress at Le Figaro, this mad cute coffee shop in the Village. Do you know it?"

"No, I'm afraid I don't," she said.

"Well, Zack offered me the position on Sunday just when I was telling him the specials. Pretty funny, right?"

"Right."

"He told me to just be myself and come and meet with you. So here I am—me—without the résumé, but so thrilled to be here!"

"Would you excuse me for a second Ms.?"

"Livingston," I said. "Sure, sure. Should I wait outside?" I asked.

"Oh, no," she answered. She picked up the phone and asked if whoever it was on the other line would mind stopping in. Two seconds later Zack walked in. "Hey, Viv!" He smiled.

"Hey," I said. I felt like I was about to get fired, and I hadn't even started yet. Zack asked if I'd wait outside, which I did.

A short while later they emerged. So-and-so invited me back into her office and Zack shook my hand and said he'd see me next week. He winked as he walked away.

Feeling much more relaxed, I plopped myself back into one of her chairs and waited for her to say something. "Well, Ms. Livingston, VH1 would like to offer you an executive assistant position in the talent and promotions department. Your annual salary is thirty-four thousand dollars and includes all medical and dental benefits. You'll need to take home the following information, review it, and stop back here with all the paperwork filled out and signed promptly next Monday." Everything else she said went straight over my head. I kept scratching the top of my hand, as though I had a mosquito bite from hell throughout the rest of her diatribe just to keep myself from fainting. I felt like this was the beginning of something amazing. I felt like the luckiest girl in the world and at the same time I felt like I was about to be sick.

"Would you excuse me?" I asked. "Where is the ladies' room?"

"Oh just around the corner," she answered. I ran in the stall, nearly tripped on the way thanks to my ridiculous shoes, and heaved. Whether it was the Bono sighting, or the fact that I just got a real job in the music business, working for a really nice man, I have no idea. Luckily, I was alone in the bathroom, I have to add. I washed up, looked in the mirror, and just as I went to crack a smile I heard Mark tell me that I was just a piece of ass, that no one would take me seriously. You can imagine. Feeling momentarily defeated, I began to dry my hands and gather my things. But I stopped and went back to the mirror. I looked at myself again, smiled, and told him to "sod off!"

(This is an approach I learned in therapy, better phrased, I think, as "vulgar" cognitive therapy. I wasn't schizophrenic, but rather engaged in a battle of the mind fuck. Mark spent four long years messing with my head and this was one of my strategies that I found worked well. In order to begin reclaiming my life and allow for the positive, well-deserving thoughts to stay in my mind once they entered. You should try it sometime—just make sure you're in a private place! I've found it to work in lots of arenas!!!)

So I went back, got my papers, thanked her for the meeting, had a janitor snap a quick photo of me and the two security guys at the entrance to the Viacom building, my new employer, and decided to surprise Patrick at his office. It would be sinful to waste this outfit! I rang my mom again—collect—I didn't have any change on me and told her the good news. She was so happy and so proud of me. She admitted that she and my father had had cable installed yesterday and watched VH1 all night, thinking that it might work in my favor and send good luck my way! (Sweet, but frightening!) Before I got off the phone, she asked if I was going to be one of those "Voice Video Jockie" kids. Ah Mom, ya gotta love her.

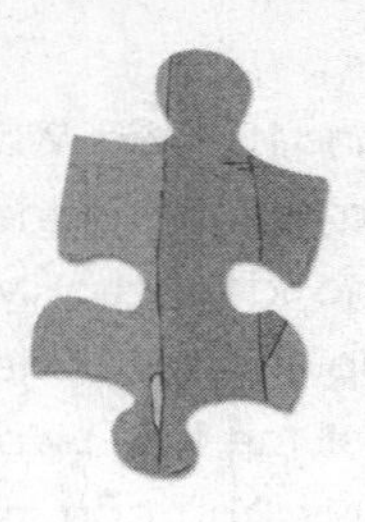

Patrick worked on the Lower East Side, which was a ways away from my, ahem, office!!! (How genius does that sound?!) And having already blown way too much do-ray-me on my taxi to my interview but still in the same nightmare stilettos, I chose public transportation option two—the bus. I waited at the bus stop for what felt like forever. I stood there with these wonderful butterflies in my stomach—the good kind that make you want to jump out of your skin and tell each stranger standing beside you the life-changing experience that you didn't let pass you by. I'm sure those folks thought I had to urinate or something. I couldn't help twisting and twitching, smiling, and making God knows what kind of facial expressions as I imagined myself working with Madonna on some "special project," escorting No Doubt to their dressing room, becoming BFF with Gwen Stefani, and coming up with some brilliant cost-effective creative idea at some big bad corporate meeting and being promoted to . . . um, how about "extremely executive assistant, talent relations"? Yes, that sounds about right, all in just six days from right now! Who could sit still really?

The bus ride was agonizing. Those big blue babies stop at every street! I also shared my seat with this awful man who evidently opted not to use antiperspirant that afternoon and must have had some kind of Greek salad just before his travels. Don't get me wrong, who doesn't love a Greek salad or feta cheese for that matter, but trust me, guys, something with this gent was just way wrong. To make matters worse, he kept talking on his mobile phone, so with his arm raised and his mouth wide open on a practically constant basis, I graciously gave up my seat.

I finally made it across town and with transfer in hand, waited yet again at another stop for the second and final bus that would take me to my man! (That sounds awfully good, doesn't it?!) I stopped in a bodega really quickly to treat myself to a "one-on-one Hostess party" (me, Mr. and Mrs. Twinkie, their friends Coffee and Cupcake, and of course, my trusted confidante, Quik chocolate milk). They totally understand me and are always so supportive during good and bad times. We don't get together much, but when we do, it's sinful!!!!

So there I am gripping this brown plastic bag covering up my treats as if they were opened containers of liquor, waiting for bus numero dos when I hear someone say, "Livingston—is that you?" I turn my head in what now feels like slow motion—certainly my hair was midair like a shampoo commercial—and much to my horrification, standing there in, I have to add this, a horrible light gray, double-breasted suit, was Mark's undergrad roommate, Fred. (Mark's friends always called me by my last name, by the way. Whether it was a football player thing or if it helped them forget that I was a real woman, not some numb punching bag with boobs—as they all knew full well what was going on and chose to do nothing—I'm not sure. My heart, for some while, nearly always skipped a beat when I'd hear a man call me by my last name, but I managed to shed that fine trait about six months ago.)

Okay, sorry, let me get straight to it. I was lucky enough to share the next thirty minutes with someone who I was unable to shed my college skin with. What I mean is, I forgot all about Zack and VH1 so long as Fred was around. I felt like I was back at Penn State on my way to a class or something. Head down, goose bumps all over, and recalling all the grossly instigating reports he would give to Mark. "Vivian looked pretty today, Mark," "Vivian wasn't too friendly today, Mark," "Vivian was talking to some guy I didn't know today, Mark." I tried real hard not to let Fred in on my inner trauma and likewise to keep most of my answers to his questions to a minimum as we stood side by side on the bus.

(I knew this sorta stuff would come up when I agreed to write this book and wasn't too sure how far I'd take it, but screw it. It's who I am, it's who I'll always be. But the key is, ladies and gents, it's my past—not my present I'm proud to say, and I think I need to really explain in a bit of a nutshell why there was nothing I wanted to hear out of or from Fred.)

This spineless, cowardly motherfucker, i.e., Fred, knew what Mark was doing to me, nearly every bit of it. He slept in the bedroom next door to Mark for three years for Christ sake. He shared the same sofa, showered in the same bathroom, barbecued in the same backyard—you get my drift. He heard the screaming, the shoving of my body against a wall by a man three times my size. The sounds of a mirror, a television, or a dish of some kind crashing to the floor, and all the pleading. He heard everything. AND HE SAID NOTHING. He saw the red blotches on my face and my arms. Ya know the kind that kids get when they skin their knees when they fall off their bikes? But mine were from the cheap mustard-colored shag carpeting in their rental house. Mark would pin me or drag me across the carpet when he was trying to prove some twisted point or another. Fred ignored the banging on the front door, the ringing of the doorbell, even the knocking on his window, as I stood hysterical and freezing, in the middle of the night just minutes after Mark threw me out on some strange psychotic whim with just my pajamas on, and my car keys in their house, along with my shoes. Fred allowed me to cry and cry outside and apologize to Mark over and over and would never do a thing. If I was going to get back in that house, it would be up to Mark. And then, of course, when I'd get back in, rush to grab my things and head for the nearest door, Fred would do nothing but stay in his room, as Mark would physically prevent me from leaving. If something crazy happened in front of him, Fred would never step in, glance my way, or dismiss himself.

I remember this one morning, I had slept over and the three of us were eating waffles at the kitchen table. Mark asked me if I had plans that evening to which I told him that I did actually. It was Sophie's birthday and a group of the few friends I had were getting together to celebrate at one of the local bars. Mark, out of nowhere, chucked his glass of milk right at my face and called me a "cock tease." He thought it was real funny that I thought I was going out, especially when I knew that that was where he and his friends would be. I remember not focusing on the humiliation of the moment, or how my clothes and the books beside me were ruined, but rather, it was the simplicity of the pain. My eyes were stinging. The force of the liquid was so hard and so fast that the pain surpassed the temperature of the cold smelly milk that was now seeping down my shirt and beneath my pants and likewise all over the floor. I remember it being so quiet afterward, it was chilling. You could hear the drops of milk hit the cold tiles on the floor and none of us dared say a word. Mark naturally regretting the action, Fred pretending that it didn't even happen, and me, well, I just sat there, utterly empty inside. I ignored any questions asked of me and the conversation between the two of them shyly lingered on. See scenarios such as this were familiar to all three of us. If it wasn't milk in the kitchen, it was books from the living room table that we often used as a desk. Remote controls were like stones, and then, of course, there were his hands. He could do anything with those.

It's not at all that I blame Fred for any of it, because I don't. I could have really gone through with those things I swore I'd do so many times: broken up with Mark, gotten the restraining order, actually have the courage to file a report the countless times Sophie or I called the cops on him, even just gone home and finished college locally after I got my head examined. But I never did. I suppose it was something that I wanted to defeat on my own. I don't know. But I was and always will be disgusted by people like Fred, who knew what was happening to me and did nothing, not even anonymously call attention to the crystal-clear abuse that was taking place. Never, not once in the course of four long years.

So, bottom line: Fred was a real stand-up guy, let me tell you, and seeing him in New York City made me want to scream. Finally, it was my stop and just as I went to say good-bye, wouldn't you know it, Fred stood up. He was getting off, too. Lucky me.

"Well take care," I said and off I walked, briskly. Consequently, I opted to postpone my party with the Hostesses and introduced them to a lovely bag woman on the corner of first and Eldridge, who looked like she, too, could use their company. "Vivian!" I heard Fred shout from behind me. "Vivian! Please wait, I know you can hear me!" (He was right. I could and I stopped, reluctantly.) "Listen," he said, "I know you probably hate me and you have every right to."

"Fred—you don't have to do this and quite honestly, I wish you wouldn't." I tried to stop him midway. I didn't want to hear anything this dude had to say.

"Listen, I just want to say I'm sorry."

"Apology accepted. Can I go now?" I said.

"No, please. I don't know why I never stood up to him. I was afraid of him, too, I guess."

"Well that's nice, Fred. I've moved on. Now you can too—conscience cleared and all."

"Vivian," he pleaded and went to grab my arm. I remember jumping back as though time had stood still and he was going to grab my hair, pull me back behind some building, and do God knows what. And, mind you, Fred had never laid a finger on me. "Look," he said. "Hate me if you have to. I don't blame you. I am just very happy to see you. You look good and I'm glad you didn't let that guy ruin you."

"Good-bye, Fred," I said, and walked away. I haven't seen him since and it's been years. That's another thing I love about New York City—it's so big, you can go a lifetime without running into a blast from your past.

I walked fifteen minutes out of my way and in the completely wrong direction. It was as if my brain had chosen to hang out back at the bus station. With my high worn way off, I opted for the closest bar. I needed a drink and my feet were killing me. Patrick who? I needed to shake the sighting off before I could see or talk to anyone. Seeing Fred made me remember things I hadn't thought of in years. It was painful.

Finding a bar downtown is about as easy as coming across The Gap in a strip mall. Lo and behold there was an old Irish pub with my name on it, just inches away. I walked inside and it was virtually empty. "Brilliant!" I thought as I ordered myself a Scotch on the rocks. I told you I needed a drink. This was no time for frilly, colored drinks with fancy names. I wanted to feel a burning in my chest and a buzz in my head within minutes. If I smoked, I gather this would have been a cigarette kind of moment as well. As I waited for my drink, I noticed the clock. It was nearly three P.M. Still enough time, I thought, to get the wind back in my sails and meet up with my man. I pulled out a ten-dollar bill from my wallet. (There was this vacant booth in the back that had my name on it, so I was pretty eager to wrap things up with the bartender.) I couldn't help but notice a photo just above the cash register. When I took a closer look, there was Jimmy, arm in arm with the bartender, a.k.a. Dad. Small world, hey?

I sat down at the booth with my back to everyone and everything. Sinatra was playing in the background—mint—and I proceeded to go over what had just happened with Fred. I didn't much care about how I treated him or what I said or even how he interpreted all of it. I was concerned more with all the memories that had passed through me. One instance, one casualty after the next, just by the mere sight of him. That really freaked me out. Had I been suppressing all these memories in order to get past them? Was that healthy? Could it happen again? Does it have to? When does a girl get a break, ya know?? That's what I was thinking. Looking back, I think I was having a mini–panic attack or something. The rush was just so heavy. My nerves had been shot by a thirty-minute encounter. I was so angry with myself for being part of something so tragic. Not in the feel-bad-for-me sense of the word, but more that "it" was all so unnecessary and had caused so much damage. WHY, VIVIAN??? Just then, I turned my head and gestured for another to the bartender. Mind you, I was now on drink two on a virtually empty stomach, at 3:15 in the afternoon on a Tuesday—very, very pretty!

Instead of focusing on the bad, I switched gears and started thinking about the good. In terms of my future, I looked at it this way: I knew I would end up proving Mark wrong, one way or another. A healthy sort of revenge that would only push me to be a better person, one who wore a coat of armor that was not necessarily made of steel. I was, and would continue to be, a better friend, a better daughter, and a better woman. My eyes now saw things that others would skip. My ears would hear things that others would miss. No, I don't think I'm super, wonder, or the bionic woman, but rather, I know for sure that I developed a sensitivity that I didn't have as a teenager and surely I would not have grown into as an adult. Not the way I was headed. You know the girl I was. There's a ton out there. The rebellious, confident, "my way or the highway," little Swiss

Miss type, where the interests, fears, wishes, and perspectives of others are not exactly on our radar screens. Now I know better.

Coming to these conclusions was making me feel a whole lot better as I sat in that pub. That and surely the last bits of my second Scotch. I liked the person I was post-Mark and I'm not too sure I would have been able to say that had he not been in my life.

I know now that when you come out of a shitty situation—and I bet this holds true for anyone—where you lose a part of yourself or something or someone who is important to you, you begin to appreciate the things you would have taken for granted in the past. Great moments become huge moments, kind gestures translate into thoughtfulness that you can't even describe, simple pleasures become valuable and the decisions you make going forward are most often thought out or devilishly spontaneous—and always for the best!

My decision to enter that songwriting contest, for example, and the words I put together that enabled me to win (unless of course I was the only one who entered, which is entirely possible); the fact that I moved to New York and took my time finding a "real job" when so many other graduates make decisions with haste because of the pressure they put themselves under, or rather what they perceive the world is putting on them. I sat at that bar, realizing that I called my own shots as they felt comfortable to me, and I felt good about that. No doubt about it, it was and is this huge sense of responsibility I have to myself, to never let an opportunity or a memory in the making slip away. When you survive something, every moment thereafter counts.

At 3:45, it was time to put my personal pep talk on hold, as I so desperately wanted to tell the good guy in my life the great thing that had happened to me today. I wanted that moment: girl tells guy great news, guy picks girl up and swings her around, girl closes eyes and spins, head falls back in sheer delight, naturally overcome by her happiness. Guy and girl leave everyone and walk off into the sunset (or moonlight in this case).

I felt a little messed up when I left that bar-shocker. I had worked through the ugly Fred drama but was heading downtown feeling a bit like a drunk driver. Although I was walking, after two glasses of Scotch, I had no business whatsoever being in those shoes! I got caught in what I like to call "Urban Quicksand" too many times to count. ("UQ" only exists when you're wearing heels and are forced to walk over the screened subway street-level grids when the sidewalks get too full. You'll get stuck in a heartbeat, and if you're not careful, you can break and/or lose the heel to your shoe, and can really humiliate yourself and not be able to get out of it. This is where you need a stranger to step in, in order for you to keep your balance and provide the base to squirm out of the "sand.")

Finally, I made it to Patrick's—by about 4:30. I was really excited. I had never been to his shop/office before. It was this wholesale hat place where you could get practically any cap, hat, or what have you, in bulk. Sometimes, Patrick would even hit the road, for weeks at a time, selling hats to distributors on the East Coast. Trust me, I doubt there has ever been or ever will be a hat salesman that comes to your door who looks anything like Patrick, and if there were, I'm willing to bet you suddenly find yourself needing a cap or two! ☺

I was feeling really good again. The walk, after a few UQ scenarios, did me good and between the wind and the Scotch I had a pretty good glow going on my face. I paused just before I stepped inside and put some lip gloss on, then I played with my hair a bit, used the reflection in the window of the store to do a quick once-over, and quite joyfully walked in.

As you'd expect, there were hats everywhere. Baseball hats (every team you could think of), ski and stocking caps, chic little berets, and very cute cowboy hats on the walls and hanging from the ceilings. Everybody in the place was wearing a hat, which was a little trippy, I have to say. I was greeted by this very big, slightly older, greasy guy who sounded just like Al Pacino and who evidently thought I was there to, but what else, buy some hats. I asked if Patrick was there and he said "Yeah," and screamed, "Patrick!!!!" in a very scary "who-hah!" kinda fashion.

"What's up?" I heard Patrick shout back and he asked me my name.

"Vivian," I said with a smile.

"Vivian is here to see you!!!" he roared.

I waited a little bit before Patrick surfaced and when our eyes met, the twinkle I was hoping for, expecting really, wasn't there. Instead, he looked horrified, donning this jerky half smile that I had never seen before. He looked confused, almost constipated, and besides being a huge buzz kill, his reaction was incredibly disturbing.

From the opposite side of the counter he said, "Hi there. Can I help you with something?" I thought he was kidding and maybe his boss was strict or something and didn't appreciate personal visits. "Sure, sure," I went along. "I'd like to see that cowboy hat up there." Chubby Al Pacino rushes in, "Does she know we're a wholesaler, Patrick? That means you've got to buy two dozen, lady."

God, what a dick, I thought. No wonder Patrick never asks me to come around. This guy is a nightmare! "Yes sir," I snipped. "I'm well aware.

Thank you." I then asked Patrick to show me the tweed berets that were displayed in the middle of the store. At least this way I'd get that annoying counter out of our way and, of course, grab a little privacy.

"Vivian, you really shouldn't be here," he said nervously.

"Obviously," I said. "I apologize but I had no idea. You always visit me at the restaurant. I just thought . . ." and before I could finish my sentence I heard this whiny voice in the background shout, "Patrick what is SHE doing here??" I turned around and it was that orange chick. I couldn't believe my eyes. She walked around the counter and got right up in my face (which besides being confrontational was really scary—she looked like she had just bobbed for apples in a barrel of terra-cotta!).

"Bonnie, please, let me handle this," Patrick said.

"What?" I said.

"Don't you get it, Vivian? That is your name right? Patrick has a girlfriend, and you're looking at her! Why can't you just accept it and be gone. You're like some freakish stalker. Don't you have any self-respect? Get a life! Daddy, please have this woman escorted out. She's not a customer!" I couldn't believe what was happening. Before I could even say anything, her greaseball cigar-smoking "daddy" was coming toward me. I looked at Patrick, who couldn't even look back at me. I could smell her father behind me.

"I'm leaving," I said, still staring at Patrick. As much as I wanted to completely lose it, I just couldn't bear getting into it there in a public place. (Plus, I didn't want any of her base rubbing off on my new "VH1" outfit.) I walked out of the store totally blown away.

Seconds later Patrick came outside and gave me the good old, "I can explain . . ."

" 'I can explain' WHAT?" I shouted. "Stay away from me!" and with that, I slapped him right across the face. (My hand actually stung for a good while afterward.)

"Please, Vivian. I'm in love with you."

"You're in love with me??? Stop it!!" I felt the tears coming and wanted to make a break for it. "Have a wonderful life. I'm sure you'll have beautiful Coppertone babies together! I don't know what ever made me think you were for real." And I walked away. He was yelling my name but having two losers in one day run after me was not quite the statistic I was looking for. Luckily, there was a cab ready and waiting on the corner and I jumped right in.

This time I did look back. I wanted a mental picture I could remember forever!

Asshole!

I couldn't cry. That's what I remember. Now that Patrick was not in front of me, I felt void. I just recall shaking my head from side to side, rolling down the window and letting the evening air run through my hair. I asked the driver to turn the radio up. "I'm Every Woman" à la Whitney Houston was on. I did my best to focus on the future, not on who I just left behind. Sure I bit my nails, felt like a huge idiot to not have seen it all coming. Wait, rather, I sort of did see this coming but didn't want to believe it. That's what was so unnerving. Yet again, I didn't follow my instincts when it came to men. (Why was and is that always such a big fuckin' problem for me? Millions of women manage to get that right—why can't I??) Before I knew it, "Wonderful Tonight" began to play on the radio and since I just couldn't appreciate Eric Clapton right there and then, I asked the driver to turn the radio off. I drank the rest of my Evian like a chick who's been lost in the desert for a thousand years and vowed to keep men out of my life. They were just way too much trouble. I remember emptying out my bag in that cab as a means and overdue way of distracting myself. Organizing receipts, gum wrappers, stupid old fortune cookie fortunes that I save each time they seem to say something relative or positive, put loose change in my coin purse—anything to keep me from feeling bad for myself. As the cab pulled up to my apartment I saw Sophie and Gabe, of all people, having a smoke on our front steps! Friends! Yeah!!! But my temporary high disintegrated the minute I realized that I never bought a bottle of water before, during, or after the Patrick debacle. Ewwwwwwwwwwww—a stranger's leave-behind—gross!!!

Real quick: Gabe is one of my oldest and dearest comrades! He lives in Vermont and we've been pretty much "just friends" for as long as I can remember. His family owned this great Italian restaurant just minutes from the house my family rented season after season. We were each other's first semi-real smooch and he taught me how to play pool and cricket. I prided myself on teaching him the fine art of French kissing, and practice not only makes perfect, but in his case, was surely no tiresome chore. ☺ We both loved to ski and snowboard (he was now an instructor), and seeing him always felt so so good. He was like a teddy bear to me! He reminded me immediately of all good times. And this, or he, rather, was a huge surprise that could not have come at a more appreciated moment!

As I got out of the cab they both hurried to put out their cigarettes, as if "Mom" was just getting home. (I still don't get it. Why smoke as an adult if you still feel as though you have to hide it?) "Look who's here!!!" cried Sophie.

"Hey there, sexy!" Gabe said and proceeded to give me a nice big yummy closed-mouth smooch. He hugged me real tight and I truly didn't want to let go. (A very *Terms of Endearment* moment for all you fellow Debra Winger fans!)

"Look at you—you're a corporate diva already!" he said. (Sophie must have given him an update.) "And where's this Patrick guy? I feel the need to kick his ass!" (Did they have ESP?) "Does he even know what he's got?"

Opting to not get into it all I replied, "What, like now I'm an 'it'? How about 'who' he's got, huh? Did you have to go to school for that instructor degree?" Sarcasm: a seemingly nifty trick. Whatever.

I helped Gabe with his things and gave him a tour of our cozy little flat. As we made it into my room, there was a Polaroid of Patrick and me lying on my desk. (He was planting a sloppy one on my cheek and my eyes were big and bright—just like my smile—as the camera went "click." Ugh! Spare me.) Polaroid in pocket ASAP. "What's that about?" Gabe asked as Sophie looked on.

"Nothing, I just don't need to hear how 'pretty' he is from you or the big 'you went for THAT type?!' "

"Okay. That's fair. But I'll be crashing here for the next few days, FYI, so if you plan on keeping him away from me, think again, sweetness." I wanted to lose it right there but faked a minor sneeze attack to warrant the red in my face and the glare in my eyes. (I thought it worked.)

Anywho, Sophie evidently knew all about Gabe's visit and they cutely both had agreed to keep it from me. I do looooove surprises! Soph had taken the night off from Fernando so the three of us could hang out like old times. They were all revved up to paint the town red or whatever color and Sophie had already devised a foolproof plan to get into one of the city's hottest clubs, Chaos. Great. Yeah, sure, this is just what I was in the mood for. I told them I needed to change and in unison they shouted "NO!"

"What? Why? It will take two seconds."

"Viv, it's just that you look so fierce! So Chaos! Just lose the blazer." (I'm sure you know who said that.)

"Yeah, Vivian—those red pants are hot!!!" (That was Gabe. What guy doesn't love tight red pants? For a second there I was feeling very Avril, circa *Footloose*. I did warn you in the beginning about my movie obsession!!!)

We walked from our place to Chaos. I did have my way with one thing as I was permitted to change my shoes. (Thank God!) Gabe, who is usually in head-to-toe Patagonia or North Face or something, must have certainly gotten a little style advice prior to packing for NYC. He was wearing black everything. Let me put it this way: Gabe in black is like me wearing some poofy floral party dress with my hair in one of those updos! Highly, highly unlikely! But it was definitely working for him. Very "Josh Hartnett at a movie premiere." The good old-fashioned boy in fancy garb, if you catch my drift. No doubt, the city chicks would dig it. I did.

"So what's the plan, dare I ask?" I said. "You know this place has got, what Soph, like a twenty-dollar cover?"

"Not tonight!" she gloated.

"Oh really, and why is that?"

" 'Cause tonight I'm Sandra Bullock's personal assistant and you are her little sister!" she said with a Garfield-like grin.

"Come on!" I said. "You've got to be joking. Who would ever believe such a thing?" Gabe just stood there laughing, either at my reaction or Sophie's Einstein-like idea.

"It works, I'm telling you. Gina, at work, did the same thing last week. Called in advance, said she was Dylan McDermott's assistant and they let her right in. No I.D., no nothing. Her name plus four was on the guest list. They were in the VIP room within minutes!"

"Please!" I said in total (envious) disgust.

"I'm telling you, just act all smiley and wowlike, and I'll take care of the rest." And with that she grabbed my hand and we were off.

I now thought to myself, all right, Fred, Patrick . . . fate could never be this cruel in one day, right!? If it doesn't work at least we wouldn't make complete fools of ourselves. Please! I crossed everything I could as we approached Chaos, walked past the toilet-paper-let-loose-like line and right up to two of the biggest dudes I'd ever seen. Sophie gave them our (fake) names, and sure enough, we were let right in, told not to pay a cover, given tickets for our coats, and escorted into the VIP room! I could not believe it! Sophie pulled it off! "You go, girl!" I laughed as we sat down at our groovy little reserved table.

"Keep it cool," she said nervously.

"Right, right. Sorry, sweets." I don't think Gabe got how big of a coup this just was. He got up to get us our drinks just as a cocktail waitress laid down our complimentary bottle of champagne. None of us kept our cool at that point. The minute she walked away we were cracking up like kids in a class once the teacher turned her back. I thought for sure we'd get busted but Sophie reminded me that since there was no way that we'd ever know anyone in the VIP room, who could ever bust us?

"True, true—sad, but true." I smiled, and with that Gabe made a toast.

"To my two favorite girls, who I'd give anything to see make out before the night is through!" Some things never change! He's been making that same toast since we were sixteen.

I'll admit it. I was fully inebriated two hours into it. I'm most often a nice buzz-e type gal. Once I catch one, I don't usually go any further. But the day's circumstances called for unladylike behavior, at least according to me. From what I remember of it, the music was insane, the guys were insane, and the vibe was, yup, insane. I don't think I'd ever experienced a night quite like that one before. All those lonely evenings of endless MTV video watching had paid off. I was a dancing fiend. So not me usually! Even Sophie was impressed. She was a bit embarrassed however when I started lip-synching every song I heard. "Okay now, Mariah, settle down" was one of the last things I remember her saying. I wish I could give you this great list of celebs I spotted, all the salacious details of the boyz I flirted with, etc., but that's the bad thing about getting bombed. Sure, I may have been temporarily fearless and danced around like Janet Jackson but I went too far, and remembered none of it!

From what Sophie told me, she danced with a few hotties that made her feel all "Fernando-who?" and Gabe was "this close" to going home with Bruce Willis's personal assistant, some cute gal in black leather pants. But when Sophie reminded him of how we got in in the first place and asked him how he thought I'd feel with him not being there the morning after . . .

"What does that mean?" I asked her, literally the morning after as I could barely keep my head up at the kitchen table, even after Sophie went out and got us coffee. Turns out I hadn't fooled either of them when

I got out of the cab the night before and when I "ripped" the Polaroid from my desk. They were both pretty sure there was trouble in paradise. Hmmmmmmmm. I guess I won't be up for an Oscar this year!

As it was, when we got home from Chaos at about 3:30 in the morning, Patrick was there. Literally, sitting nervously with Omelet on our sofa. (Never give a guy you're dating only a few months a key, by the way!) So it goes, I saw him and within seconds threw the closest thing I could find at him, which was Sophie actually, as I screamed ASSHOLE so loud my neighbors complained that very morning. Before I could flip out, I evidently passed out and Gabe was all the more happy to show Patrick the door.

He left without a fight and without leaving my key. (Another reason that giving a key early on is a bad idea.) It was either we change our locks or I get the key back. The latter option was far less expensive and so it was decided I'd retrieve it. Sweatpants, toothbrushes, undies even—all replaceable—keys on the other hand, total unadulterated bait!

Terrific!

So, my first day at VH1, I got to work in about twenty minutes. (Pretty decent commute, eh?) And was right on time—very glad not to be early and incredibly grateful not to have been late! Early surely would have freaked me out, and with Zack being there already, greeting me with a huge "welcome" smile, a ton of introductions, and even a good-luck bouquet of flowers with a note from him and his wife . . . I mean, who starts a job with such amazing karma, I'll never know! I brought along a few photos and thingamajigs for my desk and began to set up shop. Zack informed me that I needed to get an I.D., fill out more paperwork, etc., at eleven, so I had two solid hours to take everything in.

I was stationed right outside his office, which was more like a suite if you ask me. I had a great big desk with a fancy computer and a printer that I had not one clue how to use. A photocopying machine the size of a Harley-Davidson was behind me and a cozy little fridge nestled in the corner. There was a phone with about six lines at least to my right and just to my left was a television that played "our channel" (doesn't that sound nice?!) nearly 24/7. Mindy, who was Cindy's assistant, was to show me the ropes that week and she couldn't have been any more reluctant to do so. (You would have thought I had a contagious disease or something.) At the time, the whole "office politics" thing went right over my head. How could I have known that Will, Bill's assistant, was a tad lower on the totem pole than Mindy and therefore she felt as though he should be doing the training?!?!

Anywho, my brother Simon had forewarned me, the night prior, about possible coworkers with attitudes, and his advice was to simply "kill 'em with kindness." Who would have known I'd have to refer to my eldest brother the first hour I was there? Mindy was talented enough to be able to breathe aloud and simultaneously roll her eyes each time I didn't catch on to a concept, i.e., collating, call forwarding, interoffice memorandums, I could go on and on, but she was such a cow, why even give her the space in this book!!! So there! (I just stuck my tongue out at her. So mature.)

When I returned at noon from corporate I-dotting and T-crossing, Zack took me out for lunch and gave me the 411 on his department and what was ahead for us over the next few months. I asked him if it was a problem that my name wasn't Jack, Shaq, or Mack and it took a few seconds before he got my joke. (I hope it didn't take you all that long!!!) He also explained that he worked about 25 percent of the time from Los Angeles, so a big part of my job would be ensuring that his calendar was constantly updated, travel arrangements were taken care of, and that he and I always needed to be on the same page if this was going to work. Everything was about "seamless communication," he said, and if I could get that right, I would learn all about the business as I went along. "I got it," I proclaimed proudly and he smiled and said, "I know we'll make a great team!"

The rest of that day and those next couple of weeks flew by. Most of my time was spent covering up all of my mistakes and working late trying to catch up on what I'd missed while making the mistakes—you catch my drift, right?! Luckily Zack was not going out of town for another six weeks as I'd bet I would have definitely sent him on a one-way coach trip to Zimbabwe!

There were times when I felt more like an operator than an executive assistant. This man's phone would never stop ringing! I think I even developed a twitch as my heart would race each time I was on with one person and was interrupted by three other calls. I can't even tell you how many calls I lost and how many were forever lost in automatic operator hell. They don't teach office basics 101 in college, which to this day I think should be a prerequisite! And that copy machine . . . don't even get me started!!!!

But after a while (long or short, who knows) I began to feel at home and wasn't in a panic for six out of the ten hours I put in each day. Will, Bill's assistant, became a great friend and ally. I don't know what I would have done had Will not taken me on as a corporate charity case. It was a six-week program—we still joke about it today! We'd hang out after hours, order in Chinese, and practice everything from the who's who to policies and procedures, to what artists were with what labels, who managed who, what calls to patch through, which to take on my own, how to win friends and influence people (JUST KIDDING). Seriously, Will was money! (C'mon now, who of us didn't love and live for *Swingers* and Vince Vaughn, of course!)

Okay, back to what I was saying: Meeting Will was one of the best things that could have happened to me. He was a great dresser, loved to laugh, couldn't be any nicer, and through all those late nights, never once tried to hit on me. Of course, he was gay. (So typical.) All the great ones usually are. He and Sophie got on brilliantly and although he was a "cat person" we still were able to appreciate the other's four-legged friend. Will's in San Francisco now working at an ad agency, but I fully credit him with me being able to keep the job I was fortunate enough to land!

It wasn't long before I began to make "work friends" beyond Will. (Mindy was promoted shortly after I came on and to this day I still don't know why.) I began to recognize voices on the phone, master Word Perfect, and yes, even collate mass ten-page double-sided distributions.

Hooray!!! And it's worth mentioning: Zack was way on point with the "sink or swim" methodology he used with me. Without him holding my hand at VH1, I was able to catch on to the office dynamics, figure out when my two cents was worth more like two dollars, and meet the out-of-nowhere challenges that were thrown at me. Sometimes with grace and unfortunately, sometimes without! Like my first real celebrity scenario: Meeting Jon Bon Jovi at The Four Seasons to take him to the taping of *Storytellers*. The limo waited out front as I went up to his hotel room. My big responsibility was to be the friendly VH1 face, and take him and his publicist, stylist, manager, and whomever to the studio. Make sure they were on schedule, if he was thirsty get him an Evian, that kind of thing. I was a glamorous gofer for all intents and purposes, and I loved it!!

I did my best to pretend that hanging out in a black limo with JBJ wasn't a big deal. Zack asked me if I could handle it and I remember saying, "No problem, and what does Bon Jovi do again? Is it a restaurant?"

"Here's the address wiseass." And with that Zack gave me his car voucher and, as I just mentioned, the address. Oh, and one of these really cool walkie-talkie headphone devices. I felt like the VIP secret celebrity division of the CIA or something. But playing it ultra cool has never been my strong suit, especially when it really counts. I remember being a few blocks away and realizing that I had been gnawing on my nails the entire time. I begged the driver to stop for some Trident or something, and he offered me a piece of Hubba Bubba instead. Even better! I remember thinking.

So there I was, walking Mr. Bon Jovi to the car and once we got in, trying desperately not to make eye contact. (Which was sort of difficult since I ended up sitting directly across from him.) I decided to pretend like I was reading whatever it was on my clipboard and when I realized that he had actually said my name I looked up, nervously blew an extra large Hubba Bubba bubble, and before I could answer him, it popped/burst, whatever, all over my mouthpiece, which was connected to my earpiece, which was connected to my headpiece, which was connected to my hair . . . you get the picture. And what a freakin' mess!!!! I can't even go there right now—way too embarrassing! Anyway, I've moved on since then!

Now back to my story: It wasn't long before a few "perks" came my way, too. Concert tickets (along with backstage passes), movie premieres, seats to VH1 special programming, and of course, free music!!! Truly, these are the kinds of things a gal can get used to. Favors for favors, stuff like that!

My having a full-time-plus job was just what Sophie and I needed to maintain a solid friendship while she continued to date Fernando. I was running around the city, working my tail off, playing with my friends and picking up a few shifts at Le Figaro every now and then, more for old times' sake than for anything else. So our time together was more valuable and I think, too, I was becoming a much happier person. I felt good about myself and, boy, does that go a long way! I was up for things and conversations that I would have dismissed before. I think I became more tolerant of others as well. Others, yes, like Fernando, who before drove me nuts, now I just sort of disliked.

Things with my parents could not have been any better considering . . . well considering that I was not living at home, working in and around Times Square (which translated to a high-voltage danger zone to my mom), and of course, here's the big one—besides not being married—didn't even have a boyfriend! But they were proud of me. I knew that and my mother became increasingly interested in my day-to-day, which was a complete and total first!

I don't want to give the impression that I was on cloud nine, and that having a great job made me whole. Please, if it were only that easy for any of us! But, I will say, I was on my way. I knew that. Feeling like I had forever been broken, working, learning, experiencing, everything seemed to be healing old wounds. There's surely something to be said for a job well done. If you care about what you do anyway. I cared. I was passionate. I felt fortunate and the insecurities I had carried around with me for years, the things that Mark used to say to me . . . well, let's just say I was finally able to recognize, for myself, that he was dead wrong about me. (That 25 percent I mentioned earlier was now more like 8 percent.)

I will admit that things would have definitely been genius had Jon Bon Jovi scooped me up into his arms (once, of course, he got all the gum out of my hair) and I'd be yet another right hand that Zack had lost, having run off to be the full-time squeeze of one of New Jersey's finest! No dice in that department. So much so, in fact, that Patrick had been the one and only short-lived romance over the course of almost five months! That's right, my friends, twenty weeks without even a smooch!

But love, or what I thought was love, was waiting right around the corner 😮

Okay, so where was I? Oh yes, life was pretty decent. I found myself surrounded by so many different types of people, and although we each came from various cultures, backgrounds, etc., for the most part, we all shared the same enthusiasm for what we did. Many of us, more specifically, the younger set, the rookies really, hit it off, partied together, would do favors for one another. It was great. Zack was constantly on the move and I loved holding down the fort. As there was always so much for me to learn—as I said before, I was the greenest of the bunch—many of my contemporaries enjoyed teaching me a thing or two. For some it was an aspect of their position; for others, it was their individual passion for music, production, the arts, whatever it was that got them to VH1 in the first place.

I think it's because I was the eager beaver, and because I wasn't trying to outshine anyone, that people felt very comfortable letting me into their inner sanctums, both professionally and sometimes on a personal level, too. And I took every bit of it in. I felt almost like a voyeur. I watched, as certain people would move up the totem pole, and made mental notes when others would not. I was mesmerized by the powerful women of the company and how carefully they would use their femininity to get what they wanted; if it came down to it and if they had to, for that matter. I'd sit in for Zack on big meetings, taking notes and whatnot, all the while observing industry politics and all the crazy bullshit and competitiveness that goes along with it. The miserable, the jaded, they were pretty easy to figure out, but it was the stars of the group that interested me even more. What was it about their personality or their work ethic that made people light up when they walked into a room? How did they manage to get where they were? I was fascinated, sometimes more by my environment than what I was actually there to do. That was really my only wrinkle.

Sure, I won a songwriting contest and had fantasies about being a huge rock star (who hasn't, at least once, right?), but there were times when I'd question why I liked my job. (Not that it mattered but, of course, it's not like me to just sit back and let myself fully enjoy something without a tiny dose of self-involved analysis.) I mean, I had friends there who lived and died for music. After a hard day's work, they'd go to sessions, lounges, anywhere to listen to music. Sure, I tagged along some of the time, but for me it was more of a social thing, and after a while I got a bit sick of talking about a band, an album, and the sound.

That's what really freaked me out in the beginning: still feeling as though I didn't belong on some level. I was striving for perfection and those tiny wrinkles every now and again really pissed me off. But if I'm giving the impression that I wasn't having the time of my life, that's not my intention. I certainly was. But I was a tiny, tiny out-of-town fish in a very huge and insanely cool sea. And my job was really becoming my life. As I said earlier, there were no boyz to speak of at the time. When I did hang out, even with friends from back home or my family, for obvious reasons, everyone always wanted to chat about my work. And who could blame them? I had great stories, insane hook-ups, and whenever we wanted to get a reservation, or if someone special wanted to see whoever in concert, all I needed to do was pick up the phone, drop my boss's name, and, well, it was done! It was awesome and beyond clutch.

In any case, Carolyn, a big VIP in Zack's department, took a very big interest in my singlehood. She was, what, I think about thirty-six, a dragon lady when she wanted to be, but for the most part, she was very nice (especially if you didn't work for her, or so the stories go). She surely would have been Sophie's fashion icon. I rarely saw Carolyn in the same getup twice and she always looked like the slick ads I saw in magazines. Newly married, it was pretty obvious to me that, although she missed her wild days, she was very much in love. Her husband was a professional tennis player. They were nauseatingly perfect together, at least on the outside, in a Ken and Barbie kinda way. Very socially conscious, she was always on the run to one event or another. I was always comping her tickets to shows for an auction or something where she'd fuse her corporate connections with whatever it was that was important to her. (I really dug that.) Oh, and get this, Carolyn would always have a makeup artist and a hairdresser come to her office at six or so to get her all dolled up for wherever her calendar said she was going. I thought that was totally brilliant! Especially those few times that she'd have them mess around with me. ☺

Will was convinced she was doing it to get on Zack's radar, as if by befriending me, it would somehow register with him. I didn't much care either way actually. I looked up to her. She always kept her cool, she was good at what she did (special events publicity and production, by the way), and she had a mouth like a truck driver. It didn't fit her at all. I think that's what I found most amusing about her.

Anywho, she was obsessed with fixing me up; so much so that after a while it became a daily topic of conversation. She'd conduct meetings in the conference room just next to my cubicle. Usually the men outnumbered the women in her meetings (about five to one), so of course she'd give me the eye when a cutie walked in, as if to say "What about him?" I'd blush instead of signaling back, and believe me there were times when my body, each and every part of it, wanted to shout "YES!!!" But I was shy, a bit intimidated, and not exactly ready for another "relationship."

It was a few weeks later that Carolyn cornered me at the coffee machine and said, "That's it, Vivian, I've got THE man for you, and I won't accept no for an answer!" I was not about to argue with her, but used Zack's fresh coffee fetish as a temporary out. (She would have made an incredible lawyer.) Toward the end of the day, after a highly charged conversation with Sophie, who thought I was nuts not to at least inquire, I stopped by her office, sat down, and said, "Okay, you win. Tell me about him."

She stood up, closed her door, and lit up a cigarette. ("Wow, she's really into this!" I thought.) "How about you tell me about what you like in a guy, Vivian. At least this way it will be more fun for me!" Yeesh, I hadn't even thought about it myself. "Give me a few seconds, Carolyn. Your intensity is freaking me out." Her phone rang and I thought, "Yes! I'm saved, ta-ta!" But it wasn't that easy. She let her voice mail pick it up. Shit!

"Okay, Carolyn, here ya go: He's got to be taller than me. He has to be funny, caring, and kindhearted. Charming, but not arrogant. Driven, but not solely for money. Athletic, but not obsessed with sports. Hmmmmm, he's got to dig music, movies—oh, and he's got to love dogs!"

"That's it?" she said sarcastically.

"Pretty much," I said. (Figuring that surely no one could ever measure up!)

"I knew it. I knew it! He's perfect for you, Viv. And I already told him about you!"

"What?" I shrieked nervously. "Then you've got to tell me about him! It's only fair!" I said as my anxiousness took a turn for the better.

"Well, okay, he's certainly taller than you. He's very, very handsome. He's thirty, I think, and from what my husband tells me, is looking for a great girl. He was quite the ladies' man, but between family pressure and boredom he wants to settle down."

"Please, Carolyn," I interrupted, "I'm not exactly searching for a husband . . ."

"I know that!" she said. "But an amazing boyfriend wouldn't be so bad, would it? And besides, I owe his family."

"Come again?" I said.

"Sorry, what I mean is that they played a large part in getting me together with Stephen [her husband], so why not return the favor?"

"Not so fast, Carolyn. Tell me more."

"All right, all right. My God. He plays football and basketball with Stephen, so I guess he's athletic. He certainly looks like he is [she winked]. He's always talking music with me, so that little criteria of yours is covered, but I can't be sure about your movie thing."

"Well that's okay. I could live with that," I said.

"He's definitely charming and he's got a great job. I think he's in investment banking or maybe he's an attorney, I don't know. But get this, Vivian—he's obsessed with his dog!!! He carries around his picture just like you do with Benedict."

"It's Omelet." I laughed.

"Whatever," she said. "He'd like to meet you for dinner on Friday night. I gave him your work number, so he'll probably call you tomorrow. I told him to give me the day to talk with you!"

"Oh my God, Carolyn!!! You didn't?!"

"Come on, Vivian, it's going to be fantastic. He's as on top of his game as you are [huh???], and I think you'll give him a good run for his money." I started feeling like I was going on this date for her enjoyment more than for mine, but whatever.

"Go on," I said.

"He comes from a prominent family. For all the 'down to earth-ness' that he tries to play off, there's an eensy bit of pretty boy in him. That's why I think he'll like you. I don't think you're the type of woman to put up with his shit. And besides, you're beautiful, intelligent, and have a great future in front of you, which I can't figure out if you realize or not, but in any case, you'll blow him away! I'm sure of it."

"Well, thanks, Carolyn. Not for this matchmaking stuff, but for the compliments. That means a lot to me coming from you."

"Oh please, Vivian. Someday, I'm pretty sure, we'll all be working for you!"

(Nothing feels better than a compliment from someone you respect. I walked out of her office feeling wonderful.) At least until she said, "Vivian, worst-case scenario—it's only one date, right?"

(Yeah) "Right."

I ran back to her office . . . "How about his name, Carolyn!"

"Silly me," she said. "It's John." And with that she grabbed her Hermès Kelly bag, her dry cleaning, and left. "See you on Thursday. Stephen and I are off to St. Barts!!! Have fun. E-mail me!!!"

😮

Friday was only two days away. What the devil did I just agree to?!?!

Thursday afternoon, Sophie dropped off an envelope—she had problems getting upstairs. Security was always maddening and if you were not at your phone to approve your guest, they were turned away. In any case, when I opened it, it was a gift certificate for a full day of pampering. A gift from Fernando or something that she thought I would "enjoy." I mean, she could have said "needed," but I think she was trying to be polite! She even went so far as to get me the appointment for five P.M., which was only an hour or so away. With Zack out of town, I decided to get crazy and skip out early. I was so paranoid of letting Zack down, the thought of leaving a few hours early for the first time since I started felt wrong. But Will told me that I was being ridiculous and offered to cover for me should anyone notice I was gone. So off I went. 😮

I think I was the only gal without a Prada bag or a French manicure when I arrived at the spa. The lounge area was packed with impatient ladies, all on cell phones or combing through the pages of *Vogue*. They all seemed to know one another and I was the odd gal out for sure. When I was given my itinerary, I almost passed out. Over the next three hours, I was scheduled for a facial, a massage, and full body wax.

Now wait a second, how hairless did I really have to be for a blind date?! I mean honestly, how easy did Sophie really think I was, or maybe, how easy was my little Sophia? And a full body wax?? I was an upper lip kind of customer. No worries, I thought, I'll just explain to whomever that all other body parts should be left as is!

After a little bit my name was called and a semi-friendly older lady whose English had to be a third language, escorted me inside. I was told to disrobe (completely), given a key, flip-flops, and a robe to change into. In a matter of minutes, a "Gertrude" was going to come and get me. Well, okay . . .

Gertrude arrived and before I knew it we were standing in a room filled with machines that looked more like a dentist's office than any "wellness" center.

She began by telling me that the wax and facial would come before the massage and that I needed to disrobe, remove my jewelry, and lie down on the table. She'd be back in a minute. I felt a wee bit ridiculous, lying there naked (and it was a little drafty by the way) in a room that seemed oddly cramped with hardware. Where were the candles, the music? Doubtful these machines had been "feng shui-ed." Maybe they put me in a storage closet or something? "Help!" I shouted in my mind as I froze my nipples off. Just as I was about to walk out (in my robe of course) Gertrude was back. She sensed my nervousness (I wonder how), and asked if it was my first time at their spa. "Yes," I revealed.

"Usually my customers relax when I turn down the lights, turn up the heat (thank God), play some nice music, and light a few candles, and they really seem to revel in our customer base."

"How so?" I asked.

"What, you did not read any of the materials at the front desk?"

"No," I answered, "I was too busy reviewing my services."

"Okay, well, spread your legs please, Gwyneth Paltrow, Madonna, breathe please, Sarah Jessica Parker are all . . ."

"FUCK!!!!!!!!" I screamed.

"Ha, ha," she laughed. "It only hurts the first few times." I looked down, nearly crippled with pain and most likely permanently cross-eyed and saw that she had just removed the majority of the pubic hair on the right side of my body!

"What are you doing?" I cried.

"This is what is called a Brazilian bikini wax. You will love it once I'm finished."

"Finished? What could possibly be left?" I mumbled, nearly ready to faint.

"Just leave it to me, Ms. Vivian. You'll be all right."

What followed should be banned in the United States. Besides the pain, which is just incredible and fully indescribable, how about getting on all fours for a stranger who looks like your grandmother, only for her to slide wet hot wax in places that have gone untouched your entire life by anything else but toilet paper!!!!

What kind of date did Sophie think I was going on for God's sake???

She rubbed oil all over "my areas" and then baby powder and left me alone for a few seconds to relax before we went any further. If I had not seriously been in shock, I would have bolted, leaving anything I came in with behind. Before I knew it, she was back. "Now your face, let me take a look." She shined this crazy interrogation-like light in my eyes that nearly blinded me. And then made no bones about telling me all about my blackheads, clogged pores, dry patches, and hair that needed to be removed from my upper lip, eyebrows, and chin.

"My chin?" I peeped. (I couldn't yell anymore—I had almost lost my voice while in Brazil!)

"Yes, yes—have you ever had a facial?" she asked.

"No," I said.

"Well, a young lady like you should really take better care of herself. You have lovely eyes, but your eyebrows are too thick and they need shape. Surely your boyfriend does not want to kiss a hairy lip and the hairs on your chin; they are visible in the natural sunlight, you know."

"How about we just get on with it? And you did say Madonna comes here, right?"

"Yes, I have given her a facial three times. Very good skin."

Oh good.

The rest of the waxing was a cinch, compared to, well, you know. She urged me to do my underarms and legs but that's where I put my foot down.

The facial was nice—or, as I like to say, it was disguised. After a pleasurable massage of my skin and a few masks and crèmes, Gertrude was suddenly pinching and squeezing my nose to the point where I thought it was going to fall off if not be permanently disfigured. She said that this was a necessary part of the process, "especially in my case" (thanks, Gerty!), and as she poked and prodded away I finally realized why all the ladies in the front looked miserable. Chicks who are into this shit have got to be masochists!

She told me that it was a pleasure serving me (I could tell by the roll of her eyes that she was being sarcastic) and then said that Mick would be with me momentarily for my massage.

Ahhhhhhhhhhhhh. I truly thought that "stage three" would never come!!!

Okay, the door opens and there in plain sight was a vision in white. Mick was a strapping young lad who had to double as a stripper or a model by night. He was just divine! Bleached-out blond hair, huge blue eyes, and the first goatee that actually seemed to fit a guy. (Brad Pitt being the exception!) His flat-front white pants had to have been two sizes too tight and his white shirt showed off a bod like no other! (So did the pants now that I think about it!) I was ready for my massage let me tell you!!!

He opened the door and kindly moved his arm upward and out, as if we were about to ballroom dance or something. Once he cocked his head to the right and raised his eyebrows I got it. I was supposed to get up and follow him to a different place. (And believe you me, I would have followed him anywhere!)

Now this was what I had imagined. The room was navy, the light was dimmed, two candles were lit on opposite sides of the table, and the music was as soothing as was possible. I tried as best I could not to smile but I just couldn't help myself. Let me be putty in his hands!!!

"All right, Viv, I'm Mick and I'll be your masseur this afternoon. Why don't you lay that little keppie of yourz down and I'll be back in a jiff."

BUZZ KILL. Studdly muffin Mick was a puff!!! There went my fantasy. Figures! But he did give me a great massage. I conked out about ten minutes in.

Afterward I went back to the locker room to change. I glanced in the mirror real quick and I have to say, I did look pretty good. The arch in my eyebrows gave me this mischievously chic domineering look and my skin, although still a bit red, seemed to glow. Sweet!

After I had checked out, tipped the torturer and Mick (who I just knew Will would love!), I heard someone call my name.

"Vivian? Vivian, is that you?" I turned and saw Patti, a bigwig at RCA who worked on lots of projects with Zack.

"Hi!" I said.

"Is this place heaven or what?"

"Heaven, I'm not too sure about that. I just had a bikini wax," I said flatly. She started cracking up.

"Yes," she said. "They sting like a bitch, but I've got to tell ya, it drives the men wild."

"Really?" I blushed.

"Sure. Listen, you've got to meet Samantha, she heads up A&R. We're addicted to this place. Did you have a massage?"

"Yes, I did. With Mick."

"To die for, right??" she said.

"Yes!" I said and we both started laughing. I met Samantha who introduced me to Fiona and before I knew it, I was having cocktails with a handful of the who's who in the music business.

Whoever thought that a torture chamber would make for great networking?? This was genius, and besides knowing that Zack would be all over me for socializing with them, these girls were fun! We dished, complained, swapped dating dramas, and I filled them in on what I was doing that next night. I got great advice (about to open my agenda and jot it down in fact, but stopped myself. I was playing it cool!!!!). At about eleven P.M., each of us fully buzzed, we decided to jet. One of them had expensed the evening so we didn't drop a dime!

Too exhausted and a wee bit intoxicated, there wasn't enough time to fret about Friday night. I thanked Sophie for her "gift" when I got home, begged her to take Omelet out, and crashed.

When my alarm went off at 7:30 the next morning, I had more than enough time to freak out. I phoned into my voice mail at work to see if I had missed anything the evening before. Out of five messages, the first four were harmless. That was a relief. Couldn't be executive assistant of the century by screwing up something for Zack. But the fifth and final message, that was something else entirely:

"Hey, Vivian, this is John. I'm a friend of Carolyn's and your date for tomorrow night [short laugh]. Sorry that we were unable to talk today. I'll try you tomorrow, but if we miss each other, let's plan on meeting at nine for drinks at Le Cirque. I'll be at the bar. Looking forward to meeting you. All right, take care." CLICK.

Not a nervous bone in his whole damn body. Oh God!!!

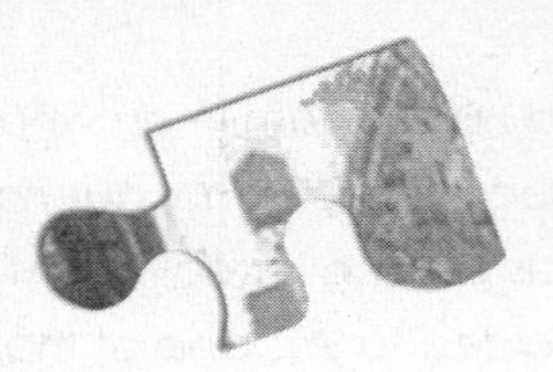

Friday at the office felt more like a stint watching paint dry. Never in my life had a day taken that long and never had I experienced an overwhelming sense of dread like I had that afternoon. I didn't want to go on a blind date. It wasn't like I was so opposed to meeting someone new. Not at all. But all the minutiae that goes along with a blind date—first impressions, having a mutual friend that nine times out of ten one usually ends up blaming for a match made in hell, then expecting the truth from that fixer—with all the "what did he say"s to the "why hasn't he called"s—it's just so uncomfortable. Kind of like a wool turtleneck sweater that rubs the skin on your neck the wrong way. Honestly, if I had had the freakin' guy's telephone number, I would have probably called and canceled. I decided that if he did indeed call sometime that afternoon, I would just make up something. This just wasn't for me. Better we meet at an event or cocktail party. Surely Carolyn could arrange something like that?

Well, anyway, wouldn't you know it: John never called and by day's end, my nails were bit down to my cuticles! No sweat, I'll just wear gloves the whole time. Such a mess!

Thank goodness it was just drinks. I devised a sure-weather "gotta go" plan. I'd arrive a little late, order one (strong) cocktail, leave my cell phone on, and have Sophie call me. (Truly original, I know!) But then I remembered: Sophie and Fernando were already gone for the weekend, for the last of a series of romantic ski retreats they had been taking together. (Thank God it wasn't a very white winter. They were closing up the house early this season—boo hoo.)

I decided to stop sweating, freaking out, and thinking myself into oblivion. Surely I could semi-manipulate Will into "working" a bit late with me that night. If I mentioned Mick and the ladies from RCA, inquiring minds would want to know, right? Then, I could maybe sort of mention that I was just a teeny-weeny bit nervous and could use just a few last-minute modern-day dating tips.

Sure enough, Will was all over my recommendation that he get a massage pronto by Mick and wanted the full-on scoop on my new high-falutin friends. I dished and dished and dished until he stopped me dead in my tracks. "Wait a second, Ms. Thing. You're nervous for tonight aren't you?" he teased.

My jig was up. "Not really. Well . . . okay so, like you wouldn't be? I just want to come off cool and collected. I plan on leaving early. That is after I get there late. It's the part in the middle I'm not sure about. What should I do? What do I say?"

"Relax. Number one . . . God it's too bad you don't smoke. That would surely turn him off."

"But I don't," I said. "So . . ."

"And it's not like you made any obvious effort when you got dressed this morning. What, did Sophie sleep out?"

"Will!!!! C'mon I'm serious!!!"

"What?! I'm just trying to say that that's a good thing! You are totally working this 'no big deal' vibe. That might take him by surprise if he's got any kind of style."

"WHAT?!"

"Vivian. Take a Valium for Christ's sake. Listen to me. I'm going to have to spell this out for you. You look great. You look sexy in an effortless kind of way. It's like you know you're a beauty so why make the effort, ya know?"

"Really?" I smiled.

"Yes. Really. And I'm sure this guy gets a lot of girls who go all out, and because you don't, he'll probably find that interesting."

Will was certainly calming me down, and in a strange way enlightening me in the ways of a man's head space. But because Will was gay, I just had to ask, "Will, honey, that may be the way you and your friends would think, but consider the testosterone levels here, okay? Doubtful that a straight guy would share the same perspective."

"Honestly, Vivian, if you weren't from Pennsylvania . . ."

"What?"

"Yes!!! Straight guys are all about the physical—trust me!"

"Okay," I said.

" 'Okay' is not going to cut it, girlfriend! You've got to believe it! You've got to own it!" he went on.

"Settle down, Mary—I've gotcha!"

"No, seriously. You drive men crazy."

"Spare me, Will. I appreciate it and all . . ."

"God, you are such a head case. And that's the other thing—the fact that you don't play games, that you don't pick up on signals—it makes you even sexier to them! What time do you have to meet him anyway?" he asked. I looked at my watch.

"Oh, God—in twenty minutes."

"Grab your coat, lose the messenger bag . . ."

"What?"

"Just leave it here, trust me. Let me see your wallet." I showed it to him. "That will do. Carry it as a clutch. I'll walk you out."

I followed him out and begged him to keep talking. He felt like a big sister. Scary, but true.

"You have to walk in confidently. You're the hot young blood of this company."

"I am?"

"You are tonight, honey." I took a deep breath. "You walk in and head straight for the bar. Don't look around, don't fidget, and strike up a conversation with another guy. Doesn't really matter who—the bartender even. Just talk. Distract yourself. Never look at the door. For all you know he could have been sitting there the whole time. He'll watch you and notice how calm and collected you are. He'll be intimidated even, if you play it right. He'll see that you're beautiful, friendly, and confident and then he'll have no choice but to approach you and that's what you want."

"I do?" I asked.

"Yup," he said.

Will's cell phone rang and I said, "Answer that now and I'll kill you."

"Easy!!!" He laughed.

"Okay, focus, Will! So he comes up to me. Then . . ."

"Then, you take a deep breath, slowly put your hands through your hair and turn around."

I couldn't help but laugh. "Sorry," I said, trying to keep my composure. This whole thing was just way too funny.

"Are you finished?"

"Yes, yes—go ahead."

"Then look him straight in the eye and before he can say anything, you say, 'You must be John.' You take the control. You have the power. Give him a kiss on the cheek and invite him to sit down. He'll be Jell-O in your hands."

"How so?" I asked.

"You've just beat him at his own game. That's how. You are the confident one. You are the sweet one. You took the burden that he can't even admit he has off his shoulders. Don't get drunk. Don't order just a salad . . ."

"But we're only having drinks."

"Please, sister," he said. "You get this right and, believe me, you'll be having much more than just dinner tonight. I have to go. Eye contact is huge, Vivian!!! Smile a lot and oh, I've been meaning to tell you—the eyebrows . . ."

"Yeah?"

"Fierce!" He gave me a huge hug and ran off. I started to giggle. For a moment, I was actually excited about what was to come in the next few minutes.

I hailed a taxi and, well, should have known better. Just because Le Cirque was just across town, literally about six avenues, that didn't equate to a hop, skip, and a jump cab ride. I had about twenty minutes to maintain the energy that Will had bestowed, review his advice, word by word, and absorb it. I could acknowledge that I was different from most women. Not just on the inside but on the outside, too. For, at that point, I never really thought too long or too hard about my appearance. That's sort of what happens when you've been in a relationship where effort on the outside psychotically translated into deviant behavior to your boyfriend. Makeup, flashy, fun clothes were a no-no, to put it mildly. (Crazy but true.) Dressing down had become a uniform of sorts for me. And it's not like I took offense to Will's remarks, but I did feel, and evidently I was mistaken, that I was dressing up for work. When I looked myself over and gazed at my current outfit of choice I realized why Will had said what he said. I was wearing a white cotton Calvin T-shirt (one size too small), black flat-front trousers, kicks, and a black car coat. I certainly wasn't dolled up and for those who didn't know me, and by the looks of my wind-blown wavy hair, you'd think I had slept in all day. Not having my bag with me meant no makeup either. Lip gloss was back at the office—SHIT—so was my phone! Wonderful!

Nervously, I tied my hair back in a knot, pinched my cheeks hoping they'd turn red, and rolled down my window. Truthfully, I had to air out. It was beginning to feel like a sauna in there. When we finally arrived, I paid the driver, hopped out of the cab, and looked just ahead of me.

Underdressed was not even the word. Too late for happy hour and just in time for the dinner crowd, I looked more like a homeless person than a patron, and I was about to totally flip out. I stood there for a few seconds and had one of my quick conversations with myself.

I focused on what Will had said, remembered how I felt when Carolyn and I had our little chat, and then I thought about Patrick. I thought about the way he'd look at me. The way he touched me and the way he would look when I touched him. If I was too fucked up to see what others could see in me, embrace the things that each had said that made me feel special and confident and complimented, then I'd better just pretend that I did. Believing it, even for the moment, would at least get me through the front door. And so would a little skin quite frankly. I unbuttoned my coat, pulled down my pants—to my waist of course! They were riding a bit high and the whole low-rise waist thing was supposedly in from what Sophie would say. So, basically, my belly button was exposed. It was probably the only fashion statement (although lame) that I had any chance of making. And besides, my period had ended a few days ago, so as far as my cycle was concerned, my belly was at its monthly low.

Whatever—I went with it!

When I got in, I did just as Will had said. I went straight to the bar. Unfortunately in this case, the maître d' didn't appreciate that I fully ignored her, which I didn't even realize I had done. Until that is, she pinched at the arm of my coat to get my attention.

"Excuse me," she sneered. "Do you have a reservation?"

"No actually, I don't. I'm meeting someone at the bar."

"Well then, don't let me stop you," she said. Followed by an insanely fake smile.

Great. So, if John was here, he just saw me get manhandled by the staff. Genius.

The closer I got to the bar, the easier it was to see that there were only a few empty seats, surrounded mostly by women, so it looked like, much to my dismay, that I was the first to arrive.

I sat down, ordered an Amstel Light, threw my coat over my chair, and made every effort to look straight ahead. After a few minutes, I heard a man say, "Excuse me." Bingo—I thought.

I went to brush my hair off my face when I realized it was up, then turned around as if it was my big phony photo shoot moment and said, "Hi, I'm Vivian" with a big cheeky grin. When I gestured to shake his hand, he said awkwardly, "Um, yeah, well, I'm sorry, I think I left my coat check ticket right over here."

"Oh, wow, sorry." I turned around, feeling like a complete idiot, and noticed the powder blue piece of paper just under my cocktail napkin and handed it back to him, sans the eye contact.

Did I mention he was probably seventy-five years old?

I took another look at my watch. John was now almost forty-five minutes late. I finished my beer rather quickly, ordered another, let my hair down and remember placing both elbows on the bar, which made for the ideal handheld headrest while I awaited my second drink, preparing for the old "he stood me up" speech I'd have to tell all my friends the next day.

A few minutes later, with my second beer nearly completely consumed, I heard another "Excuse me" but chose to ignore it. I was pretty comfortable just as I was, and I was pretty sure there were no stray coat check tickets in my vicinity.

"Vivian. Vivian Livingston?"

No way! And no time to redeem any sense of manufactured cool! I was slouched over, sweating my ass off, with beer breath, and as far as body language went, you'd have thought I'd just lost my job or something.

I turned around, with my hair in my face, and this time had no choice but to put my hands through it and brush it away. I mean, I could barely see the chap.

"John, right?" I laughed.

"Yes, I'm so sorry. Traffic was a bitch and I don't have your mobile number."

"Well, it's nice to meet you."

"You too. You've got to promise me you won't tell Carolyn that I was late—she'd kill me!"

"No worries," I said. "Your secret's safe with me."

Ya know how sometimes we compare people, well, men really, to animals? Like, if he cheats on our friends he's a snake, or if he's harmless and adorable then he's a puppy dog? Well, John was a wolf. Beautiful, mysterious, and above all else, powerful. As nervous as I was, as annoyed as I was after forty-five long lonely minutes, well, his eyes and his smile made me relax when I probably never should have. In just those first thirty seconds, I was at ease. I was myself. The whole thing was very odd. His presence brought my blood pressure down to a normal pace. Yes, of course, the two beers must have helped, but there was something about him, something that even today, I've never seen or felt with another man; it was hypnotic. His energy was invigorating, and oddly enough, he brought out the wolf in me.

He sat beside me, took off his coat, and joked that the two of us were breaking the restaurant's dress code. He was wearing jeans, brown shoe boots, and a white T-shirt with a long-sleeve preppy navy pullover. If he were ten years younger, he would have looked like a college student. He ordered a beer, I ordered my third, and we just started talking. We started laughing. And we started flirting. Who was more nervous, who went on more blind dates, who was the heartbreaker, who would kiss who first! 😮 He asked if I was hungry. Truth was I was starving, and we had my friend, the maître d', get us a quiet table off in the corner.

We ordered rather quickly as the kitchen was due to close, and of course, when the food came, the waiter gave him my steak au poivre and me his tuna tartare. (That always happens to me!) We talked a bit about work, a bit about Carolyn, and for the majority of the dinner all about our dogs. We came to realize that we were neighbors, living only blocks apart, and he asked if I wanted to take the dogs for a walk, maybe to the basketball court nearby. I was all for it.

"So, I see you got all dressed up for me, Vivian . . . ," he said as we rode home.

"Yes, I did. I was really nervous about meeting you and must have changed about ten times. I was going for something sophisticated and sexy. How'd I do?"

"You did great." He smiled.

"Yeah, that's what I thought you'd say." I was oozing with sarcasm and confidence. It was like *Invasion of the Body Snatchers, Part 2*.

We exited the cab and I chose to wait downstairs with the doormen as he went up to get his pup, "Domino." It was weird though. Looking back, it was the only awkward part of the date. I felt like the two guys who were working had somehow violated my space. They didn't really look my way and seemed to revel in the exploits of their tenant. It was as if I was the only one in that quiet lobby who wasn't in on the joke, if that even makes any sense. I sat there admiring his building. Very upscale—the entryway was larger than my parents' house. The marble floors, the great decor, and the mirrored walls. It was lovely. And I was thankful for every detail just to not have to be distracted, or rather affected, by the curious energy of those two guys that was flowing my way.

John came down a few minutes later, now sporting a Yankee baseball cap and sneakers, and of course, with "Dom," a great big black Lab who was also dying to pee and nearly ran me over. The two of them were pretty funny together. You could tell he loved his dog and you could also tell that Dom, whether intentionally or not, was just as much of an accessory for John as Sophie's Fendi bag was for her. We walked over to my place, which was far less fabulous I should add, and I ran upstairs to get Omelet. I, too, freshened up. Tossed the trousers for cargos, grabbed Sophie's treasured black pashmina scarf (she must have left it behind!), and a rubber band for my hair. I prepped Omelet for what was to come and opened the front door with a smile.

We walked a few blocks, not really talking about anything of importance. Both of us were sneaking glances at the other, that was obvious, and I couldn't have been any more comfortable with him if I tried. Just as we were about to pass a bodega he asked if he should pick up a six-pack. "Sure," I said. "Oh, and something to nosh on, too!!! Please."

Omelet chose to poop on that very corner so I was busy being a good citizen while John was doing his thing. Luckily Omelet and I were both done doing our prospective business before the two of them came out. He bought a bag of Doritos and a box of SnackWell's chocolate chip cookies, not knowing which I'd prefer, and a six-pack.

"Both," I said.

With our dogs on either side, John and I were left in the middle, each with a free hand. As a group of rowdy guys passed by we were forced to squish together, and before I knew it, we were hand in hand.

Whether it's friendships, romances, neighborhoods, school, vacations, work, it's strange how you can look back and realize how important a person or an environment was in the evolution of "you," ya know? It doesn't much matter about the amount of time, but more, the emotional investment you made in a person or a place.

I think about school, right, and I think about those years and as real as it seems to me in my memory, it's also that foreign a place to me at the same time. I know I lived there. I had an apartment, a bunch of semi-irrelevant jobs, a few hangouts, and even more safe havens (a park, a corner cushioned area in the library, a bookstore, whatever) but I was simply a passerby in the scheme of things. People came before me and after me, and I became as much of a memory to that environment as it had become to me.

Same with relationships. We tell them all (okay some) our secrets, they meet our parents, sleep in our beds, but it's only that one guy (hopefully) that we stay with forever. But what about all those "meaningful moments" (beyond insatiable sex!), those twenty-minute kisses, those yummy "I can't get enough of you" hugs, when for that little while you both think the other is the best thing since sliced bread?

And the backdrop of that event. The beach, his bedroom, a basketball court, the dance floor, a restaurant, your car. Wherever, really. We covet those memories, those places, but more often than not, we may never return to any of them again.

"Haphazard intimacy," maybe that's what I should call it. It's intimate, therefore it's meaningful. It becomes part of you. But then you move forward. What happens then? And later you remember. You hear a song, you pay a visit, or you meet up again, later, down the road.

This is difficult to articulate, but as I write and write, I can't help but feel the very emotions I did when an event was taking place. It's like I'm right there again and I'm not on any kind of hallucinogenic. (I promise!) Going down memory lane is a trip, I tell you!

I've been writing this book for months now, and I swear, I feel like I'm living my life over again, but all the characters and sets have disappeared.

Perfect example, I can't even remember the last time I paid a visit to Le Figaro. I know that all my friends have since moved on, but when I think about that restaurant and all that it meant to me, all that it did for my self-confidence and the path it eventually paved for me, it's bizarre that I am so physically and emotionally removed from it. Do we have some storage space in our souls for those places and people?

Okay, enough. It's just that I'm remembering that evening and the moment John and I held hands and the fuckin' glee that radiated through my body, but it's gone now. Hell, it was gone . . . no wait, it's too good of a story to blow right here. I'll shut up and type on. But seriously, you guys think back to a moment that was truly over the top for you (good or bad). Go ahead, put this book down even, and pick it back up after you feel the way I do.

So, isn't it really strange?

Anywho, moving on . . .

John and I were hand in hand. I wasn't thinking, "Oh gee, I hope we become boyfriend and girlfriend." Really, I wasn't. I was just thrilled to bits to feel so alive. I felt like every step we took toward wherever it was we were going was one step further I was walking away from "that girl" I didn't much like and couldn't respect. That girl who was with Mark for all those years; someone who got lost under a pile of dread and saw not a single way out.

I was finally feeling like a girl who had something to offer. I felt like I was walking into my own, if that makes any sense. (And I know that a guy you've met for a few hours doesn't do that to or for you, you do that for yourself . . . but he wasn't hurting the situation either!)

So yeah, I was happy. I tried not to look his way. The moment was mine. Kind of like a Barry Manilow ("When will our eyes meet, when can I touch you," blah, blah, blah) love song mixed with a little Salt-n-Pepa/Spice Girl estrogen if you know what I mean. Sorta sad but still triumphant. (Look, I told you all early on that I was a drama queen—I wasn't lying! I've got a theme song for everything!)

Right, so we land at these basketball courts near NYU. We park it and make a little midnight picnic. Doritos, SnackWell's cookies, and beer—

charming. It was nice and quiet and fairly well-lit, actually. To the sounds of the city (moving cars, long-distance debauchery, and a few intermittent sirens) we began to get a bit more personal. We talked about past relationships. We were both curious. If Carolyn thought we were each so fabulous, then why, really, were we each so single? I gave my stock answer: my career (what a load of crap!). And he probably gave me his: just hadn't met the right girl.

We both talked about other fix-ups that had gone awry and mutually confessed that this was, hee hee hee, definitely not one of them. (I sensed he had a larger number under his belt than me.) We talked about our families and their shared "concern" for what seemed like our all too permanent single status and the fact that we both had older siblings who had already gotten hitched, which never made any of it any easier. He seemed generally eager to talk about the trials and tribulations of his love life, which, through no fault of his own, exaggerated my desire even more to keep my private life private.

Now that I think about it, John had a lot to say for himself—misunderstood, pressured, busy, yada, yada, yada. I was definitely more of a listener that evening, which I think is still a trait I wear today. If a guy wants to talk, let him. Much easier to figure him out if he's giving you a wealth of information. Funny, most guys don't get that we women are calculating every word, eager to distinguish if we've got a player, commitment-phobe, mamma's boy, whatever, on our hands.

Anywho, I just thought he was confident, and I liked that. He was older, so back then, I thought, he had to be wiser. More time to travel through the city's social circuit, establish a reputation, and of course, figure life out. (I was young and had a lot to learn.)

He was eager to hear how I came to the city and when I told him, he thought it was "cute." He was seemingly impressed by the fact that I worked at VH1 and joked that I could hook him up with Eric Clapton tickets when he came to town. But when I talked about some of the events I coproduced, the company-sponsored tours I was working on, that I kept long hours, and was anxious about so and so, he seemed a tad condescending. As though I couldn't possibly work as hard as he did and that I perhaps didn't have a clue as to what real pressure was. When he sensed that I was a bit put off by his remarks, he parlayed them into a much more sarcastic, even flirtatious tone. (Very smart, that one.)

Before I realized it, we had slowly moved from sitting Indian style, facing one another, to a more relaxed and slightly connected scenario. Still facing each other, we were now leaning back on the palms of our hands (my wrists were beginning to get sore) with our legs stretched out, and playing footsie (how cute!). He was finishing his third beer as I was starting my second. The pups were lying down next to each other, respectfully, and about an hour had gone by.

John was big into recreational sports and was hopelessly devoted to his gym. He told me of his ritual seven A.M. workouts. "My salary doesn't make room for a gym," I said. I was a jogger with no real schedule to speak of, but come spring, I always lurked around for a co-ed pick-up game or two. He loved that I played sports and was sure he could "kick my ass" in, well, anything. I told him to settle down, that he was getting a bit too excited and "showing his cards." (Well, he was! There was not a doubt in my mind that there would be a good-night kiss and eventually a phone call however many days later requesting my company for date numero dos.) Taken aback, he asked what I meant by that exactly, so I basically repeated all of the above. (I was lit. All right. I admit it. And unfortunately, us rookies can get a bit frisky, real quick!)

"You think so, do ya?" He smiled.

"Yeah, I do."

"I bet you're wrong," he replied confidently.

"Well that wouldn't be any fun!" I laughed.

"Whadaya mean?" he asked.

"You purposely not calling me or not smooching me good night, just to prove a point. That would be lame. Especially 'cause we both know you'd want to!"

"Reeeeallly?" He laughed.

"Uh-huh!" I nodded.

I opened the bag of Doritos and gave Omelet a few. I needed to change the topic. I was getting a bit too cocky for my own good. I didn't want to force him into not kissing me or asking me out again. He seemed the type who would revel in a game as cruel and annoying as that. He was all about power and having the upper hand. Better I play into that a bit than set myself up for a month of cruel torture! 'Cause the truth was, I liked him. This whole thing needed to be construed as me flirting—not as a challenge!

But because I wasn't about to make the first move, or come across as easy, I had successfully created somewhat of a dilemma.

John came through and flirted right back. "Well, Vivian, it was you who held my hand first." Ha-ha-ha, he laughed!

"WHAT? You are joking, right?" I came back.

"Now, now, Vivian. If anyone showed their cards here, ya cutie, it was you!"

Yup. He just said, "ya cutie!" I was putty. (Not Silly Putty, more like Sadly Putty. Dah dah dah dum. ☺) He was reading my every move, every expression, and every gesture. Better that I bluff ASAP!!! For me, that meant putting an end to all the eye contact that was going on. I'd surely be exposed if this went on any longer. So I stretched out a bit, laid my head on his lap, and turned my body away from his. God knows what he would have thought if I had chosen to face the other way. Could you imagine? (Dream on!)

We had formed the letter "T." So all he had to work with was my profile. Let him think that I liked him back, I was cool with that, and it was just enough physical contact to be considered sweet, not seductive. That was what I was going for. As I began to tell him that he was delirious if he thought I grabbed his hand, Omelet jumped on top of me and began giving me kisses. Like most men, he only wanted something from me, and in this case it was more Doritos. John helped me out and fed him a few, at the same time urging me to "go on."

"Okay," I said, "I swear to you, John, I did not grab your hand first. But if you want that to be the official scenario, that's just fine, I won't tell anyone."

"You and I both know the truth, Vivian," he said.

"That's right," I teased. "We do." (I swear, you guys, he made the first move!)

Anyway, it was getting late, and believe me, as good as I felt, I wasn't about to become just another girl to fall for the likes of him right away. Sure, I fell just a few minutes after we met, but he didn't have to know that. Or maybe better put, I didn't have to show him that!

We got up, brushed off, threw out the trash, grabbed our pups, and began to walk back. I decided to just grab his hand and get it over with. And with that, he kissed my forehead and gave me a really nice and sort of long hug. "Don't look up! Don't look up!" is all I kept telling myself. We would have surely smooched and my mind wasn't as ready as my body just yet.

We carried on, stopped so Domino could relieve himself, and joked about the two seemingly different tales we'd each eventually relay back to Carolyn. There was a cute couple waiting for a taxi about a block from my apartment, friends of John's I realized, as they waved hello and I had not a clue as to who they might be. As we neared them he asked if it was okay that he introduced me as his girlfriend. "You're a riot," I said.

The two looked amused as we approached still hand in hand, and he quickly introduced me as "Vivian." The guy was very polite but the chick made no bones about her need to assess the situation, glaring at me and sarcastically pecking John on either cheek. They bullshitted for a few minutes and off we went.

"They'll be calling tomorrow," he joked.

"Lucky for me I didn't run into anyone. What kind of excuse would I come up with?" And with that, we were standing in front of my apartment and Omelet was all too happy to be home. It was a challenge for me to even face John at that point. Omelet was pulling me toward my door and I was hardly able to keep my balance.

"What's he trying to tell you?" John laughed.

"I don't know." I smiled back. There was this great "would we kiss?" tension between us. He stared right into my eyes and I couldn't help but stare back. "So, thanks for tonight," I said.

"You're very welcome," he replied, still staring into my eyes.

"I had fun," I said.

"So did I," he said.

"Well, you have my number, right?" I said.

"Yup," he said.

"So, you'll call me?" I said.

"Maybe," he said.

I smiled one last time, slightly sarcastically, and quickly said good night. I thought it best to just walk away. I didn't want to force anything and I didn't want to stand on my street for a "kiss-off." So I turned and walked to my door. I took out my key, placed it in the hole, turned my doorknob, and placed one foot inside. I just had to turn around. Had he left? Did he follow me? Was he still standing there? I had to know. And as I looked, there he was. Just as I left him, looking at me. His smile was kind. I smiled back and went inside.

Ahhhhhhh, I was "in like"!

I ran into Sophie's bedroom. I just couldn't wait to talk all about my night! But, much to my dismay, I remembered Sophie was gone for the weekend and I was on my own. So . . . I phoned my mom. Strange thing was, I almost never talked "shop" with my mother. But I just wanted to share my excitement with someone who could appreciate it. It must have been after two in the morning when I rang her. Somewhat disoriented, she answered the phone and when she heard my voice on the other end she nearly panicked.

After a few minutes of convincing her that I was all right and in one piece, I was able to say with total conviction, "Mom?"

"Yes, Vivian?" she said.

"I met a boy."

"Really?" she questioned.

"Yes, he's wonderful. His name is John. He has a dog. He lives right near me. He's real smart. Very successful and sooooooo my type!"

"And what type is that?" she asked, not really responding in the googly way I was hoping for (I should have known better).

"He's a real guy's guy, Mom."

"What does that mean, Vivian?"

"Just that he's confident, oh, and that he's taller than me!"

"I see." She finally laughed. "How did you meet him?" she asked, so I told her the story. "Well, is Carolyn a good friend of yours?"

"Not really," I said. "We work together."

"Well, what makes you so sure that she would fix you up with a nice person?"

"I don't know, Mom! [Total buzz kill] I doubt she'd intentionally fix me up with a creep."

Just minutes before, I was floating around in la-la land, but now my feet were cemented to the floor. I just knew (after I dialed) that this wasn't a good idea.

"Forget it, Mom. I was just real happy and I wanted to talk to you and tell you. Maybe it wasn't the best idea."

"Vivian, no. I am just concerned. Your judgment hasn't always been . . . well, it hasn't been very good."

"Thanks for the vote of confidence, Mom. Really."

"I love you, Vivian. Just take it one step at a time. I am very happy that you met a man. And your father and I only want the best for you. Just promise me that this time around, you'll take things nice and slow. I don't want you to wake up one morning and realize that maybe this man isn't all that you wanted him to be."

"Okay, Ma. Fair enough. I promise I will keep my head on straight. You don't have to worry. I'm gonna go. I'll call you in a few days."

"Good night, Vivian. And I am very happy that you are happy."

" 'Bye, Mom."

" 'Bye, dear."

My mistake. I should have practiced my "expectations management." I should have known better than to think my mom would suddenly step into a best friend role, one that she had never occupied before. I usually was pretty good, accepting that my mom and I were just that—mother and daughter. We would never have the kind of relationship that others had, like Sophie. She and her mom share everything, and I admit, growing up it was hard to watch. It sort of stung when I'd see them together or to hear them chitchat on the phone. It was no holds barred.

When there are times when I think my mom and I could use some quality time and she opts to see her friends, hang out with my dad, or pay a forty-five-minute visit rather than a weekend or something, well, I usually prepare myself in advance. I've learned to accept that my mother and I have limitations, of no fault of her own, or mine for that matter. It just was what it was. So if I just appreciated what I had with her, then anything more would be icing on the cake. Calling her after a hot first date with John was silly. Of course she would freak out. I'd have to marry a saint or someone she and my father had picked out in order for her to forget about Mark.

They found out about everything too late. I was in the beginning of my senior year and Mark and I had already been together something like three years. And after blaming themselves, they began to blame me. Do you know how many times my mom would ask me, beg me really, to tell her if she had ever taught me that being treated badly was okay. She still can't make heads or tails of my relationship with Mark, and in my family there was an arithmetic slash cause-and-effect mentality for everything. When they came up to Penn State after Sophie had called them, my mother couldn't even look at me. Mark and I had had a blowout like no other, and besides being pencil thin at that point, I also looked like I had been in the ring with Muhammad Ali. There was nothing I could do to prevent Sophie from making that call. I had used up all my promises to leave him, press charges, get help, whatever, and she didn't care if I ever spoke to her again. She finally accepted that the situation was out of my control.

So we can't blame my mom. She was scared for me. I was away from home and in their eyes I could fall off the dating wagon at any moment. C'est la vie.

But at least I had expelled all my post-great-date energy. Had I not phoned her, I probably would have spent the rest of the night sharing a pint of Ben & Jerry's with Omelet, watching whatever I could find on the tube until my eyes closed on their own.

I woke up pretty early the next morning and phoned Sophie and Will. As luck would have it, Sophie was back in NYC Saturday morning. Fernando had confused his weekends in his time-share, or something to that effect. I couldn't really understand Sophie's message, but nonetheless, I was able to phone Will, and then Sophie at Fernando's place, and make a plan. The three of us would meet for brunch. I went for a run prior and, like a cheese ball, jogged past the streets and basketball court that John and I had "christened" the night before. I felt great.

I walked to the restaurant at a brisk pace. It was freezing outside but also, I just wanted to see my friends! I was oozing with excitement. Sometimes retelling a great night is almost as good as the night itself. Ya know what I mean?

Rather than bore you all with the story that you already know, I walked in, found them huffing and puffing at the bar, and before I said a word I made sure the hostess knew we were waiting for a nonsmoking table.

"God, Vivian, it would be so much easier if you smoked!" Will complained.

"Good morning to you too!" I smiled.

So we sat down, ordered coffee, and I told them everything. We didn't even order until I got to the "John and I did not kiss good night" part. Sophie could not believe her ears and Will was just shaking his head from side to side.

"What?" I barked at him.

"Vivian's in loooove, Vivian's in loooove!" he teased.

"Love, please!" I said.

"Viv, my God. You're glowing!!!" Sophie said in delight.

"Okay, well, maybe there's potential here, I don't know."

"You do so know!" Will said.

"Okay, yes—he's amazing! Fine, I said it. Are you happy?"

My chocolate chip pancakes arrived before their fancy sandwiches so I let them talk as I feasted.

"I can't believe you said what you said you said and I can't believe you did what you did! I envy you!" Sophie said.

"Please, she had me as a coach!" Will proclaimed proudly.

"Okay then, this is making more sense," Sophie said.

"Thanks, Soph." I pouted.

"You're just going to have to play his game," Will went on. "He's quite the ladies' man and you are just going to have to show him that his regular game is not going to work with you."

"What regular game?" I mumbled (half a pancake in my mouth).

"Please, Vivian. This guy has broken more hearts than I have," Will bragged.

"How do you know?" I asked.

"Vivian, what planet are you on anyway? Do you not read the gossip columns?"

"Excuse me?" My blood pressure started to rise. I had no idea who John was before I met him. That was the truth. And I still didn't, even after all this lovely info, and I just knew, right then and there, that I was in trouble. Big trouble. 'Cause the more I thought about him, the more I liked him.

"Don't sweat it, Vivian," Will continued. "Regardless of what happens, you'll have had a great time, right?"

"Right," I lied back. Why were they so sure I was doomed?

"Just don't get emotionally attached and you'll be fine." Sophie smiled. Thankfully, our waitress stopped by with their brunch and so stopped my trip down the information highway. I couldn't be sure if it was the challenge at this point, or if I had been bitten by a lady-killer bug. Whatever it was, I knew that I wanted to see John again. And it was too late, I was already "emotionally attached."

I hate it when my mom is right. But maybe she wasn't. Maybe none of them were. Perhaps I would be the one who would get bored of John—however unlikely. Or maybe, dare I say, I could be the one. My mind was taking me to places I was embarrassed to share with my friends. Before I had to play John, I had to play my friends, assuring them that I was in it for the fun. For a few cheap thrills and a couple of decent meals.

But really, who was I kidding?

That next week was torture. I had to deal with Carolyn, and Zack was back in New York, so workwise, things were a bit out of control and I had to assume that every time the phone rang or I had a message, it could very well be from John! I knew better than to think he'd call right away, but it was Tuesday and we'd gone out the past Friday . . . was he too cool for even the two-day rule?

And beginning that first Monday when Carolyn came back from her vacation, she made no bones about telling anyone and everyone that she had fixed me up and with whom. It was just lovely. She cornered me by her office and she asked me for details, but I had none to speak of, or rather to share. I said it was "fun." That he was "great" and that was that.

"Well, Vivian, are you not the least bit curious about what he had to say?" she asked coyly.

"If you want to tell me," I replied. (Truth: I was dying to know what he said!)

"Well, I didn't speak to him directly. He left a message for me on Saturday and we've been missing each other since."

"So then you didn't talk to him?"

"No. But he did leave a pretty lengthy message!"

"So . . . what did he say?"

"He said that you were adorable."

"Adorable?" Funny. I had never heard myself described that way.

"Yes, and that he had a great time."

"That's nice," I said.

I walked away. It wasn't going to do me any good to beam all over her. I was so relieved. As much as my gut had thought that our feelings were mutual, Will and Sophie had totally freaked me out! He sounded sincere from what I could tell. Don't you agree?

But then why had he not called?

So two more days passed, like I said, and then finally, I returned from lunch and Zack had torn a piece of paper from my message book. "What's that?" I asked.

"Well, I picked up your phone a few minutes ago and a 'John' phoned for you."

"He did?" I lit up like such a geek. Zack started to laugh and dangle the piece of paper in front of me. "Stop it, Zack! I'm serious!" I whined.

"I doubt women get this excited when I call for them, how depressing." And with that I snatched my message out of his hand. There it was. His number, his message. "Call back." Oh God, now what?

I instant-messaged Will and Sophie the news. "DO NOT CALL UNTIL TOMORROW" came back in seconds!

"Really???" I asked back.

"YES!!!" they both typed simultaneously.

"Fine." I shrugged.

Why did everything need to be so complicated? In my mind, John wasted six perfectly good days. I mean we could have totally seen each other already. What was the point of agreeing to meet someone if your interest level was so low? What happened to carpe freakin' diem? Was I just being immature, too anxious? Great, now I was questioning myself. If I could have turned the clock back at that point, I probably would have. I wasn't cut out for this shit. Dating was a nightmare.

Patrick and I had hooked up right away—sorry, Mom, but it's true. It made everything so much easier. But then again, that was a total disaster. Maybe John was handling this with kid gloves for a reason. Yeah, that sounds about right. Taking things nice and slow.

I'm just so sure! He was calling my bluff, making me sweat it out. Was this the kind of person I really wanted to see again? YES!

That night I had a concert to attend at Irving Plaza. (Tori Amos.) Zack and I shared a car to the venue and he couldn't help but pry.

"So who's this John?" He laughed.

"Nobody," I said.

"Nobody—why do I find that hard to believe, Vivian?"

"What do you mean?" I asked.

"Well, now, don't get mad at me for saying this . . . but you've been biting your nails for the past two hours."

FUCK. "No, I haven't!" I said right back (as I removed my right hand from my mouth). "He's just some guy Carolyn set me up with. It's no big deal, really."

"Carolyn set you up?" He seemed surprised.

"Yes. Why?" I asked.

"Nothing," he said. And before I could figure out what that meant, the car stopped right in front of our destination. Just my luck.

Tori was incredible. I was perched over the second-floor balcony just awestruck by her talent and her fearlessness. I could never imagine getting up in front of that many people and doing anything. Tying my shoes would be a challenge. She was so passionate, like she had a lifetime of memories neatly wrapped up in a new record. How gratifying it must be to be able to express yourself through music and, better yet, fill theaters with people who adore your work. I just couldn't relate. I could only take it all in. Before long I was lost in her music and John was, very thankfully, *almost* out of my mind. Needless to say, the concert was more of a spectator sport for me than a business engagement. I was supposed to be meeting and greeting and such. After a few songs, Zack joined me, evidently unable to schmooze himself. We had dinner with a few people from Tori's label afterward, so by the time I got home, I was pooped.

The next day I waited until after lunch to ring John. Zack was in a meeting and I figured it was the ideal time. He picked up his own line and when I heard his voice I began to calm down. All the hype over the last week virtually disappeared. "It's me," I said.

"Well, I should have guessed you'd make me wait a day," he flirted.

"Oh, right. And you were just so busy this whole week. Put those cards away, will you, or this won't be any fun at all." I was pretty pleased with myself with that remark. Maybe I was better at this than I had thought.

He laughed for a few seconds and asked if I had plans that night. No way was I going to see him that very day. I was busy doing . . . absolutely nothing. But I had to persevere.

"Actually, I'm going out with my girlfriends."

"Well, what about tomorrow night?" he asked.

"I'm free," I said. I got goose bumps waiting for his reply.

"It's supposed to rain so the basketball courts are out of the question," he joked.

"How unfortunate," I said.

"How about we play it by ear then. I'll call you tomorrow afternoon and we'll figure something out."

"Sounds like a plan," I said. I gave him my home number and tried to end the conversation. I needed the nearest ladies' room!

"Well, have fun tonight."

"What?" I said.

"Tonight, with the girls. Have fun."

"Right, right. You too," and I hung up.

You too. You too. What was that? Such the picture of grace under pressure!

With no plans that evening, staying home and driving myself crazy was not an option. Sophie agreed to ditch Fernando for the night and hang with little old me. Turned out she needed to talk to me as much, or maybe even more, than I needed to pass the time with her. We decided to meet at some Cuban-Chinese restaurant that was supposedly all the rave in a neighborhood that I had always adored but rarely frequented, Nolita.

Nolita was a neighborhood on the rise. Great little shops owned and operated by streetwise designers, the best secondhand stores that I'd ever seen, and quaint bistros and coffee shops on every corner. Tattoo parlors, run-down pool halls, a handful of dark loungy bars and places like Alice's Grocery, where struggling musicians would play their hearts out to crowds that mixed friends with stragglers. Unexpected shops filled with wonderful imported furniture, jewelry, scarves, and rugs, and of course, those fun nostalgic haunts filled with whimsical mementos from KISS dolls, *Charlie's Angels* lunchboxes, dancing Elvis statuettes, and knickknacks from every era. To me, there was no rhyme or reason to Nolita and that's what actually made it work. A village of nomads from all walks of life just doing their thang!

I was shocked to find a line outside the restaurant and even with the brisk wind and unpleasantries that always seem to come along with a good twenty-minute wait while your stomach seems hollow, we lived through it, and much later rather than sooner we were seated.

Sophie wanted the details of my brief conversation with John and, of course, freaked out almost as hard as I did once I was through. "Well, what are you going to wear and, wait, you are going to hold out until he makes the first move, right?"

"Geez, Sophie, you're making me feel worse! Please calm down!"

"Okay, okay. Sorry."

"Don't worry about it."

After a few moments of silence, "But seriously, Vivian, what are you going to wear?"

"How should I know, Sophie? I mean, we don't even know what we're doing yet."

"Understandable," she confirmed. She excused herself to go to the ladies' room, which, for Sophie, nine times out of ten meant that she wanted to get up, see, and be seen! In her absence I couldn't help but think of what I was going to wear on Saturday night! I was involuntarily morphing into a fashion victim and I found it both frustrating yet oddly pretty fun. But shush, she was coming back!

We ordered whatever it was the two girls next to us were having. It smelled divine! "So how's work going?" I asked. It had been a while since she had talked about it.

"It's fine," she replied.

"Just fine? I thought you loved it!"

"I do, I do," she said. "But I think I need to make a move. I love retail but I want to be on the front lines of fashion; I don't want to be so reactionary, you know?"

"No," I answered. I had no idea what she was referring to. I had not reached the point of understanding the abstract dramatic and exaggerated form of the English language that many like Sophie had long since adopted.

"What I mean is . . . um . . . well, see, retail stores buy clothes from designers based on what they read and hear to be cool. They pick and choose what they are going to offer their customers based on sales almost one hundred percent of the time."

"Okayyyyyyy, and . . ."

"And well, I don't want to be part of the last moments of the fashion experience. I want to make the distinctions, predict trends, create the demand and substantiate it based on the influences in which the designer created it in the first place."

Okay, who was this really sitting across from me? Did she pick that up on television or had she read it in *Vogue*? I had never seen Sophie so serious about a topic (like her career) that actually warranted such introspection! Before I could even respond, she continued.

"I know you don't understand what I mean or you think I'm some big flake; maybe it's because you don't really pay attention to style, but it doesn't matter because you can carry it off. I love it! I always have. At home, in Pennsylvania, I just thought I'd open a shop of my own one day, ya know? But then I came to New York, and just when I think I've scored the best job ever, I realize there's so much more out there. If I have to meet one more girl in this town who's working at a magazine or styling a video, I'm just going to die! *I* should be doing that!"

It seemed as though Sophie and I were going through the same thing. Maybe that happens when you're in your early twenties. We go through school, get our degrees, think we'll just get a job, which will naturally progress into a career, and then before we know it, we're married, have two kids, and have left said jobs eons ago to be the perfect wives, mothers, or what have you. However, with age comes experience and then wisdom and, so, for us gals who are lucky to possess a wee bit of hindsight, well, nine times out of ten that is SOOOOOOO not the way it works.

But alas, we didn't know that then, sitting there waiting for our orange rice and yellow chicken to arrive. (Well, at least I think it was chicken!) But we did have each other to bounce our seemingly unanswerable questions and fragile fears off of and that helped, especially when I confessed to my own insecurities at work and what would it be that eventually I would try to take on. We were able to take solace in each other's confusion, strange maybe, but it helped!

I told her, very sincerely, that at least she knew what she wanted to do. She was certain that fashion was her life. I, on the other hand, hadn't a clue. So the only route that made sense in my mind for Sophie was to start interviewing. I could tell she felt better. (When she gets nervous or upset, her fair skin almost always breaks out in hives, the poor thing!)

"Oh, and for your information, Zack sent me to Barneys a few weeks ago to pick up a gift for his wife and, well, I spent a few hours in there. I loved it!"

"You're kidding!" she said. Her face all but lit up!

"Wait, wait, wait!" I said. "And I wasn't going to mention it, but I did sort of have an idea about what I was going to wear tomorrow." Her eyes popped out, she put her hand over her mouth and used the other to fan in front of her face.

"Oh my God!" she screamed! "I'm so happy for you!" and she leaped out of her seat and hugged me.

We were standing in the middle of an overcrowded Chinese-Cuban restaurant hugging, laughing, and crying. This was a joint where the only sounds you heard were jaded, malnourished customers either lighting up their cigarettes or proposing toasts in filmy opaque wineglasses filled with cheap merlot—chin chin!

But it was a defining moment. Better yet, a moment for us that was long overdue. It had been ages since we had had a truly meaningful heart-to-heart! Hugging her felt like home!

Avid reader, I must confess, it's been a few weeks since my last chapter. Personally, I think I put off writing because I wasn't really up to remembering the high I was on pre- and post-date two with John. You know that saying, "What goes up, must come down"? Why is that so painfully true when you think you're in love?

But it sure was fun—the up part—deliriously fun at that! Which quite perversely makes the demise of a relationship oddly bittersweet.

And yes, that's right, I used the "L" word, I know. Pretty pathetic that I couldn't even admit to you guys till now that I fell in what I thought was "love" with John that very first night. I never "went there" even with my closest friends. I couldn't—easier on the ego if it doesn't work out. But alas, I'm sure they saw right through me—most usually do.

Remember *Jerry Maguire*? Renée Zellweger's famous speech?

"I love him, Laurel, I love him! I love him for the man he already is; I love him for the man he wants to be. I love him, Laurel, I love him!"

Yup, that was me—sans the happy ending.

Older and wiser, upon reflection I can say this: Real love is mutual. It has to be, really, right? To love that person who loves you back, that must be insane!

Probably best to define my feelings for John now as "like times infinity!"

Important to note that being romanced by John was one of the high points of my dating life. Not too sure I'd have it any other way actually. I learned a lot about myself having "experienced" him. Sometimes it takes a blindside or two to wake up and smell your own coffee.

But enough, let's get to the good stuff, shall we? I don't want to skip too far ahead too soon. I haven't told you about date two yet . . . or three. . . .

I assured Sophie that I could get ready for the big date, this time around, without her. It was like pulling teeth to get her to agree that she'd stay at Fernando's. I think her dream job actually wouldn't be at *Vogue*—she'd revel being on a show like E!'s *Fashion Emergency*.

Anyway, I thought about a sexy dress, a low-cut blouse, or even lower-cut jeans, but I wanted to feel like me, not some pathetic interpretation of me trying to seduce a man based on my attire—or lack thereof. I know most men don't verbally admit this, but I'm convinced that somewhere way down in the depths of their psyche, they may even prefer to ponder over what exists under our clothes rather than having a bird's-eye view all one-two-three. What do you think?

All right, so maybe I'm wrong, but my philosophy works for me. I was never, and will never be, that exhibitionist. (Boxers over bikini bottoms till college—sound familiar?) And I just can't understand how a girl could deal with a guy who's staring at her chest rather than into her eyes.

So, I went the contemplated casual route—yet again. Vintage shirt. A bit of cream lace but mostly dusty rose satin, oversized just enough to show a little shoulder and short enough to flash my Buddha belly. I chose my good denim jeans, just out of the dryer. (I did some *Crouching Tiger, Hidden Dragon* moves an hour before pickup.) I borrowed Sophie's black coat—just below the knee, empire waist, bell-shaped at the bottom, and wore my new red boots. (I found a great pair at Barneys—my first-ever purchase there, and unfortunately not the last—on my field trip for Zack. I couldn't pronounce the name of the designer, I remember that, and found them in their after-Christmas reduced reduced reduced rack. A size too big but just in my price range, I was sure they'd be okay with wool socks!)

I was stylin', I felt good, and I felt "pretty," which is always a nice way to get started. John and I were going to a photo exhibit and then dinner. That was the plan o' action. He was meeting me at my place at seven and I was ready by five.

He buzzed up right on time and asked if he should come up. Negative. No, no, no. Not yet. I wanted him to wait for me, keep up his anticipation. At least that was the plan. I told him I'd be right down. I grabbed my bag, slipped a few Altoids in my pocket, kissed Omelet good night, and was off.

It was as if he hadn't moved from the last time I'd seen him. That great smile, those direct eyes, that confident stance—yummmmmmmmmm. But never mind that, there was a game to be played!

"Hi," I said.

"Hi," he said. "You smell like mouthwash." (Did I forget to mention that I had probably popped a dozen breath mints in the previous thirty minutes?) But it was all about confidence—no time for insecurity.

"Are you trying to dazzle me with your charm?" I asked. "Oh, and by the way, you've got toothpaste on the corner of your mouth."

He stood there mortified and I just couldn't bear it, so I confessed, "I'm kidding!"

So we were even.

"Shall we go?" he asked.

"Yeah, for sure. Should we walk?" I said.

"Why not, we're on time anyway. I hate arriving to these things on time," he said.

"Well, what kind of 'thing' is this anyway?" I asked.

"A photographer friend of mine just finished a book of his pictures. He does mostly fashion stuff and a few portraits. It's actually a show for the works in his book," he responded ever so unenthusiastically.

"That's really cool. He must be so excited."

"Probably, who knows? We'll see I guess."

"And he's a friend of yours?" I asked. (I mean if my friend was launching a book I'd be a lot more revved up than that.)

"Don't get me wrong, Vivian, I'm happy for him. It's just that there's always something like this that I'm obligated to do. Same crowd, same bullshit. That's what I like about you—this isn't your thing. And I have to say, you look great by the way."

"Thanks," I said. I couldn't really glance his way. I played with my hair to keep from fidgeting, which I think really defines fidgeting if you have hair to play with, but whatever.

Anyway, his blasé attitude toward something that to me sounded so exciting impressed me at the same time. I felt like I was strolling along with someone not really out of my league but maybe just on a different team. It was obvious that we came from two different worlds despite his moaning and groaning about how inside he was a regular Joe. Regular Joes don't have photo exhibits and parties and social calendars, no matter how hard they try. My brother Joseph was a regular Joe despite how hard he tried!

That was one thing my radar caught on date one. John's whole "thing" in his mind, or even maybe within his circle of friends, was that he was average despite appearances. But it wasn't that big of a deal, really. I mean, we all have things, shticks, armor I guess—for good or for bad. My "thing" was all about "being myself" even though at the time I hadn't a fucking clue who that really was. "Being myself" constituted taking chances for fear of being dependent on one choice. "Being myself" also required dressing down for fear of making too much of an effort and not pulling it off. I also spoke aloud before I thought about what I wanted to say; oh, and I often used a teeny-tiny bit of vulgarity, well, every now and again. I thought if I drank my beer out of the bottle, didn't belong to a gym, and went to work with wet hair, then that could be my identity: "Vivian the anti–city slicker, the tomboy with an edge." And it was all good. It was my armor.

People think we all grow out of pacifiers and security blankets.

Bullshit. As life gets more complicated, we just find different ways to stroke our nerves and insecurities. It's like having money. The more you make the more you need. Something like that anyway. If you didn't get my abstract analogy—no worries—it probably only makes sense in my crazy head.

So if John was working the "average Joe" thing, who was I to judge? More important, he made me feel like it was all about me. The moment, the evening—all of it. He was brilliant at making me feel that I was the most important thing to him. He should have been in politics!

We arrived amid the flashing bulbs of photographers outside the gallery. (What the hell was this?) From the get-go I was like a deer caught in headlights. I tried to pretend that the fact that paparazzi were an aspect of our date was A-OK with me. Yeah, right. The gallery was packed. I couldn't even see a photo. John was greeted by an army of people and I was standing there beside him praying that I, too, would know someone there. After a few introductions, John asked if he could take my coat, which was fine, until the sleeve's silk lining got caught on my wristwatch. Don't even ask.

We made our way around the room at a turtle's pace. One, because there was barely room to breathe; two, because he knew just about everyone; and three, because my boots were NOT made for walking. I could feel the blisters forming! I stopped and pretended to be awestruck by a photo of a tan naked girl on an elephant. It was refreshing to be able to make eye contact with something. John leaned down, brushed my hair away from my ear, and asked me how I was doing.

"I got chills, they're multiplying and I'm losin' control, for the power you're supplyin'—it's electrifying!" I sang.

GOTCHA! (That was a joke! ☺)

But feeling his cold fingertips just behind my ear and the way the air from his words danced on my skin, I just had to close my eyes and enjoy it.

"I'm fine. Don't worry about me," I said.

"Really?" he questioned.

"Actually, no," I confessed. "Doesn't really seem like anyone's here for the art."

"See what I mean?" he said.

"Yes," I said.

"You wanna go?" he asked.

"Uh-huh." I nodded.

"Be right back," he said. "I'll get our coats."

Thank God. The fans in there were giving me serious nipple-itis and if one more person looked me up and down, I'd have grabbed the next spring roll that passed by and tossed it!

We left eventually, grabbed a ride with a vacant black town car and went to one of his favorite Italian restaurants, Da Silvano. "Do you like Italian food?" he asked as we cuddled up against each other to "keep warm"—yeah, right.

"My favorite." I grinned.

"Perfect," he gushed. "I hope we have the place to ourselves!"

That was sweet. And I couldn't have agreed more. I should mention that Da Silvano was one of Zack's favorite restaurants. I was on a first-name basis with the maître d', over the phone, of course. Zack eats there at least two times a week and I was hoping that this evening would not be one of them.

Pulling up, you could see that we were not the only ones feeling Italian. There was a line of people waiting outside and through the restaurant's windows, I didn't see a single table. John grabbed my hand, excused us, passed the line, and shouted something or other to a man on the phone just a few footsteps away from the pretty hostess. A handshake here, a hug there, and after yet another introduction, we were seated immediately. Not bad!

The waiter came over to take our drink order. John suddenly grabbed my hand from across the table and asked "Red or white?" and without flinching, I replied, "Red." At that moment, it felt like we were a couple. Everything seemed so natural. Once he chose a wine, the waiter left and we were on our own. I loved the PDA, I loved the way he stared at me, and I loved the next words out of his mouth. "You're just so beautiful," he said.

"Thanks." I blushed.

"I really like you," he confessed.

"You too," I said. Just like the butter on our table, I was melting. All bets were off. It was getting too hot and becoming too real to keep up this whole ice queen thing and I'd never taken acting lessons. While every bone in my body was telling me that we were on the same page, it was now high time I let my guard down.

And then there she came. Some stunning superbabe out of nowhere, dressed to the nines and gesturing over to John. "Hello, handsome," she purred.

"Hi, Kim," he said. He got up and gave her a kiss on the cheek and she, rather purposefully, kept her skinny little arm around his waist as he turned to introduce us. "Vivian, this is Kim. Kim, this is Vivian."

"Hi!" I said and took a big sip of my wine that had landed in front of me just in the nick of time. They exchanged pleasantries for a few minutes and John returned to his seat as though he had just gotten back from a short trip to the loo.

Jealousy has never been a good look for me and if "Kim" wasn't a big deal to him then, well, she wasn't going to be a big deal to me either. We continued on, all the while I was secretly hoping that an equally attractive male would pretend to know me from God only knows where, approach us, and grab my ass while I nonchalantly introduced him to John, but no such luck.

We shared a huge bowl of Penne à la Vodka and finished our bottle of wine. We joked and flirted and played a fairly innocent game of footsie. We ordered tiramisu and I chose to break the silence by asking him if my lips were as burgundy as his. That always sucks about red wine. "Yup," he said and we laughed about it rather than working on wiping it away. He asked me what I was doing tomorrow (Sunday) as he thought it would be nice to take the dogs to the park. I agreed (surprise, surprise) and nervously babbled about work until our dessert could provide the necessary distraction.

We shared a cab home and John decided to get out with me rather than take it the few blocks to his place. While wondering who really was responsible for the empty bottle of wine, John put his arms around the lower part of my waist and pulled me toward him. I giggled. Back to the drawing board, I thought. We still hadn't smooched and I could tell that this was John's way of getting me to kiss him first.

I stood on my tippy toes and got as close to him as possible. "Yes?" I said.

"Yes, what?" he asked and the more we talked the closer our lips got. We each used every carefully chosen word to get closer and closer. It was like playing musical chairs. Whoever was left with the last word could be blamed with our first kiss.

I don't know what happened next, or who kissed whom, but we were kissing wildly—and perfectly I might add—in a matter of moments. It wasn't like gross "get a room"–type smooching. More like postcard material. We'd stop every now and then to come up for air or to gaze into each other's eyes, but for the most part it felt like one huge "Big Red" commercial. You know:

"Kiss a little longer, hmmmmm-hhhmmmm a little stronger, hmmmm-hmmmm-hmmmm—hmm, longer, longer with Big Red."

We hadn't a clue what was going on around us and weather was not a factor. It was sensual, long overdue, and basically incredible. Every bone in my body wanted him to come upstairs, but I just knew I couldn't do that. He was a wolf in sheep's clothing, dangerous on the dance floor. If this was going to turn into anything, it was going to be all about time.

So I said good night to John slowly and walked inside (delirious), needing a cold shower like never before! Then, out of nowhere, I tripped over what appeared to be a suitcase, placed ever so inconsiderately in the middle of the kitchen floor. I should have known something not good was up the minute my face hit the faux ceramic tiles, but as I stood up, the blood flowing from my chin was just a tad of a distraction.

Omelet, Sophie, and Fernando appeared as I looked up. As the two of them started explaining and apologizing, I began to feel faint. I sat on the nearest chair. I urged Omelet to nix his great big "hello" until I could make heads or tails of what was happening.

It was Fernando's suitcase that I had fallen over. Why was it there? Oh, because he got into an argument with his roommate sometime before or after they got thrown out of their own apartment for whatever the reason was.

I urged them both to stop talking and to bring a mirror over so I could take a look at the cut that was now bleeding so heavily that I had surely ruined Sophie's coat. I had a gash just below my chin that made no sense and that obviously needed a medical opinion. Sophie grabbed a coat and before I knew it, she and I were on our way to the emergency room. Have I mentioned my fear of hospitals yet . . . worse than tunnels!

On the short cab ride over, Sophie very reluctantly informed me that Fernando was going to need to crash with us for a while until he found a new place. "Do you mind?" she asked nervously. And what was I to say to my very best friend who obviously thought she was in love with this guy?

"Of course not. Just ask him to quit leaving suitcases in our kitchen." Relieved, she started laughing and I did, too, actually. This was not exactly how I planned the end of my evening.

Five hours and fourteen stitches later, it was over. I was inches away from a panic attack, I'll tell you that. I was seen immediately, thank God, but spent way too much time in an infirmary of sorts with a few characters I'd kill to be able to forget. Saturday night at downtown hospitals should be the next location of any "Say No to Drugs" commercial. Two girls had had an adverse reaction to their drug of choice, vomiting, freaking out. One chick was even a freaky shade of turquoise. Another old guy, definitely a grandfather, was drunk as a skunk, lying in the bed across from me wearing next to nothing (try to imagine my view) and shouting at the hospital staff. As I was leaving, a woman had come in with a swollen lip, and when I say swollen, I mean like elephant man swollen, from an allergic reaction to shellfish or something.

I told my nurse, in near tears and with my nostrils fully flared, that if I wasn't given the go-ahead to jet in a few minutes, they'd be transferring me to the psychiatric ward. I'm not too sure if it's the sanitized order, the way in which the place is blanketed with a creepy silence that only allows for sounds of pain, or if it's the sterile atmosphere that wigs me out, but whichever or whatever, I feel nauseated and anxious the minute I step foot in a hospital! She let me go and gave Sophie all my information, prescriptions, etc.

On the way home, I told her about John and the kiss and our plans for, shit, today! Guess that was not happening. "Hi, John, yeah, after you left I sliced my face open in the kitchen." Genius!

We stopped off at the pharmacy, picked up my drugs and a few Miss Piggy Band-Aids for my chin. At the time I was sporting a gauze pad that just wasn't really working for me, ya know? When we finally got home, it was nearly seven A.M. Fernando was lying in his underwear on the sofa—which fully grossed me out—and when I looked at Sophie, she immediately swore that she'd tell him to keep his sexy body covered at all times.

"Irresistible," I joked.

I got out of my clothes, brushed my teeth, and got under the covers with Omelet. Sleeping on my back has never been my position of choice (I'm a consummate spooner!) but it was too uncomfortable any other way. Omelet laid his head on my chest, which was comforting and sweet, and served as the perfect distraction. Before long I was in sleepy town, dreaming of a perfect J. Crew life with lover boy!

Let's just say it was the painkillers. (I'd hate to think I was that pathetic!)

When I woke up, I felt like I had been hit by a bus and when I went to the bathroom to take in the view (I was warned of possible swelling and such) I nearly lost it when I found that Fernando had shaved his back hair in my sink!

"Sophie!!!!!!!!!!!!!!" I screamed but only Omelet responded. C'mon now, how gracious was I going to have to be? I was livid and after running through the apartment wildly, I realized that I had slept until noon and the lovebirds were out. Just then, the phone rang. I picked it up without a thought as to who could be on the other end. I was fuming, and barked the only "hello" I could muster.

"Vivian?" I heard on the other end of the phone.

"Yes?" I replied bitterly.

"It's John. Is this a bad time?"

"No, no. Sorry. I'm just waking up."

"Good," he replied. "Look out your window," he said proudly.

"What?" I asked.

"Just look," he insisted. And as I drew the blinds I nearly fainted (again!). Lance Romance was right outside my door, cell phone, dog, two coffees, and all. He looked just as shocked as I did. (Hence the gauze pad and bed head!) "Jesus Christ, what happened to you?" His concern turning into a giggle.

"Are you actually amused by this?" I asked, still staring at him in the window.

"Open the door," he said. "I'm coming in." What the hell, I thought. I was in a flannel head-to-toe nightgown and wearing one sock that was just seconds from falling off. I mean, if I really wanted him to like me for me, this was going to be a test of a lifetime.

He came in and just started cracking up. "Awwwwwwww," he offered and gave me a hug. "What happened?" he asked. "I knew I should have come in last night!" Really?

I was so happy to see him and loved that he had just come over. No phone call or happenstance. Mr. Spontaneity was growing on me by the second. My bedroom was the warmest spot in the apartment, so I decided to have him hang out in there. That's the truth—I swear. The dogs were doing their own thing in the living room so we were really all on our own. I went over the evening's play by play and he sincerely felt bad. "I think scars are sexy actually," he said.

"Lucky for me!" I murmured back.

"You know, Vivian, had you not been on cloud nine after that kiss, you might have seen a huge suitcase in your kitchen." God—I could have strangled him! "You did turn the lights on when you walked in."

"What are you, some sort of well-mannered Peeping Tom?"

"No. But I just wanted to make sure you got in okay. Evidently I was wrong." And he started laughing again.

"Listen. I let you in here to make me feel better not worse. One more—"

"One more what?" he interrupted. He was flirting wildly, and I remember thinking that he must really like me. I was sitting beside him looking hideous and he was all happy and shit. He had on a perma smile that I just couldn't let him get away with and one that I would have happily kissed if, of course, it wouldn't have opened my stitches.

"Look at you," I said.

"Look at me what?"

"You like me," I teased.

"Yes, Vivian, I do. I thought we went over that yesterday."

"Yeah, well . . ." feeling like a bit of an idiot. "Well, it's just fun, that's all."

"It's fun?" He seemed confused. I tried to sum it up, and spin it so I wouldn't sound too foolish.

"It's like this. You spent almost two weeks trying to make me think otherwise and well, now, it's just fun to know that you do."

"Point well taken," he replied and hugged me until it hurt—literally.

After a while he took Omelet out for me and picked up a pizza and a movie. We were going to shack up at my place. We had no choice really, if we wanted to hang out that day. While he was out, I called Sophie on her cell and implored her not to come home for a while. Then I made a mad dash for the bathroom and cleaned up. (Beyond gross—cleaning up body hair that isn't yours!) As I was about to change, there was a knock at the door. John was back with *The Full Monty* and a large pepperoni pie. Perfection!

I had him set the VCR up in my bedroom. There was no way I'd be setting foot on that couch until it had been sanitized! We cuddled up in my bed, pigged out, and let Sunday drag on.

He had some big to-do the next day and had to get a good night's sleep (as if I was going to ask him to spend the night! I was actually). So he left at about eight o'clock. Forewarning me that his week was going to be hideous, he said that he would call to see how I was feeling and figure out when we would see each other again. "You are going to work tomorrow right?" he asked.

"Of course," I said.

"That's my girl!" he said. (I liked the sound of that!) He kissed my forehead, grabbed Domino, said good-bye to Omelet, took the empty pizza box to the trash, and left.

I was overwhelmed with warm fuzzies! I felt deliciously admired and when I got back to my room, I was pretty positive that I liked it much better when John was in it.

Then I started thinking, when was he going to call? What if he didn't call me soon enough and I wanted to call him? Yuck! This is why I hate relationships, why I hate being "in like"! It feels like one big settlement when you can't act or say or do or call, for that matter, when you want to! I was just fine before I met him. Having John on my brain just sucked! Consistently overanalytical and never allowing a good moment to be just that, I thought long and hard about why my satisfaction had earned a "dis" just moments after he left. Was I needy? Immature? Did I like him more than he liked me?

Hi, I'm Vivian, and I'm a freak!

I tried to look on the bright side. I met a great guy who, I think, thought I was great, too. It doesn't have to all happen at once. Oh my God. What did I mean by "all"? Da da da dum, da da dum, da da da dum, da da da da da da da dum . . .

Noooooooooo.

The phone rang again. Yes, Sophie, it's okay—you can come home now. Poor thing was quarantined from her own apartment!

But it was John. ☺

"I got back home and I couldn't focus."

"Really?" I said with glee.

"Yup. What are you doing to me?" he said.

"What are you doing to *me*?" I said joyfully and jumped into my bed. Too bad I didn't have the clapper. I needed to turn off the lights for sure!

"Hold on," I said and turned off my light and shut the door.

"Are you in bed?" he half whispered.

"Yes," I admitted.

"It's nice to know where you are," he said.

"What do you mean?"

"Now I don't have to imagine it. I've been there."

"I get it," I said.

"What are you doing?" I asked.

"I'm in bed, too," he said. Not much of a phone sex gal, I changed the topic. Presumptuous maybe, but I had to be safe.

"So, what's your week like at work?" I asked. He went on to talk about the stock market, which sounded more like a foreign language than anything else, and about his boss, some of the deals he had on the table and how much he wanted to close a few in the coming days. Being good at his job wasn't enough for him. He said he wanted to be made senior partner by the end of the year. Impressed, I went on to talk about my own ambitions—not that he asked, which bothered me a bit.

I told him of some of the special projects I was working on and was taken aback when he confessed to knowing more than half of the people I mentioned. He had this knack for making me feel almost junior to him when we talked about business. It wasn't like John was a chauvinist, but I had the distinct feeling that he didn't take my work very seriously.

Semi-unfazed, I continued. It was almost as if I looked forward to proving myself to him. A bit unhealthy perhaps, but I welcomed a challenge wherever one might be found, and if John in some way thought that I was "green" in the area of responsibility and such, I was happy to show him otherwise.

I discussed my idea of creating a new role for myself within the department. (Something that until that very moment was just a thought. I had never talked about it with Zack, Will, my parents, or Sophie for that matter, and I credited John's arrogance with allowing me to finally verbalize it.) As I was often touted for being creative and possessing a genuine understanding of the audience we were targeting, then surely I could be doing a lot more for the company than I had been so far.

What I said seemed to even things out between us and after a little bit, our conversation moved into another direction. "Are you seeing anyone else?" he asked ever so nonchalantly.

"No, actually I'm not," I responded. I have to admit, he caught me very off guard. I hadn't even thought about the idea of exclusivity. After a brief and semi-painful moment of silence, I had call-waiting and asked him to hang on. It was Sophie this time and I gave her the A-OK on coming home.

When I got back on the line with John, I asked him if he was seeing anyone, to which he replied, "What if I was?"

Ewwwwww.

"I don't know, John. What if you were?" I asked. (I didn't like the gamey tone of his voice. Should I have lied and told him yes, maybe making myself a bit less unavailable? I was back to hating the fact that I met him again. I'm such a coward sometimes.)

"If I was in something serious, then I wouldn't have gone out with you in the first place," he said.

Okay, I liked him again.

"What's serious to you?" I asked. I mean really, I wasn't his girlfriend, but he definitely made me feel like I could be, but for all intents and purposes, we were not serious. Was he involved with someone in the same way he was involved with me?

"Serious is about time," he said. "Like having a girlfriend, or living with someone, or seeing the same person during the majority of my spare time. That's what I consider serious."

"Me, too," I said. "It's odd, all these rules and definitions. I hate them," I said, sounding very relieved, I'm so sure.

"I do, too," he said. "I feel good about me and you." He went on, "And I'd like to keep this up. I want to get to know you, ya know."

"I feel the same way." Our serious tone seemed a bit awkward. I felt a lot more comfortable when we were trying to outsmart each other or when we were flirting. It was way too early to get serious, but just the same, it was nice to know that we were coming from the same place.

"Do you want to tuck me in?" I asked.

"Come again?" he said.

"My painkillers are kicking in. I would love to hang up with you just before I fall asleep," I confessed.

"You are such a cutie," he said. "Shall I sing you a lullaby?"

"Are you making fun of me?"

"No, I love this about you. You're so honest and up-front. Not afraid of putting it out there." (Please, if he only knew!)

"I can't help it," I said. "If I feel it I usually say it. I hate holding back."

"Once upon a time . . ."

"Shut up!" I laughed.

"Fine then, what's 'putting to bed' to you?" I could tell he was actually trying to say the right thing. I felt more at ease knowing that he wanted to do or say whatever it was that I was expecting. It was comforting to get a vibe from him that wasn't so confident for a change. I told him that it meant going to bed with a smile, feeling relaxed. That it had nothing to do with phone sex. He laughed a bit and told me that he couldn't wait to see me again.

"You did it," I said.

"What?"

"You tucked me in."

"How so?"

"You were honest and said something nice. Telling me that you want to see me again is the perfect way for me to fall asleep."

"I do, Vivian. Next time just you and me. No party, no crowded restaurant."

"Sounds perfect. So you'll call me . . ."

"Yes, I will."

"Good night, John," I said. My eyes began to shut despite my excitement.

"Good night, Vivian. Sweet dreams."

Perfection.

Tuck-ins are highly underrated.

I marched into work that next morning prepared for two things: the first, to be made fun of (thankfully, the swelling had gone down and I was able to remove that hideous gauze contraption from my chin but did, however, have to sport the Band-Aid look), and second, now that my thoughts about where I wanted to go careerwise were "out there," I'd have to schedule a sit-down of sorts with Zack and present my "idea."

The repercussions of tripping over a suitcase after walking into my apartment in sheer bliss were fair. I mean, as obnoxious as the next person, I would have done the same if one of my coworkers had taken it on the chin, so I took it all with as much humility as I could muster. With the afternoon nearly whipped out, after a barrage of "to do" items all crossed off my list, and with Zack finally off the phone and playing blackjack on his computer (which he always did in between the chaos), I knew I had to march in there and take a stab at moving up the corporate ladder, with or without a net.

I initially thought about presenting a plan. Showing him, on paper, what I was thinking about, how the department would stand to benefit, show how the risk could evolve into a reward after six months and so on.

But that just wasn't my style. I thought a conversation would present itself with less pressure or immediate reactions and would give Zack time to see for himself that this was a great idea, one that would only prove to help him and show him that this was something I could handle. Most important, he'd have no regrets.

So with that, I walked in, closed the door, and asked him if he had a minute. "Don't even tell me you're resigning," he said. Shocked, I laughed at him and told him that I had an idea.

"An idea. Really?" he said, very relieved.

I started out by telling him how happy I was there and how much I appreciated the opportunity he had given me, and I told him about what I had learned over the course of what amounted to almost a year. I also confessed that I wasn't the music maven that he may have thought, but that it in no way affected my enthusiasm, work ethic, etc. Rather, it enabled me to see things from another viewpoint. Where my colleagues and superiors had a knowledge and expertise about the business, I was more in touch with the public's vantage point. (I couldn't believe that it was really me who was saying all this. As much as I meant it, it was the first time I was putting my thoughts together in such a rational and systematic way. Good show, Viv!) I was the audience and I was able to separate myself from the corporate wants, needs, and obligations, and therefore, think about the ways in which I would want to experience what the channel had to offer. Basically, I could take in the objectives of the company each quarter, look at the roster of talent, and develop programs both on- and/or off-air that would capture the eyes and ears of the "viewer."

Somewhat shocked, Zack interrupted me. "I hear what you're saying, Vivian, and I'm your biggest fan," he said, "but your experience . . . other than waitressing and scheduling my meetings . . . and don't take offense to this, how can I justify promoting you?"

"Just let me finish, okay?"

"Okay." He smiled.

"I'm not saying that I could do it all on my own. But I am saying that if my administrative responsibilities were lessened, I'd have more time to work alongside you. Learn other aspects of the business while feeding you with concepts and ideas that there's no way you could come up with on your own."

"Oh, really?" he said.

"Yes. Really," I stated. "There's no way you, and Carolyn, for example, can step into my shoes, no matter how creative and how connected you are. You're in a different world, and when you were my age it was a different time."

"True," he said. "Very true."

"If I were, let's say, special projects manager or something like that, I could work on whatever you threw my way. If an idea I had was unrealistic, you or someone else here could tell me why. From there, I'd be able to rationalize your reservations and come up with something that suits you and that suits the company. C'mon, Zack, think about it."

"I love your enthusiasm, Vivian. I'll tell you that. But there are kids here who have been delivering mail and answering phones for years. Think about that. Why should I give this to you? Why not someone else who has put the time in?"

That was fair and a momentary buzz kill, but after I thought about it, I could only come up with one answer that made the most sense to me.

"Because I asked. I brought it to you. Maybe it's not the conventional way of doing things, but that doesn't have to make it undoable."

"Somehow I knew you'd say that."

I took a deep breath and took my hair out of the ponytail that was giving me a headache. "I just know that it's right, Zack. I just know it. If it's about money, I can wait . . ."

He cut me off. "Let me give you a piece of advice, Viv. Don't ever let the money card be the first thing you put down. If a company is going to promote you and give you added responsibility, then the money is a fair compensation. Whether you're working for me, or someone far less incredible down the line, never let that be an issue. Got me?"

"Yes. Thank you."

"Your review is coming up, so I'll think about your proposal. No promises though, okay?"

"Okay."

I stood up, shook his hand, and asked him if he needed any coffee.

We both laughed and I walked out feeling like I had just bit into a York Peppermint Patty. As much as I wanted this to happen, I was equally satisfied for having had the conversation. Sure, Zack was an extraordinary person who happened to be my boss. I was lucky. But I knew in my heart that I still would have proposed what I had proposed regardless because I believed it to be true and right. Ignoring my reality was a thing of the past. I had listened to my instincts rather than my insecurities, a mantra that I vowed to live by the minute I moved to New York.

I sat down at my desk and was about to call my mother, Sophie, or someone to tell them about what I had just done, but I placed the telephone back on the receiver and decided to keep the moment mine. Not for fear of looking bad should I not get the job, but rather, well, just because. I wanted to own it. Whatever happens happens. But for now, I wanted it to be mine.

The busy day had come to a close and I realized all too suddenly that John had not called. Again, I had burst my own feel-good bubble. Wouldn't you have thought that he would have called? I mean really.

As I watched everyone wrap things up and go home or wherever, I decided to stick around and bury myself in my ambition. I mean it couldn't hurt to show Zack how serious I was and it would hopefully get my mind off John. I kept telling myself to take things slow despite the fact that I was crazy about him. If it was supposed to happen it would. Yeah, right. Whatever.

So I spent the evening at my desk. McDonald's had a clutch delivery service so over a big Big Mac and large fries, I let the junk food be my fuel for thought. I came up with a list of ideas that seemed to work alongside the bands that we were promoting, the cities that were important to the channel, and the advertisers who were in bed with the company.

It didn't even feel like I was working. I enjoyed developing, albeit "pretend" initiatives that I knew at the end of the day the real people we were trying to reach would be into. As much as it was a business, I was extrapolating all the cool things that could come out of it.

Pray tell, was there a real businesswoman lurking within what I thought was a useless, untalented mess? When moments like this hit me, I can't help but think back to Mark. Proving him wrong was rewarding. Realizing a positive quality within me may seem a bit ridiculous to many, even misguided to a few, but for someone like me, an average girl with what seemed like a prognosis for little, sitting at my desk, feeling a hint of pride and possessing a bit of empowerment, I knew something good was going to come from all this. I just knew it.

Two full days had passed and that shit had still not called. I felt like I was literally playing the dating game and wanted to turn in my chips. As much as I wanted to talk to Sophie about what was happening, I couldn't. Fernando's presence within my apartment was making my skin crawl. Sure, it had been less than a week since he became an official roommate, but within that short period of time, he had already used up all my conditioner, forgotten, oh I'd say at least a half a dozen of my phone messages, burned a hole with his cigarette in the sofa, and well, you all know about the back hair.

I thought about talking to my mom but remembered how understanding she was the last time, so she was nixed. I didn't really want to open up to Will just yet either, and I knew my brothers were helplessly biased when it came to any guy I dated, so that really left only one man for the job. My little Gabe-y baby.

I phoned him on my lunch hour. We shot the shit for a bit, and just as I was about to broach the topic, I noticed out of the corner of my eye that Carolyn had paid me a visit.

"Will you be home later?" I asked him quickly.

"Yeah, till about seven," he said.

"Okay, 'bye," and I hung up.

I looked up and plastered this huge "I'm on top of the world" smile on my otherwise "I could strangle you for setting me up with such a prick" face.

"Hey, Carolyn."

"Hi, Vivvvvvvvvvvvvvvvvvvvvvvvvvv." (I had never heard anyone abbreviate my name yet still take forever to pronounce it.)

She just stared at me looking like the cat that had swallowed a mouse.

"What?" I said.

"So tell me . . . how are things goingggggg?" What was the new speech technique? Overly medicated perhaps? One too many cocktails over lunch?

"Fine, Carolyn. Really . . . great."

"Reallyyyyyyyyyyyyyyy."

"Yes, Carolyn," eye roll. "Reallyyyyyyyyyyyyyyyy."

She shifted her weight from one stiletto to the other, sort of like a big girl's version of a little girl's pout. "C'mon. I thought playing matchmaker was going to be more fun! Both of you are so tight-lipped. It's total bullshit and very inconsiderate I might add."

"Well, what do you want me to say?"

"Something! Jesus. You can trust me." (Could I?)

"I saw him this weekend."

"Annnnnnd?"

(Big sigh) "Annnnnnd, it was nice."

"Nice? Nice. Vivian, a pedicure is nice, the gal who gets me my tea is nice. But a weekend with John? Nope, 'nice' ain't going to cut it!" (Her face was turning red and I was sure the collagen she had injected into her crow's-feet and lips once a month was going to explode if I didn't give her some kind of detail.)

But then again, she already knew about our weekend. Having said virtually nothing to the dozen of curious acquaintances I work with, there was no way she could have charmed her info out of any of them . . . BINGO!

"Well, what did HE have to say, Carolyn?" (Pretty sneaky, sis!)

"To me, nothing. But he did see my hubby at a fund-raiser last night . . ."

"And?" (My heart began to race.)

"And . . . well, he's smitten!"

"No!" I jumped out of my seat and hugged her. (Way to play it cool, Vivian. When had I become such a geek?)

"I knew you'd get to him! I just knew it!" We both giggled like two preteen queens.

"Tell me everything!" she squealed.

And I did. Every last detail.

"So when are you seeing each other again?" she asked.

"I don't know. I haven't heard from him since Sunday night. What do you think about that?"

"Why are men such imbeciles? Honestly. He's probably just testing himself. Seeing how long he can go without calling you. Most bachelors don't enjoy the idea of falling for someone. They don't know how to deal."

"Honest?" I asked.

"Absolutely. Don't you dare call him. And when he does call you, and he will, put him on hold." Carolyn was good at this.

"And when you get back on the phone, don't bring up or even hint to his tardiness. That's what he'll expect you to do. And when you don't, it will drive him crazy—good crazy!"

We ew'd and ah'd for a little bit longer. She looked at her watch and nearly panicked. She was late for some overseas conference call or something. She looked at me with her eyebrows raised.

"Don't worry," I said. "I got it." I was sure my look of relief was way better than an actual "thank-you." She winked at me and strutted off.

This may sound completely pathetic, but I couldn't help but wonder: Was she born cool or was it something she acquired? Could there be hope for me?

It was pretty clear why women didn't like her. Carolyn was on top of her game. Maybe it was all an act but that never came across, at least not to me. She was a bit hard-core for my taste, meaning that there were a handful of qualities that would always distinguish her from me or, rather, me from her, and that was fine. She wasn't nice. Not unless she wanted to be. I always want to be nice. She was big into the finer things, something that I'd never really get. She teased me for choosing McDonald's over Zen Palate, deli coffee versus cappuccino, and she rarely took an interest in someone unless there was something in it for her. But still, I hoped and still do, that her "togetherness" would one day rub off on me. She knew who she was and what she wanted. I was still going through the motions.

I spent the rest of the afternoon working on my proposal for Zack. I called in a few favors from friends within the company. I knew that us "assistants" needed to stick together. We all possessed the relative dirt, the skinny, the dish, on our prospective departments. I wanted names of advertisers that we hoped to get and names of advertisers who couldn't afford us, so I called Debbie. I needed to know which bands were going on tour with the big ones, the bands who might actually break in the next year, so I called Sunny. I needed data, market research on what the "official" needs of young men and women were, so I called Robin. And of course, I needed someone to tell me how to build a spreadsheet, so I called Steven.

This was fun.

Zack popped out of his office a bit later and saw Steven and me sitting at my computer. "How ya doing', Stefan?"

"It's Steven," I said. (Zack meant well and I knew that Steven would never have corrected him, so I did.)

"Steven, of course. What are you guys working on?"

Steven was about to tell him and I quickly interrupted.

"Nothing, nothing. I couldn't find my, ummmmm, my cursor. So, well, I asked Steven to come up and help me find it." (Nice work, Vivian—not!)

"Cool," he said and went on his merry way.

"Vivian, what are you up to?" Steven asked.

"Nothing. I just don't want him to think that I don't know what I'm doing."

"But instead you tell him that you can't find your cursor?"

"Good point," I admitted. "Whatever. Just help me okay? Please?"

After about an hour it was obvious to us both that I was technologically challenged. Steven offered to build the spreadsheet for me if I gave him the data the next day. His boss was going out of town so he'd have the time.

I told him that he was a lifesaver and that I'd be forever indebted. He shrugged off my compliment, ate the last of my Milk Duds, and left.

Sophie called me toward the end of her day and asked first if John had called. "Nope," I said, rather joyfully.

"What's with you?" she asked.

"He's trying to play me. I know he'll call, Sophie. It's just a matter of time."

"I think so, too."

"Really?"

"For sure. Do you want to meet me for a drink at The Coffee Shop?"

I was a bit hesitant.

"Just me," she said.

"Yeah. When?"

"In about an hour."

"Okay."

"Don't be late, Vivian."

"As if!"

"Don't 'as if' me. An hour."

"Okay!"

I packed up my things and checked my voice mail one last time. Nada. I was just at the elevator when I realized I hadn't checked my e-mail. So I traipsed back hoping there would be something from John. I turned my computer back on, waited those few annoying minutes that seem like hours when you can't do anything but just sit there as the computer loads whatever it is that it loads.

Nothing.

Okay. No one had to know that I just did that.

He'll call. He'll call.

Friday came and I was at my wit's end. I did, however, have a foolproof game plan to present to Zack. One of the only truly good things to come out of an otherwise disappointing week. I went to Kinko's for the finishing touches and begged Sophie to handwrite my cover note for me. My penmanship is way beyond desirable or legible for that matter. She agreed after pointing out that Zack would be the first to know that someone else wrote it for me, being that he attempts to translate his messages about three times a day.

In my own defense, I was sure he would have to show it to his (few) superiors before it could be approved—always thinking positively. Besides, I wanted it to have a "personal" touch, one where no font could be compared.

After a few morning tasks, about three cups of coffee, and an impromptu "you can do this"–type speech between me, the toilet, and the four walls of my stall, I was ready.

When I got back to my desk, no sooner could I have knocked on Zack's door than he was waiting for me, as it were, right beside my desk.

"Can I talk to you for a few?" he asked.

"Of course. Gimme a second," I said.

I knew this was about my proposal. I could just tell. I had goose bumps, the good kind, on my arms and neck and back. I could feel them multiply by the second. I grabbed my bona fide "book report" and made my way into his office. I was so excited and so nervous I could barely contain myself.

"Why don't you shut the door?" he said rather seriously.

"What, Zack? Are you resigning?"

My joke didn't go over as well as I had expected. I remember thinking "SHIT!" The vibe I was catching wasn't the big promotion kind.

Here we go . . .

"Listen," he said, once I was seated. "I think you have enormous potential and so does practically everyone around here. You're probably one of the most well-liked employees VH1 has ever had." He seemed more shocked at that finding than I was just hearing it. "But the fact remains," he continued, "I talked to a few key people here and they felt quite unanimously that you aren't ready for the position you proposed. As much as we think you will get there one day, one day isn't going to be this week, this month, or this year, to be frank."

Wow. Okay, Viv, don't cry. Don't beg, but if you have to, get a little pissed.

"How am I expected to grow and learn, Zack, if I'm your errand girl?"

"Excuse me?" he said.

"Don't get me wrong. Everyone has to start somewhere and I'm grateful, but think about it. I think it's pretty amazing that I was able to see this gap and propose a solution from behind my desk, your calendar, and with six phone lines connected to each ear. I mean, be reasonable." My nostrils were flared a bit but I don't think I was tearing, at least at this point.

"I know what you're saying and I understand your disappointment. I really do, but you have to understand that half of what climbing the corporate ladder is about is patience."

"No offense, Zack, but not from where I sit. The only way I'm going to climb the ladder is if I go for it, break tradition around here, and all the while, not spill your coffee!" I stood up and slammed my proposal down on his desk during that last line. I was piiiiiissed! And since it was Zack, I half knew I could get away with it.

Just then, Will knocked on the door and Zack told him to come in. He was holding the most beautiful bouquet of flowers I'd ever seen and I turned away. I was nauseated. Zack was getting flowers as I saw my career—and my ego, thank you very much—get kicked to the curb. I got up and walked toward his window. I didn't want Will to see that I was upset. He gave the flowers to Zack and walked out, I think. Funny though, I hadn't heard the door close.

I wiped the tear that I could feel on my cheek, took a deep breath, and turned toward Zack. "Uh, it seems there's a mistake here, Will," Zack said.

I told Will not to worry about it, that I would take care of getting them to their rightful recipient once my nightmare was finished. I don't think I used "nightmare" actually, but you all know what I mean. The two of them had wide grins and cocked eyebrows. Zack urged me to take a look at the card.

The envelope was addressed to me!

Breathe, Vivian, breathe.

Just as eager not to open the card in front of them as they were eager for me to open it in front of them, I thanked Zack for doing all that he could—very sarcastically—and walked out with my flowers. I realized when I got to my desk that I had left my demonstration in Zack's office but I didn't much care right there and then, for obvious reasons.

Will followed me out and I nearly had to call security to get him to leave. I had a feeling who these might be from, and either way—should I have been right or wrong—I was certainly not going to receive this gesture in the presence of anyone but me, myself, and I. He told me I was selfish and I told him he was a queen.

The card read:

Dear Vivian, My apologies for not getting in touch sooner. I hope both you and your chin are doing well. (Are you as cute as I remember?) I would love to see you again. John

Slick Rick thinks a gorgeous bouquet of flowers was going to make things all better. Well, he's right!

Where's his number?

I have no idea where to even begin. After the flowers, I was basically on cloud nine for the next several months with the exception of a few inevitable digressions. (I've come to learn that when playing a game that's not quite you, you're destined to come in last or first, I guess, depending upon the way you view things. I'll let you all be the judge.)

I remember not calling him that first afternoon from the office. As much as I wanted to, I recalled Carolyn's strict advice all too well. Moreover, my gut seemed to say wait awhile or, at the very least, as long as humanly possible. How busy, distracted, whatever could John really be for an entire week just as a "thing" was brewing between the two of us? And that kiss—hello!!

Not calling me was not cool no matter how you sliced it.

That night I saw a movie on my lonesome, took Omelet to the park, and tried to finish a book I had started God only knows when. I fell asleep before I knew it and woke up beyond appreciative knowing I was "one night down" (as in the not calling John department).

The afternoon started out slow. Sophie was working and Fernando was not. Which equated to me getting the hell out of the apartment

ASAP. Small talk and/or quality time was not high on my priority list if you know what I mean.

It had been nearly a month since I had seen or talked to Lilly so I thought that if I was lucky I'd be able to track her down and bond! Karma was on my side. She was home—yeah!—getting over a broken heart and thrilled to bits at the idea of taking me to brunch, at the very restaurant her ex was waitressing at. I'd be the one to get her girlfriend's goat.

"Sure," I said. "I mean what are friends for, right? Just no kissing!"

We met at L'Express. Lilly looked genius! Beret, bloodred lipstick, a plunging black V-neck sweater, and I mean *plunging,* with super-long sleeves, a camel corduroy blazer, and fatigue-green velvet jeans. Her old skool Pumas kicked ass, and suddenly *my* whole glorified pseudo-grunge thing was so not working!

"You like me, don't you!" (Accentuating the "like" part) and with that I gave her a hug that she had to finally pull away from. It was so great to see her, such a change of pace. I love old friends!

Quick note: Much to my relief and less fortunately to Lilly's dismay, Amy was not working the morning shift.

We got high off espresso and full on French toast. We spent about two hours at the same table and poured our respective guts out, from Patrick to VH1, Fernando, John, and the old crew at Le Figaro. Lilly had been busy winning awards at local poetry readings and had very recently come out to her mother, having thought that Amy was the one. She said her mother wasn't the least disappointed but instead felt a sense of relief that Lilly finally trusted her. (It's nice and unfortunately all too rare when conversations like that can go so smoothly.) Anyway, Lilly was now working at an ad agency (hence the highfalutin getup), assisting the creative director, an import from England. Thankful that our waitressing days were behind us, we both agreed that a Figaro get-together was something to be planned in the very near future.

Reaching an epiphany, she stated, "He'd be great for you, Vivian!"

"Who?" I said, thinking that some glorious surfer dude was standing behind me. Not exactly, or at all for that matter!

"Garret!"

"Your boss? I don't think so."

With one guy on the table who was already working me, I told her to put Garret on hold.

In any event, what I loved most about Lilly's "Amy story" was that it was spontaneous and honest, at least in the beginning. No fix up, no one kept track of who called or kissed whom first. They spent every moment together after they first met and they seemed to encourage the other's goals. They also seemed to be on equal footing. That was until Lilly was stood up by Amy, only to find her tongue-tied with some other woman at a bar that very night. In front of all her friends and everything. You can only imagine.

Moving on, Lilly found John to be a prick once she got all the details. "Why even bother with him, Viv?" I remember her saying, and as much as I agreed with her, my heart couldn't provide me with an answer that outweighed the advice of my brain.

Typical.

We decided to walk off our breakfast and scour the 26th Street flea market. We were both obsessed with vintage T's and were in the mood to splurge. (It's always safe to splurge at flea markets. Very different and far less dangerous than designer shops in Nolita and SoHo!)

We made out like bandits, having arrived late in the day. We bought twelve shirts for fifty bucks. We spent twenty-five dollars each! Ya gotta love that! My personal fave was an old AC/DC black baseball jersey (white sleeves) and Lilly was beside herself with some kind of green cutoff tee that paid homage to The Incredible Hulk. To each her own!

We ran into Zack and his wife, Laura. They were lurking around these suspicious-looking keyboards and old guitars. We chitchatted a bit (they remembered Lilly from Le Figaro). Zack pulled me aside, wanting to make sure that I didn't take our conversation yesterday too personally. "It was a corporate thing," he said. I semi-accepted his apology but I was disappointed with him. Perhaps I was ignorant to the ways of the world. I just assumed he'd go to bat for me and hit a grand slam. Honestly, I was hoping that he picked up on the tiny fraction of guilt I passed on—mentally, of course.

Anyway, before too long, Lilly and I found our way to Sophie's shop. Sophie was thrilled to bits to see Lilly and left her customer high and dry in the dressing room. I left them there, saying good-bye to Lilly and thanking her for a great day. Just as I thought I had made a clean getaway, she hollered, "Be strong, Vivian!" I turned and winked, half knowing that at that point I didn't have it in me.

I walked for a while and stopped in a pizza place to pee. It was pretty gross but it was an emergency scenario! Minutes later, having just removed a huge wad of toilet paper from my shoe—and grateful I had only walked a single block with it on my person—I grabbed John's number from my jacket pocket. (Yes, that's right—I had carried it with me all day.) I called him at the first available pay phone and was leaving a message, as he evidently wasn't home. Just as I was about to hang up, he picked up (had he been screening?), and to make a long story short, we made plans for dinner at this sha-sha-sha-chic French restaurant on the Upper East Side. "Shall I pick you up?" he asked.

"No, not necessary. I'll meet you there," I said. I thought it best that he be kept waiting, surely not for a week, but I think a good twenty minutes plus would be fair!

I don't want you to think that this whole book is about men—it so isn't—but I do want you all to see how guys can be the benchmarks to change. The good kind of change, and notably, more often than not, and especially in my case, that's been all that they're good for! (Long term, of course!)

I can't help but shake my head at myself as I write these bits about John. Who was I then, and what on earth was I thinking?! I know it happens to the best of us, but that still doesn't make me feel too much better.

Okay, so this time around with John I decided to be the vixen. Fuck the "average" thing. What I had would be flaunted and what I didn't have, well, I'd figure something out. This was war!

Enter Sophie's asymmetrical ivory dress (fit more like a shirt, but whatever) with the tags still on. I was sure she'd understand and, if not, she'd get over it. Having just gotten my stitches out a few days before, I'd say the dress-napping was warranted!

I had black fishnets from a Halloween or two ago, somewhere, and I tracked down my black Manolo Blahnik knockoffs. A few dabs with my black Sharpie and they'd be as good as, well, sort of new. The whole asymmetrical thing presented a problem boobwise and having already committed to the outfit emotionally, there was no turning back. I had to nix the bra! 😮

After a while I realized that I was running late, of my own accord, so with my hair still wet and some remark from Fernando, "And where are you off to tonight?" I smiled politely, grabbed Sophie's black coat, and bolted.

Just as I slammed the door it dawned on me that I skipped out before my deodorant application—a major no-no for any Livingston. Fernando, of course, was already in the bathroom, door open, brushing up on his "reading" and swore that he'd only be a few minutes, which gave me way too much time to look in the mirror and doubt the whole thing. The getup, the girl underneath the clothes, and, of course, the guy. I hate when that happens!

Just as I was about to change, Fernando told me to get in there while I could, for reasons I don't care to repeat, so I did, and oh so carefully, as I was too lazy and too late to unzip and apply in the proper manner, so I pulled a Houdini and somehow managed to freshen up without a mark.

Still somewhat frantic, I also decided to utilize the mouthwash for the second time, and without a cup in sight to wash my mouth out, I did what all unladylike gals don't usually admit to: I rinsed my mouth from the sink. (Mom, forgive me!) And like a total idiot, I slammed my head on the faucet when I saw Fernando standing by the door!

Nice!

I managed to finally get to the restaurant, now about thirty minutes late. I walked in and looked around. No John. Okay?

If he left, or if he didn't show, or if he was later than me—it was over!

The maître d' asked for my coat and I gave it to him, all too awkwardly. I wasn't as ready to "work it" as I had been in the confines of my own bedroom. But when I saw a few of the gentlemen at the bar and a few of the girls at a nearby table stare me down, something told me that I had done something right. Cool!

I tried not to fidget, hoping that John was somewhere in the vicinity, and walked toward the bar. Just before I could sit, I felt a hand, a manly hand, grab my waist. I knew it was him and opted not to turn his way. "Are we a little late?" he whispered in my ear. (I loved when he did that!) I could smell the alcohol on his breath and, oddly, it was even more of a turn-on. I remember reaching my right arm above and behind me and resting my hand on his neck. I leaned his head slightly to my cheek and smiled as he kissed me. As far as I was concerned, it was just the two of us there.

I felt like a fairy princess.

We sat at the bar while we waited for our table and played with each other's hands as if we were about to read the other's palm. I ordered a White Russian. Lilly had mentioned that that was her new favorite drink so I figured I'd give it a try. John was drinking some kind of tequila. I liked mine much better.

"Turn around," he said. "You look incredible." Already gesturing for me to literally get up out of my seat and twirl around like a freakin' ballerina.

"No," I said point-blank.

"Please?" he asked all too cutely.

"Fine. But just once." I felt like a tool, but with one White Russian down and that face of his, my better judgment was already skewed.

I have to say, it wasn't half bad. I felt pretty. I felt girly—and together. I felt somewhat powerful.

He stood up, took my hand, and pulled me toward him and whispered, "I say we forget about dinner."

Okay. Now I felt like *I* was dinner.

"Absolutely not," I said and plopped back down and ordered another drink. I was *not* my dress, thank you very much!

Before long we were seated. The restaurant was lovely. Perfectly lit, genius music, and I have to say, against the dark brown leather seats and the garnet decor, my ensemble fit in perfectly. Sophie would have been beside herself! John didn't look half bad either. Sharp, tailored dark navy suit, and crisp off-white shirt. I could tell that he, too, had made an effort in the fashion department and I quite liked that.

I took a look at the menu and realized there was nothing I liked or that I had ever heard of before. Having never been brave in the cuisine department, I asked John to order me something as close to "normal" as he could. He found that amusing. I didn't.

Neither of us made mention of the weeklong no-call zone.

He ordered for the two of us and we sat there all googly-eyed and equally sexed up. I needed a moment alone to get my head together and slipped away to the ladies' room. I took a look in the mirror and saw that my hair had dried and taken on a life of its own, which sort of worked I guess. I pulled my stockings up (I hate when they're a bit too small/short and leave that ever uncomfortable gap below my crotch, don't you?). I then pulled down the dress as far as it would go—remember, I've got at least five inches on Sophie. I corrected my posture and flushed the toilet. (I have no idea why, I didn't even use it, and I'm sure no one was listening, but whatever.)

I got back to our table and John stood up. Not exactly used to anything chivalrous, I was a bit confused at first. When I sat, our appetizers were already on the table as well as a new round of drinks. (It was now time to start keeping count!)

Just as I was about to try whatever it was that was in front of me, you are never going to guess what happened. Way beyond my scope of the perfect scenario.

"Vivian? Is that you?" I looked up and over John and there was Jimmy! Remember? Actor Jimmy, bad-breath Jimmy who never called me after that first sweaty date Jimmy? Remember? And who cared really, this was SO MUCH BETTER!

Okay. Play it very, very cool, Vivian!

"How are you?" I smiled as I got up to greet him. After a kiss on either cheek and a brief hug, I grabbed his hand and introduced him to John. (This was so priceless. I swear!)

John's eyes nearly popped out of his head. Since our one and only date, Jimmy had been in two more films and had a big new television series that was due to air in the coming weeks. Anyone who watched *Access Hollywood* knew that. (No doubt John definitely did, but he was so the type that would never admit it.)

I told Jimmy that I was at VH1 and congratulated him on his obvious success. He babbled back and soon after asked if he could have my card. I don't know who enjoyed making John more uncomfortable, Jimmy or me? Those few minutes felt like hours and when we said our good-byes and I sat back down, it was now John who was forced to pretend that he didn't care.

I was now totally comfortable, nearly giddy, and it was me who felt the burden of moving on to a different topic.

I talked about work and that I was disappointed with the current situation. John said that Zack's response was probably textbook and actually doubted that he ever talked to anyone at the company. He made an effort to not make me feel that Zack wasn't my friend, and that that was the state of corporate America. "Keep your chin up," he encouraged in a somewhat cookie-cutter response, "which actually seems to be healing just fine." And he smiled.

He talked about his mother's impending birthday and that he would be burned at the stake if he went to her birthday dinner the next evening without a gift. He mentioned Carolyn's incessant inquiries about us and I told him to cut her some slack. She was just enjoying it. After a few more drinks and an awful main course, John finally asked, "So, how do you know him?"

Not quite sure how to answer I just told it like it was. "We dated when I first came to New York."

"Really," he said, very taken aback. "But I thought he was with . . ."

"Nope. It was just before that," I said.

"Oh," he said, somewhat put off.

"Come on, John, you can't think you're the only one with a résumé here?" I couldn't believe I said that, but I did.

"So, all your innocence . . . that natural . . . it's just an act?"

"I dated him, John. Does that mean I had to sleep with him? God. I mean really, who haven't you been with?!"

"What's that supposed to mean?" He seemed oddly flattered.

"Again another total hypocrisy. A guy can hook up left and right and it's an accomplishment, and the hotter the women, the more a man is idolized. I go out with one guy for half a second and all of a sudden I'm a tramp or I'm a groupie. Pleeeeeease!"

"Settle down," he said. "It was stupid of me to think that it was I who discovered you. You're unique. That's obvious."

"Was that a compliment?" I asked. I couldn't be sure. I wasn't fishing, honest. There was just something in his answer that just didn't feel right.

"Absolutely."

"Can we get out of here?" I asked. "I'm starving!"

It was true. I hadn't eaten any of my dinner.

"Sure."

He got the check, the maître d' got our coats, and we left. Instead of getting a cab, we decided to walk a bit. I knew I had seen a Ray's Pizza somewhere.

A few blocks later, cha-ching! We went in and I ordered two slices and searched like a cheese addict till I found the Parmesan. With a fruit punch, the sugary kind right from the tap, and John and I stuffed together like sardines in a booth, I was NOW in paradise!

I had left a note for Sophie to take Omelet out on the off chance that I'd get home "late," so with no obligations, the night was young! John still had to take his Domino out, so we agreed that we'd go to his apartment before we did whatever we were going to do next.

We finally got back to his place, and with my heels on, my drinks long drank, and my tummy in sheer paradise, I opted to stay in his apartment rather than join them for a walk.

I was too full to snoop around or even gather a general assessment of his place. That was unfortunate. Can you blame me, though? It was warm, my shoes were now off, I had a cashmere throw over my very bare legs and I had nestled into just the right corner of his sofa. I, the consummate lady of the night, fully passed out!

Vivian, the wild lover under the covers. Such a lightweight!

I would have paid to see John's face when he opened the door.

You kinda gotta sorta feel bad for him. You know what, though? You actually don't!

So there you have it! No sassy little love scene. Well, not just yet! That's what happens, GUYS, when you try a bit too hard to get your gals "relaxed"! It can often have the opposite effect!

I remember all too well the rush of "Oh My God"-ness that came over me as the sun woke me up, beating on my face, as if to say, "Wake up, you huge lush!" As I squinted to get a feel for where I was, it hit me immediately that I did not own a leather couch, that I was still in my dress, that I had fashioned a pillow out of the blanket, and that oh my God, my dress had indeed managed to become a T-shirt, due to a huge amount of squirming around in the middle of the night. I knew I was wearing the most "happy" pair of turquoise panties I owned, and although I was covered by fishnets, if anyone had been in the room, the image they'd come to greet was my tush. Fully expecting John to be sleeping and not seeing his dog in my peripheral, I thought that this lovely Kodak moment was to be mine and mine alone. Feeling crafty, so as to not make a single sound or draw any additional attention to myself, I slowly and quietly began to push myself up. I literally had to peel my sweaty face off the sofa. When had I become such an animal?

Before I was even halfway there (up), I heard a "Good morning!" that

I would have paid any amount of money to have been able to rewind and erase. John was literally behind me and my bum, taking in the view, and honestly, I wanted to crawl under the couch at that point and die!

I stood up, refused to face him, and immediately put my hands on my face hoping that if I clicked my heels a few times I would somehow be zapped home Dorothy-style! However, the genius I am then realized that I was still mooning him for all intents and purposes and, get this, I felt a wedgie!

What was there to do? What would you have done? I chose to laugh at myself and pray that all my jogging had had some kind of miraculous effect on the size and shape of my rear end.

I turned to him, tried to crush his head with my thumb and pointer fingers so as to not have to see his facial expression (Any *Kids in the Hall* fans will know what I mean), and had no choice but to remove my undies from my ass! I then hiked down my dress and put my hands on my hips.

"Don't say a word!" I threatened.

"Coffee?" He laughed. He also happened to have a cup in his hand.

I grabbed it and sat back down on his sofa/bed. I threw the throw over my legs and got a precious caffeine buzz going.

"How'd you sleep, J. Lo?"

Oh my God. He did NOT just say that!

Refusing to obsess about the comment, I just winced at him and burst out laughing.

This was one for the record books!

See, as much as I was thoroughly humiliated, I couldn't help but appreciate how hilarious the whole scenario was. And thank goodness I had not chosen to wear my yellow little chick-y panties. Things could have been so much worse! (Okay, maybe a *little* less worse.)

I sucked it up, both my humility and the coffee, and asked where the bathroom was.

"Right back there." He pointed. I got up, wrapped the throw around me, and headed to his more private quarters. Besides having indentations on my face, I didn't look all that bad. I washed my face, brushed my teeth (I had to use his toothbrush—simple chronic halitosis had taken over), and changed into the sweats and T-shirt that were hanging over his shower. I walked back out with my dress and hose over my arm only to find him sitting on his unmade bed and gesturing for me to come over.

I looked at my watch. It was only nine-thirty, so I tossed my dress on the nearby chair and plopped into (his) bed.

His shades were drawn, leaving this room considerably darker than the other. I was so in the mood to snuggle. We spooned and smushed under his down comforter to the sound of the streets below. I was in heaven! The more we snuggled, the more I wanted to kiss him. And from the "feel" of things, it was apparent that he wanted to do the same. The anticipation was killing me!

"Vivian," he said softly, "why don't you turn around?" But I couldn't. Of course we were about to smooch but it just felt so mechanical. I asked him instead to "get me to turn around" and from there began the most scrumptious tiny nibblings of my neck, my ears, and my cheek, until I was the filling of a John Oreo cookie.

He was the most amazing cuddler. He had the most delicate hands and the most eatable lips. It was a struggle to keep his sweatpants on.

Don't get the wrong idea. Remember that I had put on his!

John was probably the most aggressive guy I had ever been with. He definitely understood the word "no" but tried endlessly to get me to change my mind. If I had slept with him, as much as I completely and 100 percent wanted to, I would have never been able to deal with waiting another week for him to call me again. I'd be a basket case. Never mind not getting that promotion, had I slept with John and then if he had not called, I surely would have gotten canned!

He grew to accept the state of things that morning but having worked up such a sweat, among other things, we agreed that a cold shower was our only recourse.

He kissed me about a million more times and got up to run a shower. I'd take one after him. I sat up in his bed, turned the TV on but nothing seemed to get my attention. Quickly, I contemplated the pros and cons of getting in there with him.

- I'd regret it
- He'd see me naked in the light
- What would he think of me?
- Everything in my body wanted to
- I actually did need to take a shower
- I'd get to see him naked
- Who gave a shit at this point what he would think of me, I knew what I thought of myself
- I could always turn off the lights in the bathroom and bring in the candle that was resting on his bedside table.

IT'S SHOWER TIME!

I got undressed, picked up and lit the candle, opened the door, turned off the light, set the candle down on his sink and, nervously, slid the shower door open.

I'm too much of a prude to describe what happened in there—you do the math. After some time, our bodies were pruned and the aroma from the candle had gone from some kind of vanilla to that subtle burning smell when you know that it's about to go out. I laid my head back under the shower one last time assuming that it would be a fire hazard if we stayed in any longer. Just then, he held me close and just stared into my eyes. From time to time he would brush the trickling water from my face. I felt so naked. Yes, of course, I *was*, but you know what I mean.

I was sure this was love.

And I told him so.

Oh my God—of course I did not!

But you didn't have to be a mind reader. He was a smart guy.

We spent that day and many others afterward at his apartment. As the weather got nicer, we spent most evenings and weekends at the park, at his place, or at the movies. Jeans, sweatshirts, coffee, beers, whatever. Everything about our relationship was low-key. He started going to less and less of those "things," almost always conscious of the places and faces we would both enjoy. We never let more than three nights pass before we'd see each other. Even though I was always hoping it would be narrowed down to more like zero.

People knew we were dating and I just assumed we were exclusive. I cannot even tell you how refreshing it was to get past those first few weeks of trial by phone. After that shower, things were so easy. (There's a joke there somewhere . . .) I was pretty sure the game-playing and all that goes along with it was over. Now John would always call, even for no real reason, which I really liked and when I'd ring him, his assistant knew my name and would always bullshit with me before she patched me through. He loved movies almost as much as me and was a big hand holder. He was still into his fitness regimen but allowed for a few of the finer things in life—like my eating habits, thank you very much. He used to joke that I was the cheapest date he ever had. Burger King and Blockbuster and I was as happy as a pig in shit. He was a huge flirt and I was a big tease so the combination jelled nicely.

As nice as things were going, I didn't really feel confident enough to broach topics that were still gray. Love, exclusivity, meeting his friends, etc. But I figured we'd get there in time. I thought back to Carolyn's words of wisdom often and even went so far as to (I can't believe I'm admitting this!!!) not buy but flip through a few pages of the book *The Rules*. But, and no offense to anyone who's into that stuff, I just thought it was crap. Anyone who could suffocate his or her real wants, good for them. I knew I had a time clock with John. Sooner or later I'd burst. I was just hoping I wouldn't have to.

Let's see, what else? Oh yeah, he went on Rogaine and I went on the pill.

I went home one weekend with Sophie, about eight or so weeks into it, and broke the news to my family. That, yes, I had a "boyfriend." (My very first since college.) I confided to my mother and Sophie in the kitchen after dinner that I knew that I'd either marry John or he'd break my heart. One or the other for sure.

They both implored me to end it.

What do you think that meant?

They said neither of them had ever seen me so euphoric before, but Sophie's rationale (for her not so rah-rah reaction) was that I left things unsaid with John and I settled a lot. I did. She was right.

He was older than me. He had a reputation, and, well, as much as I wanted things to move quicker, I didn't want to spoil anything. In my defense, I said that I had to play the game. But to my mother's dismay, she knew she had not raised a "game-player." It was very un-me to be reactive in a "healthy" relationship of any kind.

I had had just about enough in that kitchen and was thankful that it was getting dark. My parents hated us driving back to the city at night so . . . oh well, it was time to go. And my God, it had only been a couple of months, why were they so quick to judge? Well, I know why, but still, how about a little faith?

During the ride back, Sophie defended her position. She had seen us together, seen us so happy, and I was insulted when she said that I was not myself with John because I really was when I was with him. I just knew that there were certain boundaries. And to her point, that was what was wrong with the relationship. In Sophie's mind, there shouldn't be boundaries between two people destined for each other.

I knew what she meant but I couldn't admit it. I was mad for him. I would settle if I had to until the relationship took on a pace of its own. That was my plan. She made me promise that if things got "weird," I would break it off.

"What do you mean, 'weird'?"

"I don't know, Vivian. Like, if you ever feel he's in control. If he's a jerk or if he's inconsiderate. You know what I mean. I just don't want you to have to feel that it HAS to work. At some point, and I'm not saying it's now, you have to stop being so agreeable. At some point, you have to get whatever it is that you want out of the relationship, ya know?"

"Agreeable?"

"Yeah, Vivian. When have you ever been the type to hold out on Friday night plans with friends, just waiting to see if he'll ask you to do something first? The Vivian I know would just call a guy up and ask if you were going to see each other or not. I know you really like him. It's just that you're sort of . . . I don't know. You just seem more interested that his needs are met than your own, when I just think that should be a mutual thing. Do you understand?"

"Yes."

"Look, I know how you feel about Fernando, and yes, he's no John . . ."

"C'mon, Sophie . . ." I felt bad.

"No. Just let me finish. But I say and do and ask everything and anything I want to. Not in the first week but pretty much right after. You're not the kind of girl who will do what it takes to snag a man. You won't ever have to, Vivian—you've got to see that. That's not my best friend!"

"Okay. I hear you. I really do."

"Promise?"

"Promise"

My fingers were crossed.

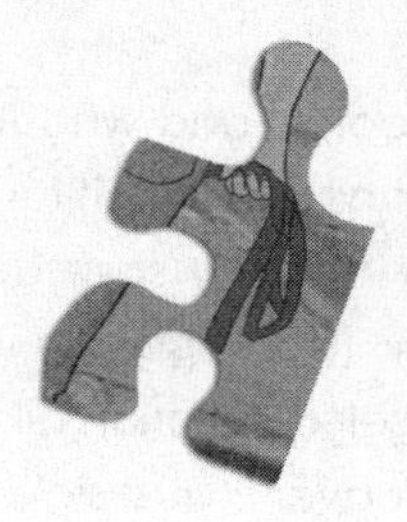

Okay. So it was like this:

I had a huge crush on John. And I guess it's hard to date someone you have a crush on 'cause you somehow somewhere don't see yourself on equal footing. But just the same, when I was with John I was on cloud nine. I was doing really well. I knew that to be true, I did.

As more time elapsed, the relationship got easier for me. Sophie would say that I was settling, but after a while I told her to stop analyzing and let me enjoy myself, and she did. Lucky for her! (JK!)

So the more comfortable I became in the relationship—I felt I had more perspective in all other areas, really—the more I could focus on other things. I was becoming more confident, more outgoing, I had more ideas and bigger aspirations. I was traveling down the road of *me*, if that makes any sense. I was realizing things about myself that I had forgotten or never really knew. Some good and, dare I say, some bad. Maybe it was all the sex; maybe it was because he seemed to like me back. Who the hell knows? I just like to think of him as the spark plug I needed and there's no real sense trying to figure out why. That's not the point. It's more about just going with it.

The one thing I can say, however, is that I still dig myself. I still like who

I've become and who I'm becoming. I still like my life, and John hasn't been at all a part of it for years!!! So, it goes to show you—and me for that matter—that my spirit according to me has next to nothing to do with one guy. (Don't get me wrong, that was a big epiphany. I didn't come to such a self-realization all on my lonesome or at the time. When it ended, I was sick over it. Just sick, but I moved on. We all do.)

So yeah, back to wherever I was—sorry about the digression but I felt it was important. Anyway, with my energy level in full gear and my love life in a rare state of calm, I was becoming very active. Taking a big bite of whatever I could sink my teeth into. And with every experience came more understanding. Things were hectic—to put it mildly—at work. We were producing endless specials, from *Divas* to the *Fashion Awards,* with after parties and press junkets. It was an insane few months.

I was everyone's brilliant "right hand" and it was getting annoying. I'm glad I was appreciated around the office and getting more and more experience under my belt, but enough was enough. If there wasn't going to be any "movement" for me at the company, perhaps there'd be a place for me somewhere else.

I felt like I was outgrowing my job as every day passed. We all need to be challenged in order to get to the next level—kind of like Zack's "sink or swim" thing. No one was throwing me into the water at VH1, and from the feel of things, everyone liked me just where I was. I wouldn't need my bathing suit for a good few more years!

My bitterness about my career was growing by the day and edging itself into my weekends. I wasn't looking forward to Mondays and I was fully living for Friday afternoons. I didn't really feel like I could talk about it with anyone. My counterparts at work saw me as the "lucky one." At least I was working for someone cool in a great department. Sophie, Lilly—they didn't really get it either. They thought my job was the bomb—free music, comped tickets, all the parties—they made me feel like I was wrong to want more. And my family, I hate to say it, but I don't think they felt that I needed to move up at all. So I did my best not to talk about it and vowed to make something happen for myself.

Look, I fully realize I was just a young'un there and all, but I've learned and I've seen firsthand that if you just accept whatever it is that just doesn't seem right, it all spirals downward from there. A slow spiral where you can see everyone moving ahead of you, and if you have a spark inside you, it's no one's fault but your own if you let it fade away.

John's take? He really didn't have one. If I wasn't saving the planet or working in some sort of Fortune 500 company, my job was sort of frivolous. Nice, right? No worries. I took care of that later.

Anyway, I realized a while back that I had not taken the "good copy" of my proposal with me after that disappointing day in Zack's office. It must have now been about four months since then, but I thought about reevaluating it and maybe seeing what else was out there for me. (I had everything in my computer, but the one that I gave Zack was so "pretty," I wanted it back!)

So, I go into Zack's office this one morning and ask if he'd saved my proposal. "Just a minute," he said and used his free hand to "shoo" me out. "Ewww," I thought. That wasn't very nice.

Will and I, both mutually disenchanted with work for different reasons, decided to take an early lunch and treat ourselves to a huge kosher delicatessen pig-out—corned beef, pastrami, cream soda, pickles—it was gross. By the time we rolled back to the office, Zack was ready and somewhat eager to see me. I asked him to give me a minute. I needed to burp, find an Altoid, and grab his calendar.

He started by telling me that he wouldn't have been able to survive the last couple of weeks without me. And as much as I knew it, it was great to hear him say it. He then pulled out my proposal. He said that as much as he appreciated the concept, he said my approach was way off. "Amateur" was his word of choice—ouch! Nonetheless, he said, it was apparent that having me sit behind my desk was to no one's advantage. I asked him to repeat that. I thought that maybe the sauerkraut from Katz's was bad or something and I was getting delirious.

Bottom line, my friends, I got a promotion! I was now the public relations and marketing coordinator of Zack's division. I got a raise, $4,700, and an officule of my very own! C'mon now, three walls are almost as good as four! I would have to interview and hire a new assistant before I could assume my new position and, well, he told me not to let him down, which I was (pretty) sure I wouldn't. Hip-hip hooray!

I phoned my mom, then Sophie, then John, in that order. I was so happy for myself. If I had a third hand I would have patted myself on the back! It felt better than sex—well, almost. My mom started to cry, Sophie screamed, and John said congratulations but that he would have to call me right back.

In the meantime, I phoned Human Resources and informed them of the change and requested all résumés they had on file. I wanted to fill my position quickly!

Sophie got us a reservation at some hot spot in the Meat Packing District and asked me for a bunch of numbers of some of my friends. We were going to celebrate. She also asked for John's number. I was a bit ambivalent at first but went along with it. I didn't think he'd be able to make it. He was leaving for Washington in the morning—had some business there and was planning to visit his family—so we'd see. I wasn't going to hold my breath. He hadn't even phoned me back yet.

Right now I was focused on my promotion! I went in to thank Zack for the hundredth time but he had slipped out already. I told Carolyn who was still there, and she was thrilled. She also confessed to knowing about it for a few days. Seemed as though Zack had worked hard to make it happen.

Awwwwwww.

I was a bit nervous to tell Will. I thought he might feel bad. But he was genuinely happy for me and was down with getting my little shindig started ASAP. We decided to skip out and get our makeup done at Bendel's before my big night. Don't even ask!

Will and I got to my "party" first—how embarrassing! But before too long, in marched a few of my friends and their friends and their friends and so on. You would have thought I was a pretty popular chick had you not known any better. Sophie and Fernando were the last to arrive. She hugged me and handed me a dozen red roses. Is she not the sweetest thing? Afterward, she took a quick look around and whispered, "I left him a message. Maybe he never heard it. It was pretty late."

"Please," I insisted. "This is wonderful. I'm so fine. If he's not a part of it, so be it."

All right, that was a fib. I was disappointed. So much so that I excused myself from the mayhem of our now very overcrowded little area and phoned my office and my apartment, hoping that John would have at least left a message. No such luck.

When Will's friends showed up, it was easy to forget that John had not. All male, all hot, and all 100 percent gay. Buzzed and boyfriendless, it didn't much matter to me what their orientation was. I danced with Michael, Chris, Frank, Scott, Tony, Justin, Jon, Steve, and Jay like they were single, straight, and in love with me! Just imagine how sad it was if you can. I believe I redefined the phrase "fag hag." Whatever. It was all in good fun.

The music was genius. One amazing song after the next. At one point, Will interrupted my little dance floor fantasy to tell me that Zack was there. As nice as it was of him to come, I told Will that he was going to have to wait. I had the music in me!

"Fine." Will laughed. "But at least rub the mascara off your cheeks. I mean, please!"

Evidently, it wasn't "sweat" proof.

I remember being urged into removing my top (of course I had a cami on underneath). It was a sauna in there and one of the guys thought my shirt would make for a great towel. Good idea actually. A lot more breathing room that way.

Then, sandwiched between Frank and Chris, all smiles, I looked over one of their shoulders and saw John pointing me out to a friend. He seemed amused and caught my glance. He gestured for me to come over and I did the same, nearly pointing the eye out of one of my dance partners. He walked over awkwardly, one hand in his pocket, the other grasping a beer. I was so happy he came, you guys. You have no idea.

"I didn't want to break up your fun," he said.

"What?" I yelled, I couldn't hear him.

So he repeated himself and we walked off to the coat check area where we could talk more easily.

"I feel bad. You left all your friends," he said, looking over to the dance floor. My guess: He was not getting that they were gay, and hell, it wasn't really my place to tell him! (Let him think they were all straight and living for me.)

"Congratulations," he said and gave me that perfect hug of his. "I'm really proud of you."

"Thanks," I said. "I wasn't sure if you were going to show up," I confessed.

"How could I miss this? It's your big night."

"I guess so," I admitted. And it really was, wasn't it? I was no longer only a participant in life. I had made a move on my own behalf. Probably the first since my decision to come to New York in the first place. It felt great. Too much emotion to sit still in fact. I grabbed John's hand and walked over to my friends. Everyone was very curious and very eager to chat John up. Zack came over and congratulated me again. It was so cool of him to show up. It really was. "I believe in you," he said.

From then on I've always made an effort to tell the people around me the nice things that I'm thinking about them. Even if it's not somehow appropriate or traditional. Zack's comment was so empowering. Why keep that feeling from someone else if I can help it? It's funny, even today when I feel like crap, like I'm just another squirrel trying to get a nut, so to speak, I remember some of the really nice compliments and remarks that have been bestowed on me. And it helps. It really does. Knowing that someone else believes in you, even if you don't in that moment, it's sometimes just the real boost you need to keep on going.

Anyway, we love Zack!

As everyone talked and drank and laughed, I took a backseat. I became an outsider for the moment and tried to make a mental note of what I had created for myself: The friends, the boy, of course, the pulse of the entire evening. I had come a long way. Sophie caught me in my little personal cocoon and winked. She got it. She knew what I was thinking and I could tell she was as happy for me as I was for myself. You're lucky in life to have a friend like that.

A little overwhelmed, I excused myself and stepped outside for some air. I thought it would get the cigarette stink off me and hopefully keep all the "you go, girl" complimentary shots from taking effect. Yeah, right! Still reeling, I walked back in and saw John scoping me out. He smiled, said something to Sophie, and grabbed my bag. Before I got to our table he was standing up and had moved a few steps in front of Will and Lilly.

"Are you leaving?" I asked.

"No," he said. "We're leaving."

And before I could comprehend what he meant, he lifted me up (think bride/groom, wedding night) turned (us) around to all of my friends and said, "Good night, everyone! You don't mind if I take my girl home now, do you?" You can imagine what my friends and what Will's friends shouted!

I waved good-bye to everyone, grinning from ear to ear, and in the arms of my boyfriend, left the bar. He whispered sweet nothings in my ear and I swear, I thought I was going to combust. Starting with my nipples first. It was so cold out there!

He wouldn't put me down until I promised him that I'd get sick if he didn't.

I will never ever ever forget that night. It was picture perfect—literally.

But alas, in the prophetic words of one of my all-time favorite songstresses, Ms. Stevie Nicks, let me quote:

"Players only love you when they're playing . . ."

That fucker!

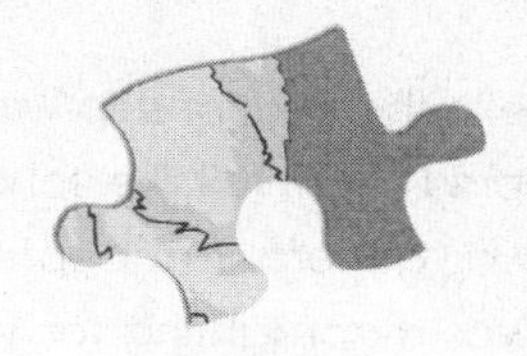

So the night was exceptional. You know what? Genius I think is more like it. (I could see what it must have looked like to the outsider and I know how it felt as the insider.) John was a regular Casanova. He knew exactly how to get to a girl's heart. And to that of her friends, I might add. The tape nearly ran out on my answering machine when I got home that next morning and pressed, "Play."

"Girl, he is amazing!"

"Loved him!!!"

"He's the one!"

Ugh! It actually made me nervous. It was all too good. I deleted them all and knocked on wood.

John went away that next afternoon for business, and from there on in, everything changed. I was now a very busy girl. With a promotion came pressure and great expectations, especially when you've convinced a number of exceptionally pessimistic people to give you a chance. I was no longer a nine-to-fiver. With no set schedule, no support staff, and endless opportunities, my calendar took on a life of its own. Events, appointments, walk-throughs, dinners, cocktails. My God!

When John eventually returned from his trip, he found he was now the one in the relationship with time on his hands. The tables were turning and, dare I say, it felt like John so-and-so was dating me, not vice versa.

It was generally accepted that my days began at eleven A.M. now that I was moonlighting for VH1 as its latest golden child. If there was a band, a venue, a freakin' caterer that was new on the scene, it would have to be me who would scoop the competition—even within my own department—and that meant lots of late nights out on the town. It was my job to be the arbiter of "new" and "fresh" and "now." I was one big walking adjective. My mind was always buzzing. I could never really "turn off." Everything around me seemed to fit into my job description. I was a lunatic!

I started drinking coffee like it was water. I had less and less time for the little things, like jogging for instance, stopping by Sophie's shop, returning phone calls in a timely manner . . . you get the picture.

And I was putting on a new kind of "freshman fifteen." What, like you think that only applies to academia? Not so. Try getting used to spending the majority of your time on your ass. Sitting at the computer, sitting through a meeting, sitting in a car, sitting at a concert, sitting at a dinner. Yeah, that part of the new job totally sucked.

I would try to explain my (new) job to my parents and they (still) could not believe I was actually getting paid. Running around Manhattan with an expense account and a car service. It was my job to make the most of the company's relationships—financial or otherwise—using resources like our talent roster, advertising/promotional budgets, or the time allotted to the company by a venue, or an act before and after events. What could we do with an artist based on his/her accessibility? How to do it in a way to please an advertiser while never appearing as though we were selling out and still maintaining the artist's integrity—even if he or she didn't have any!

I did really love it. It was just hectic. Lots of pressure. Fifty percent of which was probably self-inflicted. And John, well, his disdain for my chosen profession was becoming increasingly clear. "Much to do about nothing" is probably the best way to describe his attitude toward my stresses. He went so far as to belittle my freakin' business card. I'll never forget it. I had just gotten them, and was so proud. He barely glanced at it when I proudly handed it to him. He didn't even put it in his wallet! He left it on the bar where we were meeting friends that night, and when I spotted it as we were leaving, he tried to cover his tracks by picking it up and saying loudly, "Oops, I didn't mean to leave that," and then he stuffed it haphazardly into his coat pocket. I thought of the carefully preserved card I had from him neatly tucked into a special pocket in my wallet and how I gingerly took it out to look at it when no one was watching.

But the last straw was at dinner a few weeks after my promotion. He interrupted me.

"Hey, it's not all your department, Vivian. Don't do more than you can handle. Why don't you let Zack or Carolyn worry about the big things? That's why they take home the big paychecks, you know." We were at dinner in public and I knew John hated "scenes" but I was at my limit. The sex was great and we had fun together and all, but I could no longer block out my conversation with Sophie or my own instincts for that matter. John had never really shown interest in my work, or in my professional needs/goals, and the time had come to find out why. I decided: if he walks, he walks. I was going to stand up for myself.

I slammed my fork down in my Caesar salad and just as a few croutons flew upward like grasshoppers, I barked, "Where do you get off saying that? Do you even realize how insulting you are? You are so much more likable, and attractive I might add, when you're nice. Can't you just pretend to respect me?"

"Vivian, calm down. Please," he implored. And took a very long and nervous sip of his drink. Looking at me as he gulped, I'm guessing he sized up that I was furious, simmering like a hot pot of coffee on the stove for the last six months!

"I'm calm," I insisted as the steam whistled out of my ears.

"I had no idea I was making you feel this way. I apologize," he said. I was listening, barely. "I just see everything from a different point of view, and to be honest, I liked your old job better."

Well, at least he was being honest.

"I've been a spoiled brat since we met."

"Go on," I said.

"It was nice knowing that you were always 'present' when we were together, you used to give me so much attention. I was your focus. I was the one with all the obligations making room for you. It's just something I'll have to get used to. I'm sorry."

Okay. That was a pretty decent apology, and seemingly sincere. I decided to forgive him. But it was such a relief to finally feel like I could put my money where my mouth was with John. Like the advice I would give a friend I would now actually follow myself. I realized I had been quite the little hypocrite for a while. (As if you couldn't tell!)

We went back to his place, which was the norm at this point. (Fernando was still my guest of honor) and as I checked my voice mail in his kitchen, John went into the living room, put his Jamariquai CD on, and lit a cigarette. (Very rare, as he was more of a social smoker.) He poured himself a glass of wine, sat on the couch, tapped his fingers to the music, and put his feet up on the coffee table. I almost felt like I was spying on a neighbor or something, he seemed so far away. He must have scoped himself out through his reflection in the glass of his window a dozen times. One of his socks was annoyingly weathered by the sole and, I hate to say it, he had hairy calves. Call me crazy, but this was really the first time I could see John without my "la-la glasses" on. He was just another guy, sitting there with old socks and body hair! Can you believe it? It was strangely comforting to feel one layer removed from him that night. I was a bit over being the one who felt lucky to be with him. I seemed to have put on a new pair of pants in the relationship as it now stood, but I would soon see if John found them flattering. . . .

(You've got to wonder whatever was in that salad??? Was the dressing outdated or did it have an anchovy with attitude in its past life? For any of you who need a wake-up call in the boyfriend department and just happen to be in New York City—we ate at Ocean, by the way!)

It wasn't as if I was not as into him as I had been. To give you an indication: I still wanted to say "I love you" when I looked into his eyes, or was about to end a conversation (but I always held back). I had swiped a photo of him and his friend from his apartment, cut his friend out and placed it in my wallet without him knowing. I always looked at it when I had a few minutes to myself, sitting through traffic, during a boring conference, etc. I was way into him. Trust me. So, sure, if he had walked that night, I would have second-guessed my outburst forever. But still, for all intents and purposes, there was definitely a paradigm shift taking place. I was reclaiming my backbone as my life was beginning to take shape.

I think when you have more things going for you, and going on in your life, that which you can acknowledge at any rate, you invest less in the stake you've made in a relationship and more into the value you put in yourself. At least that's what was happening to me. And apparently, I was all too ready for it!

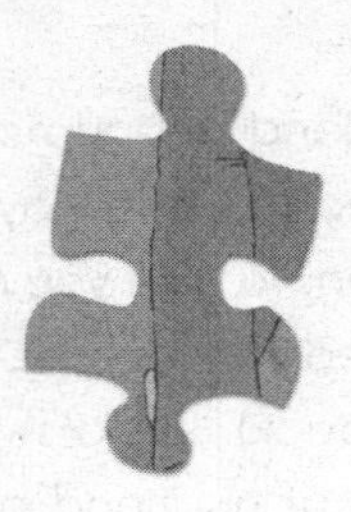

I passed out before John did that evening and scurried back to my apartment before he ever woke up the next morning. When I got to work everything seemed as it should be, until around noon when Zack asked if he could "see me," which made me feel like . . . well, you know when you're driving and a cop is driving behind you? You feel guilty for no reason. Like you've been speeding and are about to get nailed. Well, even with a boss as cool as Zack, the "see me" thing always made my stomach sick.

Thankfully, "see me" was not "you're fired" or "you suck at your job." Phew.

Instead, I was given my first official project. Where before I was always the afterthought, the throw in, or the production assistant, this time Zack was giving me a clear objective, a time line, a budget, and a goal. I needed to figure out a way to reach our male audience, get in a live show with a band that was on the brink but with no real national following, leverage the advertising dollars that the corporate parent had invested in print, and, oh yeah, I had three weeks.

The "out" was that if I didn't come up with something "fabulous" we'd simply save the money, so, according to Zack, there was "no pressure."

Yeah, right! Can you even imagine not being able to dazzle when it's the first real time it's been asked of you? Not me—no way!

I liked these little marketing riddles but, yeesh, they were usually more of a game than for real. Those next three weeks also could not have been more hectic. Not exactly "idea time," if you know what I mean. John was being a shit; Zack's new assistant, Elizabeth, wasn't catching on as quickly as we had both hoped; Gabe was "staying" with us yet again; and to make a long, long, long story very short, my eldest brother Simon and his wife, whom my family all around does not speak to, had had their first child and neglected to inform us that they were ever even pregnant. Crazy, right? Don't tell me you thought I came from Beaver Cleaver land? Hardly!

Anyway, now that I was an aunt, I had to at least send a gift, never knowing if it would even be opened. Joseph wanted no part in the whole thing. It was his ex-girlfriend who phoned him to congratulate us on the birth. Her sister was also there, in the same hospital, having twins, yada, yada, yada. So I thought it best to pick out a present from the two of us. Having never been to FAO Schwarz before and having always wanted to go, now I had the perfect excuse.

So I'm there, feeling like a really big kid in a candy store, roaming around, trying to decide between a three-foot panda bear and a Barbie town house, and I come across three young boys and their dad, I guess, playing with all these race cars. Then I noticed that the toy store had allocated almost an entire floor to the subject of "cars." The more I looked around, the more I saw the bevy of merchandise and all the guys "playing," almost using their kids as an excuse to visit this little "Matchbox" world. Interesting . . .

Right, so I get to work the next day and do a bit of research on the whole NASCAR thing. Seems as though, right before my eyes, it had become one of the country's biggest sports. Though it was still unknown to me, sort of like wrestling and the WWF, but I guess, rightly so, as the fan base is largely male.

Bingo! Male audience . . .

I have no idea where to begin and don't want to bore you with the details. I think it's best to just lay my idea on you rather than go through the motions of how I came up with it.

I nervously went into Zack's office about three days before my three-week time clock wound up. I pitched him my "Put the Pedal to the Metal" concept. (A phrase that my dad had belted into my ear the first day he taught me to drive stick.)

"Go on . . . ," he said.

"We get a venue, like a racetrack, already filled with fans, with tons of space, and eventually lure them to the stage we build for the band, just off the perimeter of the track. We partner up with a big driver or a team that already has its own fan base and give them camera time in exchange for their draw. Maybe we put a few of their cars on or near the stage, which will only make their sponsors happy, and have cool T-shirts and music and stuff to give away to all the folks who show up. Now, men love metal and music and they also love women, right?"

"Right." He laughed.

"I say we get a few girls there . . ."

"Girls?"

"Sorry, models, who can wear the latest 'racy' fashion. I don't know. Like sexy, bright colors, etc. I bet we can get a magazine to shoot the girls now that we've created a backdrop that they don't even have to pay for? Don't ya think?"

"Sure."

"Right, so between the models, the drivers, the band, the fashion, the crowd, and hopefully the photo shoot, all simultaneously, you'll have your little program! What do you think?"

I stood there, quietly freaking out, sweating like a fiend and sporting that hideous "nervous" bad breath. I couldn't stop fidgeting. I mean it all pretty much made sense to me, but Zack would be the judge. He sat back at his desk, with his two hands interlocked behind his head, and asked, "You think you can pull that off? It's an awful lot of cooks, ya know."

"With help, I'm sure I can," I said. Then I raised my eyebrows and scrunched my nose into my eyes. "I mean, I'll try." (Always know what you don't know!)

"I love it," he FINALLY said.

"Really?!"

"Really. It's a big idea. And I'll need to run it by a few people, but I like it, Vivian. I'm impressed."

This was a glorious thing. Truly.

"I'm just doin' my job," I said and strutted out of his office (think *Saturday Night Fever*).

Back at my desk, I phoned Carolyn and asked if she had a minute, to which she answered, "I have a few, what's up?"

"Nothing," I said. "Could I come by?"

"Now?" she asked.

"Yes."

"Sure. I have to leave in about an hour. Does that give you enough time?"

"Yeah. More than enough."

When I got there I could tell she was a bit disappointed to hear that I wanted to talk shop rather than talk "John." I wanted to run my idea by her and see what she thought. Before she answered me she asked what my budget was. When I told her she shouted, "Fabulous!!!" then asked, "Okay, tell me, how's John?"

"Fine," I fronted.

"What do you mean, 'fine'?"

"I just think he liked me better before everything."

"What do you mean, everything?" She was getting annoyed and needed a better description.

"The new job, the new life, the new outlook."

"You're probably right," she said. "But that's normal. You're a different woman now than you were when you met him," she said.

"Carolyn, please, it's only been six months."

"Still," she went on, "you're a 'somebody' now. . . ."

"Oh, are you telling me I was a nobody before?" That was real nice.

"Not to me, sweets, but maybe to him."

She wasn't making me feel better, but at the same time I was getting that she wasn't really trying to either.

"John's never been one to take the backseat, if you know what I mean. He likes the spotlight. What man doesn't really?"

This was not exactly big news to me. John had said a lot of this himself. I was beginning to feel that John liked having an "average" sort of "regular" gal pal, to fit his whole "regular" image that he thought he was giving off.

"It's not such a big deal, Carolyn," I said. I confided in her and told her of my misgivings with John.

"Vivian, please. I hear you. But he's John so-and-so. You're just going to let him go? He adores you."

"I don't know if it's me, Carolyn, or if it's him that's the problem. Honestly. I sort of feel like he needs the right arm-piece. Maybe he doesn't even know what he wants. I can't explain it and it's too soon to say. There's just something not right."

She winked at me and politely walked me out of her office. She was late.

John had actually left a message for me with Elizabeth while I was in with Zack. He asked her to have me call him back right away. So I did and when I heard his voice on the phone, I was far less critical of him than I had just been with Carolyn.

"How are you, cutie?" he asked.

"Fine," I said. I was waiting for him to ask me how it went with Zack. He knew I was going to give him my pitch that day.

"How'd it go?" he asked enthusiastically.

"How'd what go?" I played stupid.

"Pedal to the Metal." Wow, he remembered the name.

"Very well." I smiled.

"Good for you. I knew it!"

"Thanks," I said.

"Listen, I have this co-ed charity basketball thing tonight at Chelsea Piers—seven o'clock—you wanna come?" John asked.

"Definitely!" I said. "Can I meet you there?" I had a few things to do and would still need to go home and put my kicks on.

"If you have to . . ." I could tell he was a bit annoyed that business would be coming first but I assured him I would be there on time, blah, blah, blah.

I got all the info, got squared away, ran home, and changed into my very favorite navy tethered sweats from school, laced up my Air Jordans, threw on my last clean white tank, and my semi-grungy gray sweatshirt—fresh from my hamper! Whatever. This was all very last minute, okay?!

When I got there, I was pleasantly surprised. John was with a ton of friends, most of whom I'd never met, and they all seemed quite anxious to meet me. Furthermore, we were playing in this round robin thingamajig, and I had a few inches on most of my female competition. The vibe there was very positive. We were playing in a benefit for AIDS Education and, apparently, to participate you had to donate a bunch of money, and I really liked that John had chosen to do it.

"Why the last-minute notice?" I asked. "I would have loved the time to practice."

"Umm. Actually, I was supposed to play with a colleague of mine. But she wasn't feeling well, so I thought you'd be up for it."

Okay, that didn't sit very well. Just as I was about to ask him exactly who this "she" was, I got my answer. Little Ms. Happy Helpful, who was coordinating things, assumed I was the colleague, "Grace," and walked over with a name tag.

"No," John said. "This is Vivian." She looked confused so John explained.

"Whichever!" she smiled and gave me a crossed-out black-markered name tag. "Grace, Vivian. Honestly, John, I can't keep up!" and she hopped away with her ponytail in simultaneous step with her stride.

There was no time to get pissed at him or try to catch up with Suzy Q and maybe trip her or something. She was obviously a bit of a dimwit who meant nothing by what she said. And I couldn't have bad thoughts about her—she was a volunteer for God's sake. I slapped on the "Hi, my boyfriend is a player" scarlet letter, I mean name tag, and chose to just take it to the court, sweat it off, and be happy.

Needless to say, I kicked serious basketball ass and won the respect of John's peers! I also accidentally missed a basket and nailed Susie in the back. Just kidding. It was only a fantasy!

Afterward, a bunch of us ventured to a nearby pub for some lager and twenty-cent Buffalo wings. D-licious! John's friends were pretty decent. They all sorta reminded me of one another. Mid-thirties, Rogaine, all bachelors to the core and interested in me, my comments, and opinions when it seemed as though they had nowhere else to look. It was weird. They were great with their "hellos" and very chummy, telling me all about how "crazy John was for me," but after that, there was nothing left to bullshit about. And after they had covered all their bases, they moved on to politely ignoring me.

I didn't much mind really. I was always bad with meaningless banter. John and I actually outlasted them all, and when it was just the two of us, one on one, everything felt much better. He was very impressed with my moves, he said, and equally with my tolerance level for his friends.

"Thank God!" I rejoiced.

"What do you mean?" He seemed surprised.

"Just that they were a bit creepy. Nice and all, just . . . I don't know."

"They're just not great in front of women. Neanderthals to the core!" He laughed.

"Ha." I faked my laugh back.

"They're harmless. Prep school friends. If they don't need you for something, their interest begins to slip."

I was confused and slightly insulted. He saw my look and backtracked.

"No, no, no, Vivian. You are just not what they're used to. I mean, they're the same way with . . ." He searched his memory banks for an example.

I bit into a chicken wing and pretended it was John's arm.

"Like Carolyn. Exactly, like Carolyn!" he said, relieved.

Now, until then I had never been compared to Carolyn, and believe me, I would have seen it as a compliment in any other scenario, but there was a negative coming, I could feel it. I put the bony wing down, wiped my barbecued lips with a napkin, and waited for this incredibly charming explanation.

"Okay. Carolyn. She's great. She's smart. She's sexy. She's successful. And she married to what's his name . . ."

I reminded him. "Stephen."

"Right."

"So?" I said.

"Well, it's not like she . . . how do I put this? She sort of climbed her way up."

"Excuse me? So your friends think I'm climbing—what am I climbing? You? Or wait—you think I'm climbing . . ."

"No. Jesus Christ, Vivian! You're always so quick to judge!"

"You've got to be kidding me!" I just had to laugh.

"These guys all come from families. Established families. Same with me. Carolyn didn't. And . . . you don't either. And I'm fine with that. You know that."

"Oh, thank you. Thank you so much, John. Do you know what you sound like?"

"I'm just telling you how it is. It's not what I'm about. I've told you that from the beginning. I'm just trying to make you understand."

"I understand fine!" I grabbed my stuff and ran out of there. It was terrifying to hear him speak, and to bad-mouth Carolyn when she thought he was her friend—that she was a friend to his family. The whole thing made me sick.

I couldn't find a cab so I crossed the street and tried the opposite corner. I saw him standing by the door, looking around, talking on his cell phone. Probably leaving me a message. He was visibly upset.

I dared not move a muscle until he was on his way. I was too angry to talk, especially out in the middle of the street. Between the "Grace" remark at the game and then all of that garbage in the bar, I didn't know who I was dating anymore. And then I just had to ask . . . did I ever really know? Did John see me as an activity? Was he slumming? Did he get off on attracting and conquering women just for kicks?

He decided to walk home and I decided to follow, a good ways behind him. He was walking real slow and he shook his head a lot. He didn't really have the makings of a creep in his step. He seemed upset, which of course, made me feel bad.

One thing that I still hadn't overcome with men was questioning my own reactions. Mark told me for years and years that I was the one who was nuts, who would overreact, who would make him do or say things he didn't mean to. He rarely took the blame. It's very hard to explain, but putting the fault on me rubbed off. I knew I'd get past that routine eventually, I had just hoped it would have happened by now. Especially with everything else that was working in my favor. My life was going great. A real about-face since my time with him. But alas, Mark left his mark—for the time being anyway.

So naturally, I questioned my behavior for blocks. I thought about what a "catch" John was for blocks. I imagined just being another one of his flings for blocks and then, of course, concocting some ridiculous rationale for his remarks for blocks.

It's a vicious cycle.

It wasn't long before I sneaked up behind him, scared him half to death, and apologized for jumping to conclusions. Can you say "Ewwwwwwwwwwww"? I can—now.

We kissed and made up. It was never mentioned again. But I thought about it often. Carolyn hadn't a clue of her reputation within her circle. And it's not like Carolyn to give a crap about what people thought of her, but I had a pretty strong feeling that meant "outsiders" and not her careful group. Sadly, she would have been devastated had she had a clue, and strangely, it made me think less of her in a way. Why would her judgment be so off? Or maybe it was all the wolves she surrounded herself with . . .

Who was I to talk?

I had less than a month to pull off "Put the Pedal to the Metal." It was approved with flying colors apparently, and, luckily, I had every resource at VH1 at my fingertips. Meaning, that Zack put a staff of eight on the project, relying on other people's contacts, experience, and know-how to see it through. I would have been a sunken ship without the team, had he assumed I knew how to execute the damn thing. I was the chick with the ideas at the time! When I told my mother about it she insisted I was selling myself short, that I could do anything I wanted to if I put my mind to it. (And that made me think of John, again. Why didn't he encourage me that way?) But as much as I loved her confidence in me, Mom knew nothing about permits, production, and insurance. Nor did I, at any rate.

Zack assured me that I would get full creative credit and learn a ton in the process, and I trusted him implicitly. The location was The Laguna Secca Race Track in California. We'd be working in conjunction with the Newman-Haas racing team and Carolyn saw to it that *Marie Claire* would simultaneously shoot their fashion story as well. Get this: Newman-Haas racing is Paul Newman and Mario Andretti's team! How insane is that?! So for a week, I'd be chillin' with Paul. Yeah baby!

In pre-production I worked largely with the creative staff, developing the look and feel of the concert, producing flyers, mailers, coordinating the swag. I was cc'd on every bit of minutiae—at Zack's insistence—ensuring that I'd see the scope of the entire experience from beginning to end. I had no idea what it would take to make something like this happen. What's that Hillary Clinton line? "It takes a village." Very appropriate!

My responsibilities in Cali were of a completely different nature. In addition to the normal "talent relations" stuff, my job would also be to coax the Newman-Haas team into being as "involved" as possible. From the pre-publicity, to the shoot, to the concert. I didn't know exactly how I was supposed to do that, but Zack and Carolyn both assured me that I'd figure it out. Okay?

This was to be my very first true business trip. I'd traveled for work before, but never outside the East Coast. I was terribly excited. My nerves about the project had dissipated after the acceptance of the concept from the get-go. The rest was going to be the ride of a lifetime.

We were booked to stay at The Mondrian in Los Angeles. When I told Sophie she nearly puked. She had recently read, in *Vogue,* of course, about the Ian Schrager hotel and felt that it was her destiny to come along with me. When I mentioned that Will was coming with me, she flew off the handle and recommended herself for Elizabeth's job. She said that this trip would be something way up her alley, and not really up mine at all. And she was halfway right—until I saw the hotel!

"What about fashion?" I asked.

"What about it?" she huffed and puffed.

I felt bad. As much as I would have loved her to be there, the idea of packing a friend seemed incredibly novice. I already had to figure out how and where to stash my teddy bear (Theo). I mean, if I couldn't take Omelet, Theo was a definite!

Let me just say that while everything was beyond incredible at the office, my self-esteem had taken a nosedive since the "I'll follow you home and forgive you" fiasco with John. I felt like two different people. The young gun with all the potential in the world and the secret weakling.

What made matters worse was that I even shocked myself, having "fallen off the wagon" just after I had made such strides over Caesar salad.

I often contemplated ending things with John over that month, but I never did anything, and I can't tell you why. I knew John was a bad egg. I really did. But it was his reputation in part. To break it down: I never saw myself as part of a list before, you know? But with John I did. I was going to be just a name on a list of girls he'd had relationships with before he'd settle down, and something about that really bothered me. As much as I tried to see that if I broke it off I'd at least have a few great stories and some nice memories to take with me. But for some reason, that wasn't good enough. I abhorred the idea of being "played," and it felt as if after six-plus months I was still playing a losing game with John.

What also sucked was that I had lost the little bit of power I had claimed in the relationship. After that basketball game, and my little reconciliation scene in the street, I was a verbal doormat. Albeit a "cute" one . . . yuck! It was as though "free prick speech" was now permitted as far as John was concerned. The remarks that he would have hidden from me before, all his elitist shit, was now somehow okay. As if he felt that I had succumbed to his rationale, now that I had forgiven him for his initial comments. He seemed to think I had admitted that I wanted to be accepted into his clique. Please!

As angry as I was, I still wouldn't leave him. I ignored the situation instead and pretended that he was different. Like he wasn't like "them"—the pompous crowd he spent all of his free time with and a ton of our time bashing.

I was a joke.

To make matters worse, my friends still adored him. I know that my colleagues got a kick out of the fact that I was dating him, and I was too ashamed to tell anyone that he was not at all what he had seemed.

On the bright side, I could have chosen another Mark to shack up with, right? At least he wasn't an animal. John was a jerk, but he wasn't the devil. It was an improvement. A pathetic one, though!

Nothing is ever perfect or uncomplicated for that matter when it comes to my life. The good, the really good, seems to always come with the bad, and again, the very bad. So I was off to California in a relationship that looked great on my résumé, about to accomplish a huge professional feat, building my other résumé, for a job down the road that I would have never expected even if someone had laid it all out.

Never a dull moment.

The night before I left, John and I saw a movie and had a great Italian dinner. He was on his best behavior. Tons of PDA, a big "I'll miss you" speech, and an all-night make-out fest. (I'll leave it at that.) He almost found his way back to the glorified "incredible" category and my emotions, the whole relationship, nearly seemed real. But somehow I knew better. We were seeing less and less of each other but neither of us seemed to mind. Usually, that would be the first sign of a breakup—but he positioned it as being more mature. More quality time. Whatever.

It was hard to say good-bye to my puppy. Since he came into my life, I rarely slept without him. But Omelet seemed all too happy to be spoiled by his favorite aunt for the next week and after going over a very overzealous checklist with Sophie, I was pretty sure he was in good hands.

I flew business class to Cali—a first! Arrived at this "Mondrian" place, and immediately got what all the fuss was about. As I pulled in with Carolyn in our silver Saab convertible, Slash from Guns 'n' Roses was pulling out! David Copperfield was checking in just as we were, and to top it off, we shared the elevator with Matthew Perry, a.k.a. "Chandler Bing" from *Friends*. Hello, Hollywood!

When I got to my room, I almost fainted. Chic is not the word. Huge isn't either. I had a deluxe suite. Oddly, filled with less furniture than my bedroom. There were white orchids scattered in vases on every available table. Everything was white, actually, with the exception of the dozen long-stemmed roses on "my desk." I know, ridiculous, right? I hadn't a clue who they were from and for the moment, I didn't care. I didn't want to go back to New York—ever—and I hadn't even unpacked! The weather was about eighty degrees, my view was just brilliant, and they had all my favorite candies and goodies unpackaged and sealed in clear plastic containers lined up like artwork along the kitchen's counter. Finally, someone else held pistachio nuts and M&M's in as high regard as myself!

My king-sized bed was made perfectly, like an *Elle Décor* shoot or something. I didn't even want to sleep in it—it looked so good as is. I had two televisions, a bountiful bathroom filled with all the amenities, about four or five phones, and a decadent wine and cheese platter laid out in the dressing area. Had I woken up that morning as Madonna?!??! This was the life!

I took one look at my matching bathrobes and got naked ASAP! I found my disposable camera and, I kid you not, started snapping pictures of my room. Such a rookie, I know! There was a knock at my door and I quickly hid the camera, tied my robe, and answered it. It was Will. He took one look at the spread and started screaming! I followed suit! We both landed on the sofa and after he told me that he felt like Rupert Everett I was sure it was all right to introduce myself as The Material Girl!

We laughed until our stomachs hurt and proceeded to raid the minibar, oblivious to the tab. Six-dollar Pepsis, twelve-dollar beers, five-dollar Pringles. Scary!

"Wait, just one second," Will promptly interrupted the bingefest. "And the roses . . . ," he inquired.

"Oh, God, I nearly forgot," and I jumped off the comfy sofa, almost losing the robe.

After Will realized that he was sitting on something other than a cushion, that is my stashed camera, he called my name as I was reading the card:

> *"Vivian. Have a wonderful time in California. Remember that Paul Newman isn't half the lover that I am and get home soon. Love, John."*

Try to imagine the snapshot that Will got.

Right.

So what would you have done? What would you have thought? Smooth operator? Sincere? Time for a shrink? I had no idea what to make of it. Will was beside himself, sure that we'd tie the knot before the millennium. What a joke.

"You're not going to call him?" He was perplexed.

"No," I said.

"And can I ask why?"

"No," I said.

"Alrighty then." He couldn't make heads or tails of my comments or lack thereof and decided instead to buzz the rest of our crew, to find out what was on schedule for that evening. We were not beginning real pre-production until the morning after next so, for all intents and purposes, we were on vacation!

That evening was dinner. Apparently people in Los Angeles were not big into late nights so at the rate we were going, dinner was our only option. Carolyn made us reservations for seven at nine. She wasn't coming. She gave no explanation but Will was not surprised. Being the most senior on the project was his guess. (To put it mildly.) I didn't really think too much about it.

All dolled up, we made it, finally (Los Angeles is a tough city to navigate), to Chaya's. Leave it to Carolyn! Swanky, overpriced, and apparently an A-list destination. Not bad for our first meal. I made Will promise that he'd sit next to me at dinner. I barely knew the other people we were with and, much like Dorothy, have always preferred home to vacations without my mom, best friend, or of course, my puppy.

The food was phenomenal. I was toasted for my little "brainchild" and thanked for getting everyone out to LA for something fun to work on. It was awesome. Sitting around the table were two other men and two women: Pete, Gene, Lori, and Susan. Lori and Susan were publicists, Pete was in production, and Gene, what did he do? . . . oh, he was in programming. I got on real well with everyone. Sort of. There was something about Lori's consistent questions about John that freaked me out a bit. After a few drinks it's absolutely fine to ask personal questions—I mean, we were going to be working together for a week, it was cool—but her vibe was real dark, somewhat sarcastic and, well, like I said, she just rubbed me the wrong way.

I noticed how hungry and thirsty people can get when they are not paying for dinner. Pete was picking up the tab that night so he said not to worry, which is somewhat ridiculous considering that he was just going to expense it. But I went along with it all. I was the newbie. I had expensed dinners and such before, but never to this extreme. After being put up in a suite that could easily sleep our entire crew, I thought better to just enjoy it. Let the decadence begin! And when asked if I wanted anything for dessert, how could I refuse?

What was funny was that everyone was sure that the random passerby or the guy in the corner was "somebody," which was actually entirely possible in LA. The people-watching was out of control. Especially for us jet-lagged, over-saki'd bunch of out-of-towners. When Nicolas Cage walked in, I thought I was seeing things. Or at least a guy who looked a lot like Nicolas Cage. We actually made Gene verify it on a bogus bathroom visit.

We finally made it back to the hotel. They all decided to stay and play at The Sky Bar but I couldn't. As much as I wanted to, my eyes were closing, the place was spinning, and it was time for bed-d-bye.

I got back to my room, figured out the whole key thing eventually, unpacked Theo from my suitcase, and washed up before I crashed. I plopped down on my gluttonous bed and wished that Sophie or Joseph or Gabe was with me. This was just too beautiful a place. You had to share it. It seemed crazy that I was there for work. I noticed the flashing red light on my bedside phone and eventually realized I had a message.

The first was from Carolyn. She wanted to go hiking in the morning, get massages, and then "shop Robertson and Fred Segal." She'd be out front waiting for me at ten. Fuck. It was already two A.M. Hiking? I don't know . . .

The next three messages were from John. Missing me, then worried, then irate that I hadn't called him. I was torn. Part of me felt guilty and part of me had no desire to talk at all. It was now almost five A.M. in New York. I thought it best that I call him in the morning.

Just when I thought I would pass out, I couldn't. Don't you hate when that happens? Instead I opened a twenty-dollar clear bag of yogurt-covered (stale) pretzels and watched *The Bodyguard* on pay-per-view. And who was the one with the corporate conscience just hours ago?!

I woke up to a horrible banging at my door. I thought it was Fernando until I fully came to.

It was Carolyn all made up and ready for her perfect LA day. Hair half up, half down. Great worn-in but perfectly new T-shirt. Roomy enough to insinuate that it was a throw-on but cropped enough to flaunt her abs. Gucci messenger bag, sweatshirt around her waist. How she managed to find the chicest Nikes in town I have no idea and, of course, black leggings with not a shred of white dog hair. Nice work!

"Did you not get my message?" she asked.

But before I could answer, she made a beeline to the roses and had no problem reading the card.

"Young love . . . and thanks to me!" She basked.

I felt a headache coming on.

"Let's go, let's go!" she urged. "We've got appointments at noon and with this traffic we'll be lucky if we get a good hour hike in."

Nightmare!

She picked out my outfit and ordered me a cappuccino. I took a cold shower. It was the only place where I was somewhat sure she wouldn't bother me.

By the time we got out front I was actually semi-glad she had taken the initiative. It was a beautiful day that I would have definitely slept through. Between you and me, I had stalled quite a bit. Hiking in the desert is neither my idea of a vacation nor a morning activity. Instead, she took me to Coffee Bean and Tea Leaf, where she promised I'd never have a frozen frappa, cappa, something or other as good or even comparable again. She was right! I loved LA!

Whether I was Carolyn's pet project or she was using me for companionship, I always had fun with her and I could tell this little adventure would be no exception, and the fact that she was hell-bent on showing me the city "her way." Hey, who was I to argue?

I let her do most of the talking. She talked about her career, her marriage, and about her future. She asked me what I thought every now and again, but what she really meant was what I thought about what she had revealed about herself. If I've positioned her as this big bitch, she wasn't. To me, she was this larger-than-life character who, very simply, was very interesting to be around. She gave very sound advice when I asked for it. But basically, would never really stop for air unless I provoked her. She paid for my massage, which, I thought, was really sweet, especially after she saw my face when I saw the price tag. I discovered what "Shopping Fred Segal and Robertson" really meant and I think, looking back, that day was what tipped the scale and parlayed me into the bit of a fashionista I am today. It puts Barneys to shame. I hate to say it but it's true.

We ate at News Room, which was a blast. She knew a bunch of people there, which was sort of refreshing. (Getting a Carolyn break wasn't easy!) It also made for serious hot, hot, hot waiter watching! When we left, she explained what The Ivy was (the restaurant across the street) and I insisted on using their bathroom to get a true insider perspective. Totally humiliated, she got the car. I saw Arnold Schwarzenegger having lunch and nearly collided with his waitress. I'm telling you, Los Angeles is like a sober acid trip! You feel like you've been zapped onto a movie set or something.

I assure you I grew more used to it every minute. I got cooler after every visit. Listen, you can take a girl out of Pennsylvania but you can't . . . you know the saying!

Thoroughly shopped out, I couldn't have been happier when Carolyn called it quits. The traffic back to the hotel was insane. For sure I'd be cuffed and booked for road rage if I ever lived in this city, but that's really neither here nor there.

We got back to the hotel and I crashed—hard. The air was at a perfect temperature when I opened the door. The shades were drawn and the faint sound of one happening or another at the pool many floors below made for the perfect R&R sound track. The half-dozen chunky white orchids oozed serenity and, basically, the entire space felt like a giant cloud. I couldn't decide which white billowy piece of furniture to lay my dehydrated and sunburned body on. When I opened the second door to my bedroom, the choice was pretty clear.

I awoke to the ring of telephones . . . pretty ferocious when you've got four or five of 'em in the same space. With my bladder on the full side, I went with the dial-up in the ladies' room. Sitting down on the chilly toilet seat felt almost as good as those first few steps in the ocean, but my buzz was killed the minute I said hello.

It was John, who I realized in a split second I hadn't phoned since before I left NYC! Shit.

"Vivian?" he almost stuttered, so anxious to state my name and begin a semi-deserved tirade.

"John . . . hi. Thank you so much for the beautiful roses. You really shouldn't have," I squeaked.

"Damn right I shouldn't have. How could you have not called me?"

Before I could even respond he went on and on and on.

"If you're trying to play some little game with me you've got the wrong guy."

"John . . ." I couldn't believe his tone. He was so hot-headed, as if I was intentionally trying to push his buttons by not calling him. Was I, though? Not really. Besides the time difference, I just didn't feel that this was the kind of phone-home relationship where "I miss you" would be uttered during, in between, and after every sentence.

"Do you know how many women I could have been with last night? Do you? This is a joke. I don't need this. I don't even know why I bothered."

There was a silence. He was waiting for me to say something only to just stir things up more, but I had nothing to say. I was incredibly grossed out by his remark and after a few more seconds, I think it was clear to him, too.

"Are you there?" he asked emphatically.

"Yes," I said.

"Well, do you have anything to say?" He was egging me on.

Just then there was a knock at my door. And then another and then another.

"Hang on a second," I said.

"Are you kidding me?" he whined.

"Hang on!" I shouted and flushed (the toilet).

I got to the door and it was Gene and Lori, very ready to talk shop. I invited them in and asked if they could give me a few minutes. They fooled around in the kitchen and ultimately found a seat on the sofa as I went back into my bedroom and closed the door.

This time I picked up the phone nearest my bed.

"Listen. I've got a few people here in the other room. It's not exactly the greatest time for World War Three, okay?"

"Are you mocking me?" he asked.

"John, I'm sorry I didn't call. The pace here has been crazy and I haven't had any real time, any privacy at all, to call you."

"Please, Vivian." He chuckled.

"What's that supposed to mean?" I asked even though I knew he was yet again mocking my work, the reason for which I wasn't in New York (with him).

"Nothing," he said.

"I wanted to ring you when I got here when things died down but it would have been too late. Honestly, I can't believe how you are reacting."

"It's no problem, Vivian. I'm going out with Ken and Andy tonight and as far as I'm concerned, I'm on my own."

"Are you threatening me?"

"It is what it is, Vivian. You have a good time," and he hung up.

Not one for confrontation, regardless if I was right or wrong, tears had already begun to well up in my eyes and I felt sick to my stomach. This was all so irrational. It was. Right?

As I began the usual scenario of questioning myself, I thought about my two colleagues in the next room. If anything was going to make me look amateur, getting into a fight with my boyfriend or whatever the fuck he was at this point in front of them, was surely the way to go.

So I took a deep breath and, my God, turned down the stupid radio that just happened to be playing Paula Abdul's annoyingly upbeat melody "Forever Your Girl." No offense, Paula, I'm a big fan, but this was just so not the time.

I put on a clean white T-shirt, washed my face with cold water, and exited the bedroom.

"Is everything okay?" asked Lori, discernibly insincerely.

"Just fine," I said and opened, surely, a fifteen-dollar Corona from the minibar. I plopped down on the love seat across from the two of them and cheerfully asked, "So, what's up?"

"A lot," Gene replied. "The vans are picking us up at 6 A.M. It takes a good two hours to get to the track and with the traffic . . ."

"God, I know," I said shaking my head and trying to seem down with the California thing. My interruption was not appreciated and he went on . . .

"And with the traffic"—he looked at Lori—"we need to give ourselves the option."

"That's no problem. I agree. Can I do anything to help?" I asked.

"Yes," Lori said. "I'd like you to make sure that the rest of the crew and the freelance help we've brought on"—she hands me a stack of paper—"all are aware of the call-time and in front of the hotel at 6 A.M. sharp."

I took a moment to look over the lists.

"Can you handle that?" she questioned.

This chick was a lot nicer when she drank.

"Yes," I said. This was a big moment. Had I put my figurative tail between my legs and let her bully me, I would have been her errand girl and, I'm sure, scapegoat, too, for everything and anything that didn't go as planned for the entire production. Fuck that, I thought.

And then the phone rang. I let it ring.

"Are you going to get that?" Gene asked.

"Sure, of course. Excuse me." I leaned over and picked up the phone on my desk.

"Hello," I said. No answer. "Hello?" No answer. I hung up. Embarrassed, I wiped the hair from my face and said, "Go on . . ."

"Now there's the matter of the talent. We're assuming that the band, the drivers, the models—that their agents and managers have filled them in on it all . . . ," Gene explained.

"But that's rarely the case," Lori interrupted and rolled her eyes, then looked back at Gene. He chuckled and went on.

Did they think I didn't know from dealing with "talent"? My God. As if I had spent the last year answering Zack's phone or something? There was no doubt in my mind that I would need to earn my keep here. Being the broker of an "idea" was not the be-all and end-all. I took another deep breath.

"When we get to the site tomorrow, you're going to need to be everybody's best friend," Gene said.

"Say again?" I had no idea what he was referring to.

"Sorry, Vivian. What I'm trying to say is . . ."

The phone rang.

I picked up and again, no answer. Then whoever it was hung up. I was tempted to carry on a fake conversation just so that I wouldn't look like too much of a child and, to be honest, to keep John from looking like a huge freak, (You didn't have to be a brain surgeon to know that it was him on the end.) but I decided not to. I once tried that in high school and little did I know how loud the receiver was, but that's a whole other story. . . .

"Sorry." I was wiggling around in my seat. I felt so terribly stupid!

"No problem," he said. "It's customary that the talent is informed of the details, the promises, the compromises, a tough work schedule, at the last minute despite the assurances of their representation. As everyone will be on set for rehearsals and walk-throughs, at one point or another over the next few days, among other things, I need you to make sure that EVERYONE is informed and in agreement with what's on . . ."

The phone again.

"Shit!" I blurted out.

Lori tried to disguise her giggle and Gene attempted to complete his last sentence despite the circus. "Paper. Listen, Vivian, is this a bad time?"

"Absolutely not," I insisted. I picked up the phone and yet again, no answer and then a dial tone. When had my room turned into Grand Central stalking station? I hung up and gestured "one second" to Gene and Lori. I called down to the concierge and requested that all calls be forwarded to voice mail until further instruction.

"Now then . . ." I smiled.

Over the next hour I was handed more and more paper, packets, passes, instructions, and all the while I was only half there. Besides mortification, I was filled with dread. Dread that I was in over my head, dread that John was going to go out and find someone else. (Scary to admit, but true. I was sick with worry.) I had goose bumps and no doubt, nippleitis, in a hotel room, mind you, that was in California, that was also room temperature. There was no rational explanation other than nerves and a panic attack that kept rearing its ugly head in my mind. I was mesmerized by the red blinking message light on the phones. In every damn corner there was a blinking phone. My room felt more like a landing strip at night rather than the workplace of three urban professionals.

"I think we better go," Gene said.

"Yeah, it's getting late and we have dinner reservations, at what . . ." Lori looked at her big fancy silver watch, "eight, I think."

"Yeah," Gene agreed. "Downstairs this time, Viv. No traffic!" He was trying to make me smile.

"Right," I said. "Sorry about . . ."

Lori interrupted me. "No worries, honey, we've ALL been there." Her reassuring voice was wicked.

I walked them out, shut the door, and lost it.

I couldn't breathe. All I saw were flashing lights, papers, and a stark white room. I thought it best to run a cold shower and try to get a handle on things.

The shower was just what the doctor ordered. (Along with a few glasses of red wine. You've got to love that minibar!) I still hadn't checked my messages. What for, really? I had just succeeded in bringing my blood pressure back to its normal level and I was all too cozy lying in my bed with a lovely room service menu in my lap and Theo, of course, propped up beside me. I clicked on the television and saw that *Urban Cowboy* was now playing on TNT or some other station. It was then that I realized that there wasn't going to be anything more appealing at that moment or that evening I should say, than a bacon cheeseburger on focaccia bread, French fries, and a dose of Debra Winger to make me feel as good as new.

I rang Will and then Carolyn to tell them that I wasn't going to make the big dinner hoo-ha down below. When asked why, I lied and said that I had too much work to review and getting up at 5 A.M. for a 6 A.M. call time was going to be more than a challenge. They accepted my "resignation" and with that I prepared for what I thought would be a very low-key evening.

My dinner was delivered by a ridiculously handsome fellow who looked like a daytime soap stud or something, dressed in a very dapper cream-colored suit, who asked me where I'd like to dine. I hadn't a clue what he meant and my confusion was decidedly clear. As he rolled in what I had assumed was my down-to-earth order (I couldn't tell. It seemed as though there were three courses, all covered by white porcelain trays, lids, or whatever it is they're called.), he noticed that the television was on in my bedroom.

"Would you like to have your dinner in bed?" he asked.

And just as I said yes, I realized that I hadn't the time or the inclination to hide Theo under the covers!

I tried to get "there" first, but there was no room between my bum, him, and my dinner, to beat him to the punch.

"Will this be dinner for two?" he joked.

As I turned scarlet and put my hands in the pockets of my robe, I said "no."

I waited for him at my front door assuming he'd have to leave at some point, and as he handed me the check for my signature, I asked him if I could bribe him to keep the whole "teddy bear scandal" between the two of us.

He was really very sweet and replied, "Ms. Livingston, if you had any idea of what I've seen at this place, you'd realize your little friend would hardly make for front-page news."

"Very good then." I smiled and wished him a good evening.

"Guns 'n' Roses are with us this week. I'll need it!"

I ran back to my bedroom and there was the choicest looking burger I had ever laid eyes on. There was even a red rose in a small glass vase beside my plate of stringy fries! Oh, and I mustn't leave this out: the bell-boy had rested my ketchup in the hands of my bear!! (Seemed as though I wasn't the only person with a sense of humor in this ivory tower after all.)

Relieved to be amongst friends (Debra, Theo, and, a half-eaten cheeseburger), I reviewed my homework assignments, made the necessary calls to the staff, and felt somewhat secure with whatever tomorrow would bring. But, of course, as the credits rolled past me on the screen, I couldn't seem to ignore the flashing red light on my bedside telephone.

I tried to talk myself out of listening to my messages, but the fear of missing a call from Zack or Carolyn or something was all too great. The emotionless automated voice had no problem informing me that I had eleven new voice mail messages, so with a final bite of my burger, I hit the "star key" and braced myself. . . .

Five hang-ups. Sophie missing me. Carolyn asking what I'd be wearing to dinner. And then John's voice.

"It's John. Just call me on my mobile whenever you get this. I acted like an asshole and I'm really sorry. Please call me."

John again.

"It's me. Where are you? Call me."

John again. I could barely make out his message. It sounded like he was at a rock concert.

"It's me. I miss you so much. Call me, Vivian."

Then Carolyn again.

"I'm coming up to talk to you after dinner. Lori filled me in."

Great.

It was almost eleven o'clock. I prayed she'd opt not to pay me a visit. She had left the message over an hour ago. Perhaps I'd be in the clear.

Okay. So what to do? Do I call Sophie? Should I tell her what happened? Could I? One thing I've learned: the minute you let your friends in on how big of a dick your current man is, you can forget them ever being objective about him from that point on. Was I ready for that? Nope. Not yet.

I picked up the phone and realized I could procrastinate by ringing for a wake-up call. Perfect. I put the receiver up to my ear and dialed. Never had a telephone felt so foreign. I was near the end of my request when my second line rang. (Yeah, I had two phone lines. Pretty sweet under any other circumstance.)

I switched to the second line and picked up the call.

"Vivian! Vivian!" John shouted over the ruckus behind him. "It's me. Please don't hang up. I'm going to run outside. Hang on."

I hung.

"I want to talk to you."

"Go ahead," I said.

"I'm on my way home. Can I call you in about twenty minutes? Will you be up? I want to tuck you in."

Slick.

"Okay," I said and immediately hung up the phone.

I wanted off that phone. I didn't know what to do. I was completely conflicted. His behavior never made any sense. He always seemed to go as far as he could and then would always know when to back down and make me momentarily forget what had transpired.

I used my twenty minutes wisely. I locked the front door, straightened up, and laid out my clothes for the next morning. (Surely I'd be unable to make any sort of decision at the crack of dawn.) I brushed my teeth, used a bit of the extra toothpaste from the cap and dabbed it on the devilish little whitehead that was lurking just where Cindy Crawford has her mole, then put on some easy-listening station on the stereo and turned on the snooze timer for thirty minutes. I shut off the lights and got into bed.

A few (long) minutes passed and John had not called. I decided to call Sophie back, check on Omelet, and let fate decide if the conversation would take an honest turn.

Fernando answered, lacking any bit of thrill. I must have interrupted him while he was doing absolutely nothing.

"Wassup?" he mumbled. "Ya want Soph?"

"Yes, please," I said.

"Sophhhhhhhhhhhhhh," I heard him whine. "Sophieeeeeeeeeeee-eeeeeeeee."

After a little bit she came to the phone, deliriously happy that I had called.

"What are you up to, sweets?" I asked. "How's Omelet?"

"We're fine," she answered. "How are YOU? How's LA? Tell me, tell me!!"

It was perfect. She wanted the fluff, the glitz. I was relieved.

So I told her about the hotel, Fred Segal, Robertson, The Ivy, Coffee Bean and Tea Leaf, the weather, and the star sightings. She was beside herself.

After some time she asked about John. I told her that he had seen to it that a dozen roses were in my room when I arrived and she "plotzed."

"God, if you weren't my best friend I'd hate you! The last time Fernando got me flowers was the night we first slept together."

"So, your first date then," I joked.

"Shut up!" She laughed.

There was the second line. "Hang on a minute," I asked and I answered the other call.

"It's me," he said.

"Hang on, okay?" I replied.

I clicked over and told Sophie I'd call her tomorrow.

"I love you," she said.

"I love you, too," I said and flipped over to John.

"Hi," I said.

"Hi," he said.

"I acted like such a kid, Vivian. That's not me. I'm sorry."

"Forget it," I said. "I don't want to get into it. It's over. I have a really big day tomorrow and I don't want to stay up all night."

"I miss you," he said.

I said nothing.

"Is Theo with you?"

"Yes," I admitted.

"Good," he said kindly. "Do you like it out there?"

"I do actually."

"Carolyn must be showing you the best of the best."

"She is. We had a fun day."

"I bet," he said. "What did you two do?"

This friendly banter made we want to throw up my dinner. I knew if I didn't say something real very soon, things would be back to "normal," or dare I say, even more "dysfunctional." I had just told him that I wanted to forget it, but I really didn't. How could I?

"Vivian, are you there?" he asked. "You're still really mad at me, aren't you?" he asked.

Here we go . . .

"Yup."

"What can I do? Do you want me to come out there?"

"Are you joking?" I was shocked.

"No. I was invited to a store opening right on Sunset. I wasn't going to go. But you're there and, well, maybe it's a good idea."

As incredible as it would have been to spend whatever free time I had with a "boyfriend," and this suite—it screamed "love nest"—but there was just no way I'd have John parading around like some, some . . . whatever! If we were in love and we didn't fight and things were just unbelievably amazing, I would have jumped at the chance to be in Los Angeles with him, but alas, that was not our reality. I told him so.

"So, things aren't perfect. So what? What relationship is? And how do you know we are not in love?"

There. He put it out there. He did it on purpose. Guys know what the

"L" word means to women. Well, Dr. Charm wasn't going to get to me. As crazy as it sounds, his remark made me feel good in a quiet kind of way. And although I knew he really didn't mean it, I enjoyed that he chose to put it out there. How twisted was I???

"I'm crazy about you, Vivian. No woman has ever made me feel this way. I'm out of control. I get such shit from my friends for it. Everyone knows."

This was just perfect. I was dating a schizophrenic and he was making me nuts in the interim.

"Stop it," I insisted. He was teasing me and it was insulting.

"Stop what?"

"Please, John, a few hours ago you were going mad, you were a bachelor, you were calling incessantly when you knew I had people here. You think flying across the country is going to make everything okay? Telling me what your friends think, and jet-setting up here. Words are like arrows, John."

"It was a gesture, Vivian. I wanted you to feel . . ."

"Which part? What was the gesture?" I was so angry.

"Coming out there. I thought it would mean something to you. I think it says a lot."

"Let's just move on. I'll see you in a week. Let's just leave it at that. Please, John. It's getting late."

"I don't want to hang up like this," he said. "I feel like I've ruined everything."

"You haven't," I said. At that point, if he were a dog, honestly, I would have felt like I was petting him.

"Can you try to wake up tomorrow and think about the good things? Things with us. I want you to have a great time out there. I don't want you to be thinking about what a jerk I've been. Keep a good memory. Remember how good we are together. Is that at all possible?"

"That's possible." I was breaking down. I was full. I was emotional. It was dark and the gentle tone of his voice was indeed becoming a lullaby of sorts.

"Just call me when you can. No pressure," he said.

"Okay," I said.

"Okay. Good night, Vivian."

"Good night," I said.

As I drifted off into never-never land, I cherished the virtual security blanket that John had just laid upon me. I guess you believe what you want to believe. I could sleep knowing that he claimed to not mean what he had said, that he claimed to be sorry. I blocked out the bad, the inevitable, and focused on the good—a terrible character flaw, especially when it comes to the opposite sex.

To put it mildly, that next morning and the few days following were a living hell. I had a headset glued to my ear and a mobile phone stuck to my hand. I ran around with binders filled with papers and numbers and time lines and permits that would change and change again with every passing minute. I had gone through a tiny bottle of Advil and about four bags of Doritos in just a few days. The weather couldn't have been worse. Any glitch that could have glitched did just that. Security around the track was incredibly tight. Dealing with the endless rules and regulations was like walking through muck. Long hours made even the nicest person a nightmare and then, of course, the freakin' traffic! No one could understand why Carolyn would have put us up in Los Angeles when there was a two-hour commute each day to the venue, and that's when we were lucky! The complaints were miles long with the bickering as the sound track. At one point I had forgotten what it was we hoped to accomplish.

I had to talk to Zack. I knew I could spin it so that I wasn't tattletaleing but rather just a young'un on my first big gig. I seized a moment when our trailer was vacated and got through to Elizabeth who found Zack at my insistence and patched me through.

"How ya doing?" He seemed happy to hear from me.

"Uhhhh, hanging in, I guess."

"Tough gig, right?"

"Very."

"I hear it's going well," he said.

Amazed, I said, "Really?"

And he laughed. "Yes, really."

I was feeling better and turned down the volume on my headset—I could hear Pete screaming at someone and I was beginning to twitch.

"It's not easy, Viv. It never is. No matter how long you've been doing it. Embrace the madness."

"What do you mean?" I asked.

"Roll with it. You've got to, or it will end up rolling over you!" He seemed to think this was all very amusing. "The beginning and the middle are always a mess. You've got logistics, nerves, egos, but in the end it all seems to come together."

"I feel better," I said. "Sort of!"

He laughed. "You just do your job. Don't take on anyone else's problems. Do your thing, ask questions when you have to, and take notes. You got me?"

"Yes," I said.

"Okay, kid. I've got another call. Keep that chin up!"

"Thanks," I said. I took a few seconds and brushed my pointer finger over the small scar on my chin, remembering how great I felt before I fell. What a difference a few months makes.

I'd be lying if I said that Zack had put the proverbial Band-Aid on my worries and angst. It was a challenge to take his advice. The negative energy was like a vacuum and I was inches away from being sucked into it, but I was dedicated to the success of the event and was hell-bent on making the most of the experience. So I decided I would suck it up when need be and simply do what was expected of me. I'd sneak away every once and again and try to take it all in. It was so rewarding to see the stage resurrected, to walk around the track and see our flyers and overhear the buzz; and to sit a table away from Mr. Paul Newman as he ate his lunch in the ultra-private hospitality area was riveting. I had an all-access pass to the comings and goings of the entire space and I used it as a tourist does a map. The sounds of the engines as the cars would race by at the speed of light, God, my dad would have loved it!

Still, I was never so exhausted in my life. I had never expelled so much energy on anything before. Physically, it was like working a double shift at Le Figaro. Mentally, it was a fuckin' brainteaser. I was blown away by the ways in which people could easily take their working caps off at the end of a grueling day and hang out, gossip, and party at night. I had so much to learn.

Zack was right. After the first few days, things took shape and relationships felt real. There was a pattern to the chaos, which made for a lot less tension. The magazine was getting what they needed, the management at Newman-Haas was pleased with the additional attention their team was getting, and, at the same time, they were relieved that all the glitz and glam had not interrupted or distracted them from their day-to-day "stuff," that is, they were placing and winning. The band had arrived and "okayed" pretty much everything. And every once and again, I'd get a pat on the back for a good day's work.

The evening before the live show, I was literally threatened to start enjoying myself by my colleagues. It was hard. I can't explain it really. As much as I was the one with the "idea," I felt like such an outsider. I hated being the rookie, the new kid on the block. A perfectionist to the core, I wanted to have all the answers and the hindsight and experience to tackle a problem without asking for help. But that's impossible. No matter how good you are. No matter what it is that you do, everyone needs to learn. Some thing's are innate—production, on any level, is an acquired skill. So I accepted that and promised the crew that I'd make an appearance at, yes, the infamous Sky Bar, that evening. If for no other reason, than for Sophie, who would have thought me ungrateful of the opportunity had I not.

We made the trek back to the hotel. The crew had made plans for a big pre-show hoo-ha at the Sky Bar. I forced myself to take a shower and get ready rather than join Theo in my big beautiful bed. If only for Sophie, I needed to experience the Sky Bar at least once. Carolyn came by and lent me a sexy little dress for the evening. She assured me that everything was going to be perfect that next day and asked me if I had spoken to John. Hard to believe, but I hadn't talked to him in days. Not since that last lovely conversation. When I told her so, she congratulated me, oddly enough, "That's the way to work him!" I went along with it and laughed with her, all the while feeling pretty bad. Had I not called him on purpose? I honestly didn't think so. I was obsessed with my work. It had meant everything to me, and somewhere in the mix I had neglected my "relationship." I guess I felt as though John did deserve a call. I mean, I hadn't backed out of the relationship and I hadn't sustained my anger. I was just as guilty as him in lots of ways. (I was just a whole lot nicer!)

So, I told Carolyn I would catch up with her downstairs and planned to use my last few minutes pre-mayhem to call my "boyfriend."

I called his cellular but he wasn't there. I left a very nice message. Told him how great but insane things were and how happy I was to be at the end of a very important experience. I apologized for not calling sooner and said that I looked forward to seeing him when I got back. I gave him my mobile number and told him to phone me if he could.

And that was that.

When I got downstairs and finally found my "friends" it was apparent that the party had already started. Before I could even get a look at my surroundings, I found myself poolside, throwing back shots and being introduced to X, Y, and Z. The music was amazing, the people were beautiful if a bit strange, and everyone seemed to be worry-free. The only thing anyone around me wanted was to have a good time and forget about EVERYTHING.

The concept was fine by me.

I was dancing with Susan, Will, Carolyn, and Pete. I remember the song was a funny dance mix of "Kiss Me Deadly" by Lita Ford and we were all shouting and singing, "Kiss me once, kiss me twice, come on pretty baby kiss me deadly . . ." at the top of our lungs when my mobile rang. I don't even know how I heard it. I struggled to find the "hello" button. (I was still not a full-fledged cell phone owner! This was a rental from the hotel and, basically, it was just another piece of electronic equipment that made little or no sense to me.)

Anyway, I picked up just in the nick of time and I was happy to hear that it was John on the other end. This time I asked that he hang on so that I could find a quiet place—good luck—to have a conversation.

I found myself in the ladies' room—I seem to have an affinity for porcelain—and needing to sit, I parked it in a stall, ready to have one of those alcohol-induced fuzzy-feeling conversations.

"How are you?" I said, slurred.

"Are you drunk?" he asked.

"I think so," I said.

"Where are you?" he asked.

"At the Sky Bar," I answered.

"Great." He didn't seem all that happy to hear so.

"Don't tell me you're mad?" I asked. Still not really very serious in tone. Still not really getting that he was pissed.

"No. I like having a girlfriend who doesn't call me for days and then gets drunk at the Sky Bar."

"I can't believe you're doing this again," I said. Why I didn't know better, why I hadn't learned to expect the unexpected at this point, is still beyond me. "You can be such an ass," I said.

"Take it easy, Vivian. All right. I'm not the bad guy this time." He went on, "It's been good for me these past few days . . ."

"God, John, you're treating them like they're weeks . . . it's been four days!"

"Still, I've been out. I've talked with my friends. I've gotten some perspective." You could here the gloat in his voice!

"Is that so?"

Someone was trying to open up the bathroom door. "Someone's in here!" I shouted.

"Real classy," I heard him murmur.

"WHAT?"

"Nothing," he said.

"No, no—what were you going to say?" Whatever it was that he was implying, I wanted to hear him say it. I despise phone games like this. Especially when you are so far away and you can't get face-to-face if you feel the need to do so.

"Let's just say that I'm ready to take things down a notch or two."

"Really?" I said. "And why is that? After your convincing speech the other day, you can't expect me to think that your intense feelings can fade away because I've been busy and haven't been able to pacify you!"

"Can I be honest?" he said.

Oh God. I had no idea what he was going to say and wanted to create my own faux phone fuzz, bad reception, anything to keep him for going for my jugular.

"My friends don't think you're right for me."

"That's a shocker," I said. Somewhat relieved. I thought it was going to be something I didn't already know.

"All this time I had you up on this pedestal. Finally I found a real girl. A nice girl. And somehow I lost sight of things . . ."

"Like what things, John?"

"Like who I am. What I can offer a woman. What I deserve and what you are, really."

This was all getting incredibly sick. I was feeling emotions that I hadn't felt in years and if I had the time or the space in which to kick myself, having stumbled into yet another fucked-up relationship, I would have.

"Don't stop now, John. It's refreshing to have an honest conversation with you." I was trembling. For every ounce of anger and disgust I felt, there was just as much of a perpetual heartbreak running through me.

"You're average, Vivian. You're wowed to be working around Paul Newman. Big fuckin' deal. Paul Newman. It's sad."

"Is that so? What wows you, then? What impresses you?" His comments were so raw they were hurtful to the core.

"An exceptional woman. A beautiful woman who is on the same playing field as me. Who sees things from the same perspective as me. You don't. You never will. You're ordinary. Okay? Are you happy now? I said it."

Tears were streaming from my eyes. It felt like he was punching me in the stomach.

There was silence.

"Don't tell me you're crying. Don't try to make me feel guilty . . ."

"I'm not crying, John. I'm laughing. You haven't a clue as to who you are or what you want. You couldn't see what you wanted if it was plain straight in front of you." I meant that. The teeter-totter thing was so crystal clear. I was in, I was out. I couldn't keep up.

"You're right. I thought you had this natural beauty. I was captivated by your eyes. But, like tonight for example, when my friends said that they didn't think that you were pretty enough for me and then they pointed out girls that were incredibly beautiful, girls who would walk by me and look my way, it all made sense."

"Did it?" I was sobbing.

"It's true. That's all I'm saying. I get it now and I just want to be up-front about it. I think you're great. You're funny. You're cute. And I appreciate how hard you push yourself, but it's never going to be enough. Not for me, anyway."

"Fuck you, John." Sorry, but that's all I could come up with.

"And that mouth of yours . . . Didn't someone teach you that pretty girls shouldn't talk like that?"

"I'm average, you asshole!!!!" and I hung up.

I got up and came out of the bathroom only when I was sure that I was alone. I was a mess. I went to the sink and looked in the mirror. Where was I? Who was I? How could I have let this happen?

Just then I saw Lori. She was in the stall at the corner and, knowing her, probably sat and had popcorn in there while I was crying my heart out.

"Hi," I said. And splashed cold water on my face.

"Looks like little Ms. Perfect couldn't hang on to her man."

I looked up. I stared at her, certain I had imagined that she had made such a brutal comment. She pulled her dark lipstick from her purse and, as if I wasn't even there, puckered up and put a fresh coat on, staring straight into the mirror.

I was horrified.

She finished her application, put the lid on the stick, turned my way, and said, "Not such a hotshot after all. Welcome back to the planet Earth, bitch."

I couldn't even respond.

She plopped her makeup back in her bag, turned around, and walked out.

I sobbed until my eyes felt like they were bleeding. I wanted to go home. I was through. I wasn't meant for relationships. I got burned every time and could never react when I would see it coming. I hated myself. Who was I kidding? I wasn't cut out for all of this.

I used the freight elevator to get back to my room. I made sure my hair was sufficiently covering my eyes because I didn't want to see anyone. I felt like I was going to pass out. I felt so alone it made me shiver.

That evening was a turning point for me. Truly. I can look back on it now and see a theoretical sheet of ice freeze over every ounce of my existence. A new suit, if you will. I sat in one of the fabulous chairs in my fabulous room of the fabulous hotel that I was staying in because of my fabulous job and I made myself stop crying. It was as close to an out-of-body experience as a woman like me can get. (A self-professed nonbeliever in anything that I can't control or rationalize.)

Instead of looking in a mirror, it was as if I stepped outside myself and took a seat just across from me. I took a long hard look at who I was at that moment. Seemingly, a defeatist to the core. A masochist maybe on some level. I saw a girl who had taken on too much—made herself too vulnerable—and I vowed that that was going to end right there and then.

When it came to matters of the heart, why bother? Why not accept my limitations? I thought back to Mark, to Patrick, and, of course to John. Each of these men had something to hide in the beginning. I was certain of that. And in some perverse way it was sexy. It was a turn-on. And of course, here's the ultimate cliché, it was a challenge. And look where it got me—same emotions, same torment, just different kinds of bruises.

Women with their heads on straight repel themselves from men like these. It was somewhere in my makeup to be attracted to them. Hoping always for the best. The only person to be angry with at this point was myself. I was always staid, I was always repressed, I always forgave. It was pathetic.

Going forward, because I'd be kidding myself if I could rule out men entirely (I just love them too much), things would go my way. I decided nothing would be real, nothing would be substantial or long-term—this way, how could I lose? I'd never let them in and always kick them out. If I loved falling in love so much, I'd fill up a lifetime with "best parts." Since I may not be making much sense here, let me break it down vis-à-vis one of my favorite analogies—anything pertaining to food!

If I wanted pizza, it would be fine to only eat the crust. I'd lick the icing off a tray of colorful cupcakes. With a frozen Italian ice, I'd flip it and scrape the bottom, and I'd eat only the cookie part of a Twix bar. I'd eat only the centers of buttered pieces of toast, the chocolate crunchy part of a Carvel ice cream cake, and, of course, the whipped cream on top of my hot chocolate.

The deal was this: men were at my mercy! I'd be with who I wanted to, when I wanted to, how I wanted to—no judgments, no consequences, no prisoners. I would go straight for "the best parts" and leave any real emotions at the door. (This may be the chapter, Mom, where you stop reading the book! I promise it was just a phase.)

Now, as far as the rest of my life was concerned, I'd be damned if I let Mark, Patrick, John, this chick Lori, anyone who ever thought I was nothing, think they had me figured out. I'd go on to divide and conquer. I knew that I had made it this far on my guts, my instinct, and, most importantly, as myself—my nature. I was able to acknowledge that and although I may not have been built for a long love, I most certainly could make something special out of my life.

I had good friends, a wonderful family, a dog that I adored, and if I had "success" with my job, what more could I ask for?

Unable to sleep through the remaining few hours that were left before "call time" I packed my things, reviewed my notes, took a shower, watched television. I finally left the hotel at sunup and walked up and down Sunset Boulevard until businesses began to open and there were more than a few pedestrians in the street.

I was the first patron at Coffee Bean and Tea Leaf and sipped my iced whatever as I walked back to meet up with the crew. When I caught sight of the van, and subsequently the crew, I realized for the first time that I'd find myself again, face-to-face, with Lori. Strangely enough, it somehow felt inconsequential. I'd also have to explain what had happened the night before with my disappearing act and all. Hmmm. David Copperfield was a guest in the hotel . . . nah, that wouldn't work. Besides, I'd bet almost anything that Lori was all too happy to fill them in.

Carolyn and Will came scurrying over to me before I knew it. Genuinely worried and concerned, they wanted to make sure I was okay, and, naturally, they wanted to know what had happened. And who could blame them really? It was just about ten hours ago that little old me was dating one of the city's most eligible bachelors.

I assured them that I was all right and that I really, really didn't want it to get in the way of what I had worked so hard for this past month. They agreed and promised to back off—temporarily. When I saw Lori, I really just saw through her. Maybe she resented that I had the job that I had or that I had come up with the Metal Pedal concept. Maybe she hated me because she was burnt by John, maybe it was because she had always wanted to date him. I really didn't give a shit. She was as close to the personification of "misery" as anyone or anything I'd ever known and all I knew was that she hated being her. That's enough payback that anyone could ever hope for.

So for the next two hours I pretty much kept to myself. I hated not having anything to do on the road and knew that I'd begin to crumble if my downtime went longer than a few minutes. Meaning, I'd romanticize John, wonder if I could have done anything differently. Even sadder, what I could do to get him back. So looking out the window was out, staring into thin air was a no-no, and absolutely no listening to the lyrics of the sappy songs on the radio. Just across from me I saw Susan struggling to keep her eyes open as she read the *Los Angeles Times.* That was a good idea especially since I hadn't slept the night before. Maybe I'd catch a few z's if I attempted to read the financial section of the paper.

It worked!

I woke up just as our van pulled into the track. The sun was shining in through the windows and the sky couldn't have been more blue. Pete and Gene, seated behind me, were all but too ready to get the show rolling. Where my stomach was in knots they were more like players before a big game.

"Let's go, killer," Gene said. "Today's your big day! Woo-hoo!"

I smiled back.

As I was gathering my things, they passed me right by as did Will, Susan, Lori, and all the rest. From my window I could see that at this point bygones were bygones. This group, that for the past week had been huffing and puffing all the way home, quite literally, were now all partners in crime—supportive, helpful, and ready to take the place by storm.

"You ready?" I heard from behind me. I was startled and too nervous to recognize any one voice.

"Too much coffee maybe?" the voice said again.

I turned and saw Carolyn behind me. "Sorry, I had thought it was just me." She gently hit my bum with what felt like a magazine, urging me to get going. I wonder had she not been there if I would have ended up hiding under my seat.

I put my sunglasses on and very slowly moved toward the door. As I stepped off the van she whispered in my ear, "You've got nothing to worry about. Be proud and enjoy it." Before I could thank her or even acknowledge her comments, she was already on her walkie-talkie and her assistant had brought her over a hot cup of coffee.

People were pouring in from every direction. The cars were all either being prepped or taking test laps around and around. It was as if a small pilgrimage of music, fashion, and race car aficionados had made its way to our van. The day had started without my permission and before I knew it, there was no time for nerves, not a moment for self-pity. A dream realized was taking shape and Carolyn was all too right: if I didn't focus, it would all pass me by.

I'd love to get into how perfect everything was—every detail. I still think it's the best work I'd ever done, maybe because it was the beginning of something bigger, who knows? But I dare not bore you all with minutiae. I mean, really, you've already made it this far. How about I sum it up instead?

Okay. Everything was in place. After the final race of the day, the band had already rehearsed, and the sound check went smoothly. The crowds were beginning to gather. All the somebodys were on the set to do their thing and the production guys were giving the thumbs-up to the technical crew. At this point, the fashionistas had gotten practically everything that they wanted pre-performance so as the lights went up and the cameras started shooting, I stood just offstage and marveled at the scene. I was in tears (what else was new really?!!) as the MC finished the introductions, the crowd cheered, and the band began their first song.

For that hour plus, I was congratulated over and over again. Everyone seemed to make it their business to pop over, stand beside me, say something over the "airwaves." It felt absolutely wonderful. I wish that feeling for everyone. But the best was yet to come and this, I swear, is a true story . . .

"So I hear this was your big idea, eh?" someone said.

"Yup," I said, still staring out toward the front of the stage. As I said, not that any congratulatory remark was not appreciated, but it was pleasantly becoming a pattern and for some reason, in this instance, I just didn't physically acknowledge the comment.

"Not bad," the voice said again.

"Yeah," I replied and noticed Carolyn and Will on the other side of the stage, pretty much directly opposite me, looking as if they had just seen a ghost. With their eyes bulging out of their heads it was difficult to discern whether these were good or bad looks, so over my headset, I asked them, "What's up? Everything okay?"

To that, Will mumbled what sounded like, "Take the crown!"

"What crown?" I said.

Again, "Take the crown."

"What?" I started laughing. They looked like they were both in pain and trying desperately to contain it.

"TURN AROUND!" Carolyn proclaimed and hit her forehead, insinuating that I was a complete idiot.

So I did just that. And standing next to me, wearing a white lightweight long-sleeve polo shirt, a Newman/Haas baseball hat off to the side, and with his striking baby blue eyes barely hidden behind gray-shaded and oddly crooked aviation-type glasses, I kid you not, was none other than Mr. Paul Newman.

Not one to play it cool ever, my mouth surely dropped to the floor.

"Hiya, kid," he said flatly.

"Hi . . . Paul, uhhh, Mr. Paul, Mr. Pewman, I mean Newman . . . Mr. Newman."

"Hi." He laughed. "It's Vivian, right?"

"Yes." I laughed. This was really too much.

I could see from the corner of my eye Will and Carolyn both quietly freaking out, almost becoming a human pretzel if that makes any sense. Clenching each other, trying so hard not to scream or jump up and down and much like a kid in a classroom, I was trying desperately not to let their odd game of Paul Newman Twister give me the giggles.

"Say," he said.

"Yes?" I said.

"You wanna take a ride?"

"A ride?" I said. What was he talking about?

Then in my headset there was Will's voice, "Take the ride, Vivian, take the ride."

"Hang on one second," I said to "Paul" and took my headset off.

He then pointed just offstage to this light blue scooter. I raised my eyebrows, confirming that I understood what he meant and, hey, what girl in her right mind is going to say no to Paul Newman? Sure, I'd miss the end of the concert, but you and I both know how often VH1 reruns their programming!

Together, we maneuvered backstage and down the steps to his "wheels."

"You might want to get rid of all that stuff . . ." gesturing to my headset, the sweatshirt around my waist, the clipboard.

"Right," I said. "Of course."

I looked for someone I knew to hang on to my things but no one was around. Naturally, they were all busy working. But, just then, as I was about to leave everything with a security guard, I saw Lori talking to a few journalists a little ways away. I pointed her out to "Paul" and he said, "She's with you?"

"Uh-huh," I said. "Let me run and give this to her, I'll be right back."

"No need," he said. "Hop on."

So I did. And with my one free hand, I held "Paul's" shirt. We scooted right up to her and, naturally, everyone and their mother had taken notice, figuring out who it was that was about to interrupt their conversation.

"Lori," I said. "Would you mind hanging on to this for me?"

She just stared for a minute, not believing her eyes and not saying a word. She was so angry. I swear I thought she was going to flip!

"Sure . . . of course." She winced.

I threw her my things and before I could say "thank you," we were moving.

I held on to him now with both my hands and just started cracking up! I had no idea where we were going, when I would be getting back, and, of course, I couldn't have cared!

"Have you ever been in a race car before?" he asked as we rode past tons of people, cars, and cameras.

"No," I said.

"Good!" He laughed.

I didn't get what was so funny. That was until we stopped at the track itself, just next to a silver car that looked, to me anyway, like a Lamborghini or something. I think it had cobalt blue stripes from front to back but I can't really remember.

"Your car, Mr. Newman," said a rugged young gentleman in a candy-apple red flight suit, and handed him a key.

"Thank you," he said and gestured for me to unleash him from my nervous grip and step into the passenger side of the car.

"You're serious," I questioned.

"Sure!" he said.

The same guy who gave Paul the key gave me a helmet and made sure I was buckled in all safe and sound and tight!

I was inside the car, quietly freaking out, waiting for Paul as he took some photos and signed a few pictures for a small group of bystanders. The interior of the car looked like that of a plane. Not that I've ever seen a cockpit, but you can imagine.

He got in, buckled up, and asked me if I was ready. I winked at him as he started the car.

We were off before I could even blink and I couldn't help but laugh, more like cackle really. This was just way too much!!! We went faster and faster, around and around. At one point we were at one hundred sixty miles an hour! (I looked at the dashboard.) He looked at me a few times and laughed and I urged him to keep his eye on the track! I could see the headlines already:

SOME GIRL AND PAUL NEWMAN PERISH IN RACE CAR ACCIDENT

I loved the rush and the power. I have never been able to do the speed limit since and wasn't even sure if the whole thing was really happening! If his arm hadn't brushed mine as he shifted or something, I don't think I would have ever known for sure. When we began to slow down and my "ride" came to a close, I thanked him profusely.

"Don't mention it," he said coolly.

We both got out of the car and with helmets in hand, I had to just steal a moment and gave him a kiss on the cheek. There were even more people around at this point, waiting to catch a glimpse of, let's face it, this bit of our American royalty.

I don't know how they pulled it off, but Will and Carolyn managed to be there, to watch as Paul's car did its final lap and pull in toward the staging area. Not only did they snap a few action shots, they called my name, held up their camera, and just after my little smooch, I asked Paul if he'd mind if my friends took our picture.

"Not at all," he said.

CLICK!!!

I was so thrilled I could burst. I couldn't help but cry again as Will and Carolyn screamed with delight.

I had changed my flight in the wee morning hours and instead of riding back with everyone, partying my face off, and leaving for New York when initially planned, I had a cab meet me at the raceway and take me to the airport just a little while after my P.N. experience.

Will helped me with my things and walked me to the gates. He couldn't understand why I wanted to leave, why I wouldn't want to stay in LA for the weekend, hang out for a bit and bask in the glory. I couldn't describe it any way other than to just tell him that I was "full." (Again another food analogy!)

"I don't understand you," he said disappointedly.

"That makes two of us," I said. I gave him a kiss good-bye and got into my cab.

I put my sunglasses back on and rolled down my window once we got on the highway. The breeze felt perfect and I couldn't have been any happier to finally be on my way home.

Later, and as though she even cared, the straitlaced young woman at the ticket counter greeted me, took my information, and asked, "Did you enjoy your stay in Los Angeles?"

It took me a few seconds to come up with an answer . . .

"It was an experience."

I carried on, my heart broken but my body filled with anger. I did my best not to let John's remarks linger but I'd be lying if I told you that they didn't haunt me. I never went into detail about "that evening" with anyone but Sophie. It was too painful and, honestly, I was ashamed for having fallen for him in the first place. I did, however, keep to my promise, and steadfastly committed to a life of pleasure and achievement.

I went on to produce a handful of other events for Zack and racked up quite a reputation for being a creative "out-of-the-box" thinker, which I loved. Although uncharacteristic, I began to utilize my connections, big time. Playing with the city of New York, experiencing everything it now offered me and, I hate to admit it, pretty much everyone I had an interest in. Fearless of rejection, it's easy to go for what you want and get it, especially when all you want is to have a good time.

I dated a musician, a football player, a photographer friend of Lilly's, Zack's trainer, an actor/comedian who lived on the West Coast, "befriended" Gabe from time to time . . . I could go on and on. It was as if I was reliving those four wild years most girls have in college in nearly half the time. I'm not proud of it. And if this wasn't an autobiography, I assure you, I would really, really, really play this all down. It's not as though there was a new guy every night, I'd say every month was more like it. 😮 And ironically, this "new" version of me seemed to bring even the biggest of big shots, the token commitment-phobes, the lady-killers, to their knees. I've never been treated so well by men that I treated so poorly. Such a joke!

I ran into John once, while at a bar checking out a band a few months later. Luckily I was with that musician friend I just mentioned. John's presence made me very uneasy, but there was no way I was going to leave on account of him. It was not until Henry (the musician) left me alone to go to the loo, that John walked over to me. We looked each other straight in the eye. I was too angry to say anything and he was too cocky to say the first word. Imagine if you will for a second how creepy it was. He came toward me from across the room and simply stood in my face among a crowd of strangers. It was not until Henry came back a couple of minutes later and put his arm around me that I was able to unlock myself from John's gaze. Just thinking about him makes me cringe.

And if you can even believe it, Fernando was STILL living with us, but I didn't have the heart to burden Sophie with my frustration. She was growing more and more disillusioned with her career; interviewing for entry-level positions at magazines, but to date, none had ever come through. As my professional life was kicking into high gear, I felt guilty and was pretty sure, by the looks of things, that my displeasure would outlast their relationship. It felt as though she was getting bored. She loved meeting the friends of my "friends" and, from time to time, seemed not at all too thrilled when hopping on the bandwagon was not really an option. I left it all alone. I never wanted Sophie to have me to blame for anything that did or didn't happen with Fernando.

Anyway, as I said, I was a changed woman. I made myself believe that this new lifestyle of mine was "me" all the while I knew it was really for shit. I may have been fooling the people around me, but inside I felt like a fraud. I desperately wanted to fall in love and live happily ever after, but I never thought I'd be able to pull it off. But it was fun; maybe "entertaining" is the better way to put it. And to make matters worse, between my work and dare I say, my men, I felt this twisted sense of confidence. I was such a mess but I didn't look like one. That was another thing, after a tryst with the trainer (It's a painful experience to date someone who is in better shape than you.), I was much more conscious of what I ate and made working out a part of my weekly regimen. I actually joined a gym. (With a great corporate rate I was able to afford it.) And then there was Sophie's employee discount that we happily took advantage of. I splurged from time to time on whatever piece of clothing I thought I had to have, and with a roommate who lives and dies by the pages in *Vogue* and thinks nothing of revolving debt, I was slowly morphing into quite a little clotheshorse.

My mother knew something was off. I was happy; I looked good and didn't really have a worry in the world. I was born a sensitive neurotic; qualities that never really fade (I don't care what anyone says) despite therapy, sex, and medication. But as much as she pried, she couldn't figure it out. Thankfully, like all of us, she went with the "no news is good news" thing after a while, rather than a maternal interrogation that would have surely done me in.

So that was that. I was living life on the edge, of course, a place I have always felt most "safe." I was temporarily placated, keeping busy, enjoying my life, my downtime with Omelet, racking up story after story, and leaving what is best defined as "damaged goods" in the doldrums of my subconscious. Nice, right!

But it's always when you least expect it that life seems to let you know who's boss . . .

Late one Friday afternoon, I snagged a few tickets to a taping of *Saturday Night Live*. They were actually meant for Carolyn but she had to go out of town unexpectedly and I was more than happy to take them off her hands. Sophie and Fernando had other plans, so Will, Lilly, and a friend of mine from home who was in town, joined in. A fan since I was allowed to stay up past 10 P.M., I was never so excited to go to anything. Our seats were on the main floor and the skits were hilarious. I think it was Alec Baldwin who was hosting. We had an amazing time. We were even lucky enough to get on the "list" for the customary after-party, which that evening was being thrown at Barolo. Hobnobbing with the cast and crew was quite an experience and one that I didn't want to end. Lilly, quite literally, had to drag me out of there.

Close enough for us each to walk home; it must have been 3 A.M. when I turned the corner of my street. Just yards from the front of my apartment building, I saw all these lights and crowds and chaos. There were fire trucks and police cars filling my narrow street. Not good. I remained calm. As I got closer to our building, I saw Sophie and Fernando amid the sea of people standing about in shock. That's when I started to run. As I got closer I saw that Sophie was in hysterics. I hugged her shaking little body and before I could ask what had happened, I looked up at our building and saw that it was being eaten by flames. My heart sank. I tried to calm her down, but I was freaking out myself. It was all so frightening.

With madness and sirens and this immense heat surrounding us, I finally had the sense enough to ask the obvious questions. "What happened?" She could barely form sentences, but eventually told me that our apartment had caught fire. The flame of a candle caught the curtains in our living room that was blown inside from the wind, she thought, and in an instant, our place was torched.

Automatically, I started screaming for Omelet. Sophie kept apologizing but my ears weren't even registering what she was saying. I freaked out. I dashed for the door but there was nowhere to run. The entrances to the building and those surrounding were blockaded off. Try as I may, no one would let me through and no one would listen to me. I felt like a lunatic, kicking and screaming, pushing and shoving, until I fell to the ground weeping. All I could imagine was Omelet, forever my puppy, forever my companion, scared and trapped and I could do nothing. I stared hopelessly and helplessly at my apartment.

Minutes felt like hours. Hours felt like days. I threw up at one point and when Sophie kneeled down to help me, I shoved her away in disgust. I blamed her. I blamed her idiotic boyfriend who I was sure was reckless and thoughtless as usual. And then I blamed myself. I should have kicked him out months ago. A policeman asked me if I needed to call anyone. Someone who could pick me up. The flames were relentless and he doubted that any of us would be able to get back into our homes for quite some time. I never felt so alone. I called my parents and sobbed. They were leaving immediately and would get a hotel room for the time being.

Sophie tried again to talk to me but I would not have it. She asked if I wanted to leave with her, wherever it was that she was going, and I ignored her. I'd stay, at the very least, until there was a shell to see. How could I leave my Omelet??? I didn't know how. It was then that the very policeman who had offered his help a few minutes earlier, urged me to look toward my apartment. I brushed the hair and dust from my face as he helped me get back on my feet.

Out of the building's doorway came this huge firefighter, in that black and yellow uniform, smoke everywhere, covered in this hopeless black soot with what looked like a gray-coated Omelet in his arms.

"Could that be your pet, miss?" he asked.

Sophie began to cry Omelet's name and I lunged for this man and my dog and refused to let go. Omelet was visibly terrified and squirming to be let free. An emergency crew came toward us and laid down a blanket for the fireman to place Omelet on. He kept licking my face and I think I peed my pants I was so excited. After a little while, once the medics said he was fine, incredibly enough, he was back on his four precious feet and standing beside me. I was given a fireman's jacket to keep warm and decided to stay put until my parents arrived. Sophie wanted to stay but I told her to leave with Fernando, to go get some sleep, and to call me on my cell phone later. (Yes, I had by this time entered the twenty-first century and gotten a cell phone.) She was riddled with guilt but I was still so angry. For the first time in my life, I wanted her as far from me as possible.

As it was, the fire started just after 2 A.M. and burned until almost 6 in the morning. I had phoned my parents moments after Omelet was rescued, so fortunately they didn't have to deal with that on the ride down. But when I saw them, I became hysterical again. I had lost everything. I had the clothes on my back and my Omelet. I was full of despair. We didn't have any insurance or anything like that. I would have to start over. But each time I saw Omelet everything else just felt like details. Important details, but still, just that. My father spoke to a few of the officers and firemen on the scene as I held my mom's hand like a fourth grader. The owner and superintendent of the building showed up and demanded answers but there was no "official report" as of yet. I had known nothing of a tragedy like this. It didn't matter who I knew, what I did, where I worked, I realized that the world could chew me up and spit me out if and when it saw fit.

My dad was finally able to find a hotel that welcomed animals. After an expeditious check-in and as they made one phone call after the next, I eventually passed out. Omelet and I both nestled under the covers in the king-sized bed in my parents' room.

That next Sunday was the longest day I can remember. I recall waking up and for a split second not having a care in the world. And just as I began to sit up, it was as if everything came crashing to a halt. I didn't even know where to begin. My dad was there. He said that my mom had gone out to get me some clean clothes, that my brother Joseph would be meeting us at the hotel in a few hours, and that Omelet had been walked. He let me have a few minutes to wash and wake up and after that, everything was downhill.

He was very upset with me, for a number of reasons. Why had a man been living in my apartment? Why did we not have any kind of renter's insurance? What, if anything, had I put in my savings account? What kind of lifestyle did I have, coming home at 3 A.M. on a Saturday night? Get this: Why was Sophie using a candle anyway? "We are living in modern times and we have electricity!" It went on and on and on, that was, until my mother opened the door and insisted my dad back off for a while.

But he was all too right. I had next to nothing put away. It never dawned on me that anything like this could ever happen. I was at a loss for words, which as you are probably aware, is a rarity. I had worked so hard to make my parents proud and earn their respect. Now I would have to ask them to bail me out, an independent woman's worst nightmare. Especially coming from a huge "told you so" kind of family.

I called Zack at home and told him what had happened. He urged me to use my remaining vacation days to deal with everything. So I took that next week off. My father had a conversation with my landlord and, luckily, the building was insured. Talk about a huge weight being lifted from your shoulders! We would not get our security deposit back but considering everything, I felt that to be way more than fair.

Joseph finally arrived, which temporarily took the focus off of me. My dad needed to get back to Pennsylvania for work on Monday so he requested that Joseph stick around and help me get my life in some sort of order. He gave me four thousand dollars. Rather he wrote Joseph the check now that I think about it, to rent an apartment, buy a few things, and he expected to be paid back within eight months. (Five hundred dollars every four weeks.)

I couldn't apologize enough. I was so sorry to have involved them in the whole ordeal. I told them how much they meant to me and how much I appreciated their generosity. "You're lucky we are in the position to do so," my father barked.

"I know, Dad. I know."

My mother was the "good cop" if you will and pulled me aside to "translate" for my dad. She said he was just very concerned and, of course, thought that I should just come home already. He cared about me and loved me, she said, and that he'd come around eventually. I knew all that, but I still felt terrible.

I phoned Lilly and told her what had happened. She said that I could stay with her as long as I needed to, which was incredibly sweet. She and Will met Joseph and me for dinner that evening, just after my parents left. I also phoned Sophie and asked if she was all right. You could tell in her voice that she wasn't. I hated the idea of her being all alone (Even if she was with Fernando. To me it was the same thing.), and urged her to come by the hotel, meet us for dinner and to talk. Reluctantly, she agreed to meet me on Monday morning.

I have to admit, it was really nice to have my big brother in town. No one compares to family when you're in crisis mode, and for some reason New York City never felt so foreign. I asked him to keep himself busy while Sophie and I talked. So by the time she got there, he and Omelet were out. I'm sure he was using him as his "wing man"; he always loved the attention he'd get from the ladies whenever he'd take up with Omelet.

Sophie cried, apologized, swore to make it up to me—you can imagine. She took full responsibility for what, once I had all the facts, was really just an accident. We always lit candles in that apartment. It was just a huge freak of nature that a small rush of wind from the window (that was just opened a crack) would wreak so much havoc. She assumed "we'd" look for apartments that week and that's when I came to the realization that it was probably best that we each go our separate ways. At least and only as far as a home was concerned. It was time we had our own places, I told her, while also confessing that our previous living situation was really pretty rough on me. She apologized but asked, of course, why I had never mentioned it before. I told her that it wasn't like it was horrible, incredibly irritating was more like it, and, quite honestly, I knew she loved Fernando and how could I ask her to make him leave? It was a bit awkward for a few minutes but we got through it. She was a little freaked out at first, at the whole idea. Knowing how pricey it can be to live on your own in New York, or now having the choice to make it official and shack up with her man.

Although it may be more expensive, which of us hasn't spent pretty much every night with our "better halves" when things are going well? Come on, it's a lot easier than taking the plunge and really living together. A high-priced security blanket if you will, always knowing at the end of the day, you have a place of your own if need be.

I assured her that she could stay with me, once I found a place of course, as long as she needed to. But I insisted that it was because I treasured our friendship, that the idea of living together again was probably not the best idea. She asked if my parents hated her, and I told her not to be silly, but did share my father's Neanderthal remark about the candle, which we both laughed about and said, "was so him!"

Joseph stayed with me that week. We must have looked at thirty apartments, none of which I could afford or were worth what they were asking. Sound familiar? So, I decided to take Lilly up on her offer and stay with her for a while. Fernando and Sophie found a place together on the Upper East Side very quickly and it was a relief to know that she was okay.

Lilly had a tiny, tiny, tiny railroad apartment in Chelsea. Her futon made for a decent bed, and closet space . . . well, that wasn't really an issue—I didn't bring anything with me. There was a park nearby for Omelet and my commute to work was even easier then before. But it sucked. I felt like we were fully putting her out and that maybe I was being too fussy and should have just taken something and gotten on with things.

Fortunately, luckily, thankfully, and every word in between, Will had great news for me about two weeks into my stay with Lilly. Apparently his friend was going to Brazil for a few months and was looking to sublet his apartment. Will said it was lovely. A one-bedroom walk-up in Nolita. He said that I'd love the decor and, even better, it was only eight hundred bucks a month! I didn't even need to see it to say yes! Within three days Omelet and I were in. And Will was absolutely correct. The place was phat! I now had three full months to look for the right place and was finally living in the neighborhood I had always loved!

Carolyn's assistant, Lexi, lugged this big garbage bag over to my cubicle the day after I had moved in. When I asked her what she was doing, she replied, "It's her housewarming gift to you." Puzzled, I open the bag. It was filled with designer hand-me-downs. "To fill your closets," she said. It was one of the best gifts I had ever been given. I walked over to her office to thank her but she was on the phone. I stood by her door and waited for her to stop yapping. Instead of letting me say a word (what else was new really), she put her hand over the phone and said, "Please, I can't stand looking at you in that hideous outfit every other day!" I laughed. "Now get out of here already!" she said and went back to her call.

So Carolyn.

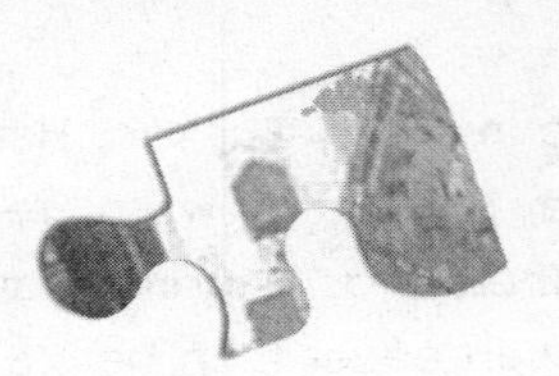

It was a Sunday afternoon, while walking Omelet through our old digs, that it dawned on me to pay a visit to the fireman who had rescued my puppy. It had been nearly a month and, frankly, I was a bit embarrassed that I had not thought of it sooner. The firehouse was just around the corner and not wanting to go in empty-handed, I scrambled to find a suitable thank-you gift. But how can you really ever express in a present, gratitude too large to be measured? Surely my sincerity, presented in mere words would have been ample had it come in a more timely manner. Having just passed a florist, I decided to buy a dozen white roses, Omelet's signature color, and hoped that they would be received well. (First time I ever bought a man flowers.)

Anxiously, I entered the station, and introduced myself to the first man in navy I encountered. He recognized Omelet immediately, which I thought was very sweet, and I just assumed that he was our hero. As I began to thank him, he confessed that he was not the man I was looking for. He had been there, but it was "Jack" who had coaxed Omelet out of our bathroom that morning. Proud of his friend, he went into detail telling me about the rescue effort. It gave me a gulp in my throat.

"Is he here?" I asked. I took Omelet off his leash. He was so curious and so excited to walk about.

"Actually, no," he said. "He's not due for a few more hours. He's on the night shift."

I was bummed. "Oh, well," I said. "That's too bad."

"Yeah, well you should come back another time, maybe tomorrow morning? He should be here then."

"I've moved downtown since the fire, ya know," I said. "And I have to work tomorrow and I wanted to be with Omelet. Shoot."

Omelet had made his way back by this point.

"Maybe some other time then?"

"I guess so," I said. "Well . . ." I hadn't caught his name.

"Mike."

"Well, Mike . . . could you give these to Jack (handing him the flowers) and tell him that Omelet and Vivian stopped by. Tell him how much I appreciate what he did."

"No problem," he said.

Omelet then made a mad dash to the entryway of the station. I was sure he'd seen a cat or something and got nervous thinking he'd run into the street. But before I could shout his name or run after him, it was evident by the looks of things that he wasn't in any danger. He had nearly toppled down some random man. He was jumping up and down, wagging his tail back and forth and licking this guy who had simply walked toward the entrance of the station.

"Sorry," I called, and did my best to help this poor man out of the clutches of my strange dog. But he didn't seem to mind. I couldn't even tell if I knew him. At this point he was down on one knee and had dog all over him. His messenger bag was on the ground and his only identifiable trait was his worn-in gray and white New Balance running shoes.

"Easy, Omelet, easy boy!" the man said.

Huh?

Mike walked over with the roses.

"Now you can say it yourself," he said.

Jack.

Omelet finally came and sat next to me and "Jack" then came to his feet, brushed himself off, and looked my way.

Immediately I became awestruck and stood there, flowers in hand. He had the kindest and most beautifully imperfect face I'd ever seen. Maybe it was a case of hero-itis? Who knows? But I was at a loss for words.

"Hi." He smiled.

"Hi," I said eventually.

(Silence)

Mike walked away and his movement interrupted my "trance."

"Sorry," I said. "These are for you. Thank you. Thank you for rescuing Omelet."

But I was still holding them. Never handing him the bouquet.

He brushed my words off. "It's my job," he replied, not acknowledging the flowers.

"Really, from what I heard, it was a very dangerous thing you did. Omelet means the world to me and I . . ."

"It's nothing. I understand. You don't have to thank me, Vivian."

He had said my name . . .

Still holding the flowers, "I'm glad we caught you. Mike said you wouldn't be here for a while. I was about to leave."

"Yeah, I decided to come in early today," he said.

"Well, it was a good thing I guess. For us," I said nervously, petting Omelet as a means of distraction.

"For me," he then said.

I knew immediately. I was sure that this man was going to be a part of my life.

He had already rescued my dog and perhaps he would eventually rescue me . . .

This time, there was no hurry. No "best part." Taking it slow had never come naturally. I had always wanted to dive in headfirst, say it all, get the confirmation; this was not the case with Jack. There was no tension. It was replaced instead with a foreign sense of calm. I took the time to get to know this gentle man, this "older" man, this genuine man. It was as if the moment I looked into his eyes, life took a chill pill. Forgive my lack of eloquence, but that's what it felt like. The rush that ran through my system during our very first dialogue provided all the assurance I needed. Everything else from there on in was governed by process, not by me and not by him.

He had the most lovely weathered olive skin. Faint little lines that stemmed from the corner of his eyes like rays of sunlight. He had a Grecian nose, broken, he told me, twice while in school. He had great dark, almost wavy hair, and adorably bushy eyebrows and a small chicken pox scar that rested on his right eyelid and that you could only see if you spent lots of time kissing him. ☺

His eyes were blue, navy really, and he had funny lips. Big and brooding. (He said he was often teased as a kid but was always assured by his two older sisters that the girls would appreciate them one day. NO DOUBT!) He was a big guy though he had a smallish frame. Oh, and he had great feet!

I gave him my new home telephone number that afternoon and he rang the next evening. I was still somewhat behind on things at the office and his schedule was pretty brutal so a week passed before we saw each other again. In the meantime, though, we had great phone! People asked me if I was using a new moisturizer and Carolyn was sure I was getting laid. But I was just happy. Plain old happy.

He was so impressed with my work and, most of all, how much it meant to me. (And that, of course, was a breath of fresh air!) He was born and bred in New York, extremely tight with his family, and thought me independent for settling in a new city. I made sure he understood that mom and dad were less than three hours away, but he urged me not to downplay it. He told me that he had never met a woman that had more problems taking a compliment than me. I couldn't argue that.

He was a third-generation New York City firefighter (part-time). He loved what he did but naturally felt a sense of obligation not to put a wrench in the family business. He never got his degree, something that he didn't really regret. He majored in architecture in college but stumbled into fine art. He loved to work with his hands (I can attest to that), much to the surprise of both himself and his family; he grew as fond of sculpting as he was skilled at it. He lived in Brooklyn Heights and had a small studio space in Cobble Hill (also in Brooklyn). Let me see, what else can I tell you about him . . . He was obsessed with his niece; he hated karaoke, lived in jeans and wore pleated pants until I felt comfortable enough to make the introduction to flat- and tab-fronted trousers. Oh, and he was a fine Italian chef! Jack was one of those guys who was into relationships. Admitting that at twenty-nine, he had never spent more than a few months at a time being single. (Join the club!) He had his heart broken once but other than that, had yet to fall head over heels. He was a rather low-key kinda guy. He had a set schedule within the department and lived within his means . . . easily satisfied and appreciative of most simple things. He would sell some of his art and help out at his brother-in-law's painting business and would use the extra money to travel, taking trips with his friends and what not. He was a runner. Marathons. Since his early twenties. I could go on and on, obviously.

As much as we were alike we were just as different. He was not big into the bright lights of the city. He didn't paint the town "Jack" if you know what I mean. For a city boy, he seemed more like a country mouse. I loved his friends, felt comfortable with his family from the beginning, and, well, if there was ever a Mr. Perfect, as far as I was concerned, Jack was it for me.

He was the first man I ever talked to about Mark.

He was the first guy I ever left alone with a family member.

He was the first guy who seemed to love every inch of me for no other reason than it was part of the package.

And he was the first guy who told me he loved me and I knew really meant it.

We've been together for about two years, pretty happily. Although I struggle from time to time, wondering when he'll figure me out. (Some things haven't changed.) Too much of a good thing still freaks me out.

Wait, I've got to tell you about our first kiss . . .

Date number three. I know, I was surprised, too. I don't think either one of us wanted to rush into anything. It was not like the desire wasn't there from the very minute we met, trust me, but as I said before, from the onset, we moved about like turtles. Anyway, I decided to take him out. I wanted the focus off of it being just the two of us. Dates one and two were over dinner, a bottle of wine, and a quiet setting. I thought we could use an atmosphere with a little pulse, some music, you know. So we went to one of my favorite haunts, Joe's Pub. Jack doesn't love to dance, unless it's slow, which I later figured out, so when we got there he thought it best to occupy a small table in the far corner that had just opened up. Still, it was groovy, dark, and although a lot less private, oddly, much more intimate. Probably because we were forced to get close and focus on each other if we were going to communicate at all. To say it was "loud" in there was an understatement.

A few friends from work were there, as it turned out, and I was all too happy to introduce him, or shall I say, show him off. He was just so delicious. Like a gentle giant who had just gotten back from an Eddie Bauer photo shoot! We must have been there for about three hours. Talking, laughing, telling our most favorite stories and some of our most embarrassing moments. We had already reached the hand-holding stage, date two. (He does this great thing where he just softly tickles the face of my hands when we are separated by something like a table.) As the bar began to mellow out and the crowd began to sprinkle off, I think Jack got a bit more comfortable. He did the tickling thing for the first time, which sort of took me by surprise. I visibly cringed in that great way and, apparently, gave him some sort of look that he interpreted as "kiss me!" He leaned in to kiss me, he says now, not thinking it was the ideal moment but not wanting to let me down. (Whatever!) I naturally did the same, not wanting to make him feel like his timing wasn't right. But we did have this small table between us, chic and candle-lit of course, but still a barrier that required me to reach behind my back and push up off my chair with my fingertips. Had I taken a Pilates class, maybe I'd be able to pull it off. ☺ I closed my eyes thinking "Finally! This is it!" and cocked my head to the left waiting for the big smooch. Instead I heard him shout, "Holy shit, Vivian! Don't move!" Bug-eyed as you can imagine, and to the sound of girls screaming "Oh my God!" and pointing at me, I realized way too late that my hair had caught on fire. And before I could move, some man that I had never met jumped across our table and literally "put me out!"

You don't really know what the true definition of "humiliation" is until you've been through that, I swear to you.

The smell in and of itself is the most disgusting thing, especially if you color your hair! Not only did I burn off the majority of my hair below my shoulder on my left side, but I also lost most of my left eyelashes and part of the corner of my left eyebrow.

We didn't kiss until date four!

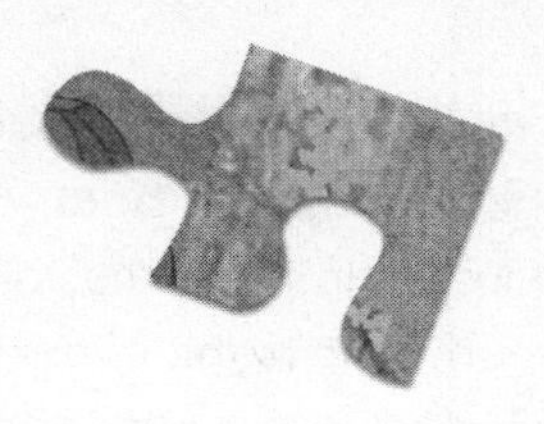

So, I had finally stumbled into that groove; where your life just seems to move forward, like a road trip where you can't believe you've been in your car for "that long." In the good way. No traffic, great weather, a genius mixed tape, your favorite junk food, and, wow, you didn't even have to stop, lost, asking for directions. On paper, everything was as close to perfect that I had ever known . . .

My relationship with Sophie was completely on the mend. At least in my head. What I mean is that she was in a good place, as was I. I no longer felt that I had to hold back. She had landed a job as an editorial assistant at a magazine and, you'll love this, she finally saw that there could be life after Fernando!!! They parted ways about two months into her gig in the fashion closet. (She managed "samples," clothes that were lent to the magazine by designers for photo shoots. If there was ever a dream job . . .) Seems that once she felt really "on to something," really strong, really excited about herself and her future, she took a second look at her present. It was such a relief to finally be able to feel like I was participating in the life and times of my best friend, rather than like a cautious spectator.

I had found a studio apartment just short of those three months in my sublet. It was actually in the same building, ground floor, and for the first time I had a tiny little backyard to play in! Great for lazy days, perfect when I just didn't feel like taking Omelet out for a long walk and thoroughly romantic in the evenings. A little wine, a few stars, and Jack. You dig? I tried over and over again to create a little "enchanted forest." I'd buy potted plants, rosebushes, you name it, but after a while I felt more like a murderer than a horticulturist. I decided to stop wasting money and purchased a piece of an old rickety white painted picket fence, just enough to lean against the small stone wall of the building behind mine. (Anything and everything is for sale in NYC.) And in some strange way, it "worked." Without the right light or enough sleep, there were times when I'd swear I lived in the country! I had a shoe box of a kitchen, but for as much cooking as I did (none) it really didn't make that much of a difference. Jack and his cousin built a bunch of shelves and some storage space for me. There was one tiny closet, more for coats and umbrellas than anything else and, fire or no fire, regardless if your budget is big or small, us gals know how to accumulate "stuff." The ceilings were pretty high, which made the room feel larger, and my bathroom was the bomb! It had these beautiful turquoise mini ceramic tiles on the floor, on three of the surrounding walls, including the one in my shower. There was also this adorable tiny arched "peekaboo"-type window embedded in the shower wall. It was too small for any psycho to fit through but large enough to fit my shampoo, razor, and soap on its ledge. The apartment had character; that's what I really loved about it. It also had a roach problem, but after the repeated efforts of an exterminator, Omelet and I soon became its only tenants.

My parents came down to "approve" this time around, and were pleasantly surprised. That was until they figured out how much I was spending. Eleven hundred bucks for a safe, clean space of your own in a decent neighborhood with a "backyard" (That my dad just thought was more of an "architectural error," not exactly the "backyard" he had expected!) was a pretty good deal. But they just didn't get it. However, once I handed them back their envelope, and was no longer in their debt, what really could they say? I also made sure to hide all my candles before their visit. Thought it best to prevent an argument! It took a while to furnish it and give it my signature style: crowded. I frequented the flea markets as much as possible and all too often brought home things that Sophie and Jack couldn't believe I actually paid for. But I reminded them each that "One woman's trash is another woman's treasure!" And if they'd prefer, they could always give me their credit cards. I really had some great times there. Every once in a while, I even felt like a grown-up.

Will had left VH1 at that point, on to producing commercials at an advertising agency based in San Francisco. The city wasn't the same without him. But I was happy for him. He had given himself a "deadline" at VH1 and committed to making a change should he not be at a certain level at a certain time. I admired that he stuck to his guns and after hearing about how much he loved his new life, I was really inspired and very proud of him.

A few weeks after Will left, Carolyn announced that she was pregnant. She was having a boy and pledged to all us ladies that she'd raise a good one! Watching her go through a pregnancy was absolutely hilarious. She had to eat right, quit smoking, her feet got too swollen for her Manolo's, and she complained and complained about the clothes afforded to women in the maternity world. We'd lunch from time to time, where she'd often go into explicit detail about her visits to the doctor. That's just about when my fear of having children went into high gear; if there was a drawer or a shelf, in my apartment or Jack's, it had been condom-ized!

Zack had gone through two assistants since I had been promoted and I found myself wearing my old hat from time to time. It never really bothered me. I joked that I was evidently "irreplaceable" and I always felt so indebted to him, if he needed an extra hand, how could I refuse? Otherwise, my professional life was pretty hectic. I traveled a lot, at least for me. Jack joined me on two separate occasions. We camped at the Grand Canyon, after a business trip to Las Vegas. That was fun. And he met me in Jamaica after a concert I was there to co-produce that featured Kid Rock and P.O.D. (Which was almost too much fun!) There was one other instance where he was supposed to meet me in Seattle for a long weekend, but his niece came down with a pretty mean case of the chicken pox and so he decided he should stay. I told you he was a great uncle. (And I really loved that about him.)

Sophie and I had the chance to experience California together, too. I was there on business and she took a few days off. All she had to do was pay for her airfare. The rest of the trip was on me, if you know what I mean. ☺ She was in her glory, I kid you not. If I hadn't grown up with her, I'd swear she was a California Girl!

So as you can see, there was a time when the only thing I could complain about was the fact that I had no complaints. Being an inherently overachieving risk-taking emotional windup toy, I'd get a bit itchy every now and again. I was entering my mid-twenties and the idea that "this was my life," as great as it was, still scared the shit out of me. I couldn't remember a time before when something wasn't wrong or when change wasn't around the corner. The familiar, albeit a little masochistic, was still the familiar, ya know? I guess it would have been safe to say that I'd yet to feel comfortable in my own skin, and I'd often wonder what it would take or if I ever would. I struggled with "deserving" the life I had created for myself.

Why was drama always so sexy? Dare I stop and smell my own roses? I couldn't.

We were just rounding out winter in New York and spring was still a few weeks away. It had been rainy and cold and basically depressing for what felt like forever. Carolyn was out on maternity leave, every third person was sick in the office, and I had worked without a weekend for almost a month. I had entered that point in my career where most things felt like I had done them time and time again. Jack was a little disgruntled as I had yet to make use of the time-share he had in Vermont, and Omelet was having "stomach" problems (to put it mildly). Basically, I was walking around as though I was strung out and it was one of those Fridays where "TGIF" was an understatement.

It was about two o'clock and the day felt like it was going to go on forever. Jack had made "reservations," and as much as I wanted to see him, I was way more into sweatpants and pizza than heels and a menu. On the bright side, the restaurant was nearby and we were meeting early, so with all things being said, it could have been worse. I took two Advil, caught up on my paperwork, and figured I'd return e-mails and make long-distance calls until quitting time. I figured wrong. Zack called in a bit of a panic, Rosalie, his new assistant, wasn't feeling well, join the club, he couldn't get a messenger and begged me to hand deliver a package to a "new client," that was all too important and couldn't wait for whatever it was until Monday. Perfect!

I grabbed my coat and scarf and tried not to be so miserable. At least it wasn't raining and, hey, my decision to sport my new spring shoes turned out to be a good one. I found a smile and looked at this new task as a way of making the day go faster. I picked up the package from Zack's office, let him thank me about fifty times, and was all the more thrilled when I saw that I was headed to the most southern part of Manhattan. (This equated traffic and, I'd bet, the majority of my afternoon with a few angry NYC cabdrivers.) The minute I stepped outside, Mother Nature had a moment and the rain began to come down as if I had just stolen its boyfriend. No umbrella. My new shoes. Great. I stood in the pouring rain waiting for a cab. No cabs. So I walked to the subway station and tried to stay positive, because I was "this close" to completely freaking out. The cars were empty so I was able to find a seat, but, and somehow there's always a "but," the air-conditioning was on full alert. With a twenty-minute train ride ahead, already feeling like shit, and now I was soaking wet, I knew I'd have to stop at the pharmacy on the way home for cold medicine. I warned you guys . . . it was a bad day!

Finally! My stop. But the torture continued as I almost forgot the package on the damn train and then had to walk another seven blocks. It was still raining. (Did I mention the new shoes had heels?) At this point, I looked and felt like a wet rat. My silly long scarf was being dragged through every puddle imaginable and yet again I wasn't wearing waterproof mascara. I finally find the freakin' place, and go to the wrong floor. Rosalie wrote "14" instead of "4." When things get perpetually worse, I usually end up laughing. It's my way of keeping my cool. But this wasn't a "usual" day.

So I finally get to my destination. I find an all too miserable receptionist and do the best I can to be pleasant. I tell her that I was instructed to hand deliver the envelope that I managed to keep dry by the way. But she let me know that that wasn't the procedure. That everything was to be left with her. I quickly glanced at her digs. She was more of a pack rat than me. I could just see her not getting in touch with its recipient for whatever the reason and me taking the blame soon after. I politely explained my situation. She didn't much care. About five minutes go by and she decides, I guess, that if she just lets me through she'll have more time to reapply her lip liner and tease her hair. Ultimately I was given the go-ahead.

Please visualize: I am a wrinkled, miserable, wet mess. I even have sound effects. (My new ruined camel shoes squeak with every step.) I've been instructed by the Poison groupie of a receptionist that it's the conference room, farthest to the left. I enter, rather abruptly, and see before me a huge, long, somewhat dark space with about fifteen suit types, maybe there was one woman, all sitting around a large oak table. It was "corporate" if there was ever a word. I was mortified. Okay, get ready for this one. I ask for Mr. Whomever, who identifes himself and stands up. Much like a bride with a train, I had my scarf, trailing after me, soaked in the city's winter gook. I proceed toward him to give him the bone-dry envelope and my heel got hooked in the stupid thing. I am now sniffing the carpet and hoping that I died during the fall. Where were my bridesmaids? After a collective "oh" from the crowd, the man rushes over to me and asks if I'm okay. I refuse to answer. He puts out his hand to help. I play dead. I can't even bear to get up. So after lying there for about three minutes, I get up and he helps me to a seat. I hadn't even said a word yet. I take another look around, as if someone would have missed what just happened, and after seeing I'd say about fifteen people smirking, trying their best not to laugh, I put both of my hands to my face and start cracking up. Which eases everyone else's tension and they do the same.

They offer me a cup of tea and I decline and request hot chocolate. I wasn't trying to be difficult, but I could smell that someone else was drinking it. The one woman asked me what I did at VH1 so I told her. She asked if I liked it and I said that I did up until about five minutes ago. I figured I was the comic relief they all needed to finish up their day. I left the package, decided to hold my scarf rather than wear it as I left, and called Zack to let him know that my mission was accomplished.

Jack called just as I got back and asked if I'd be disappointed if we just stayed home. With the rain and all, he thought it would be nicer if he made dinner at my place. How psyched was I? We had the most relaxing weekend. The perfect kind; where you sleep late, stay in your pajamas, watch TV, and smooch. Could you ask for anything more? We came across this odd Patrick Swayze film festival . . . We watched *The Outsiders,* then *Dirty Dancing,* and finally *Ghost.* During the big "pottery scene" Jack reminded me that he himself had a studio and, embarrassed, I quickly turned the channel. That's about all I remember . . .

Thankfully, the sun was shining that Monday morning when I reported back to work. I was rejuvenated and a bit more optimistic than the Friday before and expected it to be just another ordinary day sans any delivery duties. It was Lilly's birthday and the night called for dinner and drinks at eight. I remember stopping off at the card store on my way to work and then, of course, dashing to the office. For some reason, every time I go card shopping I always have the sudden urge to pee and am never "allowed" to use the establishment's toilet. (As if . . .)

As I got off the elevator and headed directly for the bathroom, Zack was at the coffee machine (surprise, surprise) with some odd guy I'd never seen before.

"Hey, Viv," he said. "I want you to meet . . ."

"One sec. Zack, my bladder is about to explode!" I said while en route.

Ahhhhhhhhhhh.

I assumed I'd meet whomever by our kitchen, but they were gone by the time I got there so I stopped by Zack's office. Rosalie wasn't there yet, surprise, surprise, so I just walked in.

I opened the door and saw him standing in front of his desk, casually leaning against it, sipping his coffee.

"Where's your friend?" I asked. "Sorry, you know what happens when

I go card shopping," and I held up my little Hallmark bag for proof. "I had to go!"

He shook his head, raised his eyebrows, and reached his arm out, gesturing for me to look behind my shoulder.

Fuck.

"He's behind me, isn't he?" I laughed. I had forgotten how big his office was.

"Yup," he said.

I turned around and saw that it wasn't just one "him" but three and one woman. I hadn't yet had my coffee so it took a second for me to put it together. This was part of the crew I'd "stumbled upon" quite literally on Friday. Mr. Whoever, that woman with the questions, the dude with Zack by the bathroom, and some other guy with red hair.

"Take off your coat," Zack suggested. So I did. "Why don't you sit down?" he said. So I did.

"Hot chocolate?" the woman said and the four of them laughed,

What was going on?

Leave it to Zack, my friends. As it turned out, the urgent errand on Friday was a hoax. The important "client" was a new media company called Forever After, Inc., and one of the founders happened to be an old college roommate of Zack's during his graduate stint at Maryland. As it were, the company was in the process of launching a Web site where you'd follow the life and times of a twenty-something young woman living in New York City. Somehow Zack had it in his head that they might find me "amusing." It turns out that they did. They offered me a job at www.Vivianlives.com. And the rest, well, I guess that's now herstory!

epilogue

So that's how it all happened. Pretty crazy if you ask me.

I can say now, very matter-of-factly, that I'm still as neurotic as ever. With age only comes certain kinds of wisdom and more facial hair, which bites. But like most of us, I pick up and dust off every time I fall and try to remember where and why I tripped in the first place. I still yearn to live life large and always seem to be making decisions as if I need to make up for lost time. Go figure.

I have no idea if Jack's the one. I react to the world around me in much the same way as I did when I was nine, and still have less than a grand to my name in savings. Shows you what I know!

But I can say this: life has a very funny way of coming full circle and has a wicked sense of humor, never offering instructions or a protractor for that matter. (Remember those!)

Maybe we're all dreamers in our own way and I'm too self-absorbed to see it. Maybe not. Maybe there are some of us, the average gals, who surprisingly find the traditional blasé and seem to wear our experiences in much the same way a boxer dons his belt. (Noteworthy: from what Sophie tells me, belts are back!)

In any event, thanks for reading my book. I really hope you liked it.

I guess I'll catch you on the flip side or maybe in a random support group. You really never know! Be good and go wild every once and again, for old times' sake!

All my love,

vivian ☺

acknowledgments

There would be no autobiography without a great many people who have inspired it, supported me, and possessed the foresight and bravery to take a chance. This includes first, "Jon-e G" and Seth, without whom the world would have probably never even met Vivian. The many talented and generous people who, like me, could feel Vivian's pulse, beginning with only a concept. Namely, Leja, Alex, Richard, Nick, Stacee, Pam, Hilary, Caedlighe, René, Gina, Tatum, Tizzy, Marty, Fred, David, Ric, Amy, Nikki, and Betty. A very special and heartfelt thank-you to my editor, Allison Dickens, whose creativity, patience, and trust made this a pleasurable experience and led me toward an accomplishment that I can be proud of. To my friends, past and present, who, when I looked back, provided more than enough memories to fill these pages. I love you and I miss you. Specifically, to my "Sophie," my dearest friend and for sure my better half. I adore you. To the dedicated and very special group of women who have been loyal to Vivian both online and offline (the "Vivsters" and "Viv-heads" as I affectionately call them). You all make me forget that this is a "job" and remind me how right it was to take this road in the first place. And finally, to Mr. Dove. Without whose immeasurable love and "wicked" support, well, I can't even imagine . . . I love you, you know.

about the authors

Vivian Livingston is a sassy, twenty-something singleton who lives in New York City with her beloved pampered pooch, Omelet. Her life—the ups, downs, and everything in between—is chronicled on the Web site that bears her name: www.Vivianlives.com. This is her first book.

Coauthor Sherrie Krantz is one of Vivian's best friends and the founder of Forever After, Inc., the company that created www.Vivianlives.com. Before starting her own business, Sherrie was a public relations executive at both Calvin Klein and Donna Karan International. She, too, resides in New York City.

at's me at Le Figaro waiting tables to get by. Still masqu
s a "starving artist" and unable to accept a more approp
dline like, shall we say, "starving waitress." Such the po
d wait. obviously too broke to visit the hairdresser' nice

say "CHEESE!" say "I can't believe I actually had this photo taken!" nerd to the core!

"you think you know, but you have no idea." After one "show" or another. Feet throbbing, underarms sweating, and still, never really believing I actually got paid to rock out!!

Thank you, Will! Not for the flowers, but for ensuring that one of the worst weeks of my life will forever exist on film!

okay, now we're talking. . . . yeesh! i mean shopping. i've gotten pretty good at that —— à la sophie.

Ahhhhh, sweet nothings . . . somebody pinch me! wait, don't!

Book cover shoot: four hours sitting stationary under hot lights in tight jeans with a face cake full of makeup . . . I was way ready to call it quits!!! (I'm so not cut out for this **@%!)